BOYFRIEND LESSONS

SOPHIA SINGH SASSON

THE SECRET HEIR RETURNS

JOSS WOOD

MILLS & BOON

First Published in Great Britain 2022
by Mills & Boon, an imprint of HarperCollins*Publishers* Ltd
1 London Bridge Street, London, SE1 9GF

www.harpercollins.co.uk

HarperCollins*Publishers*
1st Floor, Watermarque Building,
Ringsend Road, Dublin 4, Ireland

Boyfriend Lessons © 2022 Harlequin Enterprises ULC
The Secret Heir Returns © 2022 Joss Wood

Special thanks and acknowledgement are given to Sophia Singh Sasson for her contribution to the *Texas Cattleman's Club: Ranchers and Rivals* series.

ISBN: 978-0-263-30379-7

0522

MIX
Paper from
responsible sources
FSC® C007454

This book is produced from independently certified FSC™ paper to ensure responsible forest management.

For more information visit: www.harpercollins.co.uk/green

Printed and Bound in Spain using 100% Renewable electricity at CPI Black Print, Barcelona

BOYFRIEND LESSONS

SOPHIA SINGH SASSON

This book is dedicated to all those who've ever wondered—what's wrong with me?

The answer is absolutely nothing.

You are perfect as you are, and I hope you find that special someone who thinks so, too.

One

"So you just left?" Caitlyn Lattimore said incredulously. She was used to Alice's crazy dating experiences, but this one made her sit up in the pool lounger.

Alice slid her oversize sunglasses on top of her wavy blond hair, refilled her chardonnay glass and topped off Caitlyn, who had barely touched her first glass.

"The man ordered two appetizers, lobster for dinner and a bottle of wine from the reserve list. Then he pulls 'the left my wallet at home' crap. No, thank you. I told him I was going to the bathroom and then asked the waitress if I could escape through the kitchen door because he was a creep."

Her dating stories get scarier by the day.

Alice grabbed the bottle of suntan lotion and rubbed her arms. "I need to find a better dating site."

Caitlyn reached for the sunblock. It was early June, and the sun was strong. One touch of UV and her skin would turn shades browner. She had a number of Lattimore events to attend in the next month, and her makeup artist had just spent days perfecting the right shade of foundation for her. Alice called them rich girl problems, and Caitlyn agreed. She'd won the lottery when the Lattimores adopted her twenty-four years ago. Even now, they were sitting by the sparkling blue pool of the Lattimore ranch, their wine bottle perfectly chilled and a staff member readily available should they need anything else. Alice called it the Ritz Lattimore, but it was home for Caitlyn, one she loved not because of the luxuries, but because her family lived here.

"I wish I had your chutzpah. If that had happened to me, I'd have paid the bill and spent the night seething." Caitlyn said.

"Darlin', for that to happen to you, you'd need to actually go out on a date. To leave this gilded cage and venture into the smog and filth we mortals call the real world."

"You sound just like Alexa."

Alexa had left Royal for New York City, and then Miami, when she went to college and never looked back. She'd been home recently, though, for Victor Grandin's funeral.

Alice raised a brow. "I was sorry to hear about Layla's grandfather dying. Victor Grandin was such a pillar in this community."

"He was. Alexa came home for the funeral and I suspect Layla would like Alexa to stay permanently, because her cutthroat lawyering skills will help our two families."

"Is this about that letter that came at the funeral? You never told me the full story."

Caitlyn's stomach roiled. "Turns out Heath Thurston is making a claim against the oil rights to the land beneath the Grandin and Lattimore ranches." It wasn't the claim that worried Caitlyn but the effect it was having on her family.

Alice leaned forward. "See, this is what happens when we don't see each other for a month—I miss all the juicy gossip."

"It's more than gossip. Those oil rights include the land that the Lattimore mansion is built on. Heath claims Daniel Grandin fathered Heath's late half-sister, Ashley, and that Daniel's dad gave Heath's mother Cynthia the oil rights. He says he found some of his mother's papers supporting the claim."

Alice's mouth hung open. Even she was speechless after that. The thought of what losing their family home would do to her siblings had consumed Caitlyn every second for the last month, since Victor Grandin's funeral.

"How did Ashley die?"

"In a car crash that also included her mother, Cynthia."

"Why did Victor Grandin Sr. give Cynthia the oil rights and not Ashley?"

"We don't know. And my grandfather signed the document, too, so he knew about it. Now he doesn't remember a thing, so Victor Grandin Jr. hired a private investigator for the two families to look into why they might have signed over the oil rights for our lands, and whether Daniel really fathered Cynthia's child."

Alice sat back, speechless once again. "Have you ever met Heath or his twin brother, Nolan?"

Caitlyn shook her head.

"I went to high school with them. They are hot. I'm talking freshly seared steak hot. I'd forgotten about

Nolan, he left Royal but if he's back, that changes the dating scene." She wiggled her eyebrows at Caitlyn. "They're both single."

Caitlyn smiled. "There's enough drama in my family without me trying to date the men trying to destroy our ranch."

Caitlyn chewed on her lip. Alice was right about one thing—she needed to get a life; she was tired of her image as the quiet, shy woman who startled when a man sneezed next to her. Even though the last part was right. "Maybe I should sign up for one of these dating sites. Not all of yours have been that bad. What happened to the guy who sent you flowers and took you to meet his family?"

"He was fine, a bit boring in the sex department but I was willing to deal with that until he took a call with his mother while he was on top of me."

Caitlyn had just taken a sip of her wine, and it went flying out of her mouth, spraying all over the pool lounger. She covered her mouth in embarrassment.

Alice smiled and handed her one of the rolled hand towels from a basket on the table. Caitlyn wiped her mouth and the pool lounger. "You know not to do that to me when I'm drinking," Caitlyn said, laughing.

"Sorry, I forgot about that endearing habit of yours."

"The guy actually talked to his mom while you were in the middle of having sex?"

Alice nodded. "What's worse is he talked to her for a good two minutes, and wanted to continue on like it didn't make a difference."

"How could you not tell me about this?"

"That happened on the day of the Grandin funeral. I was so embarrassed I couldn't even think about it." Alice shook her head. "You and I need to meet men in real life. It's hard to suss out the creep factor online. It's singles' night at the Lone Star nightclub. How about we get all dressed up and go?"

I'd rather face down a pack of hungry wolves.

"You know that's not my scene. There aren't enough cocktails in the world to get me comfortable enough to talk to a strange man. It seems safer to start out with online chatting."

Alice shook her head. "Dating sites are not for you, darlin'. You need someone who's vetted, get some practice in before you go out into the world of vultures and mamas' boys."

Caitlyn nearly spit out her drink again. "I'll skip the mama's boy, but I could use someone who has the backbone to withstand the Lattimore siblings. The last time I went out on a date, Jonathan asked if he could have the guy's Social Security number to run a background check. The time before that, Jayden followed me to the restaurant where I was meeting a blind date. He didn't like the look of the guy, so he stayed parked on the street the entire time I was at dinner and followed us home."

Alice put her hand to her heart. "Your brothers are super sweet."

"No, they're overprotective. They don't pull that stuff with Alexa."

"Because she moved away." Alice took a sip of her wine. "I do have a nice, decent guy with whom you can practice your flirting skills." Alice smiled cheekily, and Caitlyn narrowed her eyes.

"There has to be something wrong with him or you would've dated him."

Alice laughed. "That would be really weird. I'm talking about Russ."

Caitlyn raised a brow. "Your brother, Russ? I thought you said he wasn't into serious dating."

Alice shifted on the lounger. "He's not, which is why he'd be the perfect person to practice your conversational skills. You two really haven't hung out, so he's like a strange man."

Caitlyn bit her lip. She didn't want to offend Alice, but she'd never felt a spark with her brother, Russ. He was a nice enough guy, but he was just so *white*. Not that she had a problem dating white men. Her biological mother was white, but in the last couple of years she'd struggled with her identity, along with most of the country. Despite her closeness with Alice, her best friend didn't understand Caitlyn's struggle with being a woman of color. Alice had never been asked where she was from, as if her brown skin automatically meant that she was exotic or foreign. Caitlyn had struggled with that over the last two years, debating her own identity. Was she Black, white, both or neither? Whenever a form asked what her race or ethnicity was, she left it blank, because none of the categories fit her. That was the one thing she and Jax had in common. Her ex-boyfriend was also biracial, and he'd understood some of the things she'd struggled with. Yet it hadn't worked out with him, either. Maybe she really was a lost cause.

"Caitlyn, what's the harm? It's just Russ, and you could use the practice."

"I don't know.... Have you asked Russ?"

Alice shook her head reluctantly. "Look, he's coming home after months of travel. I was going to have dinner with him on Friday. Why don't you come? It'll just be the three of us. Low-key. No pressure. I'll be there to back you up and fill in if you stammer over your words or spit out your wine."

Caitlyn threw her dirty hand towel playfully at Alice. *What do I have to lose?* She was bored by the endless conversations about the fate of the Grandin and Lattimore ranches in her house and of making excuses about why she didn't date more. Ever since Layla Grandin and Josh Banks had gotten together, her family had been even more determined to see Caitlyn out and dating. She was tired of being pitied by her siblings. It was time to get over what had happened with Jax. It had been a year since they'd broken up. She'd been on a few dates since then—all failures, thanks to the scars Jax had left. She knew intellectually that Jax was just a bad dating experience, but it clung to her, haunted her thoughts at the most inappropriate times. It was time to replace those memories, even if it was with something meaningless.

"Come on, Caitlyn, what's the worst that can happen?"

She sighed. *That I'll hate Russ but you'll fall in love with the idea of me and Russ and it'll affect our friendship.*

"I'll order Italian from your favorite place," Alice said coaxingly.

"I'll come to dinner. As a friend. I'm not dating Russ."

Alice beamed. "Who said anything about dating? Think of it as a practice session."

"You've got to be kidding me." Alice glared at her phone.

"Trouble?" Caitlyn asked as she arranged the cutlery on Alice's table. Alice lived in a charming row house in the center of Royal. She had decorated it in a comfortable cottage style with soft pastel colors and wood furniture. Caitlyn had come early to help Alice with dinner preparations. She enjoyed the easy way she could make a salad in Alice's kitchen. At her house, the staff took it as an affront if she prepared her own food, feeling that they weren't meeting her standards.

"Russ is late, and he's bringing a friend to dinner."

Caitlyn smiled. While Russ was supposed to be her practice date tonight, it would serve Alice right if he brought another woman home with him. Caitlyn had suspected, but she now knew, that Alice hadn't told Russ she was setting them up.

"I'll set another place at the table," Caitlyn volunteered, her voice sugary sweet. "Don't worry, you have enough food to feed the entire block." If Russ was bringing a woman, Caitlyn could sit back and watch the two of them interact and take notes. The churning in her stomach slowed, and she opened a bottle of wine and poured two glasses. She didn't like to drink when she was anxious, but the evening was looking up.

"How dare Russ bring a woman." Alice seethed.

"Did you tell him he was here to give me boyfriend lessons?" Even as she said the words, Caitlyn realized how ridiculous the idea had been all along. There was no such thing as practicing dating skills. Was there?

She took a large sip from her glass, picturing herself taking notes as she watched Russ and his date converse during dinner as if she were sitting in a classroom. The idea made her giggle.

A half hour later, when the doorbell rang, both Alice and Caitlyn had polished off equal parts of an entire bottle of Bordeaux, and Caitlyn was looking forward to the evening.

Alice opened the door and greeted her brother. Caitlyn waited patiently on the gray leather couch, not wanting to interrupt the inevitable whispered shouting of

Alice berating Russ for spoiling the date setup that he didn't know he was participating in. She felt bad for Russ and even worse for his poor date, who would have no idea what she had done to incur Alice's passive-aggressive wrath.

"I can't believe it's you!" Alice's squeals made Caitlyn sit up.

Before she could react, they all walked in, and Caitlyn nearly choked on her drink as she caught sight of the most beautiful man that she'd ever seen.

Two

Dev Mallik knew the moment he walked into Alice's apartment that Russ was going to hate him by the end of the night. He and Russ had been quite the pair in college, Dev with his dark hair, brooding green eyes and generally standoffish nature and Russ with his baby blues, dirty blond hair and the kind of aw-shucks face that made women stalk him after their relationship ended. Russ always got the girl and Dev was stuck entertaining the friend.

But their arrangement suited him just fine. He had enough drama with his family—he didn't need relationship issues to compound them. He preferred women who were vivacious, confident and ready to forget him after one night. Which was why Russ had convinced him to come to dinner at his sister's. Apparently, Alice was prone to setting Russ up, and the last time he'd dated one of Alice's Royal friends, he'd ended up not being able to come home for six months in order to avoid running into the woman at the doorstep to his condo building. So, he'd brought Dev along tonight to distract the friend from Russ's irresistible charms.

Except, one look at Alice's friend as she put a hand to her delicate mouth and Dev's knees buckled. Before him was the most stunning woman he'd ever seen. She met his gaze and her deep brown eyes, brimming with innocence and laughter widened.

She stood slowly, and he noticed the wineglass in her hand tip forward, so he stepped toward her and placed his hand on her elbow to steady her arm.

Impossibly, her eyes widened some more, and he found himself mesmerized. Her lips parted and though he knew he was being rude, he couldn't help staring at how perfectly pink they were against her tanned skin. What would it be like to run his fingertips across their lusciousness?

Someone cleared their throat—Dev couldn't be sure whether it was Alice or Russ—but it seemed to jar the beautiful woman. She stepped away from him.

"Dev, this is my friend Caitlyn."

Caitlyn. He rolled the name on his tongue. The beautiful name suited her.

He smiled. "Nice to meet you." He extended his hand. She set the wineglass on a side table and took his hand. Her skin was silky soft and warm. It was the kind of hand he wanted to feel on his naked skin, and he held on to it a little too long.

Alice said something he didn't hear, and Caitlyn took her hand back.

"Russ, you remember Caitlyn," Alice introduced them.

Russ stepped forward. "Hey, Caitie, nice to see you

again." Caitlyn winced at the nickname. Russ stepped toward her and enveloped her in a hug, and a twinge of jealousy pricked at Dev. Had Russ dated her before? Or was she one of the ones that Russ crudely categorized as *too good to screw with*?

"When did you get to town, Dev?" Alice asked.

"Today. I called Russ, and he spent the afternoon moving me from the Royal Grand Hotel to his condo."

"Well, of course!" Alice turned to Caitlyn. "These two were inseparable in college. It's been years since I've seen you, Dev. What gives?"

Dev smiled warmly at Alice. He'd always liked Russ's sparky little sister. "Right after college, Dad sucked me into the family business. After that it's been one thing after another. Thought I'd come to Royal to take a break from family drama." That was another thing he liked about Alice and Russ—while they may have their sibling spats, they were genuinely close and affectionate with each other. Their parents lived in Arizona and generally stayed out of their lives, but they supported Alice and Russ in whatever the duo wanted to do. Dev couldn't imagine his parents being so hands-off. As much as he loved his heritage, he envied the freedom Russ had to chart his own course.

His Indian parents interfered in everything, from what he ate for breakfast to what he wanted to do with his life. He'd just had a nuclear-level war with his family to come to Royal. He was looking forward to focusing on himself while he was here. It was time for him to pursue his own goals.

"He wants to open a restaurant here," Russ chimed in. "I'm going to help him."

"What type of restaurant?" It was the first time Caitlyn had spoken, and unlike Russ and Alice's Texas twang, she had the clean-cut accent of a finishing school graduate and a voice that was as sweet as a glass of perfectly chilled iced tea on a hot day.

It took him a second to remember what the question was. Russ slapped him on the back and jumped in. "Some hoity-toity fusion Indian cuisine. You should talk to Caitlyn—she's Royal upper crust."

Caitlyn narrowed her eyes, clearly not happy with the description. "We could use a nice Indian restaurant in this town." She gave him a warm smile, and a zing went through his body.

Alice handed the men a glass of wine each. "So, what're your plans?"

"I'm here for a month to scope out potential locations and do some market research. I understand there are already a lot of fine dining establishments here so I'll have to get to know the town to see whether there's room for another restaurant." His comment was for Alice, but he couldn't seem to take his eyes off Caitlyn. "Maybe a Royal native can give me a hand?" *Why waste an opportunity to mix business with pleasure?*

"Alice and I can take you around," Russ said affably, and Dev gave him an irritated look. Hadn't he brought Dev to entertain the friend? Then why was he butting in?

"Why don't we get dinner on the table? You guys were late, so the food is getting cold." Alice grabbed Russ's arm and took him to the kitchen.

A small smiled played on Caitlyn's lips, as if she was enjoying a private joke.

"What's so funny?" Dev whispered as he and Caitlyn stepped toward the dinner table. He needed to know what could bring such a beautiful smile to her kissable lips. Alice had pulled Russ into the kitchen, and they could hear furious whispering but not what was being said.

Caitlyn looked at him with mischief in her eyes, and heat licked deep in his belly. She lowered her voice. "If I had to guess, Alice is telling Russ right now that he needs to tell you to focus your attentions away from me. I'm supposed to be Russ's date tonight, although he doesn't know it."

Dev bit his lip so he didn't laugh out loud and catch Russ's attention. Caitlyn was staring at him, her eyes locked on his, and dancing with amusement. He bent his head and whispered in her ear, "Russ figured Alice would try to set him up, so he brought me here to entertain the friend." He caught a whiff of her fragrance, a muted vanilla and lavender. It was sweet and sexy and kicked up a fire deep in his belly.

He noticed a slight blush on her neck and ears and smiled.

"Ah, so you're his wingman." She took a tiny step away from him and sipped her wine.

"More like the distraction." He stood almost a foot taller than she, so he bent toward her to whisper, "Though I suspect that Russ has been trying to set me up with Alice for a bit now."

Caitlyn's smile dropped. "Would you like to go out with her?" Her voice was measured, but he heard the disappointment loud and clear.

"I've always seen Alice as Russ's little sister and therefore my little sister. I can't imagine dating her."

Her smile reappeared. "I agree completely. I've known Russ as Alice's brother, so it's hard to think of him romantically."

"So why did you come here tonight?"

Caitlyn sighed. "I need practice talking to men."

"Tell me you're kidding."

She shook her head. "I'm not good at making small talk and playing the dating game. Since Russ is exceptionally good at it, Alice thought it would be nice for me to practice with him."

He stepped closer, to see if she really was as skittish as she made herself sound, but she looked up at him, her eyes flirtatious, even challenging. *If this is what she calls shy, why isn't every man in Royal lining up to take her out?*

"So you were hoping to practice what, exactly, with him?"

Her neck and cheeks turned that delectable shade of pink, and he resisted the urge to place a hand on his heart.

"Just conversation. You know, flirting and small talk."

"Well, you don't seem to have any problems talking to me. Dare I say we're even flirting a little?"

She raised a brow. "Are you saying you're enjoying talking to me?"

He leaned in so his lips were almost touching her earlobe. She didn't back away, but he heard the sharp intake of her breath. "I'd like to do a lot more if you'd let me."

The pink in her cheeks deepened. "I mean talking, of course," he said cheekily. Though that was far from the truth. While he did want to talk to Caitlyn, what he really wanted was her alone to see exactly how pink her cheeks could get.

She took a long sip of her wine and gazed at him from under her lashes. Alice and Russ sounded like they were making their way back to the dining room with dinner. "You know what, you're right. I don't have trouble talking with you." She chewed on her lip and glanced toward the kitchen then back at him. "Can I ask you for a favor?"

Whatever you want, Caitlyn, you'll find me more than willing.

"I'm intrigued."

"Will you give me boyfriend lessons?"

Three

Caitlyn couldn't believe what had slipped out of her mouth. *Did I just ask a complete stranger to give me boyfriend lessons?* What was wrong with her? Had she had too much to drink? She looked down into her wineglass as if it would tell her how much she'd had. She calculated that she'd probably drunk a little more than two glasses. Not enough to blame her rash decision on alcohol.

It had been so easy to flirt with Dev, even for a short time. She'd never felt at ease with a date like that. With Dev, there was none of the paralyzing nervousness she felt when she met new men. She and Alice had just been talking about dating lessons, and then in walked a man she had no problem talking to, despite the fact that she was insanely attracted to him. If she could get comfortable with him, then she wouldn't have problems with other men. As a bonus, he was only in Royal for a month, so there was no chance that there would be awkwardness any time they saw each other in town. Nor would she have to avoid him like she'd had to avoid Jax over the past year.

Alice had arranged them around her rectangular dinner table so that Caitlyn was sitting across from Russ and next to Dev with Alice across from Dev. Alice had ordered a beef ragù ravioli in rosé sauce, steamed vegetables and garlic bread from the local Italian restaurant Caitlyn loved. It was a family favorite because of it's good food and unpretentious interior. Caitlyn had prepared a Caesar salad.

"This sauce is excellent," Dev said.

Russ scrunched up his nose. "I personally prefer the one from Primi Piatti. This one is too creamy."

"The creaminess comes from good-quality cheese. Most places just use cheap mozzarella." Dev scooped some sauce on his fork and licked it.

Caitlyn didn't want to stare, but she couldn't take her eyes off the way his tongue flicked out and licked the edge of the fork. A warmth pooled deep in her core, a feeling totally unexpected sitting at dinner. It usually took more than staring at a handsome stranger to get her going. A lot more!

"They also use Grana Padano in this sauce. That's what gives it the depth of flavor," Dev continued, and Caitlyn had to force herself to focus on what he was saying.

"You know your food," she said admiringly.

"In a different life, I would've been a chef."

"Why not in this one?"

Their eyes were locked together, and Russ and Alice faded from her consciousness.

He shrugged. "It's complicated. But that's why I'm

opening a restaurant. I want to start a chain of high-end Indian fusion restaurants."

So he's Indian. Caitlyn had thought as much from his name. He was slightly darker skinned than she, but those green eyes—*oof.* His hair was thick and wavy and she wondered whether he'd like it if she ran her fingers through it.

"Why choose Royal for the first one?" Alice's voice broke through, and Caitlyn looked at her guiltily. She'd been completely focused on Dev beside her and had been ignoring Russ. Not that it mattered, because he seemed to be busy staring at his phone.

"Because Royal is far enough away from my family that they can't drop in on me. And from what Russ tells me, this town has the deep pockets and foodies to support a new restaurant. In a place like Vegas or LA, where new restaurants open every day, there won't be any buzz. I'd have to work ten times as hard to get attention. A town like Royal is full of wealthy—" While Caitlyn was studiously cutting a piece of ravioli into perfect square bites, she could feel his eyes on her. "—discerning individuals who appreciate fine dining."

Caitlyn looked up to see that he was indeed staring at her, a sparkle in his green eyes that sent her nerves tingling.

"Plus, the start-up costs in Royal are relatively low," Russ chimed in. "There are a number of places that went out of business in the heart of town, and their space is dirt cheap. I'm friends with the local Realtor. I'll set it up for you."

"Those businesses were lifelong Royal residents," Caitlyn said, irritated. "Mrs. Lowrey owned the little tea shop. It was passed down to her by her mother, who started it when she first moved to Royal in the 1920s.

There's a hundred years of history that just got erased when they foreclosed."

"Russ didn't mean to sound so insensitive," Alice quickly jumped in. "Caitlyn tried to help those businesses get loans—even hosted charity events and got the wealthy ranchers to open their tight purse strings to help."

"What happened?" Dev asked, sounding genuinely interested.

Caitlyn shrugged. "We were able to keep several of the Main Street small businesses open, but a number of the older residents just didn't have it in them to keep going under the circumstances."

Dev smiled kindly. "You cared enough to do something about it. That counts for a lot."

"So, Russ, tell us, how is work going for you?" Alice said loudly, trying to get Russ's attention away from his phone.

Russ launched into a monologue of how he'd scored a major win. He worked as an investment banker, and while he was New York–based most of the time, he was back to take some "chillax" time.

Caitlyn found herself thinking about how she'd brazenly asked Dev to be her practice boyfriend, embarrassment mixing with anxiety and fear as the night went on. What must he think of her? She'd known him all of two minutes and had asked him to give her boyfriend lessons, like they were middle school children. Now that she had time to think, she wondered how best to extricate herself from the situation. Perhaps not mention it? Tell him she was joking? How could she even bring it up again?

When dinner finished, they all helped Alice pack up what was left of the food. Caitlyn was acutely aware of

Dev moving around her in the dining room and kitchen. Alice took Russ to the kitchen to help her put away dinner—and probably to yell at him.

Caitlyn sat down in Alice's seat at the table so she was across from Dev. She didn't want to sit close to him again. All through dinner, she couldn't help glancing in his direction, and she hadn't missed Alice's glare every time she'd done it.

She took a sip of her wine, wondering where to start the conversation.

"So, how do I get in touch with my practice girlfriend?"

She clapped a hand on her mouth, but it was too late. The wine spluttered out of her mouth, across the table and onto his hand. She grabbed the napkin on the table and began mopping his hand and the table all at the same time, too mortified to even look at him. "Oh my God, I'm sorry. I'm so sorry."

He placed a hand on hers, stilling her frantic movements. She looked at him. There was a wide grin on his face, his eyes dazzlingly green. A warmth spread from her chest to her face. "I'm so sorry," she repeated in a small voice.

His hand was still on hers, and he stood and leaned over the table so his face was close to hers. Her entire body pulsed. His aftershave smelled like heaven, the scruffy five o'clock shadow on his jaw inviting her to rub her hands on it. "When we go out on our first date tomorrow, can you do that again? It's the sexiest thing I've ever seen."

She looked at him in horror. "I'm so sorry, it's a terrible habit."

He lifted his hand from hers and placed a finger on her lips as if to shush her. The feel of his finger made her lips tremble. He shook his head. "Don't ever be sorry for doing that again."

Alice cleared her throat, and both of them jumped back, as if they were teenagers caught by their parents.

"Dare I ask what's going on here?" Her voice was a little too high, and Caitlyn knew she was pissed.

"I did that thing I do when I get caught off guard while drinking wine," she said sheepishly, hoping to soothe the irritation etched on Alice's face. "Dev was helping me clean up."

Russ set down a stack of plates. "Uh-oh, you got the Caitie shower," he said. "We've all been victims."

Caitlyn wanted to crawl under the table and hide. Alice shot Russ a look. "Well, I have tiramisu for dessert, and Russ brought home a lovely ice wine that we opened."

Caitlyn wasn't hungry for dessert and wasn't sure she could stay much longer in Dev's company without incinerating and asking him to teach her more than just conversation. "I'm sorry, I have to leave. Since I knew I'd be drinking, I asked my brother to give me a ride, and he'll be heading home soon."

"Oh, stay. You can take an Uber later," Alice insisted, but Caitlyn shook her head. She was already planning to take an Uber—she'd used her brother as an excuse to make her escape.

Once Caitlyn had left, Russ decided it was time to play one of their old college games that involved a lot of drinking and a rehash of the most embarrassing/frustrating moments of their lives. Alice wasn't too keen and neither was Dev, but Russ's exuberance was hard to ignore. After a while Alice held up her hands. "I think we're out of alcohol."

Russ booed her. "Guess it's time to call it a night."

"Before you do…" Alice turned to Russ. "What did you think of Caitlyn?"

Russ cocked his head. "Caitie? What's there to think about?"

Dev tried not to laugh. "Well, I thought she was fantastic."

Alice glared at him. "Caitlyn was supposed to be Russ's date."

Both men laughed, much to Alice's chagrin.

"Sis, you really should let me in on these plans of yours. Though I will admit Caitlyn isn't the shy little creature I remember. She's really come into her own."

Dev caught the note of interest in Russ's voice, and his heart seized. Was Russ interested in Caitlyn after all? If they'd been at a bar and interested in the same girl, they'd flip a coin. But this was different. Russ knew Caitlyn, and if he was interested in her, Dev couldn't stand in his way. Even though Caitlyn had seized his interest in a way he'd never experienced before. It wasn't just her stunning body or looks. Normally he couldn't stop thinking about what it would be like to take the woman to bed, but with Caitlyn, he'd been genuinely interested in getting to know her. There was something about her—perhaps it was the genuine innocence—that tugged at his heart strings. She seemed sincere and authentic, like she said what she meant and every sentence wasn't a calculated step toward some hidden goal. Russ wasn't the right man for her—he was a ruthless investment banker with a golden tongue when it came to lying to women to get what he wanted. Dev hated to think of Caitlyn, with her charmingly naive request for boyfriend practice, in Russ's hands. He shuddered. The man wouldn't think twice about taking advantage of her.

"So you interested in her?" he asked Russ more insistently than he'd intended.

"Dev, your tongue was hanging so far out of your mouth, I'm surprised you weren't licking the plate instead of your lips," Russ said.

Dev punched him playfully but thought hard about his words. "Yeah, I think I like her—that's if you're not interested in her."

His heart stopped as he waited for Russ's reply, but Alice jumped in. "He is absolutely interested."

"Excuse me?" Russ glared at his sister, and Dev sat back. Even if Russ was interested in Caitlyn, there was no way he was going after her now and letting Alice win. Dev knew his friend well enough to know that Russ hated the way Alice interfered in his love life and how judgmental she was about the women he dated. Dev understood. His own family was constantly presenting the "biodata" of eligible Indian women from around the globe with the expectation that one of them would catch his attention. None had. Not like Caitlyn. At the thought of his family, a shiver went down his spine. They would never approve of Caitlyn. He shook the thought away. He wasn't marrying her. There was no reason to ever bring his family into their potential relationship.

Relationship? He'd just met the woman tonight. They hadn't even had sex and Dev was already contemplating a relationship? *One step at a time, Mallik*, he told himself.

The first step was getting Caitlyn's number from Alice.

"Alice, Russ isn't going to date Caitlyn because you're setting him up with her."

Alice glared at Dev, and Russ sat back in the couch.

"I'm goin' to let m' man Dev here have her," he said insolently, his Texas accent a little slurred.

"Neither one of you deserves her," she said icily. "I don't know what I was thinking, bringing her into this vipers' pit. That girl is way too good for either one of you. I'd hoped you—" she used her finger to stab Russ in the chest "—had grown up some."

Dev sat up and struck a more serious tone. "Seriously, Alice, I do really like her. She seems like a nice person, and I promise you I'll treat her well. Plus, she asked me to be her practice boyfriend, so I feel like I should at least text her to let her know I'm interested."

Alice's jaw dropped. Literally dropped. "She did what now? What else did she say?"

"Nothing. We didn't really get a chance to talk, what with you trying to insert Russ into the conversation. I don't even have her number to follow up and ask her out on a practice date. Any chance you'd share it?"

Alice narrowed her eyes, and he cringed at the ice-blue glare. "Not a chance. If I have anything to do with it, you aren't getting anywhere near Caitlyn."

Four

Caitlyn awoke the next morning to a text message from an unknown number on her phone. She threw back her comforter, groaning at how bright it was in her room.

When she returned home from Alice's house the night before, she'd found her family, minus Alexa, who was back in Miami, and the Grandins gathered in their living room. They were meeting to discuss their favorite topic: Heath Thurston's claim. They'd rehashed everything they knew, which wasn't much. The private eye had confirmed that Daniel was very likely Ashley's biological father, because the timing fit. But they still didn't know why Victor Grandin had given the oil rights to Cynthia and not to Ashley if it was supposed to be her birthright. Even more puzzling was why Augustus Lattimore had signed the papers. Jonas Shaw, the PI, was also working on finding out if the documents Heath Thurston had shared were legitimate.

Layla and Josh had been there as well, and Caitlyn had spent the entire night studying them surreptitiously, wondering if she'd share something like that with someone. Dev kept coming to mind, but she pushed the thought away.

After the Grandins left, her parents went to bed, but Jonathan, Jayden and Caitlyn stayed up talking. For once it was not about Caitlyn's dating life. None of them liked the idea of sitting around doing nothing while the PI did his work. Jonathan suggested they go through every single piece of paper that related to the property. Augustus, Ben's father and Caitlyn's grandfather, was so forgetful, even their father, Ben, couldn't be sure that he hadn't hidden something in the attic and forgotten about it.

Jonathan had hauled the boxes down from the attic. They'd already been through all the files in the study and Lattimore offices. It was time to unearth what had been hidden away. They had started going through the dusty, cobwebbed boxes. They found some interesting historical pictures, a lot of dead spiders and even a dead mouse in between some old books. They'd given up at the first light of dawn and Caitlyn had taken a quick shower to get the dust off, then crawled into bed.

She had several text messages from Alice but ignored those. She needed to give Alice time to calm down.

Then she saw the text from an unknown number.

How's tonight for a practice date? Dev.

Dev? Had she given him her number? She rubbed her eyes and reread the text. His number wasn't saved in her contacts, so they hadn't exchanged numbers last night. Then she saw the texts from Alice.

Russ got your contact info from my phone and gave
it to Dev.
Has he texted you?
DO NOT go out with him.
Call me when you see this.

She turned her attention back to Dev's text. What
did he mean about a practice date? Her brain was a little
foggy from the whiskey she'd shared with her siblings.
It took a minute for last night's memory to make her sit
up in bed, wide-awake. She'd asked a complete stranger
for boyfriend lessons. *What have I done?*

She stared at the text message and her heart jumped.
It had been so easy to talk to him, the usual feelings of
dread and anxiety hadn't overtaken her. Then there was
the image of Dev's green eyes, his tall frame, the way
he'd licked that sauce off the fork. Warmth stirred deep
in her core. She'd be crazy to go out with him. Surely
there were better ways to practice her dating skills? She
took a breath and typed out her response.

"So what exactly is a practice boyfriend?" Dev
asked.

Caitlyn stopped before taking a sip of her water. How
could she explain it to him when she hadn't been able to
come up with an answer herself, despite having thought
about it all day.

"Are you ready to order?" Caitlyn was grateful for
the too-attentive waiter of the RCW Steakhouse, one
of the fine dining restaurants in Royal. Dev had suggested it, and now he sat back in a collared shirt with
the top button open and khakis. He looked effortlessly
perfect—not too dressy, but not too casual.

Meanwhile, she'd shown up in her standard ladies'

luncheon outfit—a knee-length pale pink sheath dress with a boat neck. She'd tried on every outfit in her closet. To ease the incessant fluttering that had taken hold in her belly ever since she'd texted Dev to accept his invitation, she'd chosen a familiar outfit. One that boosted her confidence and made her feel in charge.

"Tell me about the menu and specials." Dev asked the waiter with a healthy dose of amusement in his voice. The waiter launched into a description of each steak on the menu, finally ending with the special of the day, which was brisket.

"What do you recommend?" Dev turned to her.

"The steak," she quipped.

They both ordered French onion soup for an appetizer and prime rib for dinner, and then Dev let out a laugh. "Maybe I've been in New York too long, but steak houses there don't just serve steak. This is a really nice place but their menu could use some variety."

Caitlyn smiled. "This is a ranchin' town and RCW is a local favorite. I come here at least once a week."

"Does this town really need another fine dining restaurant?"

"It could." Caitlyn said quickly. "A lot of meetings and business gets conducted in restaurants. For example, the hospital board likes to come here for lunch. The women all order salads, minus the steak. They really come here for the whiskey. On that front, this place is the best in town, and if you want to attract the old ranchers, you need to make sure you offer premium alcohol at your restaurant."

He smiled and pretended to take notes. "Looks like you might be the one giving me lessons…on how to succeed in Royal."

Her cheeks warmed. What had come over her last

night at Alice's? Maybe it was the wine, maybe it was the fact that she'd been unbelievably attracted to Dev. Or just some plain old crazy had come over her.

She went on to talk about wine, whiskey and bourbon, the drinks of the town. She wasn't usually this talkative, but she didn't want to go back to talking about what practice dating meant. The conversation flowed through dinner. Somehow, she didn't feel the tension that usually tightened her muscles on these dates. Dev's easy smile put her at ease.

"So what do you do?"

The dreaded question. There was no avoiding it. *Time for the spiel about all the important work I do to make it sound like I have a real job.*

She met his gaze and regretted doing so. His face was so open, his eyes warm and inviting. She remembered how he'd reacted when she'd spit her wine out at him. When that had happened with Jax, he'd made fun of her, repulsed like she'd thrown up on his good shoes. That's the way all men reacted. But not Dev.

She sighed. "I'm basically a socialite. As you gathered last night, my family is wealthy. After college, it was hard to focus on a job or career because my parents needed so much from me. Serving on the various boards that we get invited to, planning charity events, hosting events, etc. I'd be lying to you if I said that I was saving the world. I've just been untethered. I came back home after college and my family needed me, so I put my plans aside."

Every time a man found out that she didn't have a regular nine-to-five job, there were two types of responses—the guy either assumed that she wanted to live off her family money or that she was husband hunting. She couldn't decide which was more offensive. She searched Dev's face for which category he would fall into.

He reached out and put a hand on hers. The weight felt good on her hand, comforting. "Being there for your family is something to be proud of. Big families are complicated, and it takes an inordinate amount of work to keep people and business contacts on your side. Don't ever be apologetic for that."

Tears stung her eyes, and she blinked. "Do you also have a big family?" she managed to choke out.

He smiled. "I have big personalities in my family. I have one brother and one sister, both married with children. And parents who have a rather large business that they want me to take over, much to the discontent of my siblings."

She raised an eyebrow. She couldn't imagine fighting with her siblings for the family business. Part of the reason she took on so much of the family social work was because no one else wanted it, but it was an important part of keeping their standing in Royal and making sure that their ranching business got what it needed.

"Your siblings want the family business, but you don't want to give it to them?"

His lips tugged into a smirk as if the very idea was funny. He shook his head. "Ma and Dad grew up in India, where the eldest son takes over the family empire and takes care of the family. That's me. But I don't want to just inherit my father's wealth. I want to do something on my own, if only to prove that I can successfully run a business. That's why I'm in Royal. My siblings are more than happy to take over the family business, but they have a tendency to live lavish lives, and Dad is worried they'll run the business into the ground. He doesn't trust them, so I'm left playing the peacemaker between my father and siblings."

"Wow. So, what happens to your family business if you successfully launch your restaurant chain?"

"That is a question I refuse to think about. I'm hoping that me being out of New York for a month or so will give my sibs a chance to show Dad that they can step up. I love my father, but he's hard on all of us. Maybe if I'm not there, he'll see my sister's accomplishments. She really has a head for business, but my dad has refused to appreciate that."

Is this guy for real? Most men saw her attachment to her family and her constant focus on them as a sign of immaturity. But here was a guy who truly understood what it meant to love, care and sacrifice for his family.

"Are you going to miss your family while you're here?"

He shook his head and laughed. "I'm so done with family drama. Don't get me wrong, I would stand in front of a bullet for my family, but I need a mental break. That's why I chose Texas for my first restaurant. We have no businesses here, no reason for my family to appear. I need a break from family crises."

Caitlyn's heart fisted. She'd been about to share her own family's dilemma with him, but it was hardly fair.

"So, if you're done stalling with small talk, want to tell my why you need boyfriend lessons?"

No, I want to talk about anything but that.

He was looking at her with such a sparkle in his eyes that her heart jumped and she lost the few words she'd formulated since the start of dinner. *Who asks such a gorgeous guy to be a practice boyfriend?*

"I find it hard to date." She swallowed, trying to get the words out of her dry mouth. "When I'm with a man, I get stiff and quiet. I need some practice dating, getting comfortable with small talk and flirting. You're the first one I've met who I didn't get all tongue-tied with. I didn't mean to spring it on you like that. I'd had a little too much to drink."

"Well, you haven't touched your wine tonight, and I don't see you having any trouble talking to me."

A fact that hadn't gotten unnoticed by her.

"Which is why you're the perfect guy to be a practice boyfriend. I'm comfortable with you and…" *Can tolerate the experience.* She stopped herself from saying the last part out loud. How could she explain to Dev the fear she felt every time she got close to a man? She couldn't even explain it to herself. *Cold fish.* Those were Jax's words but others had said a variation of them to her. The therapist she'd seen had called it a fear of intimacy. A fear that had come from what had happened with Jax.

The sex was fine, but it hadn't cured her inability to connect on an emotional level. She'd seen what Layla and Josh had, how they understood each other and the way they supported one another. Josh knew what Layla needed, and she intuitively took care of him. Was it too much to want the same thing?

He leaned forward. "So am I just meant for conversation or do we get to practice other things, too?" A smile twitched on his lips, and while she tried to maintain eye contact, her heart skipped erratically. Her eyes involuntary dropped to his lips. They were so firm and lush. What would it be like to feel them pressing on the sensitive parts of her? Heat gushed deep in her core, and as she lifted her gaze and watched his eyes darken. She knew without a doubt that he could see what she was thinking.

We can practice anything you want. Wait, what? She

broke eye contact and took a sip of her wine to do something other than think about him and her naked. She wanted to go out on dates, practice her conversational skills, learn how to get to know someone so she could connect with them emotionally. If she had sex with Dev, then their physical relationship would overshadow everything. She couldn't deny the attraction she felt to Dev, but what if she let things get physical and he also found her lacking? *No, that won't do. I have to make it clear to him that this is a platonic relationship.*

"Well, I was thinking I can keep you company as you do your research on the restaurants in town. I can show you around, introduce you to the movers and shakers, and in return you can teach me how to…"

"How to…?"

"Dessert?" Dev shot the waiter a dark look, but he didn't get the message, handing them the dessert menus. Caitlyn quickly declined dessert, and Dev followed suit. She didn't fully trust herself with him yet, it was best to end the date on a high note.

As Dev pulled out his wallet, Caitlyn waved to the waiter, pulling out her own credit card. "I should pay."

He shook his head. "Absolutely not. I invited you to dinner." When Alice had refused to give him Caitlyn's number, Dev had called in a favor with Russ to get her information. He hadn't been able stop thinking about her since last night. She was even more beautiful than he remembered from the night before. *Why would someone like her need a practice boyfriend?* Men should be falling over themselves to get a date with her. He'd just spent the last hour and a half enjoying talking about Royal, the history of Texas and foods from around the world. She was intelligent, witty and grounded. Not at all like the socialites he'd met in New York whose main focus was making sure they outdid each other, whether it was fashion, jewelry or Manhattan parties. She was the first woman he'd met in a long time whom he wanted to get to know, not just take back to his bed. Although *that* was something he also wanted to do. Eventually. As long as she was okay with the idea that their relationship was temporary. He had enough going on with his life that he wasn't interested in any type of long-term commitment. But while he hadn't planned on an affair in Royal, it would make his time here a lot more interesting.

"Yes, but you only invited me because I asked you to be a…practice boyfriend." She tripped over the last words, and he smiled.

As their server made his way over, Dev held out his card to the waiter, who plucked it out of his hand. "I asked you to dinner. Because I wanted to see you. Practice or not. Besides, this is a business expense, I'm here to check out the competition."

Caitlyn smiled widely, and he found himself smiling back, completely taken in by the sweetness in her eyes. "This place is a Royal institution. They'll be on of your main competitors."

"Russ has been telling me for years that there's no place like Royal to open a restaurant. Lots of deep pockets and a real appreciation for good food."

"He's right."

The waiter returned with the credit card receipt a little too efficiently. Dev was hoping to get some more time with Caitlyn. "Do you know a place where we can get coffee?"

She paused, and he was sure she was about to refuse him, but then she nodded.

As they walked out of the restaurant, he placed his hand at the small of her back. A gesture he hadn't even thought about until she stiffened. He removed his hand. *Did I do something wrong?*

They walked down the main street. The daytime heat had dissipated, so the night was warm but the slight breeze made it comfortable. The sun had set, but the last rays clung to the sky in hues of dark orange and purple. Old-timey streetlamps threw seductive shadows on the bricked sidewalk. It was the quintessential main street of old-town America. He longed to take her hand or tuck her arm in his, but he resisted. As they walked, she pointed out the various local businesses, most of which had closed for the day. He marveled at how she knew the names of each of the owners and their life stories.

She stopped in front of a red brick building with an old-fashioned sign that read General Store.

"Now if you are serious about opening a restaurant here, you need to make friends with Ol'Fred. Don't call him Fred. He likes to be called Ol'Fred."

"With the Texas twang?"

She smiled. "Yes. His family has been in Royal since the town was founded, and he not only knows all the landowners in town, anything you need to get things done, he's the man. He knows all the building contractors, the city inspectors and the permit architects at the county. And if you need a certain brand of tonic water for some spoiled brat cousin that even Amazon doesn't carry, he can get it for you."

They were standing underneath a streetlight, which emitted a soft golden glow on her face. He turned to face her, unable to take being so close to her and not touching her.

"Caitlyn, cards on the table. I like you. I want to

spend more time with you, and not just because you can give me a crash course on all things Royal. What exactly do you want from me?"

She swallowed but didn't avert her gaze. "I don't want to be pitied because I usually can't get past a few dates. I want to learn how to open up to a man and have meaningful conversations, not just small talk. To connect on an emotional level."

He stepped closer to her. She stiffened but didn't step back.

"Is that all you want? To connect emotionally? What about physically, Caitlyn? Do you need practice with that?" His voice was low and thick, and he couldn't help it. She looked so devastatingly sexy and vulnerable that he wanted to—no, he *needed* to touch her, to let her know that she didn't need any help connecting with him, or anyone, for that matter. If she was having problems, the fault was clearly with the guy for not seeing the intelligent, caring person she was.

"I… I…don't know," she said helplessly. Her eyes darkened, and she dropped her gaze to his lips and her face tipped upward slightly.

"Then let me help you make up your mind."

He stepped closer and ran his hands down her bare arms, enjoying the soft, silky feel of her skin. He watched her face. She closed her eyes, and her lips parted slightly. Goose bumps sprang up on her arm, despite the hot night, and he knew she was feeling the same electric connection he was. He gently took her hand.

"Open your eyes."

She did.

"I'm going to kiss you now."

Her eyes widened. He bent his head and kissed her

softly, just barely touching her lips, savoring the feel of her. He felt the slight pressure of her lips as she kissed him back and opened her mouth to him. He wanted more than anything to deepen the kiss, but he didn't want to scare her off. He put his arm around her waist to steady them. She felt so right pressed against him, and he couldn't help but pull her closer so he could feel the crush of her breasts against his chest.

That's when it happened. For the first time in his life, a woman pushed him away from her like she couldn't stand his touch.

Five

What have I done?

She hadn't meant to push him away so rudely. What she'd wanted to do was kiss him hard then untuck that stiff shirt and run her hands all over his chest. She'd pressed herself against him and felt the same heat that pulsed between her legs in his pants. And that scared the hell out of her. She didn't want to risk being rejected by him. *A cold fish.*

He stepped back from her and held his hands up. The streetlamp lit his eyes, which were filled with horror. "I'm sorry I misread things, Caitlyn. I didn't mean to kiss you if you didn't want it."

Didn't want it? That's not the problem. She wanted it *too much*, with a fire and intensity that didn't make any sense. It was just a kiss. He was just a guy.

She shook her head. "No, I'm sorry. I didn't mean to do that."

"Kiss me or push me away?"

Both.

"Push you away. I don't know what came over me.
I've never done anything like that before."

"Am I so bad a kisser?" he said lightly, placing a
hand on his chest where she'd pushed him. He looked
so devastatingly, boyishly handsome, her heart fisted.
She'd expected him to get angry, to yell at her, utter
some expletives. She had wanted the kiss. He had
warned her that he was about to kiss her. She wanted
to lie to him and tell him that she'd changed her mind
about him being a practice boyfriend. That she didn't
want to see him anymore. This non-relationship was
already too intense.

But isn't that exactly what I want?

"It's the opposite problem, actually. It was just so…
good."

"Now, that's a more interesting answer." He stepped
closer to her. "What do you mean?"

"Do you mind if we walk?" It was too disconcert-
ing, having him looking at her. As irrational as it was,
she couldn't help feeling he could read her thoughts.
She didn't want him to know how out of control he
made her feel.

"Lead the way."

As they walked down the main town street, she re-
sumed her informational session on Royal businesses.
She was avoiding the conversation. She knew it, and
Dev knew it, but he let her go on, asking her questions
about Royal and about her family. Familiar, comfortable
topics. When they reached the tack shop, she stopped.

"This is where everyone in town buys their fancy
equestrian items for the horses they ride in shows."

"Do you ride?"

She nodded and looked wistfully at the shop. Dev was in town pursuing his dream, and yet hers was stalled.

"What is it?"

She turned to him in surprise. "Nothing."

He rolled his eyes. "I have a sister and a mother, so I know when a woman says 'nothing' it really means 'everything.'"

Now it was her turn to roll her eyes. "Oh, please, don't mansplain me. Sometimes it also means I don't want to talk about it, or more importantly, I don't want to talk about it with *you*."

He smiled. "C'mon, I'm your practice boyfriend. If you can't tell me, then who?"

The laughter in his voice was infectious, and it made her smile at her own ridiculousness. "Fine, if you must know. I have this plan—more of a dream, actually—of starting a horse-riding program for foster children on the Lattimore ranch. I've been around horses all my life, and it's been an amazing experience for me and a teaching tool in how to care for an animal, how to feel one with another living being."

She pointed to a belt buckle in the shop. It was a big silver buckle studded with rhinestones. "That buckle costs what most foster families make in a month. They can't afford to send kids to horse riding camps. We have all these horses that we hire staff to ride because no one has the time to groom and ride them. Seems like such a waste."

"So what's stopping you?"

"I can't just open up the Lattimore ranch and ask kids to come on over and ride horses. I have to get permits, inspections—it's a whole process."

He raised an eyebrow. "I get it. You pissed off Ol'Fred and he's standing in your way."

She smiled. "Ol'Fred has been offering to adopt me since I was a little girl. He'd do anything to help me."

"So then?"

"It's just life. I have all these obligations and board commitments. It's hard to find the time."

"Sounds like excuses to me."

"What?" *How dare he?* He didn't have any idea what her life was like.

He turned to face her. The light from the tack shop threw shadows across his face. He raised his hands like he was going to touch her, then crossed them. "You seem like the type of woman who knows how to get things done in this town. If you want to open this camp, I bet you could make it happen with a snap of your fingers. So, what are you waiting for? What's stopping you? The real reason, not the one you're telling yourself and everyone else."

She wanted to give him an angry response, but the warm look in his eyes and the crease on his forehead melted her heart. She was looking for genuine connection. What had her therapist said? That she put up blocks, hid behind her conversation talking points. Normally her dates didn't care to probe past what she said. They were too focused on how the night would end and whether she'd accept an invitation to their bed. But Dev wanted to know more. He wanted to talk about things she hadn't prepared for.

She swallowed, then looked into the tack shop window to avoid his gaze. "I'm the youngest in the family. I have two brothers and a sister. They've looked out for me my whole life. Made sure I'm successful in whatever I do."

"You've never done anything on your own."

She shook her head. "It's not that. I've planned many charitable events and social programs. You're right. I can do this in my sleep. But I've never done anything this important. Since the pandemic, the foster program has been overwhelmed. And it's not just the stories you expect—kids who are abandoned, abused or neglected. It's kids whose parents love them but lost their jobs and couldn't make ends meet. The state forcibly took the kids because they were living in cars and homeless shelters. Neither the parents nor the kids want to be apart, but the state has to put the kids in a stable home. Then there are cutbacks to the state program so the families who foster get little support and are overwhelmed themselves. These kids are moved from one family to another. And even when the kids find a good family, they feel they have to be loyal to their birth parents and don't know how to process the emotions they feel toward their foster parents."

Tears sprang to her eyes as she thought about the kids she'd met. She volunteered at the child protection services office, babysitting kids who were waiting for placement. Playing with them and giving them the attention that the social workers who were busy finding them families didn't have the bandwidth for.

"I want to give them something that's stable. A place where they feel safe and can connect with a living being without the complications of a label like 'foster dad' and 'real mom.'"

"Is that how you feel about horses?"

She startled. "What?"

"A horse only needs water, food, shelter and grooming. No complicated human emotions with horses."

A bitter taste swirled in the back of her throat. Was

that why she'd always gotten along with horses? Because they didn't expect any real feelings from her? No, that couldn't be true. She loved her horses, talked to them, bonded with them. They sensed when she was sad or angry. But they didn't expect as much from her as a man, that much was true. Yet she wasn't about to admit that to Dev. They'd already gotten a little too close for comfort.

She sighed. "Horses sense feelings and emotions. They need love, which is why a riding program for kids is so perfect. They have so much love to give, and they just don't know where to direct it sometimes."

He bent his knees so he was face-to-face with her, forcing her to look at him. His eyes were soft, even a little shiny. "You are a wonderful person, Caitlyn. I hope you know that. To care about something other than yourself is something very few people know how to do."

Then why am I such a cold fish? she almost blurted out. She tried to smile at him, but tears threatened to spill out of her eyes, so she turned her gaze back to the tack shop window. "I was ready to start my program, but there's an issue with my ranch. I don't want to start the program and have to take it away."

"What do you mean?"

Could she tell him? "It's exactly the type of family drama you don't want to get involved in."

He laughed now. "As long as it's not *my* family drama, I don't care. C'mon, spill it."

She told him about Heath Thurston's claim.

"Let me get this straight. Ashley might be the blood relative, but Cynthia is Ashley's mother, and the oil rights were given to her."

"Correct, which actually makes the claim stronger, because Heath and Nolan are Cynthia's sons, so they directly inherit from their mother. But there are still some things that don't make sense, so we've hired a PI to find out."

"I'm sorry, I'm not a rancher. Why does Victor Grandin, is it?" She nodded, so he went on. "Why does he get to give the oil rights to your land to cover up his son's sins?"

"That's the baffling part. My grandfather signed the papers so the rights beneath our land are included."

"Didn't you say you live with your grandfather? Why not ask him?"

"Augustus is ninety-six years old and has memory issues. We've tried asking him, and each time we get a different story. We're trying to find out whether the signature is even genuine."

"So how does this affect your horse camp?"

"If the claim is real, and Heath and Nolan Thurston decide to exercise their rights, they'd be digging wells right where the stables are. We'd lose the stables and horses. I can't do that to those kids. While all this could take some time, I can't let them fall in love with something that then gets yanked away from them."

"Is that what happened to you?"

"What?"

"Is there something that got taken away from you?" he asked softly.

Her heart beat wildly in her chest, and her palms felt greasy. She was the most privileged child she knew. A biracial baby adopted by a wealthy, loving family who doted on her. There was absolutely nothing that she could have asked for in her life that hadn't been handed to her. The only thing she'd ever lost was Jax, her high school best friend and perhaps the love of her life.

She shook her head. "I'm the story every foster kid

dreams of. My parents adopted me when I was a baby. My family, including my siblings, love me like crazy. I couldn't ask for anything in my life."

"Does that make you feel guilty?"

"What?"

"That you were given a chance with your family that the foster kids don't have? Is that why you want to open the horse ranch?"

She took a shuddering breath. *How did he know?*

"It's okay to feel guilty, for having it all, you know. To even feel resentful for it. You didn't ask for it."

This time she didn't stop the tears that squeezed out of her eyes. All her life, she'd been told how lucky she was, to be grateful for the gift she'd been given. That's why she'd returned home after college to take over the Lattimores' charitable and community work. To give back a little bit of what she'd gotten. Yet all she felt was guilty. For having it all. For not giving back enough. For not saving all the other kids, the majority of them Black, from the fate the Lattimores had saved her from.

Dev lightly placed a hand on her arm then extended his other arm, inviting her to step into his embrace. She couldn't resist. Stepping close, she placed her cheek against his chest and immediately felt his warmth strengthen her.

You know Royal has a ghetto? It's where people like me live. Where your butler, gardener, cook and Ol'Fred live. Jax had said those words to her when he'd gone off to college. It was his way of telling her there was a whole world she needed to see. The real world. He hadn't said it with malice, but it still hurt.

Dev was almost a foot taller than she was, even with her heels. Yet she fit perfectly against him. She focused on the beating of his heart, which seemed to be racing as wildly as hers. Closing her eyes against the rise and fall of his chest, she took deep breaths to push Jax out of her mind. Here was a man who wasn't obliged to be with her. He was here because he wanted to be. No one was forcing him.

"How about we make a deal?"

Caitlyn stepped back from Dev, blinking away the remaining tears in her eyes.

His green eyes sparkled. "How about I agree to be your practice boyfriend and help you figure out how to make your horse camp happen, and you introduce me around town and help me set up my restaurant?"

She smiled. "What exactly does being a practice girlfriend entail?"

He grinned. "I like how you turned this around on me."

While she'd pulled back from his embrace, his hands were still loosely on her arms, and she liked them there, liked the weight of his touch, the slight smell of soap and aftershave. Maybe it wouldn't be that bad an idea for him to be a full boyfriend. What if she slept with him? What's the worst that could happen? Their relationship would end the same way her others had? So what? Dev was only going to be in Royal for a month. He'd told her at dinner that he planned to open the restaurant, then return to New York to his family business before continuing to establish a chain of restaurants. He wasn't planning on living in Royal. He wasn't going to be a long-term anything, and she planned to be a lifelong Royal. If along the way he could help her get more comfortable with men, that's all she needed. Wasn't that the point of boyfriend lessons anyway?

"Here's what I can offer you as a practice boyfriend," Dev said, and Caitlyn followed the smooth, thick sound of his voice, letting herself get pulled in. He was a man—he would ask for the thing all men wanted. And she was ready to say yes.

"We can spend time together, go out on dates and get all the conversation time you want."

She nodded, waiting for the next part. Because suddenly, that's the part she really wanted.

"I'm not going to touch you without your permission. And I'm not going to sleep with you."

"Wait, what?" She hadn't meant to say that out loud. It had been in her head but had come out most unexpectedly.

He smiled. "I've never had to entice a woman into my bed, and I'm not going to start now. We'll keep it a platonic relationship, unless…"

Her throat closed. "Unless?"

He leaned over, his lips oh so close to hers but not quite touching. "There's a lot more that I can teach you other than conversational skills." She sucked in a breath, wanting desperately to move an inch forward and press her lips on his. But he seemed to be moving away.

"But if you want more, you're the one who's going to have to seduce me."

Six

She sat up, hot and sweating, in her own room with its pastel-blue ceiling and soft gray walls. She'd been dreaming about Dev giving her lessons in bed. The kind of lessons that made her breathing heavy, her body sweaty, and matted her hair to her head. Caitlyn rarely dreamed, but when she did, they were vivid and visceral. But this dream was crazy. It didn't take a genius to figure out what it all meant.

As if he could sense her thinking about him, her phone buzzed with a text from him.

Going to check out a restaurant on Colton Street at 9 am. Are you free to come with me? Practice brunch date afterward?

It had been less than twelve hours since she'd seen him, but the idea of going out with him filled her with excitement. She texted him back then sprang out of bed. With only forty-five minutes to get dressed, she wouldn't have time to wash her hair, which was a bit of a production. She did a quick conditioner wash to get the sweat out, then pulled it back into a ponytail, forgoing perfectly straight hair that she usually re-curled into perfect waves. Her hair was naturally curly, but not the tight curls or long locks Alexa had. She often envied her sister's perfect hair.

She chose a sundress, one of her favorites that she usually wore around the house, a peacock-blue dress that wrapped around her with a deep V-neck and a hemline that ended right before her knees. Her smart watch told her the day would be hot, so she knew better than to wear makeup. It would just melt and make her face look splotchy. Plus, she didn't have much time, so she settled for a swipe of lip gloss and threw on strappy but flat sandals in case there was a lot of walking to do.

She took one last look in the ornate full-length mirror in her walk-in closet and had to admit that she liked this new look. If she didn't know better, she'd say she looked like one of those flirty girls on the cover of a fashion magazine. She normally dressed so business-like. Her hair was always perfectly pressed and styled, never in natural curls, as it was now with nothing but a scrunchie. Caitlyn wasn't vain, but she knew that she was generally a beautiful woman, having been blessed with big eyes, a small, straight nose and lips that fit her face perfectly. Her skin color ranged from a beige to a golden brown, depending on her summer tan. Looking at the bottles of different-colored foundations on her dresser, she quickly took an extra minute to put on sunblock. She had a series of Royal events on her calendar where it would definitely not be suitable to show up without makeup or with wild hair. But the morning belonged to Dev.

Dev had offered to pick her up, but she chose to drive into town. Against her father's wishes, she'd opted for a Tesla Model 3. It was dwarfed on the road and in her driveway by the bigger cars, but she liked the electric car among the gas guzzlers in town. It was Sunday, so she didn't have any meetings, but she did want to stop by the child protection services office to see if they needed her help later in the day. They'd been short-staffed lately, and she often found the social workers there on Sundays. She helped them with filing or photocopying so they didn't spend their entire Sunday working.

She arrived five minutes late. Dev had asked her to meet him inside the restaurant, but he was waiting by the door for her. She pulled to the curb. He had been leaning against the brick wall of the building, one leg bent, his eyes on his phone. He wore a V-neck T-shirt and jeans. His hair looked perfectly mussed, with soft waves that kissed his brow. He looked up when she arrived.

"That's not a legal spot. There's a parking lot in the back." He gestured to the little driveway a few feet away.

"I know. But don't worry, I won't get ticketed. Sorry I'm late."

He came around the front of the car as she collected her purse and opened the door. Or tried to. It was locked. He grinned, and she unlocked it. When it clicked, he tugged again.

"These car manufacturers make it really hard to be chivalrous."

"That's because chivalry is dead. Instead, those gentlemen of yesteryear are replaced by creeps that try to carjack and assault women, which is why car doors automatically lock."

He shook his head as he extended his hand to help her out of the car. She didn't need help but liked it. It gave her an excuse to touch him.

As she brushed past him, he whispered, "You look amazing, by the way." She warmed, not at the compliment but by the thickness in his voice as he said it.

He let go of her hand, then held his out. She looked at him, confused.

"Am I supposed to give you something?"

He smiled. "Your car keys, so I can park it in the lot."

She laughed. "Actually, this car has no keys. It runs off the app on my phone. Is that what women in New York do? Hand you their keys and say 'park the car'?"

"Not exactly, but they are used to a certain amount of male chivalry."

She shook her head. "My car is fine here. I know the cops on the parking beat—they never ticket my car."

His eyebrows rose. "Well, don't you have the town of Royal wrapped around your little finger."

"It's amazing how much appreciation a few charity events, and bagel and coffee at the precinct buys you."

He did a mini bow. "You are truly the princess of Royal."

The door opened, and a man in a suit stepped out of the restaurant. He was tall, lanky, with sandy blond hair and blue eyes. He smiled widely as he saw her. "Miss Caitlyn, I had no idea you were the friend Mr. Mallik said we were waiting for."

"Greg, it's so nice to see you," Caitlyn said genuinely. "It has to have been over a year since you were last at the ranch. Your dad told me you'd gone into commercial real estate."

He nodded proudly. "And doin' real well, thanks to Mr. Lattimore's recommendations, miss."

"Greg, we're the same age, please call me Caitlyn."

Dev looked at Caitlyn. "How do you two know each other?"

"We live in the same town—a lot of us know each other."

Greg piped up, "She's bein' too kind. My daddy works as a ranch hand on the Lattimore estate. I grew up workin' every summer at Miss Caitlyn's."

"Greg, please call me Caitlyn."

He turned slightly red at her second request, seeming unsure whether it would be more offensive to heed her request or undo his very traditional father's strict request to call everyone up at the mansion by Mr. or Miss or Mrs.

"Let me show you the place. It used to be…"

"…the old Stevens brewery," Caitlyn finished.

Greg nodded. "Miss…sorry, Caitlyn here knows more about Royal history than anyone. Well, except Ol'Fred."

Caitlyn realized that she was interfering with Greg's carefully planned spiel, so she deferred to him to tell the rest as Greg showed them the space. The brewery had been closed for almost a decade. The Stevenses had been an old couple who ran it for nearly thirty years. When they died, they left the brewery to a nephew who lived in Los Angeles, and he put it up for sale. It had changed hands a couple of times—a local rancher tried to open up a steak house, which competed with the RCW Steakhouse and it became a town feud. The rancher gave up on it and sold the property to a chain restaurant. It didn't do very well. The leftovers of the red icon still hung over the old wood bar. The place was in rough shape, having been on the market for several years with little maintenance. Someone had swept up recently, but the old wooden floors were caked with mud and dirt, and the stale smell of old water, dead mice and long-ago yeast still hung in the air.

Dev asked Greg several questions about the sale terms and the condition of the kitchen equipment. Greg had done his homework, and Caitlyn made a note to tell his dad just how well he was doing. She knew Mr. Hodges was always tough with him. Caitlyn hadn't really known Greg when they were growing up, even though she visited the stables daily. *You never socialize with those who aren't in your stratosphere.* Jax had said that to her when he had first returned home from college. At the time he'd said it with a laugh but she later learned that he'd meant those words.

"How about I leave you two to discuss it? I'll just be two doors down at the café when you're done. Let me know and I'll lock up," Greg said, smiling.

Dev turned to Caitlyn once Greg had left. "If I didn't know better, I'd say the lad was crushing on you."

Caitlyn frowned. "What? No! Greg's just…he's Greg."

"Greg is an all-American male, and he has a crush on young Miss Caitlyn." Dev added Greg's accent when he said her name, and she laughed.

"So what you do think of the place?"

They stood in the center of what was supposed to be the dining room. Caitlyn had never been in this place before, but she'd heard about it from the locals when it was the brewery.

Dev was deep in thought. "It's nice. It certainly has good bones and old-world charm, but it's just so…"

"Just so…"

Dev clicked his fingers as if trying to find the words. "…Texas," Caitlyn supplied.

He grinned. "Yes. Exactly. Like the RCW Steakhouse."

"It's the kind of place old men would come to eat bloody steak and smoke cigars."

They both laughed at that. "I need my place to feel like you're coming to eat at a relative's house. It's different, it's not everyday, but it's homey."

"And you're looking for that in Royal?"

"Would you eat in a place like that?"

She nodded, acknowledging the trap. "I think the younger generation of Royal is not quite as big on stuffy and formal restaurants. They are well traveled and appreciate new and refined cuisine."

Dev nodded. "Well, this is the first of three places Russ had prioritized for me to see. Let's hope the other ones are better."

"You'll find something," Caitlyn said reassuringly.

They looked at each other for a moment. "I really like this look on you," he said.

"What look is that?"

His lips twitched. "This natural look, like you don't have a care in the world."

"This Caitlyn usually doesn't step out of the house."

"Why not?"

Why not indeed? She shrugged. "I just feel like it's an expectation, you know. I'm a Lattimore, and I need to represent the family." Even as she said the words, she knew they weren't true. Her parents had never put any pressure or expectations on her, and her siblings certainly didn't act that way.

"Are you sure it's not body armor?"

"What would I need body armor for? I have everything I could possibly ask for." She didn't like the pitch of her voice when she said those words, even though they were true.

"Well, I like all your looks, Caitlyn, but this is definitely my favorite." He stepped closer to her, and she felt a slight tug as he wrapped one of her curls around his finger.

"I like your hair natural."

He was close to her, and she breathed in the spicy scent of his aftershave. It was seductively woodsy. Why did she want a platonic relationship again? He was nearly a foot taller than her, so she was looking up and noticed a tiny shaving cut on the side of this jaw. She touched her finger to the cut, and he froze, then stepped back from her.

"Wait, you got to touch mine, but I don't get to touch yours?" she said playfully, marveling at the seduction that had naturally crept into her voice. It was as if she was someone else entirely. His green eyes darkened, and her insides melted.

She lifted her fingers and touched his hair. He sucked in a breath, and she smiled, feeling a surge of excitement. His hair was soft, not textured like hers, but thick and naturally wavy. He didn't use a lot of hair product. She liked that. What would it be like to run all her fingers into his hair and tug? Would he like it?

He cleared his throat. "Are you done fondling my hair?"

She retreated her hand and stepped back several

paces suddenly embarrassed at the naked lust that she was sure was written all over her face.

He closed the distance between them. "Caitlyn, don't get me wrong. I want you to touch my hair. I want you to touch a lot more than my hair." His voice was low and thick and his eyes dark pools of molten heat. Her own skin was enticingly warm and tingly. "I'm doing my best to be a gentleman here, but know this…" He bent a little closer so his lips were mere inches from hers. His breath was so close to her mouth that she wanted to suck it in. "…anytime, anyplace you want me, you can have me. No questions asked."

She did suck in that breath, unsure of what to say or how to react. Deep inside, a voice screamed, *Take me now, put me against the bar, lift up my skirt and show me just how much you want me.* But that voice stuck in her throat. He waited for what seemed like an eternity, then straightened and stepped back from her. The silence stretched between them until he broke it. "I guess Greg is waiting for us. Let's give him the keys and I'll take you to brunch."

She nodded and followed him out, knowing the moment was lost and wondering if she was falling into the same old patterns again.

Seven

"This could be the set for a horror movie," Caitlyn said.

They were sitting in Dev's rental car waiting for Greg to show up. It was early in the morning, but the place they were visiting was clearly deserted. They had unbuckled their safety belts but felt it best to wait for Greg before they went exploring. The structure before them looked like it had been a diner once. The large neon sign had stopped working, but the letters were visible. The windows were large, and beyond the coat of dust and grime, they could barely make out gingham curtains. The parking lot was spacious, with no spaces for handicapped parking, indicating the place had been closed a very long time.

"I think Russ is purposely setting me up with these terrible properties to punish me for moving out to the hotel."

"Was he mad?" Caitlyn asked.

Dev nodded. "He took it as a personal affront to his hospitality. Never mind that the guy's idea of break-fast is still Froot Loops, 'cowboy style,' as he calls it, meaning dry, because it's too much to keep fresh milk in the fridge."

"You should do something to make nice with him."

Dev nodded. "I promised him we'd go out one night. Apparently, there's some Lone Ranger nightclub that he's dying to take me to."

Caitlyn felt an irrational bubble of anger. "The Lone *Star* is a meat market. It's where singles go to hook up."

Dev looked at her, his green eyes mischievous. "Would it bother you for me to go there?"

Caitlyn looked toward the diner so he wouldn't see her eyes. He had an uncanny way of reading her. It had been two weeks since the first night they'd met and she had seen Dev almost every day, either to look at a prop-erty with him when her time allowed, or at dinner. They were almost in a routine. He texted her each morning asking what her day looked like then suggested a way for them to see each other. Yesterday she'd been tied up all day, so they'd met for coffee in between her after-noon meeting and her dinner charity event at the Texas Cattleman's Club. Caitlyn had wrangled with whether to invite Dev as her date rather than showing up alone yet again, but she had ultimately decided against it. There would be too many questions—ones she wasn't ready to answer yet. She didn't need any more gossip among the Royal residents. They still asked her about what happened with Jax and they'd broken up a year ago.

Jax. The other reason she hadn't invited Dev to the gala last night. She hadn't known if Jax would be there. On the off chance he would, she wanted to face him alone. They hadn't seen each other since *that* night, but she knew it was time for them to talk. They'd spent too long avoiding each other. In an odd way, spending time with Dev made her less nervous about the difficult conversation that lay ahead with Jax.

Despite the sexual tension that simmered between them, it was easy to talk to Dev. Maybe it was that he didn't let her get away with canned answers. He always pried and probed until she felt coaxed into talking. She'd shared more of herself with Dev in two weeks than she had with any other man. Even Jax. She knew Dev was only here temporarily, but she didn't want to share him with someone else, even for one night.

"What would you do if I said I don't want you to go?"

He didn't answer, so she looked at him. He was staring at her. Since the day in the old Stevens brewery, their time together had been physically distant. While she enjoyed spending time with him, she was reminded of her physical attraction to him and could no longer ignore the sexual frustration she felt.

"Why don't you want me to go, Caitlyn?"

The ball was in her court. She understood that. But she couldn't help fearing what would happen if she took the next step. She'd never had such an easy rapport with any man. They flirted, laughed, shared deeply personal thoughts, and she finally understood what her therapist meant about her needing to open up. She didn't want to lose that. What if they slept together and it didn't work out? As it is, there were a scant two weeks before he left Royal. Maybe friendship was all she should take from him.

"I don't want us to practice anymore. I want to be with you, physically." The words tumbled out of her before she could stop them. His darkening eyes mesmerized her and she leaned forward. He didn't hesitate, and closed the distance between them. His hand cupped her cheek, and he pressed his lips firmly to hers. His tongue flicked across her bottom lip, and she lost all rational thought. Her entire body quivered, her core hot and desperate for his touch. This time she didn't hold back. She let her tongue tangle with his. When the kiss wasn't enough, she twisted her body and tucked a knee underneath her so she could get even closer to him.

The kiss broke and she moaned in protest, but Dev pulled back and cleared his throat. "Greg is here."

She noticed him adjusting his pants, and she looked down to see that her wraparound dress was twisted so her ample cleavage was on full display. She didn't miss Dev's appreciative glance but sat back in the seat and quickly adjusted her dress.

Greg tapped on the window, and Dev and Caitlyn looked at each other and smiled.

The diner was in such rough shape that they couldn't really go inside. When Greg unlocked the door with a set of old-fashioned keys, the lock was so rusted that he had to force the handle, which in turn led to the door splintering on its hinges. The wooden flooring inside had significant cracks, and none of them felt like testing whether it could hold their weight.

Greg smiled apologetically. "As I said, the property is in rough shape, but there are really no more options on the west side of Royal. This is at the very edge. I know this building would have to be a teardown, but this property comes with fifty acres of land and a barn that's in usable shape."

Dev's eyebrows shot up. "Fifty as in five zero."

Greg nodded, and Caitlyn had the urge to giggle at Dev's wide eyes.

"This is Texas, darlin'. That kind of land is not uncommon." She smirked.

"Yeah, I'm used to New York properties, where we talk in inches, not acres."

"It's a pretty nice parcel of land—flat, clear lot. I know the ladies' auxiliary has been rentin' it regularly for their clothing drives."

"That barn has an entrance through *Piedmont Road* right?" Caitlyn confirmed.

Greg nodded. "But you see that little footpath there?" He pointed to the other side of the parking lot. "That'll lead you right through the trees and to the barn. You might want to go see it since you're already here."

Caitlyn turned to Dev. "I've been in that barn once. It's actually pretty nice. Maybe the restaurant can be situated there."

Dev raised his brow. "Really?"

"No harm in checking it out," Caitlyn said.

"Well, you folks go ahead. I'm gonna have to do some callin' around, see who I can get to come board up that door," Greg said. "It won't be right to leave it like that." He handed them a set of keys. "These will open the side entrance. Drop them off in town at the real estate office when you're done. Now you be careful walkin' around."

Dev still looked skeptical, but Caitlyn grabbed his hand. "C'mon."

She took him out back. Thick shrubbery overwhelmed the narrow footpath. "Are you sure about this?" He looked pointedly towards her bare legs and sandaled feet.

She nodded. An idea had come to her when Greg mentioned the barn, but she wasn't sure Dev would understand it until he saw the space.

She led him through the thicket of trees, and they emerged in a field that had long ago browned and dried up. A large red barn stood about two football fields away.

"Wow, that looks like it could be on the cover of *Farm and Country*."

Caitlyn was pleased that the barn was the one she remembered. From the outside, it looked like a quintessential farm barn—tall with a sloping gray roof and white cross-hatched windows. The once-red paint was now a dull maroon, and as they got closer, they could see that the wood siding on the barn was cracked and peeling in several places. They walked around to the side, past the big front doors, as Greg had instructed, and to a side entrance. They unlocked the padlock, and the door opened easily.

Inside, the cavernous space smelled like earth and pine cones. It must have been recently used, because rubber pavers had been added to the floor, and several six-foot tables were set up in the center of the room. There were a number of cardboard boxes here and there but overall, the space was neat. The artificial pine cone smell came from several tree-shaped air fresheners that had been hung across the wooden slats delineating the hayloft. Caitlyn smiled. Only the ladies' auxiliary would try to freshen up a barn. She walked over to the double front doors and deftly unlocked them from the inside, throwing them open and bathing the barn in sunshine and fresh air.

"So, I have a crazy idea."

Dev smiled, "I can't wait to hear it." There was no snark in his voice, just pure interest, and she tried not to notice how alluring his emerald green eyes shone in the sunlit barn. There was no doubt in her mind that he was more interested in picking up where they left off in the car. Not that she wasn't. The barn was deserted, after all, and oddly romantic.

"This town has plenty of upscale restaurants. What if you opened a family Indian fusion restaurant? Imagine dining tables inside where parents can sit and enjoy a nice meal. And outside, you set up a playground where the kids can run around, get some fresh air. You can even have an indoor-outdoor kitchen. Build a tandoori oven outside where your chef can bake fresh naan."

"Someone's been doing their homework on Indian cuisine."

She smiled shyly. She had been doing a lot of research, but she wasn't about to admit just how much time she'd spent trying to learn a little more about his culture. She'd learned that *chai* meant tea, so saying "chai tea" was redundant. Just like *naan* meant bread, so saying "naan bread" was the same thing. She'd realized that he spent so much time asking about her that she hadn't learned much about his heritage from him.

"I like the concept, but to renovate this space will require a lot of resources. I was banking on creating a luxury brand. I don't see the clientele from RCW Steakhouse, or a lot of the ranchers in this town, sitting down to eat in a barn. In New York, yes, people would drive hours to have this type of experience, but not here. They'd feel like they were in their own backyard. I think upscale is the way to go."

He wasn't wrong on that front, and her heart deflated.

"Hey, what's wrong?" He stepped toward her and bent down so he could look her straight in the eyes. How was Dev such a mind reader? She shook her head, not trusting herself to speak.

"It's written all over your face." He placed his hands on her bare shoulders, and his touch heated her insides.

"I guess I want you to find a space here in Royal so you don't leave."

He smiled. "You're enjoying my company that much, huh?"

She lifted her face so she could meet his gaze. She ran her fingers along his jawbone, then across his bottom lip. His lips parted, and she grabbed his chin and pulled him toward her. Their lips crashed, and every single second she'd spent holding herself back from being with him destroyed the last threads of inhibition still holding her together.

She wrapped her arms around his neck and pulled him closer, pressing her body to his. With her flat sandals, she had to go on tiptoes even with his head bent. She fit perfectly into him, and just as she felt the hot heat between her legs, his erection pressed hard into her belly. His hands went around her waist. She thrust her hips forward, unable to control the maddening need for him.

He moved his hands to her butt and bent down and lifted her. She wrapped her legs around him, enjoying him hot and hard between her legs. She'd never wanted anything as much as she wanted him inside her. Her panties were wet with need, and her core throbbed painfully. He carried her to one of the folding tables, then set her on it. He hadn't broken the kiss, and she searched wildly for his hand, but he was ahead of her.

As she plundered his mouth, he put his hand on her knee and ran it up her thigh. She moaned, arching her hips instinctively to encourage him. Her hands were still around his neck, and she ran them down to his chest. He put his palm between her legs, pressing against the silk of her panties, and she moaned. The warmth of his hand provided temporary relief. She pulsed against his hand, then broke the kiss. "More, Dev, I need more."

He didn't hesitate. He slipped the fabric of her panties aside and put his thumb on her core. The rush of heat that flew through her belly was so intense that she sucked in her breath. His lips moved from her mouth to her neck as his thumb circled her clit. "More," she said hoarsely. She needed him inside her, filling her, pumping into her, releasing her.

He slipped a finger inside her but kept his thumb on her core. She gasped and grabbed a fistful of his shirt, unsure if she could keep her balance on the table. Her entire body throbbed with pleasure. "I need you," she begged, so close to the edge, she couldn't stand it. She thrust her chest forward. His mouth moved down her chest. He pushed down the v-neckline of her dress and she reached down and undid the knot holding the wraparound dress in place. The front of the dress opened and he pushed the lace bra aside. His mouth gripped her nipple just as he slid another finger inside her, and she lost her mind.

When the last waves of ecstasy finally subsided, she dropped her head on his chest, feeling satiated yet wanting more. He extracted his fingers from her, and a moaning sound of protest escaped her lips.

"I'm sorry I didn't wait for you," she said, somewhat embarrassed. She'd been so caught up in her own pleasure that she really hadn't considered his. She hadn't been prepared to orgasm so quickly. It almost never happened to her.

He kissed her ear, and another ripple of pleasure tore through her. She extended her arm and touched him through his pants. He was still hard, and she started to unbuckle his belt. Maybe her unlucky streak with men was over. If she could keep Dev hard this long, after she'd already orgasmed, maybe there was hope for them. Maybe she wasn't a cold fish after all.

Her hands trembled as she tugged on the belt. Dev put a hand on hers.

"Caitlyn, no."

She froze. He didn't want her. He'd pleased her because she'd asked—no, begged, no, *accosted*—him for it, but he didn't want her back.

She pulled away from him, adjusted her bra, pulled her underwear back in place, and re-tied her dress. Her breaths were coming faster than they should but she couldn't slow down the beating of her heart. It was happening again. Why had she forgotten that this was what happened every time? Why did she think things would work with Dev? *Because things have been different with him.*

"Hey, are you okay? Did we go too far?"

She couldn't meet his gaze. There was no way she was letting him see the tears brimming in her eyes.

She shook her head, unable to speak. She hopped off the table, nearly tripping as her feet landed unsteadily. He caught her and lifted her chin so she was forced to look at him.

"Hey, what did I do wrong?"

The traitorous tears wouldn't stay put, and his face crumpled. "Oh my God, did I hurt you? What did I do? Please say something."

Somehow, she was making things worse. *Why can't I get hold of myself?* The one thing she could always do was put on her armor and extract herself with dignity.

She took a breath. "If you didn't want to be with me, you just had to say so."

"What? You think I don't want you?" He pulled her into his embrace and held her tight, pressing his body against her. "Does it feel like I don't want you?"

It sure doesn't.

"Then what is it?"

He kissed her forehead tenderly, then trailed kisses down her cheek. Despite the doubt flooding her thoughts, her body responded immediately, wanting, needing him. She pressed against him, her body seeking reassurance that she did indeed turn him on.

"I don't want our first time to be in a barn. Call me a hopeless romantic, but I want it to be special." He kissed her neck. "I want to take my time, treat you the way you should be treated." He nibbled on her earlobe, his breath warm, and her entire body molded itself to him. She moaned sinfully. *I don't want to wait. I want you right now.* "I want to see you naked. I want your hands all over my body. I want us to have the whole night to enjoy each other, not just this stolen moment."

How could she argue with an offer like that?

"Tonight," he promised.

Eight

"No, Ma! I haven't seen her biodata, and I'm not interested," Dev said, his face reflecting the frustration he felt. His mother was on a video call with him, so he couldn't even fake that he was in the middle of a meeting. Ma had caught on to that trick and insisted on scheduled video calls.

"Dev, your younger siblings are married. I talked to *Pandit-ji* and he said the stars are aligned for you to marry."

"I'm only twenty-eight, Ma. It's the time to build my business, not get saddled with family obligations."

"Your father was married when he was twenty. Do you think he built his empire by himself? Why do you think a wife is a liability?"

Because I've seen how my siblings' spouses have drained them, financially and emotionally. He loved his brother and sister, but he'd witnessed them slowly giving up their goals in favor of what their spouses wanted. His brother hadn't wanted children, yet his wife convinced him to have two. She was pregnant with her second when the first was barely two. His sister, the cut-throat businesswoman, had agreed to quit her job and stay home to help her husband with his elder-care duties. He didn't want to be forced to make the same choices. He had a specific plan for his business. First the restaurant in Royal, then a chain across the United States. He needed to be a free agent, not saddled with a wife.

So what're you doing with Caitlyn? He pushed that thought aside. He'd been honest with Caitlyn from the beginning about how he planned to leave.

"It doesn't matter anyway. I'm dating someone." He knew it was a dangerous thing to admit to his mother, but it would temporarily get her off his back. At least buy him some time until he was back in New York and could avoid her in person.

"Very nice, very nice. Can I see her picture?"

He rolled his eyes. "How about asking me what type of person she is, Ma? Why is it straight to the looks for you."

"*Aaare*, you think I haven't learned your type by now? You want the impossible in a woman. She has to be intelligent, she has to be kind and caring, she has to be this, she has to be that. All the goddesses in the Vedas combined couldn't meet your requirements for a woman. If you selected a girl for yourself, then she must be something. So, I want to see her picture."

He knew why his mother wanted to see Caitlyn's picture. First to make sure she was real and he wasn't just making an excuse. Second, so she could see what attracted him. He knew it was a bad idea, but maybe complying would get his mother off the phone faster.

He'd already texted Caitlyn to see if she wanted to come with him to check out a restaurant location, and she'd just texted him back asking what time. He wanted it to be as soon as possible. He was eager to spend more time with her. But first things first.

He pulled up her picture on his laptop. She was on several local committees and boards, and many of them had a picture of her on their website. His favorite was a standard yearbook-style picture where she had only the slightest smile on her face. It was meant to be serious, but he loved that photo. She looked so innocent and sexy, wearing a strand of pearls around her long, elegant neck, her makeup minimal and her wavy hair down around her shoulders. It had only been a few hours since he'd seen her, but he was already anxious to see her again. He had the whole night planned out.

She'd sparked an idea this morning, and he'd called Greg, who had found a promising place. Dev had already been to see it and was going to take Caitlyn there in the evening. Then they'd pick up Italian from her favorite restaurant and bring it back to his hotel room, where he hoped to have her to himself all night and all day tomorrow.

He shared his screen with his mother, who gasped.

"*Wah!* You have good taste. She is beautiful."

He didn't know why, but his mother's approval sat well with him, even though he hated that fact. He was trying to become an independent man, but somewhere inside was still a child who sought his parent's approval.

"Is she Indian?"

He flinched. He'd hoped the conversation wouldn't come to that. He knew how his parents felt. They expected him to marry someone whose ethnic background was from India. Even though he and his siblings had been born and raised in the US and lived like Americans, his parents firmly believed that someone who wasn't Indian couldn't understand the closeness of their family and their values. Dev had disagreed even before he met Caitlyn but even more so after getting to know her. She knew exactly what it meant to put her family's needs before her own. She'd been doing it all her life. In many ways, she lived her family values far better than he did.

"No, she is not."

"She's definitely not white. Then what is she? Mexican?"

He winced. Typical of her generation, social standing and general lack of tact, his mother did not feel the need to filter her bluntness.

"No."

"Dev," his mother said warningly, and he knew her patience was wearing thin.

He sighed. "She's biracial, Mom, half white, half African American."

His mother was silent. When she finally spoke, it was worse than he'd braced himself for. "Are you trying to punish me?"

He stayed silent. It was a rhetorical question. He studied his mother's pinched face. She was only forty-eight, having married when she was eighteen and had him when she was twenty. Yet she looked like she was in her thirties, her face unmarred by wrinkles and perfectly made up with eyeliner and dark red lipstick. She wore diamond solitaires in her ears, and her hair was dyed perfectly in shades of black and reddish brown where the gray would have been. Dev got his green eyes from her, but when they stared at him from his mother's face, he felt a chill down his spine.

"Do you know what it will do to our social standing if you marry a Black woman?"

He didn't bother correcting her as to Caitlyn's race. In truth, he didn't know how she identified. For all he knew, his mother might be right. He'd only just realized that he hadn't bothered to ask.

"You are the most eligible bachelor in our community. You can have any desi girl you want from around the globe. I get no less than three offers a day for you. For good girls, educated girls, beautiful girls. Girls who know our language, our culture, and can teach it to your children. I've given you a lot of slack thinking you just need some time to go do some *maasti,* and if that's what this is, I'm fine with it. But I will tell you in no uncertain terms that you will not marry a girl who is not Indian."

"Ma!" he said, exasperated. "Who is talking marriage? I'm just dating her." It was the coward's way out of the conversation, but he was in no mood to have it right now. He knew how his parents felt, and there was no point in battling with them unless there was a reason to do so. He was nowhere close to marrying anyone, and Caitlyn was far from a contender. It was clear from their conversations that she was tied to Royal. She had no interest in traveling or leaving her comfort zone.

Appeased, his mother gave him a small smile. "Have whatever fun you want. You know I'm very modern thinking that way. As long as you know what we expect of you."

How could I not?

He managed to get his mother off his back by scheduling their next video chat and with a promise that he would read the biodata she'd sent of the latest wife prospective. The biodata was a résumé-like dating profile with a picture, their likes, dislikes, education, etc. He'd wait a day to pretend as if he'd studied it, then send an email to his mother saying he didn't like it. Since the next video call was a few days from now, that would give her enough time to calm down.

His phone pinged, reminding him that Caitlyn was waiting for an answer from him. He quickly made plans to see her in a few hours.

"Who are you texting with?" Alice asked suspiciously.

Caitlyn guiltily clicked a button on her phone to darken the screen as Alice leaned over. They were in Caitlyn's bedroom, which remained largely unchanged from when her mother had redecorated it during her teenage years. A queen bed with a gray upholstered headboard stood in the middle, decorated with an elegant silver-and-gray comforter and pillow set. A small couch stood underneath a bay window with end tables on either side and two chairs across for a cozy sitting room. But the two women were sitting cross-legged on the bed like they had when they were in college. Alice and Caitlyn hadn't gone to the same high school, as Caitlyn had been in private school and Alice had gone to the public school. Yet they'd met in college and instantly bonded over their Royal roots. More than once, Caitlyn wished she'd become friends with Alice instead of Jax.

"How many have we gotten done?" Caitlyn asked, changing the subject.

Alice rolled her eyes. "What does it matter, we have like a million more to do. I can't believe I let you talk me into this."

"It's for a good cause." They were making brown bags for the foster kids. The snacks fed the kids on the weekends when there was no school breakfast or lunch. Normally, the high school kids packed the bags, but it was prom weekend, so they'd been short on volunteers and Caitlyn had agreed to pick up the slack. One of the Lattimore charities she oversaw funded the snack bags. She knew Alice wasn't really complaining—she had offered to help.

"I still think you need to give Russ a chance."

"Alice, he's not interested in me."

"Listen, I know Dev. Russ always brought him home for Thanksgiving because his own family didn't celebrate the holiday. He's a nice guy, he really is, but he's never going to be serious about anyone until his business is established. He's pretty much said so to me and Russ."

"Who said we're getting serious? I just asked him to help me practice my conversational skills and get comfortable around men. Didn't you tell me that's what I need to do?"

"Hardly! I told you to date a nice guy. Like Russ."

"The guy who personifies the love-'em-and-leave-'em motto?" Caitlyn said with a tinge of annoyance in her voice. Alice sometimes forgot how much time she spent lamenting Russ's dating exploits.

"He's changed, and he's ready to settle down."

"No, *you're* ready for him to change and settle down. There's a difference."

Alice glared at her, and Caitlyn softened her tone, well aware that she'd be just as defensive if someone tried to tell her that she was wrong about her brothers. "Listen, Russ is a great guy, no doubt. But it's a little hard to think of him as anyone other than your brother. There's no spark, you understand?" Alice didn't look convinced.

"I don't want this to affect our friendship, Alice. How would you feel if I tried to set you up with one of my brothers and you didn't like him? Could you please let this go?"

Alice sighed. "Okay, I'll lay off Russ. Will you tell me whether the mystery man you're texting is Dev?"

Caitlyn sighed. "Yes."

"I knew it!" Alice screamed.

"A mystery man, huh."

Caitlyn groaned as she turned to see Alexa in the doorway. Her long black curls were loose, and she was wearing a gray T-shirt and bike shorts, her standard gym uniform. The last thing Caitlyn needed was for Alexa to get involved with the conversation regarding Dev. It was so rare for Alexa to be home, she didn't want their time together to be about her dating life.

Alexa homed in on Alice, knowing she was the weaker link. "Nice to see you, Alice." She sat on the bed and picked up one of the bags to fill, so Caitlyn could hardly object. "So, you have a mystery man. Looks like a picked a good weekend to make a trip home. Spill."

Alexa had always intimidated Alice a little. It was the lawyer in her—she had a way looking at you like she could read your mind. Alice shifted on the bed. "That's what I've been trying to get out of Caitlyn, but it's a secret mystery man. Maybe you can get more out of her."

Devious. Caitlyn glared at her best friend as Alexa turned to her. Caitlyn knew it was fruitless—Alexa would hound her until she gave in. "As Alice well knows, the not-so-secret and utterly unmysterious man is Dev Mallik, Russ's best friend. I met him at dinner at Alice's house."

"So dish some more. What's he like?" Alexa pressed.

"He's nice. He's in Royal to open a restaurant, and

I agreed to show him around town. We've gone out to dinner five or six times and talked on the phone a few times. No biggie."

Alexa and Alice exchanged glances, which irritated Caitlyn. They were both supposed to be on her side. "What is it?" Caitlyn asked.

"You met him two weeks ago and you've already been out with him five or six times," Alexa didn't bother to hide the surprise in her voice.

She had actually seen Dev more than that, but Caitlyn wasn't going to add fuel to the fire. Each date had been more frustratingly platonic than the last. Dev had stayed true to his word. While there was the inadvertent hand or shoulder brush, until this morning there hadn't been anything sexual. They'd sampled all the Royal restaurants like a pair of food critics and decided that Dev had his work cut out for him. If he wanted to compete in the Royal restaurant business, he'd have to offer something extraordinary. Dev had talked about the chef he'd lined up for his restaurant and the dishes they were working on together, and Caitlyn was impressed and genuinely looking forward to the new place in Royal. The only hiccup had been that Dev hadn't liked the places Russ had lined up for him as potential locations, and he'd gone through Greg's list too.

Then this morning happened. She didn't know whether it was the knowledge that he might leave earlier than he was planning, or the sexual tension that had been simmering between them, but she'd been ready to take things to the next level with him. She needed to see whether her practice relationship could turn into a real one. Tonight would be the test.

"Earth to Caitlyn." Alexa snapped her fingers.

Caitlyn turned back to the conversation. "So what

if I've been out with him a few times? I'm helping him get to know Royal, and he's helping me with my conversational skills. It's not like we're headed down the aisle. It's a temporary friendship."

"For you, darlin', that many dates is a serious relationship," Alice chimed in.

Caitlyn shot Alice and Alexa an irritated look.

"I'm just worried that you're getting involved with someone who's going to be leaving town in a couple of weeks," Alice said.

I'm worried about the same thing. "He's planning to stay a little longer." She didn't know if that was true, but she hoped she could convince him to stay longer if things went well tonight.

"For how long? Once he finds a location, he's going to leave and go back to New York," Alice said.

"And he'll be back occasionally to check on his restaurant," Caitlyn said, hating how defensive she sounded. "We can see each other then."

"I thought you said this was temporary," Alexa said softly, and Caitlyn cursed under her breath. Trust the lawyer to find the flaw in her argument.

She knew it was the norm in her family to baby Caitlyn, but she was a grown woman now. She knew how to handle her affairs. *Just like you handled Jax*, a condescending inner voice jibed at her.

"Look, I know you guys mean well, but trust me to make my choices. I know full well Dev is not from around here, and that he's going to leave. I know whatever I have with him is short term. I don't need you guys to explain it to me like I'm a teenager with a crush."

Alice cleared her throat. "There's something else you should know about Dev."

She shifted on the bed, and Caitlyn lost her cool. "Out with it, Alice."

Both Alice and Alexa raised their brows but wisely didn't comment on Caitlyn's tone.

"Russ wanted to set me up with Dev, because he's a nice guy and Russ knows I want to settle down and get on the marriage train. Dev confided in him that he can't marry someone who isn't Indian. Apparently, his family is quite traditional."

Her heart fisted. She and Dev had never talked about marriage, but somewhere in the back of her mind, she realized they'd actively avoided the topic. He talked about his family and all the expectations they weighed down on him but never what it meant for his romantic future, just his professional one.

"Wow, let's just hit pause here a second, guys. Everyone's been harassing me to get out more. I go out on a few dates and here you are evaluating whether he's marriage material and questioning whether we have a future together. Haven't we fast-forwarded a bit too much?"

Both Alice and Alexa had the grace to look sheepish. "Sorry, darlin', I just don't want to see you hurt, and aside from Jax, I've never seen you spend so much time with one guy," Alice said. "Russ said all Dev can talk about is you. I'm seeing things moving too fast and just want to make sure you don't get hurt."

Alexa nodded. "I'm glad you're out and dating. It's time you moved on from Jax."

"How many times do I need to tell you that I'm over Jax?" Caitlyn tried to keep her voice level. She knew she'd fallen apart after Jax, but could anyone really blame her, given their history?

Alexa leaned forward and took Caitlyn's hand in

hers. "When you were six years old, you loved this old horse called Shooting Star."

Caitlyn nodded. She remembered that horse clearly—he was an Appaloosa, a beautiful white horse with brown dots and a sandy blond mane.

"You loved that horse so much you rode him every day, rain or shine. But he ended up with colic that wasn't treatable, and the vet recommended we put him down. You were devastated. No matter how hard we tried, you refused to believe that Shooting Star couldn't be cured."

"I was ten," Caitlyn said defensively. "And as I remember, he was eventually put down."

Alexa squeezed her hand. "Do you remember that you spent two days and two nights sitting by his stall, refusing to let the vet take him? You were adamant that he would heal on his own, that your sheer force of will could cure him. Daddy didn't want to forcibly remove you, so we took turns staying with you until you fell asleep out of sheer exhaustion. That's when we were finally able to take Shooting Star."

"I don't know what all this has to do with Dev." Caitlyn shifted on the bed. She wanted this conversation to be over with.

"It has to do with you, Caitlyn," Alexa said gently. "You have so much love in your heart, and you give it all to the people you care about. Sometimes you give too much. Even though I wasn't here, I could tell that things were moving too fast with Jax, but I didn't say anything, and I wish I had."

Caitlyn softened her voice and looked directly at Alexa. "I'm not a fragile baby. I know I'm loved and that I have an amazing support system…" she blew a kiss to Alice and squeezed Alexa's hand "…but you guys need to trust that I can take care of myself. I'm doing exactly what I set out to—I'm going out with someone where I know there's no chance of a future, so I can relax and get some flirting practice." She injected just the right amount of casualness in her voice, but her stomach churned painfully.

Had she really thought through where things were going with Dev? She'd been so focused on how easy it was with him, convinced that it would end at any second, that she hadn't really considered the opposite possibility—*what if it went well?*

Nine

"Little thing like you should not be carryin' those big boxes," Ol'Fred bellowed. Caitlyn set down the boxes containing the snack bags they'd packed.

Ol'Fred stood where he always did, behind a wood checkout counter. His place looked more like a gas station pit stop than the fancy places that surrounded him, but Ol'Fred's shop had been here since the day Royal was founded, and no one told Ol'Fred how to run his general store. He carried basic groceries, knickknacks, tools—anything that someone doing real work in Royal might need on an urgent basis. He also carried specialty drinks, high-end whiskeys and wines that forced the elite of Royal to trudge to his store. It was the only place in town where every resident of Royal could shop.

"I'm not as fragile as I look. Can I leave these here? Yolanda said she'd pick them up in the morning."

"You don't have to ask. Y'know I'd do anything for

the kids." He called out to one of his store hands to take the boxes.

Ol'Fred pulled out a can of Fanta and handed it to her. Caitlyn smiled and popped the tab, careful not let the fizz spill over. It was their tradition since she was a little girl. Her mother never let her have the orange drink because it was full of sugar, so Ol'Fred would sneak it to her.

"You just missed Jax."

Caitlyn looked around the store. "Don't worry, he's gone." She didn't know whether she was relieved or disappointed. They'd done the avoidance dance for a year—she needed to get it over with.

"You never did tell me what happened with you and Jax." Ol'Fred's tone was fatherly.

Caitlyn leaned over and kissed Ol'Fred on the cheek. "What do you always say, one day a rooster, the next day a feather duster? That was mine and Jax's relationship."

"Guess I'm gonna have to leave it with you."

She thanked him for the Fanta and walked out of the store. Just as she opened the door, she bumped into someone, dropping the almost-full can of Fanta. She murmured an apology and bent down to pick up the can before it made more of a mess.

"I see Ol'Fred is still taking care of you."

She froze. A knot formed and twisted in her stomach. She took a breath then stood. "Jax."

He smiled at her, but she couldn't bring herself to do the same. He was wearing his standard-issue basketball shorts and a T-shirt. His hair was freshly close-cropped.

They stood for a moment, staring, each unsure what to say to the other. Jax spoke first. "Listen, I think we should talk. We've avoided each other long enough. We can't leave things like this."

She nodded. Wordlessly, they walked to the park, to their bench. It was the place where they used to meet to do their homework; it was the place where he'd told her that her father had paid for his tuition to her exclusive private school so she'd have a friend; it was the place where they'd met when he first came back from college; it was the place where they'd first kissed. It was only fitting that it be the bench where they finally closed their relationship.

Her throat was tight. She didn't know how to begin, what to say. He didn't seem to have that problem.

"Look, Caitlyn, I'm sorry about the last time we were together. I shouldn't have left like that, and I shouldn't have said the things I did. I hope you didn't dwell on it."

She'd played that night in her mind for months after their breakup.

"Did you mean it? What you said?" She hated the high-pitched tone of her voice, but she needed to know whether they were words of anger or whether he'd truly meant them.

He was silent. "We've been friends for a long time, Jax. I need you to be honest with me."

He sighed. "Look, your father might have paid for my tuition and asked me to be your friend, but he didn't make you my best friend. You did. You were the only one who was nice to me at that high-brow place. I felt intimidated by that crowd, being one of the few Black kids, being the only kid who didn't summer in Europe and on and on. But you gave me confidence— you treated me like I belonged there. That's why we became best friends. It had nothing to do with your father paying my way"

She gave him a small smile. "You were the only kid in school I liked. It was easy to be your friend."

"The only reason I told you about your father paying my tuition is because I didn't want you to find out from someone other than me. What I didn't tell you is that you weren't just my best friend. You were also my childhood crush. But my ma worked for your family. If things didn't go well between us, it would've meant ruin for my family. I had no choice. I could only be your best friend."

"That's what brought us back together when you returned home after college"

"But that's just it. Four years had passed. I was a different person than I was in high school. And I hoped you had changed, too."

"What exactly does that mean?"

"Remember Declan Grayson?"

Her cheeks warmed. "That was high school, Jax."

"It was junior year. You were so in love with him. You did anything he asked of you but then, just like that, you dumped him. I tried talking to you about it, but you wouldn't tell me a thing."

"It that what this is about? Some old high school secret…"

He shook his head, but before he could say anything, she jumped in. "You want to know what happened with Declan? He was a high school crush. I went out with him, and he wanted to go further physically than I cared to. I told him I wanted to wait and he didn't, so I dumped him. Pardon me if I didn't feel comfortable talking to my male best friend about how I hated some other guy's groping."

The knot in her stomach twisted painfully. Perhaps this had all been a bad idea. What had she hoped to gain from this conversation? She knew what the issue was, had experienced it ever since high school.

"I knew all about it, Caitlyn. Declan told the whole school you were a prude and some other not-so-nice words. That's not why I bring him up." He sighed. "You put your heart and soul into everything you do. Including relationships. You went all in for Declan. You hardly knew him, and yet you were making little hearts in your notebook and writing *Mrs. Caitlyn Grayson*."

Heat rose up her neck and to her cheeks. She should have known Jax would've noticed her schoolgirl notes. "I was sixteen, Jax. Give me a break."

She wished she had the Fanta can that she'd just thrown away to clear the nasty taste in her mouth.

Jax rubbed his neck, a gesture she knew well. "What are you trying to say, Jax? Just spit it out."

"When I came back to town, I wanted to give us a chance. I didn't want to go through life wondering what might have been with you. But you wanted to pick up as if no time had passed. It was like we went from catching up over coffee to being engaged in one day. You didn't even bother to get to know me."

"I do know you, Jax. We spent four years together."

"When we were kids."

He gave her a small smile. "I'm not that person anymore. Do you know, for example, that I led a Black Lives Matter protest in DC? Or that I took the LSATs to see if I can get into law school to become a civil rights lawyer?"

That stung. Caitlyn narrowed her eyes. "You'd only just gotten into town—we hardly had time to talk."

"That's my point exactly. You didn't bother to get to know me fully before jumping into our relationship. We'd barely begun, and you were already showing me off at every Cattleman's Club event, dragging me here and there every single weekend. You were even making wedding plans."

Caitlyn shook her head. "That's not true, Jax. I was enthusiastic about our relationship because of our past. Just like you, I'd thought about us on and off through high school, but I didn't want to ruin our friendship. We weren't strangers."

"But we were, Caitlyn. We were old friends who should have taken the time to get to know each other, but we jumped right into a serious relationship without going through the dating part first. I'm not saying it was all you. I did it, too. I came back and found you grown into a beautiful woman and couldn't help falling into the fantasy you painted for us. After six months it just all came crashing down, the reality of what we'd been doing."

"So it's my fault. I put too much pressure on our relationship."

"That's not what I'm saying. I think it was both our faults. We let things move too quickly."

She shook her head and stood. "Are you done with what you had to say?"

He hung his head, then nodded slowly. "I'm not handling this right, but I want you to know that I care about you very much."

Just not enough. That's the part he didn't want to say, but she understood. She wanted to tell him that she'd trusted him, as a former friend, as her boyfriend, and that he'd broken her heart. But she couldn't bring herself to do that. The all-too-familiar knot in her stomach had grown and risen up to her throat, choking her. At least he didn't refer to her as a cold fish again.

"Thanks for the talk. Have a nice life," she managed

to cough out, then walked away as quickly as she could without breaking into a run.

One thing was for certain—she wouldn't make the same mistakes with Dev. She wasn't getting into anything serious with him.

Ten

It was the first time he'd picked Caitlyn up from the Lattimore ranch, and Dev couldn't help be impressed. The ranch seemed to be an endless sprawl of perfectly landscaped lawn and picturesque barns. No peeling paint and rusted doors here. The one-mile drive from the front gate to the mansion was lined with perfectly trimmed hedges. Russ hadn't been kidding when he'd pitched the idea of Dev opening a restaurant in Royal—the kind of wealth here put the fancy Manhattan penthouse circle to shame.

The property he'd seen today had the potential to make not only his dreams come true, but also Caitlyn's. He couldn't wait to show it to her. He'd already spoken to the chef and restaurant manager he'd lined up and walked them through the space on video. They agreed with his plans. All he needed was for Caitlyn to get on board.

They'd only known each other a short time, but he'd connected with her on an intellectual and emotional level. She understood the two parts of him, the one that belonged to his family and the one that longed to be an independent man. Getting into business was the perfect way to keep her in his life. It would give him time to sort out their romantic relationship.

She was waiting for him under the portico of a circular driveway. She looked stunning in a strappy ice-blue dress with a crisscross design that gave him a peekaboo view of her lovely back. The dress ended midthigh, showing off her shapely legs. It was the kind of sexy dress he'd never seen her in before. Her hair was left loose around her face, not straight and pressed as it normally was, but curly and wild, just the way he liked it. She was wearing flat shoes, and he was glad she had thought practically.

Before the car fully stopped, she tapped on the window. He unlocked the car, intending to get out and open the passenger side for her, but she yanked open the door, got in and smiled. "Let's go."

"In a hurry to get out?"

"Yes!" she breathed. "If my siblings find out you're picking me up, trust me, they'll be all over us and will monopolize the entire evening. You can forget any plans you may have."

Is that the only reason you don't want me meeting your family?

He punched the accelerator, eager to get to their destination. "Listen, your idea this morning gave me one of my own. So, I asked Greg to look, and he found the perfect place."

"That's great."

"But I need you to say yes to make the place work."

"Why me?" He caught the tentative fear in her voice but pushed it aside. He was being mysterious, after all.

He reached over and patted her hand. "You'll see."

Greg had given him the keys to the small ranch. Dev wanted privacy to explain his idea to Caitlyn. He had no idea how she'd react. He hadn't let himself fully consider what he would do if she said no. Because in that case, he was out of options in Royal and would have to move on. Already he'd spent more time here than he should have. Although he'd given himself a month, he'd seen most of the properties that would have been suitable for his restaurant in the first few days, but he'd kept looking. Not because he didn't have other places to go, but because he wanted to see where things went with Caitlyn.

He'd come to that realization after talking with his mother. He rarely shared information about who he was dating, and he knew his mother would have an issue with Caitlyn not being Indian, but he'd told her anyway. He'd told her so that his mother could start getting used to the idea of Caitlyn. He'd told her because he'd never met a woman he felt as comfortable with as Caitlyn. The fact that he hadn't even slept with her and was thinking these thoughts made it all the harder to ignore his feelings for her. She understood him, really listened to what he wanted without trying to impose what she wanted. Tonight was the ultimate test to see if she felt as strongly for him as he did for her. Would she go along with his plans? Would she be willing to share and mold her dream with his?

"We're going to the east side of Royal?"

He nodded. "Yes, we've exhausted everything on the west side, so I asked Greg to expand the search to all of Royal. Why? Is that a problem?"

She stayed quiet for a few minutes, as if formulating her thoughts. He snuck a look at her and saw frown lines on her forehead. "East Royal doesn't have the social demographics you're looking for to support the luxury restaurant you're envisioning."

He smiled. "You mean it's the poor part of town."

"Yes," she said quietly. "And I don't mean it disparagingly, I just mean that's where the working-class families live. They can't pay the type of prices you're considering. The wealthy ranchers on the west side aren't really going to drive to a high-end restaurant on this side of town."

"I have an idea for that," he said.

"Now I'm really intrigued. You know, Ol' Fred's shop is the only one on Main Street that's for regular people and not there to cater to the hoity-toity of Royal. It would be nice to have another place like that in Royal."

"Aren't you one of those hoity-toitys?" he asked playfully.

She nodded. "I absolutely am. Which is why I really want to do that horse camp. I know my family participates in boards and charities, but that stuff barely scratches the surface. Half the time I'm not even sure where all the money goes. I want to do something where I can see the results in front of me, not on a piece of paper."

He smiled. "Any news on the oil rights claim on your ranch?"

She shook her head. "We're still waiting for the private eye to find whether the deed Heath Thurston has is valid. We looked through our own family papers but haven't found anything."

She sighed. "I just want this to be over with so I can

start working on my camp. I thought by now we'd have some resolution."

"Maybe it's for the best?"

"What do you mean?"

"I could fund my restaurant from my trust fund. Or by simply selling one of the cars my father has gifted me that mostly sits in a New York garage at a rent that constitutes most people's annual salary. But I didn't touch any of that money. Do you know why?"

"Because you want to be your own man."

"That's part of it, but it's a lot more than that. Everything in my family is intertwined—our home, our finances, our social lives, you name it, and it's all one big happy family. The problem with that is there's no room for real disagreements. If I want to go against my family, I can't. This is my way of ensuring I have an escape chute if I need it."

He pulled into the driveway of the small ranch Greg had found for him. He parked the car and looked at Caitlyn.

"You really think you're going to need an escape from your family?"

"I'd rather not find out."

She shifted in her seat. "I can't imagine a scenario where I'd need to flee from my family."

"There are a lot of expectations in my family that may not exist in yours."

"Like who you marry?"

His heart slammed into his chest. He didn't want to talk about this now. He wanted this evening to be about them and their relationship. He needed to know whether she felt the same connection he did. Whether her heart was going in the same direction as his. It was too soon to contemplate the future with a woman he'd

only known for two weeks. He knew that intellectually, but his gut and his heart said something different.
What he and Caitlyn had was special. Unique. Wasn't
it? Sitting here with her, it certainly felt that way, but
the conversation with his mother had unsettled him.
He'd found himself anxious to make sure that Caitlyn
shared his feelings about their relationship, that she was
also seeing a future for them.

She was waiting for a response.

"I will marry whom I want," he said firmly.

"Your parents don't get a say?"

"Does your family get a say in who you marry?"

She paused then shook her head. "They'd never stand
in the way of my happiness. They do have strong opinions about who I date, and I'm sure any man I bring
home will have to stand up to a CIA-level interrogation,
but ultimately they'll support my decision."

He wished he could say the same thing about his
family.

"Let's go see this place."

It was nice sized property, nestled on a relatively
flat area of land bordered by trees. They drove up to
the ranch house, which was a charming, sprawling one-
level.

"I don't know this property. Who lived here?"

"From what Greg told me, it belonged to a Mr. and
Mrs. Fredrick. They left the property to their son, and
he's recently decided to sell."

He opened the front door and they stepped into a
large foyer with hardwood floors.

"You want to convert the house into a restaurant?"

He nodded and pointed out the various rooms. "It's
already got a large kitchen. I'd only have to put in commercial appliances. The rest of the house can be easily

converted into a dining room. The smaller rooms can be for small private groups."

She peeked into the formal dining room. It was a cozy space with a rectangular dining table that sat ten people. "I can see my family eating in this room. And the house has so many windows, it feels bigger than it is."

He nodded.

"I like the feel of this place. I can totally see seating on the porch and the back deck, and a beautiful dining room on this main level with the current bedrooms as private meeting areas for business dinners. But the Royal elite still aren't going to drive all the way over here."

"I have a plan for that," he said. But the plan hinged on her. His stomach flipped. The next few minutes would tell him how she felt about him. In a way, the next moments would decide whether or not he stayed in Royal.

"Looks like the old owners took really good care of the house. The floors are polished, the baseboards are clean…and they're mostly moved out. Why hasn't it sold yet? The real estate market in Royal is pretty strong."

"Well, there's a rather big catch that's in the property covenant."

She raised a brow, and he led her to the back door and opened it. She gasped. The twenty-acre backyard held two riding rings and two large barns. There were a couple of horses turned out into the rings, a black horse and a white one with black spots.

Caitlyn gasped. "I was not expecting this. Those horses are beautiful." She pointed to the black one. "That's actually a mustang—a pretty well-bred one, from what I can tell. And the other is an appaloosa." Her voice caught.

He placed a hand on the small of her back. She stiffened slightly. "What's wrong, Caitlyn?"

She shook her head. "Nothing. I used to have an appaloosa when I was a little girl. He died."

He placed an arm around her shoulders. "I'm sorry."

"It just brings up a painful memory."

He took a breath, wondering if now was the time to bring up his plans. *What the hell!* "Well, maybe it's a sign."

"Of what?"

"That this horse is meant to be yours."

She looked up at him, frowning. "I don't understand."

"The catch with this place is that it comes with those two stables that can take a total of twenty-some horses and those two beauties there. The owners want someone who will agree to take the horses and keep them together. Apparently they're bonded—whatever that means."

"It means they're attached to each other. Horses that bond together are hard to separate. They get sick if you do."

She was staring at the horses. "Let's go see them."

He pointed to the stairs leading down from the deck. As they approached the ring where the horses were roaming around, the appaloosa stopped and considered them. When they were within a few feet of the ring, the black mustang snorted, whinnied and reared.

Dev put a hand on her shoulder to hold her back. "Careful, Caitlyn, I don't know anything about these horses."

She smiled back at him, and his knees went weak.

The setting sun backlit her in soft orange and yellow hues. *How can one woman be so stunningly, perfectly beautiful?* Despite his busy afternoon, there wasn't a moment that had gone by without him thinking about their morning together. Had that just been this morning? It seemed like a lifetime ago that she'd pulsed against his fingers and thrown her head back in such abandon that he'd nearly lost it. He'd been with enough women to know how to control himself. That he'd almost lost it with her told him there was something special about Caitlyn. Something so special that, for the first time in his life, he was intimidated by the thought of a night with her. What if he couldn't control himself? What if he couldn't live up to her expectations? What if he couldn't give her what she deserved?

He pushed the last thought out of his head. He didn't even know if she felt the same way about him. Before he started making plans, he needed to know that they were on the same page.

"Trust me," she said. "Stay back a little."

There was no way he was going to let her walk so dangerously close to the horses. He walked right behind her, ready to leap if the horses decided to jump the fence.

She began talking softly to the horses. "Good boy. That's right, you're a good boy." The appaloosa snorted and scuffed the earth with his hind leg. The mustang hung back.

Caitlyn bent down and tore some of the grass from the earth. He did the same. "Not the grass—get the clover that's growing." She un-fisted her hand and showed him the green plant. She approached the horse slowly. When she got to the fence, she extended her arm. The appaloosa sniffed, then clopped over to her. He buried his nose in her hand, then ate the offered clover.

She petted his head and then rubbed behind his ear. The mustang whinnied, then joined his friend. Dev offered the clover he had picked to Caitlyn, and she fed the mustang. *Maybe this will go better than I thought.*

"Who is taking care of these horses if the owners moved out?"

He smiled. Trust her to be worried about the animals. "Greg said there's a ranch hand that comes by to feed, water and turn them out."

She rubbed the mustang's back. The horse was practically rubbing up against the fence begging for Caitlyn's touch. Dev knew the feeling.

"Well, he's not doing a great job. The horses need grooming. Looks like they haven't been brushed in ages. I'll call Greg and ask to talk with the ranch hand."

"You can do one better."

She turned to look at him, and the appaloosa buried his nose in her neck. She automatically smiled and started rubbing the side of his face. Insanely, he felt jealous of the horse.

He cleared his throat. "Here's my idea. What if this was your horse camp?"

Her eyes widened. "What?"

"What if my restaurant wasn't just a restaurant but a riding club? We board horses for the rich and famous, and when they aren't riding those horses, you run your camp. This property is cheap enough that instead of renting like I had planned, I can buy it. This place can be ours. We can run it together. You run the stables, and I'll run the restaurant. I'm thinking I'll even create a café portion where I can serve up more family-priced dishes. Upscale restaurants in New York do that all the

time—they have food trucks with better-priced dishes."
He stopped. He'd been so busy pitching his idea that he
hadn't stopped to look at her face.

She stepped away from the horses, and they began
galloping around the ring.

"Caitlyn?"

She was turned away from him, so he placed a hand
on her shoulder. "What is it?"

"Don't you think we're moving a bit fast?" Her voice
was small.

"It's a business partnership," he said carefully. "Your
idea this morning really resonated with me. I want to
put my restaurant in this part of town. I want to create a place where everyone is welcome and can afford
to eat. If we board some expensive horses, it'll attract
the rich, and there's plenty of space here for you to run
your camp without worrying about the claim on the
Lattimore land."

"What exactly do you mean by a business relationship?"

Why was her voice so cagey? *Did I move too soon?
Am I reading our relationship all wrong?*

"It's whatever you're comfortable with, Caitlyn. We
can co-own the land. I can run the restaurant and you
run the stables. This is just an idea, one I hoped we
could work on together."

"What happens when our personal relationship
ends?"

She said when*, not* if. He moved around so he was
facing her. The sun had set quickly, and it was getting
dark pretty fast. She refused to meet his eyes, and her
body was so straight and stiff, it was as if one touch
would send her fleeing. He put his hands behind him
so he wouldn't be tempted to touch her. He could sense

her fear. He'd felt it himself after realizing why he'd shown his mother her picture. He was falling in love with Caitlyn. For the first time in his life, he was thinking about a future that included more than just his business and family.

"You tell me. How far do you think our personal relationship can go?"

She still wouldn't look at him, intently studying the horses. "We hardly know each other, Dev."

He moved so he was in her line of sight. "Ask me anything you want to know. Go on—what is it that you want to know about me?"

"Is your family expecting you to marry someone Indian?"

He sucked in a breath then nodded. "Yes, but what they're expecting and what they'll get are two different things. I told you, I know I'll have disagreements with my family. They want me to marry someone they approve of, and the whole reason I want to be financially independent is that I don't want to be hostage to their standards. I want to marry the person I love."

"And how does this hypothetical love of yours fit into your plans to jet around the country building your empire?"

Her words were a knife in his gut. This was not at all how he'd hoped the conversation would go, but now that it had started, he had to finish it.

"Caitlyn, let's not talk in circles." He placed his hands gently on her shoulders, the lightest of touches. She stiffened but didn't move away from him. "Please look at me." She lifted her face, and his heart clenched painfully. Her brown eyes were shining, her nose and face flushed.

Had his words caused her grief? What had he done

that was so wrong? Or was she misinterpreting what he was saying?

"I don't want there to be any confusion between us. What I'm saying is that I love you. I want to be with you. All this—" He gestured around them. "—is me trying to commit to you. I don't have everything worked out, but I don't want to. All I want to know is that you feel the same way about me and we'll figure out the rest together."

"Don't you think this relationship is moving a little fast? We've only known each other for two weeks and you're suggesting…"

Could she twist the knife any deeper into him? She hadn't said she loved him back. Hadn't even acknowledged that he was making a grand gesture.

"What? What am I suggesting that's so scary to you?" He hated the annoyance in his voice, but he was fast losing control over his emotions. She didn't love him back. She didn't even see a future with him.

"We've only known each other two weeks. I told you the reason I haven't started the camp at my family ranch is because I don't want to start something and then have it yanked away from these children. They have nothing permanent in their lives. You blew into town with the intention of starting something here and leaving. How do I know that doesn't include me, too?"

"Because I'm telling you right now."

She stepped close to him, her mouth set in a firm line. "Can you tell me you'll stay in Royal if I ask you to?"

"That's not really fair."

"Why not?"

"You're not even ready to commit to a business proposition, but you want me to change my entire life plan and move here?"

"That's the point, Dev. Your plan is to open a restaurant and leave, but my life is here in Royal."

"So you expect me to upend my entire life, let go of all of my plans and move here to Royal?" He immediately regretted the hostility in his voice. He hadn't meant for the conversation to go this way. Perhaps he had jumped the gun.

She sighed, and a tear streamed down her cheek. He brushed it away with his finger. She grabbed his hand and kissed it. "I can't do this, Dev. I'm sorry, I can't."

Eleven

"I don't understand, Caitlyn." Alice was sitting on the pool lounger staring at her. This time Caitlyn was the one who'd drunk most of the chardonnay that sat between them. It had been two days since she'd seen Dev. After she'd refused to talk anymore, he had dropped her at her house and left. Since then, he hadn't texted or called. He hadn't responded to the text she'd sent that night saying she was sorry.

Alice had come over unannounced when she'd heard the story from Russ. "You know he's planning to leave tomorrow."

Her heart lurched. The last couple of days had been a jumble of emotions for her. The conversations with Alexa and Alice, with Jax, and then with Dev had all crashed into one tightly knotted tangle that she couldn't separate no matter how hard she tried.

"Look, I know I was against you and Dev getting

together, but I can't see you like this. Russ says Dev
is a mess. He's never seen the poor guy like that." She
moved from her pool lounger to Caitlyn's. It was a rare
cloudy and cool day so they were both in their sun-
dresses enjoying the weather. Alice put an arm around
Caitlyn. "What happened, darlin'? Did things not go
well in bed?"

Trust Alice not to mince words. "Not this time. We
didn't even try." Though that was not completely true.
That morning in the barn was imprinted on her. She
hadn't forgotten how her body had responded to him.

Alice waited patiently. Caitlyn's throat was tight.
"It's Jax. I saw him, and we talked."

Alice hugged her tighter. "Oh, darlin', why didn't you
call me? What did that rascal say to you?"

"Nothing that wasn't true. He pointed out that I
jumped right into the relationship without even getting to know the man he'd become. That I put so much
pressure on the relationship that it was inevitable for it
to fail." She filled Alice in on their entire conversation.
"He didn't say anything about our last night together,
but he didn't need to. He blames the pressure I put on
him—that was clear."

Alice gasped. "That little turd. How dare he?" She
turned toward Caitlyn and squeezed her shoulders. "You
listen to me. When he came back to town, you're the
first person he asked about. He was just as hot 'n' heavy
into it as you were."

Caitlyn hiccupped as the tears rolled down her cheek.
"He's right, though. As soon as he came back to town
and we started dating, I was hearing wedding bells. I
put my entire life on hold for Jax. And I'm doing the
same thing with Dev, putting my plans for the camp on
the back burner."

"That's not what you're doing. You put your plans on hold because of that claim on the Lattimore land, not because of Dev."

Caitlyn shook her head. "When Dev took me to that ranch, I realized that I should have been the one to have found it. He's right, it is the perfect place for my camp, but I was so focused on Dev that I didn't know the ideal ranch went up for sale. I missed it completely."

"Caitlyn." She picked up the bottle of wine and topped up both their drinks. Caitlyn gulped a big sip of her wine. She knew that determined look on Alice's face—she was about to get a lecture.

"You are the most loving person I know. You dedicate yourself to the people and the projects in your life. That's why you stuff snack packs in your free time and run yourself ragged doing all the Lattimore business your siblings don't want to take on. That's who you are. Jax wasn't just some guy you dated. You two had been best friends. It was hardly as if you were startin' at the gate. Jax wants to blame you because he doesn't want to take responsibility for himself."

"He said it was both our faults. If I put too much into the relationship, he didn't put enough." She could tell she'd taken the wind out of the rest of Alice's speech. "But that doesn't change the fact that I'm falling into the same trap with Dev."

"It's hardly the same. He wanted to buy that place for you because he's committed."

"How do I know that? How do I know that he'll stick around? That the first time his family calls, he won't go running?"

Even as she said the words, she remembered him telling her that he loved her. That he was setting up his own business so his family didn't have leverage over him, so he could marry who he wanted.

"Caitlyn, do you hear yourself? What are you so afraid of? What do you have to lose?"

Everything. She had everything to lose. One bad experience with Jax and she'd become a cold fish. What would happen if she let Dev burrow even deeper into her heart than he already had?

"What do Dev and I really have? We've been playing a childish game where he pretended to humor me with boyfriend lessons." She spat out the last words, feeling ridiculous saying them out loud. "I don't want to repeat the mistakes I made with Jax. If it was real with Dev, he would've called me. Instead, one thing goes wrong and he's acting the exact same way as Jax."

"That's not fair, Caitlyn. It's really not the same situation."

"I'm done talking about this." She was done thinking about it, too. For two days she'd sat around the Lattimore mansion, moping. She'd started on this ill-thought-out endeavor with Dev because she was worried that Jax had ruined her for all men. Dev seemed to have brought out the sexual desire she thought she didn't have. But was it Dev, or had she finally conquered her demons? There was only one way to test her theory.

"Listen, I could use a night out. Do you want to go to the Lone Star?"

"Are you sure that's the best place for you to be right now?"

Caitlyn nodded. "I need to be someplace where I don't have to be myself."

Twelve

"I'm not sure this was a good idea." Alice grabbed her arm. Caitlyn shook it off. Whatever curse Jax had put on her had been broken, and she was determined to enjoy it. She'd managed to talk to half a dozen guys tonight, flirted, even danced with a couple of men. All without feeling the familiar tightness of panic in her chest. Maybe that's one thing Dev had been good for—being a practice boyfriend. That's all she had asked of him, after all.

"I'm not drunk, Alice. I'm perfectly in my senses and doing what you've been telling me to do for ages—letting loose."

The Lone Star was packed. It was a Friday night, and the smells of beer, peanuts and sawdust filled the air. The place was decorated like an Old West saloon with cowboy hats and horseshoes on the wall, a big, polished wood bar and a square dance floor. There was even a mechanical bull in one corner that was getting good use.

"Can I buy you a drink?"

Caitlyn turned to see a tall, muscular man with dark hair and thick eyebrows. He looked vaguely familiar, but Caitlyn couldn't remember where she'd seen him before. Alice placed a hand on Caitlyn's arm. She sighed. Alice was right. Partying all night wasn't Caitlyn's thing. She'd come here to test a theory, and she'd proven it. There was nothing wrong with her, never had been.

"I'm sorry, but…" She stopped. She didn't know what compelled her to, but her eyes suddenly went to the door. Her heart stopped in her chest. *How could he possibly be more handsome than I remember?* Dev walked in behind Russ wearing jeans that showed off his long legs and an untucked T-shirt. Hadn't he said Russ wanted him to come here to pick up women? Two days since they'd last spoken and he was already cutting his losses and moving on?

She tugged on her ear, a signal to Alice that she was happy to talk with the guy. They had a system. A tug on the ear for *go away, I am interested in this guy*, and a touch on the nose if she needed Alice to rescue her.

She turned to the handsome stranger and put a hand on his arm. "I'd love a drink. Beer will do."

He nodded and gestured to the bartender. It took Caitlyn and Alice the better part of half an hour when they'd ordered their drinks, but this guy had no trouble getting the female bartender's attention.

When they had their beers, she took a sip, then turned to him. "I'm Caitlyn," she said.

"Heath." Her pulse quickened. It couldn't possibly be the same Heath, could it?

"Yes, I am that Heath Thurston," he said, as if reading her mind.

"By that I assume you know I'm a Lattimore."

"The door isn't that far away, if you'd like to run."

Actually, what I'd like to do is throw this drink in your face. She took a breath and lifted her beer. "It's nice to meet you."

He clinked his beer mug with hers. "Mighty nice of you not to throw that in my face."

She smiled. "I considered it, but then I figure it's better to get you drunk and pump you for information."

He threw his head back and laughed. She snuck a look at Dev, who was staring right at them. A pleasant zing went through her at the murderous look in his eyes. She forced herself to turn back to the conversation with Heath. Perhaps she could find out more about his plans.

"It's nice to meet you, Caitlyn. I know I can't be very popular with your family right now."

"Yeah, they don't take kindly to having our home threatened."

Heath leaned over. "Listen, it's not my intention to cause chaos in your lives. I just want to do right by my sister's memory."

She nodded. "I can understand that."

"Tell me, Caitlyn, what is a beautiful girl like you doing in a place like this?"

His eyes sparked. He was flirting with her. She glanced at Dev, whose eyes were still fixated on her. Were her feelings for Dev real or just a rebound from Jax? Could she have the same chemistry with another man? Heath was certainly attractive enough.

"You think I'm beautiful?"

He smiled and she leaned forward, putting her elbow

on the bar so their faces were barely an inch from each other.

"I think you're stunning."

"Well, you're not that bad yourself."

She leaned in farther, and mentally scanned her body for the heat and lust she should be feeling. Heath was devastatingly handsome. She hoped that the morning at the ranch with Dev had also unlocked the mental block her therapist claimed was her problem. Surely sitting this close to someone as handsome as Heath should have her as hot as bothered as one look at Dev.

Alas, she felt nothing.

Russ slapped Dev on the back. "You stare at her any longer, bud, and your face will freeze like that."

Dev rolled his eyes. The Lone Star was the last place he wanted to be, but Russ had insisted, and Dev didn't have the will left in him to fight. He'd spent the last two days wallowing in self-pity, asking himself how he could have misread the situation with Caitlyn. The first woman he'd fallen for and he'd managed to screw it up royally.

He glanced toward her again and caught her eye for just a second. She looked stunning in skintight jeans, a strappy red sequined top and high heels that made her entirely too sexy for a place like this. Why was she sitting so close to that guy? Why was she leaning into him as if she was going to kiss him? He clenched his fists. *That man better not lay a hand on her.* How could she let another man touch her? What did that guy have that he didn't?

Then it happened. The man kissed her. The bubble of anger that had been growing inside Dev boiled over.

He stood and made his way to them. He pushed the man away from Caitlyn, breaking their kiss.

"Whoa, man! What the hell?" the man muttered.

"Dev!" Caitlyn screamed.

"What are you doing, Caitlyn?" Dev demanded.

"That is none of your business." Caitlyn said.

He looked daggers at the man who had been kissing the woman he loved. "Beat it."

"Listen, I don't want trouble, but it seems to me you're the one that should leave."

Dev glared at the man. He moved toward him, but Caitlyn grabbed his shoulder. "Dev, don't!"

He looked at her. Did she want to be with this loser? Had she already moved on from him? Had he just been a practice boyfriend all along so he could prepare her for the likes of this guy? She met his gaze, then sighed. "Heath, it was nice meeting you, but I need to talk to Dev."

She opened her purse to pay for the beer, but he waved her away. "Don't worry about it. Least I can do…considering."

She nodded.

Considering what? He wanted to ask her, but there were more important things on his mind. Like what was bar guy offering Caitlyn that Dev couldn't. *Royal.* The answer slammed into him. The man was from Royal. He could offer her the one thing Dev couldn't.

"Come on, Dev, let's find a quiet spot to talk. Just give me a sec." She turned to Alice, who was a few stools down on the bar, talking to a man, and whispered something to her. Alice turned to look at him for a beat, then nodded.

Each corner of the bar was louder than the last, so they decided to take the side exit and step into the alley.

It was dark, lit only by the light spilling from the apartment building windows on either side. It smelled of tobacco smoke and something sweeter.

"What were you doing in there?" Even in the shadows, he could see the anger in her eyes.

"Me? What were you doing kissing that guy?"

"Excuse me? What's it your business who I kiss?"

He stepped back, the anger that had consumed him just moments ago replaced with a cold ice that seeped into his veins. Who was he indeed? "You know what, you're right." He shook his head. "I'm the crazy one. What was I thinking? All you wanted was a practice boyfriend, somebody to warm you up so you could go out with guys like him." He waved toward the bar door, then turned away from her.

"I guess you're done practicing with me."

Thirteen

The last thing Dev wanted to do was leave Caitlyn standing in the alley, but he'd already made his play. It was her turn now.

She made a strangled sound, and he closed his eyes. "Dev, don't go."

He hadn't even realized he'd been holding his breath until she said those words. He breathed out. She came around so she was facing him. "I need to tell you something."

That was not what he was expecting her to say. Especially not with that look of pain etched on her face. Instinctively, he put his hand on her shoulders. "Hey, are you okay?"

She nodded. "Can we go someplace and talk?"

It was getting late, and most of the Royal cafés and restaurants were closed, so he drove in silence to his hotel. He was curious as to what she wanted to say, trying not to hope that she'd changed her mind. He handed his car key to the valet and directed her toward the hotel lobby.

She shook her head. "I want to talk someplace private. Can we go to your room?"

He sucked in a breath. "Caitlyn, are you sure?"

"Just to talk," she reiterated.

He shook his head. "I can't promise you that. I'll stick by what I told you on our first date. It'll be up to you when you want to move on from practicing, but being together in a hotel room is more than I can handle."

A pinkish tinge rose from her neck to her cheeks, and he tamped down on the heat that rose deep in his belly. She led the way to the elevator, and they went up to his room. When he'd checked in, all the suites were already taken, so he was in a standard room that had one large bed, a small desk and a little round table with two chairs.

It was hard to ignore the bed that took up most of the space, but he walked resolutely to the small table. "Let me order drinks from room service. Do you want something to eat?"

She shook her head. "Just coffee."

He ordered a pot and sat across from her. She bit her lip. He waited patiently.

"My best friend in high school was a boy named Jax. We never dated in high school, but there was always something between us. What I didn't know until just before Jax went off to college was that my father had paid for his tuition so that I'd have a friend. It broke my heart."

His heart lurched for her. She looked up at him, gauging his reaction. He gave her a small smile. "When

I was in high school, I was a bit of a pimply-faced, chubby little boy."

That brought a smile out of her. "I have a hard time picturing that."

"I'll show you my parents' Facebook account which has documented my teenage years in embarrassing detail. Anyway, I did not secure a date to the school dance. My dad didn't want me to stand around alone all night. So, he hired an escort to take me to the dance, thinking I'd be the cool kid. Except half the geeks in the exclusive New York private school had the same idea and the escorts knew each other, so they ended up spending the night hanging out with each other while I stood in the corner."

The smile on her face was much bigger and more genuine, and it pinged his heart. He'd fallen hard for her. Would she break his heart?

He softened his voice. "I don't think my dad would intentionally try to hurt me, just like yours wouldn't. They're convinced that they know what's best for us. What they don't realize is that in trying to protect us, they hurt us even worse."

She blinked, and a tear rolled down her cheek. She looked so innocent and full of pain, his heart squeezed painfully. He wanted to reach over and brush the tear away. Instead he tentatively placed his hand on hers. He didn't want to move any closer and scare her away. There was more to the story, he could tell by the deep breath she took, and he wanted to give her the space she needed to tell it her way.

"Jax went away for college, and we didn't keep in touch. I was mad at him for keeping my father paying his tuition a secret. Then he came back to Royal and by then I'd forgiven him. We reconnected. He admitted that he had loved me all through high school, but his mother had warned him to stay away from me because she worked for my family. He wanted to know if I'd felt the same way, and of course I did. Jax had been my best friend for years. He knew me—I could talk to him. We already had feelings for each other. It made sense to explore whether what we had was deeper."

He nodded—he understood perfectly. He'd never met another woman with whom he connected the way he had with Caitlyn. With other women, when he told the story about the high school dance escort, they were horrified and what followed was a discussion about how inappropriate his parents were. How could he tolerate their intrusiveness? He'd never met an American woman who could understand why he still lived in his family home at the age of twenty-eight when he was gainfully employed and, in their words, "not a loser." Caitlyn hadn't asked him to explain any of these things when he'd told her.

"Our relationship moved pretty fast. In hindsight, I didn't bother to go through the steps. I was just so excited to get my old friend and high school crush back." Her voice cracked, and he squeezed her hand even as his own stomach roiled.

"Jax was my first. I've been with a few men since him, but it's all ended in the same way."

He felt the tremor running through her body and he longed to take her in his arms, but he didn't want to lose this moment. He sensed that what she was about to tell him would explain her behavior. There was no way that he was the only one who had been feeling their connection.

"Jax and I planned a special night. It wasn't his first time, but he knew it was mine, and he wanted it to be a good experience for me." She visibly swallowed. "I don't even know how to tell you what happened. I'm not sure I understand fully. Jax tried so hard to pleasure me, but it just wasn't working...for the both of us..." Her voice cracked again. "We tried again a few times, but it just got worse. He started having problems, too. When we broke up, he told me that he'd never had a problem being with a woman, but I was a...a cold fish."

She hung her head. How could any man be with Caitlyn and think of her as anything but the passionate woman she was? He wasn't sure if there was more to the story, but he also didn't want to scare her away by getting too close.

"I've spent months in therapy trying to figure out what's wrong with me. My therapist encouraged me to date, and I did. But the same thing has happened each time I've gotten close to a man. My therapist calls it a fear of intimacy."

"Caitlyn..."

"No, Dev, don't say anything. Don't tell me that I'm wrong or how I'm beautiful or that I turn you on. I've heard that before. The problem is not with you, it's with me."

You're wrong, Caitlyn. Just thinking about that morning in the barn aroused him. How responsive she'd been, how wet and hot her body got with his touch. Dev had been with enough women to know that there were different levels of attraction he himself felt with each partner, but not once did he question the red-hot chemistry Caitlyn ignited in him.

"The last time you and I met...at the ranch... I had bumped into Jax that day. He lives in Royal too but we have been studiously avoiding each other. He finally decided he was ready to talk. He said that I had put too much pressure on our relationship. We moved so quickly, going from old friends to a serious relationship in one step. It was too much too fast."

"Oh, Caitlyn." He squeezed her hand, at the same time aching for her and relieved to find out why she'd reacted the way she had. He had moved too fast, pushed her to make a commitment when she wasn't ready. He was doing exactly what Jax had accused her of doing.

He pushed his chair close to hers, cupped her face and wiped away her tears with his thumbs. "I'm sorry I put pressure on you, that I rushed things."

"I don't want the same thing to happen to us that happened with Jax."

He nodded. "I understand that, Caitlyn…and…"

A knock on the door interrupted him, and he swore under his breath. He'd forgotten about room service. He let the man in to set up the coffee service on the little table, glad that he'd thought to also order some cookies. Caitlyn looked a little pale and he wondered if she'd had dinner. The room service attendant poured the coffee while Dev signed the check, and then the man left.

Caitlyn automatically added cream to his coffee and sugar and cream to hers. They'd had coffee so often together she knew exactly how he liked his. With a twinge he thought about how lovely it would be to spend breakfast with her. But if there was anything their conversation had taught him, it was that he would lose her if he pushed too hard. She was running scared.

They finished their coffee in a comfortable silence, then he poured her another cup. "Caitlyn, I don't ever want you to feel like I'm pressuring you. I've never had a serious relationship like you had with Jax. You're the first woman that I feel like I've ever connected with. You get me. You know me. You understand me."

He couldn't read the expression on her face, and the coffee burned down his throat. Caitlyn was the first woman he'd loved and hadn't been afraid to tell. What she'd just told him solidified his feelings for her even more. He hadn't imagined their attraction, hadn't over-estimated their chemistry or their connection. She felt what he did. But he also knew that there was only one way to convince her of that.

"But if friendship is all that you can give me, I understand, and accept."

Fourteen

Caitlyn stared at Dev. So, it was also happening with him. She'd admitted her deepest, darkest secret. The one only her therapist and Google knew about. What had she really expected? That he would take her into his arms and insist on proving her wrong? *Yes!*

She hadn't planning on telling him so much. But once she'd looked into his eyes, she'd realized that he was the only man who had ever told her he loved her and meant it. Jax had said "love you" once in a while, but it was in the way she said it to her siblings. He'd never told her he was in love with her.

Her brain screamed at her to call an Uber and go home. To save herself the humiliation that was sure to come. But she was frozen in her chair. He was looking at her expectantly, waiting for a response to his offer of friendship.

With every ounce of courage that she had, she stood. Her legs felt unsteady. Dev stood, too. "Caitlyn…"

"I have more than enough friends. I don't need another."

He stepped back, but she closed the distance between them. "What I need, Dev, is a lover. A man who can turn me on, who can show me that I'm not the passionless woman I think I am." His eyes widened, and she gave him a small smile. She stepped closer until she was well into his personal space.

Her legs felt like rubber. She wasn't sure how much longer she could stand. That's when his arm went around her, pulled her close. His head came down, and his lips seared onto hers. She met his kiss with a fervor of her own. Her body was on fire, and he was definitely aroused. She stepped back and lifted his shirt. He helped her get it off. She ran her hands across his muscular chest. He inhaled sharply, which spurred her on. She kissed his chest, ran her fingers over his nipples.

"I showed you mine, now you show me yours," he said cheekily and took off her shirt. She unclasped her bra, eager to feel her body naked and raw against his. He cupped her breasts and ran his thumbs over her nipples. She moaned, enjoying the feel of his hands on her. He bent his head and kissed the spot between her neck and shoulder, and her body pulsed with desire. She placed her hand on his erection, and his hardness made her even wetter than she was. He wanted her. There was no awkwardness; she was enjoying his touch, not dreading it. In fact, she wanted—no, needed more of him.

She unbuckled his pants and slid them down, then kicked off her high heels and discarded her jeans and panties.

"Do you have a condom?"

He nodded and opened a drawer to retrieve it. He went to open the packet, but she stopped him. "Not quite yet." She smiled then pressed herself against him. She wanted to feel the full length of his naked body against her bare skin. He cupped her butt and lifted her up. She wrapped her legs around him and moaned as she felt him hard between her legs. He rubbed against her wet core and let out a guttural moan. Then he put his mouth to hers.

They were rubbing against each other, she hot and wet, he hard and strong. His shaft pressed against her clit, sending waves of ecstasy through her body. She wanted him so badly, she began writhing against him, inviting him to plunge inside her.

He walked them over to the bed and set her down. He took a deep breath, and she looked at him, taking in the fierceness of his erection. "Dev, please I need you inside me."

He shook his head. "Not quite yet." She hated that he was using her words against her. He put his mouth between her legs, and she lost it. His tongue flicked across her clit, then went in and out of her. His arms were beside her, and she grabbed onto them for support, bracing herself for the explosion about to go off inside her. She dug her fingers into his skin as he licked and sucked her. "Hmm, you taste amazing." He pressed his thumb against her clit as he flicked and sucked with his mouth, and she lost her mind. The pleasure that rocked through her body was sensational. She screamed and lifted her hips, and he cupped his mouth over her sex and sucked.

When she came down from her orgasm, her core was still throbbing. She grabbed his shaft and rubbed him against her clit. He moaned. "Caitlyn, oh my God,

I can't hold out much longer." That just spurred her on even more. She grabbed and stroked him and could feel him pulsing in her hand. He stopped her, then quickly placed the condom on himself. When he entered her, she was sure she was going to shatter into a million pieces. He felt amazing inside her. She was already wet, but now her body molded itself to him, gripping his hard shaft as another orgasm pounded through her. She had wanted to do it with him, to finish the second time with him, but she couldn't wait. With her nails digging into his back, she tightened around him, giving in to raw, beautiful pleasure.

When she finally stopped pulsing, she noticed he had gone soft inside her. For a second, fear gripped her. Had it happened again? Had she managed to turn him off?

He smiled at her. "I'm sorry, I wanted to go a little longer, but I just couldn't hold off."

"You finished?" she asked shyly.

He pulled out of her and removed the condom. "A little too soon for my liking, but we have all night for me to make it up to you."

He grinned at her.

"We do have all night? Don't we? You're not going to up and leave me again, are you?"

Caitlyn shook her head. There was no place she wanted to be other than in Dev's bed. She crawled under the sheets, and he joined her. She turned around so he could spoon her. Impossibly, he was hard again, but she wanted a moment to feel his body against her. To take a breath and process what had just happened. She'd seduced Dev, had made him hot for her, and he in turn had lit a fire in her body.

As they snuggled in together, she finally understood what her therapist had been trying to tell her. There really was nothing wrong with her. She needed to connect emotionally with a man to feel comfortable with the physical part of their relationship. That's why the kiss with Heath hadn't roused her, the way Dev did just by looking at her. She had opened up to him, shared herself with him and felt connected to him. Maybe she'd even fallen in love with him. The thought filled her with warmth, and she pressed close to him.

"Hmm, you keep doing that and I'm not going to be satisfied with just holding you."

She turned around to face him. He kissed her on the nose. "I wish you'd told me earlier about what happened with your ex. I can't believe that any man would think of you as cold. You are passionate, kind, caring…any man would be lucky to have you."

Her heart pinched. That day at the horse ring, he'd told her he loved her. Had his feelings changed? Had she managed to drive him away from her like she always did?

"I'm sorry for the way I reacted the other day when you suggested a business partnership."

He ran his hand down up and down her back, and her body responded immediately, involuntarily curving into him.

"I was just overwhelmed with the suddenness of the idea."

"Was it that or something else?"

There he was again, refusing to let her get away with the words she'd crafted. "What do you think it was? These days you seem to know me better than I know myself."

He smiled. "I doubt that." He pulled himself closer to her so his lips were almost touching hers. "But what

I think is that you didn't like the fact that I was proposing a business relationship and not a personal one."

She shook her head. "That's crazy. We've only known each other for a few weeks—I wasn't expecting anything. You just took me by surprise, and I guess I didn't understand why you'd want to tie us together permanently without knowing where our personal relationship was going."

He kissed her briefly. "Where do you want it to go?"

She didn't hesitate. "You are my happily-ever-after, Dev. That's what I want."

"And where shall we live happily ever after?"

"In that ranch you found. We can make it a home. I can see some cozy farmhouse-style furniture, maybe curtains instead of the wood blinds that are there. I can take in horses and run my camp. You can see about turning that old Stevens brewery into your restaurant. You know, the more I think about it, maybe some remodeling could really make that place work. The location is so perfect, and…"

"Caitlyn," he interrupted gently. "You know I can't live my life in Royal."

She blinked. "I know. It was just a thought." He kissed her nose. "I'm not saying we can't come back here often to see your family, but my family business is based in New York, and if my restaurants are successful, I'll have to travel around."

She extricated herself from his arms and sat up. She'd known this conversation was coming and had been avoiding it. She hadn't had the words before, but now she understood why his plans for the ranch had bothered her so much. "What do you expect me to do? Stay by your side as we hop from one place to another?

Or stay here in Royal, waiting for you to come home when your schedule allows?"

"I hadn't thought about it. We only just got together. Give us a chance, and we'll figure something out. My family has a private jet. We live in the same country. I have friends that make things work with partners in India—we'll find a way."

She wasn't sure she believed him. She wouldn't ask him to stay in Royal with her. He wouldn't be happy here. But she wasn't sure she could be happy anyplace else.

He ran a finger slowly from her lips, down her neck, between her breasts and down her legs. She was already wet and throbbing for him and more than happy to forget about the looming decisions between them. She had Dev right now, and his mouth was doing that thing he was so good at. She wasn't going to ruin it by thinking about the future. Tomorrow would come soon enough to ruin things.

Fifteen

When he opened his eyes, Caitlyn was next to him, naked and bathed in morning light. They'd had quite the night, finally falling asleep when the sun came up. He stared at her face, wondering how he was ever going to let her go. He was glad they'd put off having the conversation about the future last night. He hadn't wanted to ruin their first night together, but even after she'd fallen asleep, he'd stayed up thinking about what she'd said.

He couldn't ask her to follow him around while he set up his business. Nor could he move to Royal. While it was a charming town, it didn't feel like home for him. He'd seen his siblings give up their dreams for their spouses. He wouldn't do that, nor would he expect Caitlyn to do that for him. But he was having a hard time finding a happy medium. Wasn't he jumping the gun anyway? Caitlyn hadn't even told him she loved him, and here he was trying to figure out how to make their lives work together.

Caitlyn murmured something unintelligible, and he kissed her forehead and left the bed. He checked his phone to see what he had on the schedule and cursed under his breath when he realized he had a video call scheduled with his mother in a few minutes. He had overslept.

"What's got you lookin' like you got bit by a box full of mosquitoes?"

He turned and smiled at her. She was sitting up in bed, holding the white sheet to her chin, and he loved her innocent smile and big eyes. This was the Caitlyn he wanted to wake up to every morning—rosy cheeked and looking at him like he was her whole world.

"I guess you can't take the girl out of Texas." *Literally.*

She smiled. "No, you can't." She lifted an eyebrow toward the phone he was holding.

"I have a video call with my mom in five minutes."

The look of blissful pleasure on her face was replaced with panic. She scrambled out of the bed and began looking for her clothes. "I need to get out of here."

He stepped toward her and pulled her into his arms. "No, you don't. I want you to meet my mom."

She shook her head. "Not looking like this, I can't. And I need to prep, figure out what I'm going to say. I need to research some Hindi words and…"

He placed a finger on her lips. "No, you don't. You just need to be yourself, like you are with me. Don't put on the armor. It'll just be a quick hello."

"I still can't have her see me wearing your bedsheet!"

He smirked. "Fine, put on clothes. It'll be nice to take them off again."

She gathered her clothes and raced into the bathroom just as his phone rang.

"Hi, Ma!"

"Dev, *beta*, how are you?"

They chatted for a few minutes. Dev tried to keep the video focused away from the bathroom door so he could properly introduce Caitlyn. His mother talked about the cuteness of his niece and then the latest drama of his siblings. Against his hopes, his brother had not really stepped up to help his father. His sister was handling things well, but things were falling apart at home for her. "It's time for you to come home, son. I don't want Maya's marriage to suffer because of the work she is doing for your father. I think he sees how capable she is and he'll give her more permanent responsibility."

Dev sighed. What his mother didn't know was that if Maya's marriage was suffering, it was because she was finally beginning to realize everything she'd given up for her husband. Her long-buried resentment was surfacing. He'd seen it since the day she quit her job. But now was not the time to discuss all that. He heard Caitlyn carefully opening the bathroom door and saw her peeking out. He waved her into the room. She'd pulled her hair back into a ponytail and washed her face. She looked incredible.

She gestured with her hands to leave but he shook his head.

"Why are you shaking your head?" his mother demanded. Caitlyn froze.

"Ma, you remember Caitlyn, whose picture I showed you? She's here, and I want her to say hello to you."

His mother immediately switched to Hindi, even though they'd been talking in English. "You know that is not how things are done. It is not proper to introduce me to a girl you are sleeping with."

"Ma, she's much more than that, and I think you know it. I wouldn't introduce you to someone unless I was serious about them."

His mother sucked in a breath. "Guess I have no choice but to meet her."

Caitlyn was already strapping on her heels. Before she could bolt, he gestured to her. "Ma, meet Caitlyn. Caitlyn, meet my mother."

Caitlyn glared at him quickly, then turned to face the camera and smiled.

"You are even prettier than the picture Dev showed me." His mother said.

He let out a breath. He didn't think his mother would be rude to Caitlyn, but she could be passive-aggressive.

Caitlyn smiled. "It is so nice to meet you, Mrs. Mallik. I had hoped we would meet under better circumstances."

His mother smiled. "My son is known to be very inappropriate, but we shall cover for his inadequacies, shan't we."

Both Caitlyn and his mother smiled and continued to make small talk. His mother asked about her family, and, immediately at ease, Caitlyn told her all about them. They talked a little about the charities they were each involved in. His mother even took one of Caitlyn's suggestions for a children's charity.

He was glad to see Caitlyn at ease with his mother. He wanted them to get along, to know that Caitlyn could fit in with his family.

"Tell me, Caitlyn, do you identify as a Black woman or as a white woman?"

Dev sucked in a breath. At least his mother had asked diplomatically.

She smiled. "It's a great question. Until a couple of years ago, I would've said both. But the truth is, my family, the Lattimores, is Black, and whether I realized it or not, I've been treated like a Black woman most of my life."

"As a woman of color myself, I understand, my dear. So tell me, how will your children identify?"

"Excuse me?"

"It's something to think about, isn't it? Take my grand-daughter for example, beautiful child she is. My son married an Indian woman, but my granddaughter calls herself Indian American. When she makes little pictures of her family, she colors herself a different shade than her parents, even though she looks exactly like them."

He knew where his mother was going, and he wasn't going to let his mother sow doubt in Caitlyn's heart. "Well, we should get some breakfast, Ma, so I'm going to steal my girlfriend back."

"No, wait. I'd like to respond to that." Caitlyn took a breath. "There's no answer. All my life, I've felt like I didn't know how to describe myself. I wasn't white or Black. Personally, I think it's sad that we still define people by the color of their skin. I hope my children won't have to deal with that at school. But if they do, I'll tell them what my mother told me. *It doesn't matter. All I want is for you to love who you are.*"

"Your mother sounds like a good woman." Dev knew that tone in his mother's voice, and he was glad Caitlyn wouldn't recognize it for the condescension it was.

"It's time for us to go, Ma."

His mother switched back to Hindi. "Dev, she's a

nice enough girl, but it doesn't change the fact that she's not Indian. It's time for you to come home and stop wasting your time in that backward Southern town." She hung up, and he took a breath to compose his face.

"She hated me, didn't she?" Caitlyn said quietly.

He shook his head. "No, she didn't hate you. She hates the fact that you're not Indian. That's something I'll work on with her." He tucked his phone away and cupped her face. "You did great."

"She has a point, you know."

"What do you mean?"

"What you wouldn't let her finish saying. That our backgrounds are very different. You don't know what it's like being Black, and I don't know what it's like to be Indian."

"So what, Caitlyn? How does that matter now? We have a lifetime to get to know each other's cultures and traditions."

She sat on the edge of the bed. "Until a couple of years ago, it wouldn't have mattered much to me, either. But one thing Jax made me see is how blind I'd been to the fact that I am Black, and that it affects how I see the world and how people treat me. It affects the responsibilities I have to my community as a member of the privileged class." She paused and swallowed. "It will affect how your family treats me."

"Listen, I've dated my fair share of Indian women, and let me tell you that what I value as a person is the same things you do. That's what's really important."

She shook her head. "Just now, your mom wanted to tell you what she thought of me, so she switched into a different language. That's how it'll always be. Your siblings married within your culture. I'll be an outsider in your family."

He sat beside her and took her hand. "I won't let that happen."

"Then you'll be an outsider in your own family."

He couldn't deny that she was right. It would take a long time for his family to get used to speaking English at the dinner table. They'd made a pact to only speak Hindi at home to make sure the next generation, his nieces and nephews, learned their language. But surely that was a small thing to overcome.

He leaned over and kissed her cheek. "I'll teach you the language. Don't worry too much about it."

"I don't think it'll be that easy."

He shifted so he could cup her face and make her look at him. "No, it's not going to be easy. But you know what's nearly impossible? Finding that one person who gets you and supports you and will be there for you. What we have is worth fighting for." He gazed at her. "I've been with my fair share of women, and the connection we have, it's nothing like I've had before. In my culture, we believe that there is one person who is made for us, our soul mate. You're mine, Caitlyn, and I'm willing to do whatever it takes to make it work."

Her eyes shone. "Are you sure, Dev? I know how much your family means to you. I don't want to be the one that comes between you and them."

He kissed her briefly on the lips. "You won't."

She turned her face and kissed his hand. "As long as you stand by my side, we'll face it together. My family won't be that easy, either."

"Is it because I don't speak with a Texas twang?"

She smiled. "Yes, and you're not a rancher, and you're not from Royal."

"That's a problem for you, too, isn't it? That I'm not from Royal."

She took his hands in hers. "I love you, Dev. I think I've loved you since the moment I spit my wine in your face."

A feeling of warmth and relief flooded through him. "I love you, too, Caitlyn. I promise you, we will figure it out. Finding love, that's impossible. Figuring out where to live and how to make a business work, that's just logistics."

"You make it sound so easy."

She leaned over and kissed him, and he kissed her back. A slow, sweet kiss to let her know that he loved her and that he was willing to fight for them.

"How about we spend the rest of the day together, forget about our families and just enjoy the fact that we have each other?"

She nodded. "Can we start by ordering breakfast? I'm famished."

He bent his head and kissed the spot between her neck and shoulder that made her break out in goose bumps. "Can I feast on something else first before we start breakfast?"

She murmured her approval and took off his shirt. He happily obliged and took off his jeans as she shed her own clothes. He wanted to take his time, but she had other ideas. As soon as his clothes were off, she grabbed his erection. Her hands were soft but her touch firm, and he nearly lost it. How could it be that her merest touch set his body on fire? He was usually much more reserved, but found it hard to hold himself back with her.

"Caitlyn, one second…"

She shook her head. "I don't want to take it slow. I want you now."

The fire in her eyes matched the one burning through his body. He knew what this was about. The conversation with his mother had deflated the bubble they'd created around themselves last night, believing that a declaration of love was all they needed. They both needed an immediate and urgent reminder that it was real between them, and that it was worth it. Or perhaps he was the one who needed reminding. He couldn't admit it to her, but she was right about the fact that it wouldn't be easy with his family and he'd have to give up part of his own relationship with them to be with her. He needed to be strong. His family always had a way of pulling him back in, of sucking him into their fold and their needs. What he needed was Caitlyn.

She pulled his arm with one hand while the other stayed firmly on his impossibly hard shaft. She lay back on the bed and guided him inside her. She was slick and he tried to tell her to take it slow, but she wouldn't listen, arching her hips to take him deeper inside her. Somewhere a phone rang, but he ignored it. He kissed her and she moaned, moving her hips. He matched her movements, feeling her tighten around him. The sensation was too much for him, but he held on as long as he could, determined to make sure she finished before he did, though it was hard to hold on with her tight around him and moaning with pleasure. She lifted her hips as her orgasm took over, and he couldn't hold himself back as she vibrated and pulsed against him.

"What's that ringing?"

He registered the same phone ringing that he'd noted when they got started, but where was it coming from? It wasn't his cell.

"That's my cell phone," she exclaimed.

The ringing stopped and she relaxed against him, but a minute later, it rang again. He slid out of her, seeing the panic on her face.

"I better get it, make sure it's not an emergency."

She scrambled out of bed, and he smacked himself. He'd forgotten the condom. How could he have been so stupid and not protected her? He knew he was healthy and didn't doubt for a second that she was, too, but he should've been more responsible. He'd gotten caught up in the moment and lost his mind. He'd have to tell her, make sure she took whatever precautions she needed to. How would she react when he told her? If this had happened with any other woman, he would've been freaking out. Actually, this would never have happened with another woman. But if it had to happen, he was glad it was with Caitlyn.

She answered the phone. "Sorry, I wasn't near my phone." She was breathless. "I'm on my way. I'll be there in fifteen minutes."

She looked at him as she clicked End on her phone. He was already pulling on his clothes. "What's wrong?"

"The private investigator found something about the claim on our ranch. The Grandins are coming over—the whole family is gathered. I need to go."

Sixteen

"I'll drive you."

Caitlyn sighed. Was she ready to bring Dev into her family fold? The Grandins were like family. If she took Dev with her, he'd meet all of them. *What if they don't like him? What if they scare him off?*

She pulled on her jeans and checked her appearance in the mirror. She couldn't show up looking like she was doing the walk of shame. Even though she was.

"I don't have to meet them. I can just drop you off."

She looked at him as he was fixing his own appearance. He pulled on a fresh shirt and ran a comb through his hair. There was a five o'clock shadow on his face, but he managed to make it look like it belonged there.

"Caitlyn, I need to tell you something."

She turned to him, her stomach clenching at the hollowness of voice. *What's wrong now?*

He swallowed. "I'm so sorry, I forgot to put on the condom that last time."

She almost laughed. How could she have forgotten? She was so careful. Almost without thinking, she looked at her phone for the date. *Crap.* Of course it was the time of the month when she should be even more careful.

"I take full responsibility. I know we have to go now, but I want you to know that I will be there for you, that…"

She put a finger on his lips. "The responsibility was as much mine as it was yours. If something happens, we will figure it out together."

He gave her a quick kiss, and all she had to do was look in his eyes to know that he was all in with her. He'd introduced her to his mother. While he made it out to be no big deal, she knew it was. It was clear from the overly casual way his mother had asked her some pretty deep questions about her family. The very fact that his mother had known about her before she and Dev had even slept together meant his feelings were serious. If he could take a gamble on her, she needed to make the same commitment to him.

"I want you to meet my family. There's no time like the present." Plus, she knew her family would be better behaved in front of the Grandins.

He placed his hands on her shoulders, forcing her to look up at him. "You don't have to, Caitlyn. I want to meet your family when you're ready. I'm in no rush."

She smiled. "Let's do it."

When they arrived at the Lattimore mansion, her family was gathered in the living room. All eyes turned to them as they walked in. Her grandfather Augustus was sitting in the large wing-back chair that was his spot in the family room.

Every time she saw her grandfather, it was hard to believe that he wasn't the same person he used to be. While he was still the tall, physically imposing figure she remembered from her childhood, his mind was not what it used to be. Her grandmother Hazel sat with Caitlyn's father, Ben, and her mother, Barbara. There was an antique silver pot on the coffee table, which she knew held the special brew coffee that her grandparents liked. Royal Doulton teacups, the service set from her parents' wedding, were set out along with little sandwiches, scones and pastries. Caitlyn's stomach rumbled, and she remembered they hadn't eaten breakfast.

Jayden was sitting opposite her parents, but Jonathan was pacing behind the couch. Their living room held three grand sofas and several chairs.

She was holding Dev's hand, and he squeezed it as a silence fell over the room. Caitlyn straightened, trying to stand as tall as she could. "Hi, everyone. This is my...this is Dev." *Boyfriend* seemed like the wrong word for him. Jax had been her boyfriend. Dev was so much more.

Jonathan was the first to speak. He made his way toward them. "Welcome, Dev." He held out a hand, and Dev shook it.

Before anyone else had a chance to speak, the Grandins arrived. Victor Jr. was accompanied by his son Vic, and his daughters Chelsea and Layla. Their younger sister, Morgan, hadn't come. Layla's fiancé, Josh, was there, and for once Caitlyn didn't feel the ping of jealousy that she did when she saw them. They all greeted each other, and everyone gave Dev a not-too-subtle once-over.

Layla sidled up to Caitlyn when she was alone for a second. "Who is that handsome stranger with you?"

"Someone I care about," she answered honestly.

"Well, whoever he is, hold on to him." Layla winked at Caitlyn, then went to help herself to the refreshments.

Dev handed Caitlyn a cup of coffee with some pastries on the saucer. "Why don't you sit and have something to eat?"

"Could you hear my stomach grumbling?"

He smiled. "I have a feeling you're going to need your strength for this meeting."

She had no doubt. Usually when the Lattimores and Grandins got together, there was chatter and merriment, but today, everyone found a seat pretty efficiently, many forgoing food or coffee.

Jonathan placed a large speaker in the center of the coffee table. It looked like an octopus, with cables that connected to multiple mini speakers that he spread out. It was the conference room telephone. "I have the private investigator, Jonas Shaw, and Alexa on the line."

Caitlyn had never seen everyone so quiet. She and Dev had chosen to stand behind the couch where her parents were seated. Her hand trembled slightly, and she set her cup on a side table. Dev handed her a small scone from his own plate, but she shook her head. Her appetite had vanished. He took her hand and squeezed it.

Jonas Shaw's voice was deep and crackly over the speakerphone. "I know you folks are anxious to know what I found, so I'll get right to it."

The room stopped breathing, but all Caitlyn could think about was the secure feeling of Dev's hand on hers. What if she found out in two weeks that she was pregnant? How would she feel? *Why aren't I freaking out about it?* Was she crazy to believe that he was committed to her?

Jonas cleared his throat. "As y'all know, Ashley Thurston was born about nine months after Daniel Grandin had an affair with Cynthia Thurston. You guys hired me to investigate the legitimacy of the papers that Heath Thurston is using to claim the oil underneath both your lands. I found a lawyer that used to work here in Royal. He's long dead now, but his daughter had his old papers. I went through them and found a copy of the paper Heath Thurston has."

The room took a collective breath. Until now, their entire strategy had been to refute the authenticity of the papers Heath Thurston had produced with Victor Sr. and Augustus's signatures.

"What about Augustus's signature on those papers?" her father asked.

"I'm afraid that's more bad news. Among the lawyer's papers was a logbook. Each person who visited the office signed in. On the day the papers were signed, Augustus's name was in the log, along with his signature. The same signature that was on the papers."

Silence hung like dead weight in the room, then Alexa spoke up. "Did you check to see if Augustus could have been there for other business? Maybe he was using the lawyer for something else?"

Caitlyn hated that they talked about her grandfather like he wasn't in the room. She looked at Augustus. The scowl on his face suggested he didn't like it, either.

"I checked, but I couldn't find anything related to Augustus. I reviewed the logbook for the month before and after, and Augustus didn't go to the office on any of the other days. Looks like his signature is legit."

Alexa and Layla asked Shaw several more questions,

trying to find a way to dispute the information he was giving them, but it was of no use. It was pretty clear that Heath Thurston's claim was real and both of their ranches were in danger. Once Jonas had hung up, her father turned to her grandfather.

"Daddy, do you remember Victor asking you to sign something?"

Augustus frowned at his son. "Why are you askin' me? And who was that on the phone besmirching my name? Why don't you ask Victor? Where is Victor anyway?"

Her grandmother stood and placed a hand on Augustus's shoulder. "Darlin, Victor can't be here right now."

"Then I'm not staying, either." Her grandfather rose from the chair, surprisingly agile for his age.

"I think I better take him back to bed," Hazel said.

When they'd left, everyone began talking at once.

"Augustus had no right to sign over our land to pay for Daniel's sins," Ben grumbled. Caitlyn had never seen her father so riled up.

"Excuse me, but how do we know that your father isn't the one that put my grandfather up to this?" Chelsea exclaimed, tucking her long, flowing hair behind her ear. As the eldest daughter of the Grandin clan, Chelsea was fearless, and not afraid of butting heads with anyone.

Jonathan spoke up, his tone sharp and cutting. "Augustus isn't the one who had an affair and a child out of wedlock."

Caitlyn noted the fear and anger on the faces around the room. Their families had been friends forever, and they were turning on each other.

Layla chimed in. "I don't for a second—"

"Everyone stop!" Caitlyn cut in, surprised at the

strength in her voice. Since she rarely spoke, everyone turned in surprise.

She made eye contact with everyone. "Now is not the time to turn on each other. Our only hope in getting through this is to work together. Both our properties are at risk here."

Alexa's voice crackled over the phone. "Only if there is oil. What if we can prove there isn't?"

Heads all around the room started nodding, obviously liking Alexa's line of thinking.

Victor Grandin Jr. spoke up. "I'll get Jonas working on that." He picked up his phone and left the room to make the call.

"It seems to me that what we need is a good lawyer," Caitlyn stated. "Our current ones don't have the personal investment we need to make sure this goes our way."

She didn't have to say more. All eyes turned to the phone.

"Alexa, we need you and your brilliant mind," Layla said softly.

"I know you weren't plannin' on coming home soon, honey, but this is too important," her mother said.

Alexa sighed. "I'll represent us on this. Caitlyn is right. We have to work together. Right now the most important thing is that no one from either of our families has any contact with Heath or Nolan Thurston. Is that understood?"

Caitlyn tensed and gave Dev a sideways glance. He didn't know that the man in the bar last night had been Heath Thurston.

"We don't know what the brothers' next steps are, and what we don't want is to inadvertently give them information that helps their case," Alexa continued.

Everyone nodded solemnly even though Alexa couldn't see them. Barbara invited the Grandins to stay for brunch, but everyone seemed to have lost their appetite. The Grandins rose to leave.

"I think I should go," Dev whispered to Caitlyn as everyone said goodbye to each other.

She grabbed his hand. "Don't."

He shook his head. "I think you need to focus on your family right now. There will be plenty of time for them to get to know me. Right now, they need you to process the news they just got, and you need to be here for them."

She smiled at him, unwilling to let him go but loving him for being so considerate and understanding that her family needed her. "I'm sorry about our day together."

"There will be plenty more." He gave her a chaste kiss on the cheek, then slipped out quietly.

"Where'd your fella go?" her father said as he poured himself a cup of coffee from the fresh pot that one of the kitchen staff brought out.

"This wasn't the best time to bring him," Caitlyn said.

"There's never a good time," Jonathan said gruffly. Her brother was sporting his signature jeans, T-shirt and cowboy boots. "I kinda wanted to talk to the guy."

"What, so you could get his social security number?" Jayden piped up. He picked up a sandwich and tossed it in his mouth, much to his mother's chagrin. She handed him a plate, and he promptly set it down.

"Have you been researching him?" Caitlyn could see her brothers cyberstalking Dev. "Did Alexa tell you about him?"

"Relax, sis. He seems like a solid guy." Jayden said.

Jonathan cleared her throat. "I still have some questions I'd like to ask him."

Caitlyn shook her head. "This is why I didn't want him sticking around."

"Caitlyn, did you know that his siblings are both married to people from their culture?"

"Yes, Jonathan, I know that. I don't see what that has to do with me dating him."

"Oh, Caitlyn, darlin', I could see clear as day that you two are in love with each other. You'd never have brought him today if you weren't serious about him." Her mother patted the seat next to her, and Caitlyn went to her.

"Why do I feel like you're all ganging up on me?"

Her mother put an arm around her. "We just want to make sure you know what you're doing."

"I'm not a child, and for your information, he introduced me to his mother today."

"And how did that go?"

"It went fine."

"Has Dev talked to you about whether his family is willing to accept someone outside their culture?" Her father put a sandwich on a plate and handed it to her.

"Are you guys willing to accept him? He's not Black." She set the plate on a side table. Her stomach was churning, and she couldn't imagine eating.

"You know that doesn't matter to us," her mother said.

"There's no point in talking about this when we don't know anything about his family. We've barely known each other for three weeks. Aren't you all always on my case about getting out more and dating and getting over Jax? Well, how am I supposed to do that when the first man I bring home gets the Texas inquisition?"

Her siblings had the courtesy to look sheepish. Alexa called out and everyone suddenly remembered she was still on the phone. In her take charge voice, she asked everyone to sit down so they could discuss what their next steps should be. Only Alexa could command a room even when she wasn't in it. After a while, Caitlyn stood, grabbed the plate her father had given her, loaded it up with sandwiches and left. Talking to death about what lay ahead wouldn't change the situation. One thing hit her with certainty—she wouldn't be able to open her camp on the Lattimore property anytime soon. The legal machinations Alexa was talking about would take forever, and Caitlyn couldn't keep putting her camp on hold for that long.

Then another thought punched her in the gut. Dev was supposed to be leaving town today, and not once had he mentioned staying.

Seventeen

Caitlyn breathed a sigh of relief when Dev texted to ask if he could pick her up a few hours later. She had already washed her hair and blown it out. She went to one of her favorite boutiques in town and, much to the amusement of the shopkeeper, picked out a red dress that was unlike anything she owned. The neckline was scandalous, and that's exactly what she wanted. She wore it without a bra, as it was meant to be worn. The dress cupped her breasts and tied in the back, then came around the front of her body like a wrap and ended in a bow.

She shivered with excitement at the thought of Dev loosening that bow and unwrapping the dress from her. She wore it with a pair of strappy heels and a new silk thong. She closed her eyes and imagined Dev's hand on that thong, and her core throbbed with anticipation. As she looked at herself in the mirror, she barely recognized the woman in front of her. Her cheeks were flushed, her skin glowed and the dress looked like it belonged on the cover of a fashion magazine.

She was ready just as Dev pulled to the front of the house, which was eerily quiet after the drama of the morning. Dev exited the car to open the door for her and looked at her quizzically. "Isn't it a little hot to be wearing a coat?"

She gave him a smile, then looked around to make sure there were no staff or siblings lurking nearby. She took off the raincoat she'd thrown on and twirled for him.

Dev whistled appreciatively.

"I can't be seen wearing something like this. I bought it just for you."

He touched her partially bare back and kissed her on the cheek. "You look sensational," he breathed into her ear, and her heart fluttered at the hungry look in his eyes. He looked back toward the front door of her house. "Any chance your family is gone? I don't think I can drive with you looking like that."

She shook her head, smiling. He sighed and got into the driver's seat. "I was going to take you out to dinner, but I'm not sure I can share you with anyone else tonight."

"There is no way I'm going out on the town looking like this. I have a reputation as a stuffy Lattimore to keep up. This dress is just for you."

The wolfish smile he gave her and the dark hunger in his eyes made the dress totally worthwhile.

"Why don't you drive to the corner of Main and Porterhouse? My favorite Italian restaurant is there, and we can get some takeout. I'll place the order now and it'll be ready by the time we get there."

Once they picked up the food, he turned down Porterhouse Street. "Wait, the hotel is on the other side."

He smiled. "We're not going to the hotel. Just wait and see."

He pulled up to one of the new condo buildings that had been built at the edge of town. He turned to her. "I rented a place here. Didn't feel right to keep taking you to a hotel room."

She refused to think about what that meant. He'd rented a place. That was a sign that he wasn't leaving anytime soon.

The condo he'd rented was on the top floor of the building with a great view of the neighboring ranches. The space was light and airy without being ostentatious. There was an open kitchen, living room, dining room and two bedrooms. It was sparsely furnished with basic but tastefully modern furniture.

"How did you get it set up so quickly?" It had only been a few hours since she'd last seen him.

"Well, I only had a suitcase to move. The place was already furnished and ready to rent."

He stepped behind her and circled his arms around her. He kissed the back of her neck, and a shiver of anticipation zinged through her.

"It definitely needs some homey touches. Maybe you'd be willing to help?"

Setting up house with you? Sign me up!

"So you plan to stay in Royal?"

"For now."

There was that maddeningly unclear answer. *What does* for now *mean?* Before she had a chance to ask, he trailed kisses down her neck and to the bare spots on her back. He cupped her breasts and moved his thumbs over her nipples, and all thought left her mind as heat flooded her body.

"Now, how do I unwrap this dress and get to my present?"

She undid the bow in the front of the dress, her body electrified with the anticipation of what was coming.

Suddenly the doorbell rang. Dev cursed under his breath, and she looked at him quizzically. "Expecting someone?"

He adjusted his pants and yelled, "Coming." She began rewrapping the dress. "My mom said that she was sending a package, so I told the hotel to send the courier over here when it arrived. I assumed they would leave it by the front desk."

When her dress was rewrapped, Dev went to answer the door, and Caitlyn moved out of view. She didn't want anyone seeing her in that dress, even if it was just a courier.

"Dad, what are you doing here?"

Wait what? Who!

"Surprise!"

This was not happening to her. Pulse racing, Caitlyn looked for the raincoat and realized it was on the other side of the room. She couldn't get to it without crossing in front of the door and being seen. Would it be better to hide in the bedroom until Dev's father left? Hiding was not a good idea. With her luck, he would decide to stay the night and then it would look even worse for her to be caught in the bedroom.

The man who entered the apartment looked nothing like Dev. He was half a foot shorter and lean, with thinning hair and round glasses. Despite the heat, he was dressed in a business suit. Regardless of his small size, he had a booming voice, and Caitlyn could see Dev shrinking right in front of him.

"Your mother was worried about you. I came to take you back to New York with me. Our jet is at the airport. Things are…" He stopped when he caught sight of Caitlyn.

"Ah, I see you have company." He eyed Caitlyn, and she shrank back, wishing she had hidden in the bedroom. "Sorry, I should have called. I can come back."

"No, it's okay, Dad. I want to—"

"No, no, son. You paid for the night, you should enjoy yourself."

It was as if someone had seared her with a branding iron. She raced to the kitchen to collect her coat, threw it on and picked up her purse. She couldn't stay one more second. This was not the way to meet Dev's father. "I need to go," she mumbled.

"Caitlyn, wait, no, don't leave." Dev caught her hand as she tried to race past him and put an arm around her. "Dad, this is Caitlyn, my girlfriend."

Her father's eyebrows shot up. "I see why your mother is worried," he said.

"Dad! Don't be rude. Caitlyn is important to me."

"No, it's okay, this is not the right way for us to meet. I'm sorry." She pushed Dev aside, wanting nothing more than for the floor to open up and swallow her whole.

"Let me drive you home."

She met his gaze, her eyes pleading. She couldn't take any more embarrassment. She shook her head, "Dev, please, take care of your dad. I need to go. I'll take an Uber." She turned on her heels and left.

"Dad, you can't just show up like that."

"Why not? Because you're ashamed? And what is

this about you moving from the hotel and leasing an apartment? I thought you were here to open a restaurant. Where is the restaurant? What have you been doing?"

Dev took a breath. He knew things looked bad from where his father stood. He was a traditional Indian man, and it was bad enough that his first introduction to Caitlyn had been in his apartment, but to have her dressed as she had been was a double whammy. He needed to calm the situation before things really got out of hand.

"Dad, let's start over. Why don't you come and sit? Let me get you a glass of water and then we can talk."

Temporarily mollified, his dad took a seat at the glass dining room table. Dev eyed Caitlyn's dinner favorites and sighed. He handed his father a glass of water, then plated the food for both of them. It was a practice in his father's business to serve tea and refreshments before every meeting. It irritated Dev, who considered it a waste of time and money, but his father had a saying that rhymed in their language. Translated, it meant that if stomachs are empty, words are, too. It's how business was done in India, and it went beyond hospitality. He hoped this time, it reduced his father's crankiness.

"*Beta*, I came to take you back."

"Dad, I told you when I left that I need to chart my own course."

"I understand that. I did the same thing when I was your age. Your grandfather was dead set against me coming to America. He even refused to pay for my ticket. Your mother and I came here with nothing. We stayed with relatives, and I used my savings and sold your mother's jewelry to buy my first business. From that I built up an entire empire. I understand your need to be your own man, and I want to support you."

There was a big *but* coming, Dev could feel it, and he braced himself.

"And I will support you, *beta*. But I need your support right now." His father sighed, took off his glasses and rubbed the bridge of his nose. All his life, his father had seemed larger than life. The great Vishvanath Mallik, the man who reduced competitors to tears after filling them full of tea and mini cucumber sandwiches. Right now, all Dev saw was how shrunken his father looked, and the bags under his eyes.

"I know you have pushed me to consider your sister and brother to run the business. What you don't know is that I have given your brother, Khushal, several chances. He likes the lifestyle but not the work. Your sister, Maya, is very capable, but this job comes at a cost. You know that her in-laws are old and live with them. The last three weeks that you've been gone, her marriage has suffered. Her husband has told her in no uncertain terms that she can't keep working the hours she's been working. Their household is falling apart. That's why I'm here. I had hoped to handle things without you, give you a chance to pursue your own dreams, but I'm getting to be an old man now. I can't handle it all. I need your help."

Dev's stomach knotted. "Dad, I've told you that we need to hire more executives. You have to trust people outside the immediate family."

"You haven't lived like I have, son. You don't know how vulnerable family enterprises like ours are. One mistake and the entire business can fall. I told you how your uncle inherited my father's factories in India. I was so busy running things in America that I trusted him to run the factories that were my inheritance. He ran them into the ground. Factories that your great-grandfather built under the British rule, when hardly any Indians were allowed to own property and have wealth. Those factories survived colonialism and crumbled because of some bad decisions. I can't trust someone else."

It was an argument that he and his father had been having since Dev had graduated from business school. He'd felt totally unprepared to be the CFO and COO of this father's company as a new graduate, but his father had never been convinced to hire someone for those roles.

"Dad, Maya is a grown woman. Don't you think she should make her own decisions? She loves working—she went to Harvard Business School. When I don't know how to handle something, I call her."

"Her husband came to me directly, and I promised him that I'd bring you back so Maya could return her attention to their marriage."

"Don't you think that's unfair of Neeraj? I've only been gone for three weeks, and he's already coming to you. He, and you, haven't even given Maya a chance."

"Dev, this is not up for debate. You know how your mother and I feel about marriage. We wouldn't have what we do if it weren't for your mother. Maya has the same responsibilities to her family."

"Aren't we her family, Dad?"

"Once married, a woman's priority is the family she marries into."

"Dad, the world has changed, and we aren't in India anymore. You have to give up these old-fashioned beliefs."

"Does this have to do with that girl?"

Dev straightened. "No, Dad, this is much bigger than Caitlyn alone…"

"Because if it is, let me tell you that your mother

and I are not going to let you throw your life away on a girl like that."

Dev dug his nails into his hands, trying to formulate his anger into a respectful sentence. "You don't know Caitlyn. What you walked into today was a private romantic moment."

"Look, Dev, I know you think me old-fashioned, but I'm not that traditional. Maya dated, and I don't expect your future wife to be pure and virginal, but I do expect her to have some decorum, family values and…"

"Caitlyn has all that and more in spades. Like I said, you caught her at a bad moment, but she comes from one of the most respectable families in Texas. She herself is on the board of the local hospital and several charities. She tirelessly supports her family every—"

"Your mother told me all about Caitlyn. The issue is not whether her family is respectable enough and if she herself has good values. It's whether she is willing to leave her family to come support you and your dreams. Your life is in New York. Will she leave her life in Royal to come be with you?"

Dev's mouth went dry. *No, she won't.*

Eighteen

Caitlyn turned off the phone so it would stop buzzing. It was Alice, who had heard from Russ, who had shown up to Dev's new digs to find his father there. Dev had not texted or called. She knew he needed time to talk to his dad and smooth things over, but it had been more than six hours since she'd left his place. Caitlyn couldn't shake the feeling that things were not going well with his dad.

Worse, she couldn't help wondering if his father had succeeded in doing what she feared most. Had he convinced Dev to go back to New York? To give up on Caitlyn?

It was late into the night and she was exhausted. She checked her phone again. No calls from Dev. She turned off the phone and tucked herself into bed. There was nothing she could do tonight.

She slept fitfully. This time she dreamed that she was

naked in bed with Dev and the Lattimores and Grandins all walked in on them and accused her of colluding
with Heath Thurston. She woke up in a cold sweat and
realized it was only 4:00 a.m. She checked her phone
and cursed under her breath when she saw ten missed
calls from Dev. He'd called right after she fell asleep.

Unable to return to sleep, she opened her laptop
and pulled up the listing for the ranch Dev had wanted
to buy with her. Her stomach clenched when she saw
"under contract" on the listing. Someone had put an
offer on the place. She slammed the laptop shut. It was
a sign that she and Dev weren't meant to be. She'd
planned to buy the place and surprise Dev with it, but
clearly fate was also shitting on them.

It was too early to go riding. She didn't want to show
up at the barns and screw up the morning chore schedule. She decided to go for a swim.

After a few laps, Caitlyn heard Alexa as she came
up for a breath.

"You training for the Olympic team?"

Caitlyn propped herself on the edge of the pool where
Alexa was standing. "Woke up early. It's too hot to run
and too early to ride."

Alexa was in jeans, a loose t-shirt and carried a paper
cup.

"You took the early morning plane from Miami?"

Alexa nodded. "I need to review all the family papers and whatever Jonas found."

"I know this whole legal business is horrible but the
silver lining is that you'll be home more now."

Alexa tilted her head. "What's going on, Caitlyn?
You only swim like that when you're upset. What's
wrong?"

She bit her lip. The last thing she needed was Alexa's

judgment. "Any more news after the bombshell yesterday?" Had that only been yesterday? She still couldn't
believe how much had happened in one day. She'd gone
from waking up to the promise of a new life with Dev
to having the rug pulled from underneath her. In all
that, she hadn't even stopped to think about what the
call with Jonas Shaw meant for their family's future.

"No real new information, but what Jonas found
is pretty damning for us. We need to figure out what
Heath Thurston wants out of all of this, but we also need
to be careful about how we approach him and Nolan."

"I know it was my idea, but are you really okay with
taking this on?"

Alexa shrugged. "I have been thinking about this
since it happened. This is too important to trust to an
outsider. But I can't stay in Royal. My life is in Miami.
I'm going to need your help." She took a breath. "Caitlyn, the family is going to need you in the coming
months. This fight with the Thurstons is going to be
tough. And Grandpa is getting worse. Dad tried talking to him alone yesterday, and he doesn't remember
what he may or may not have signed."

Caitlyn took a breath. "What do you need help with?"

Alexa smiled. "We all know how much you do for the
family, and we appreciate it. I'm counting on you to help
me fight this claim. I can only stay for a short time. Can
you help me with sorting through Grandpa's papers?"

Caitlyn smiled and nodded. Maybe it was a good
thing that the little ranch had sold. Her place was right
here with her family. They needed her. She exited the
pool and got dressed, opting for the most conservative
clothes she had, which was most of her closet. Despite
the heat, she settled for a pantsuit with a white collared
shirt. She added her pearls and drove into town to her

favorite bakery. She'd called ahead for an order of coffee and pastries. When they'd come to Dev's rental condo the previous day, he'd put her name on the list with the front desk so she could get a spare key anytime. Dev tended to sleep a little later, so she picked up the key in case he didn't answer her knock. She hoped she was early enough to offer them breakfast. Though what had happened the day before was tough to overcome, she owed it to their relationship to talk to Dev face-to-face.

She knocked on the door, but there was no answer. She used the key to enter. The place looked exactly as it had yesterday, but something was amiss. She set breakfast on the counter and noticed both bedroom doors were open.

She walked to the first door, her legs rubbery. The bedroom was pristine. The bed looked like it hadn't been slept in. She peeked in the second bedroom, and it looked the same. Had Dev and his dad woken up really early? Something about the tight corners of the bedsheets bothered her. She doubted that Dev, who had grown up with household staff, could make the beds so well. She walked into the room and threw open the closet door. She raced into the other room and found the same thing. She looked in every corner of the condo.

Dev was gone.

Nineteen

Dev cursed at his phone when he woke. His wireless charger hadn't quite connected, so the phone hadn't charged and was now dead. He placed it on the charger again and went to get dressed. His parents owned a penthouse triplex on the east side of Central Park. His room was palatial by any standards but especially New York City standards—it held a king-size bed, his exercise equipment, a deluxe desk decked out with all the technology he could ever want and an en suite bathroom. Looking around the room he realized just how frat boyish it looked with his clothes from last night on the floor and the dark leather furniture. He made a mental note to ask his mother to call the decorator to redesign the room. He walked into the shower and let the ten body jets and rain shower wake him up. He hated waking up this early.

After arguing with his father for hours, he'd finally

agreed to get on the family jet and come home for a few days. He'd called Caitlyn multiple times, but she hadn't answered. It was too complex to leave a voice mail. He'd just keep trying. He didn't want to leave things the way they were, but after talking with his father he'd realized that he had to come home and deal with whatever was going on with Maya. He was her older brother and had always protected her.

His phone was ringing when he exited the shower. It was his sister, Maya, calling to tell him that she was in the dining room downstairs. It was barely 7:00 a.m., but he shouldn't have been surprised that his sister had heard he was back and was ready for a fight. He sighed and threw on a collared shirt and dress pants.

"Maya," he greeted his sister as he walked into the dining room. His parents' penthouse suite spanned the better part of the top floor of the forty-story building, plus a portion of the two floors below. The dining room was on the topmost floor and had a floor-to-ceiling view of Central Park. The staff had set out coffee and pastries. His parents were late risers and typically didn't come down to breakfast until 8:00 a.m.

His sister was five-seven and dressed like the New York power broker she was in a smart white dress suit that looked like it should be on the cover of *Businessweek*. She gave him a warm hug and a kiss on the cheek. More so than his brother, Dev felt close to Maya; even when they were kids, he'd been both her best friend and protector. He'd vehemently disagreed with her choice of husband but had ultimately supported her because she'd asked him to. In fact, he couldn't think of a time when he hadn't done what she'd asked.

"I see Dad couldn't live without you."

She poured him a cup of coffee with the amount of

cream he liked and selected his favorite chocolate crois-sant from the pastry basket that his parents' staff had set out for them.

He sighed. "Apparently your husband can't live without you."

She looked down, tears shining in her eyes. "That's why I came early. I wanted to talk to you before Ma and Dad wake up. I need your help, Dev. I don't want to put you in an awkward position, I know you're supposed to have this time to explore your dreams, but I really need my big brother right now."

His stomach turned. Maya was tough as nails. Whatever was going on was bad, and his sister needed him.

His phone rang. He looked down at the display. It was Caitlyn. He looked at Maya's teary face. He couldn't take the call. He silenced it.

"Hey, Maya, you know I'm here for you. Whatever you need."

Twenty

He wasn't answering her call. She hung up without leaving a message. A deep ache settled into her chest. Everything she'd been trying to ignore came rising to the surface and soured her mouth.

Yes, he'd called her last night, but to say what? That all it had taken was for his father to show up and he'd left without even saying goodbye?

She walked to the windows to stare out at the neighboring ranch. She watched the cattle grazing in the fields. What was Dev doing? Was he looking out at the Manhattan skyline wondering how foolish he'd been to think he could live in Texas?

Tears streamed down her face. Her phone rang and she looked down eagerly, only to find it was Alice. She answered, hoping Alice had some information about why Dev had left so suddenly, a small part of her hoping there was a family emergency that had compelled him.

Alice insisted Caitlyn come over to her house. When Caitlyn appeared at her door, Alice pulled her inside and gave her a long hug.

"Darlin', I'm so sorry."

Caitlyn hadn't realized just how much she'd been holding in, because suddenly her body was racked with sobs. Alice held on to her. When her tears finally subsided, Alice put her on the comfortable couch and went to make them coffee. Caitlyn remembered that the last time she'd been sitting on that couch, Dev had walked through the door. It was the first time she'd seen him, and she'd nearly spit out her wine. Was it just three weeks ago that her biggest problem was that she had trouble talking to men and needed boyfriend lessons?

Alice returned with a steaming cup of coffee and handed it to Caitlyn, then sat beside her. Caitlyn curled her legs underneath her and turned to face Alice.

"Dev called Russ last night when he couldn't get hold of you. He had to go back to New York with his dad."

Caitlyn nodded and took a sip of the coffee to see if she could loosen the lump in her throat.

"Russ said he was really broken up about it and was even debating showing up at your house, but Russ talked him out of it. He didn't want him getting shot prowling around your house in the middle of the night."

"What was so urgent?" Caitlyn managed to choke out.

Alice shrugged. "He didn't say, just that he had to leave but he would call you."

"You were right all along." She filled Alice in on the conversation she'd had with Dev's mother and the disastrous meeting with his father the day before.

"I think your boyfriend's father mistakin' you for a hooker beats me sleeping with a guy who took a call from his mama while we were having sex," Alice joked, and it brought a small smile to Caitlyn's face.

"I didn't even know you owned a dress like that."

Caitlyn smiled wistfully. "I didn't. I bought it just for him. I refused to even go out to dinner looking like that."

Alice rubbed her arm. "For what it's worth, Russ said he's never seen Dev like this with any other woman. I think his feelings are genuine."

"It doesn't change the fact that his responsibilities are to his family."

"And what about yours?" Alice asked gently.

"What do you mean?"

"If Dev had gotten hold of you last night and asked you to come with him to New York to sort out his family drama, would you have gone?"

The question slammed into Caitlyn like a freight train at full speed. She didn't even have to think about it. She filled Alice in on the meeting they'd had with the private investigator. "We can't keep hoping that claim isn't legal. I have to be there for my family. This is devastating them. Even Alexa flew in this morning."

They were silent for a while, then Alice finally spoke. "I'm your friend, and one hundred percent on your side. But don't you think it's hypocritical to expect Dev to drop his family obligations when you're not willing to do the same? He's the eldest son, and you're the baby of the family. Imagine the pressure he's feeling."

Alice had just voiced what Caitlyn had always known deep down inside. She was asking Dev to make a sacrifice that she herself wasn't willing to make.

Her phone buzzed, and she looked down to see that Dev had texted. Tried to reach you. Had to come back to New York. I'll call you soon. I promise.

Alice leaned over to read the text. "You need to talk to him."

Caitlyn shook her head. She wiped the tears that had fallen on her phone and typed, I can't talk about this. I understand why you had to leave. I love you and always will, but we were foolish to think we could make this work between us. Your life is in New York and mine in Royal.

Alice placed a hand on Caitlyn's. "You can't send that text. You have to talk to him."

Caitlyn shook her head. "What good will that do? I thought talking to Jax would help me come to terms with our relationship, but the only thing it did is sow more doubt about my bad relationship skills." She wiped the tears from her face. "What will Dev say? That he loves me but that his family comes first? And what will I say back to him? That my family is more important than his? That he needs to give up his family obligations when I'm not willing to do the same?"

Alice took both their coffee cups and set them on the table. She hugged Caitlyn, who cried into her friend's shoulder.

The only thing left to do was to was accept the fact that the love of her life was gone.

Dev looked at the text Caitlyn had sent and cursed under his breath.

"Did you see the biodata of Anjali Verma?" his mother asked from across the breakfast table. His father was sitting at the head of the table, his face hidden behind the *New York Times*. As far as Vishvanath Mallik was concerned, the matter of Caitlyn had closed when he'd gotten Dev to agree to come back to New York.

Dev set his fork down on the plate with unnecessary

force, and it clanked loudly enough to get his father's attention. Maya had already left, and while Dev had agreed to help her, he couldn't deal with her problem until he addressed his own.

"Ma, you can send the biodata for every girl around the globe, I'm not going to look at them and I'm not going to marry any of them."

His father sighed. "Is it about that girl?"

"Caitlyn is the love of my life," Dev said, not bothering to hide his anger.

"Dev, you know that we are very modern-thinking parents, but the one request we have is that you marry someone Indian," his mother said quietly.

Dev took a breath. "Ma, you've always taught me that the most important part of our culture is our family values. That we take care of each other, and are always there for each other."

"And an American girl can't understand that. How many of your *gori* girlfriends understood why you were still living at home? How many of them would be comfortable with us living with you in our old age?"

"That's what I'm trying to tell you, Ma. Do you know that Caitlyn lives at home with her parents? That she works day and night to make her family's business successful?"

"It's not the same. Indian girls have a different level of respect for their elders that I've never known American girls to have."

"Actually, Ma, you're mistaken if you think that just because a woman is Indian, she's okay with the concept of a joint family. The last girl you set me up with—remember Priya, who I went out with for a few weeks?"

His mother nodded enthusiastically. Priya was one of the few women that Dev had agreed to meet from the endless biodatas his mother sent. She was an NYU law student, and Dev had thought she sounded interesting.

"I liked Priya. Her mother just called me last month to say that she's still single," his mother said encouragingly.

"Well, I'm not surprised. She specifically told me that she had no interest in being with a man whose life revolves around his family and that she will never agree to live with my or her own parents. She thinks her grandparents ruined her childhood. Oh, and she also doesn't want any children, and she'd like a husband who is willing to fly around the world with her, because she's going into international law and expects to have clients all over the globe."

Even as he said the words out loud, a thought he'd buried deep in the recesses of his brain surfaced. Wasn't he hoping Caitlyn would do the same thing? Wasn't he planning to open a national chain of restaurants and go from city to city setting up his business?

His mother gasped. "*Hai*, what a liar Priya's mother is. She assured me that she raised her daughter with very strong family values. Don't worry, the biodata I sent today, that girl…"

"You're not hearing me, Ma!"

His mother gaped at him. His father cleared his throat then slapped a hand down on the table, making the cutlery rattle on the plates. "We are not going to argue endlessly." His voice dropped. "Let me put it this way, Dev. You have a choice to make. That girl or us. You decide who is more important to you."

Dev sank back into his chair. He hadn't thought his parents would go this far, but they had, and with it, they'd sealed his fate.

Twenty-One

Caitlyn sighed when she saw who was calling. For the last week since Dev had left, she'd spent most of the time either wallowing in self-pity or tediously going through her grandfather's papers, a task no one else seemed to want to do. It suited her just fine, she didn't want to be around people. She'd canceled several meetings and even postponed her volunteer shift at the children's services center. She didn't need another reminder of how spectacularly she'd failed. The only thing she'd accomplished this week was to help Alexa with sorting out the family papers in preparation for the battle that was coming with the Thurstons' claim.

She answered her phone. "Hi, Greg."

"Miss Caitlyn, I'm glad I got hold of you."

Caitlyn didn't even have the energy to correct him.

"You remember those two horses at the Frederick ranch you called me about?"

Caitlyn sat up. "Yes. Did you talk to the ranch hand about brushing them more often, and making sure that—"

Greg cut her off. "Yes…the new owner asked if you would possibly meet him at the ranch today round 7:00 p.m. to tell him what he needs to do with the horses. He's never owned horses before."

Caitlyn sighed. It was probably one of the city people from Houston or Dallas who showed up in Royal thinking they'd like a country house. She had seen too many of them who liked the idea of owning horses and then trusted ranch hands to take care of them. She'd rescued four horses who had been neglected like the ones at the Fredrick ranch.

She was inclined to say no but then thought of the horses. She didn't want them suffering because she was too busy mourning Dev to help them.

"I'll be there."

"Thank you, Miss Caitlyn."

She hung up and got herself out of bed just as someone knocked on her door. She opened it to find Alexa. Her sister was dressed in black pants and a light blue top—her lawyer clothes.

"Wake up, sleepyhead." She smiled. "I came to say goodbye. I'm going home."

"Aren't you already home?" Caitlyn said, rubbing her eyes.

"Cute. Anyhow, one of my clients has an emergency, and I need to go back."

"But what about the Thurston claim?"

"I don't have to be here physically to work on it. I'll come back when needed." She put her hands on Caitlyn's shoulders. "You know my life is in Miami, right? I've already been here too long. I need to go back."

Caitlyn nodded. She'd hoped her sister would come back for good, but she'd made her own life in Miami. Alexa had never let anything stand in the way of getting what she wanted.

"I'll be here to help with whatever you need." She hated how sad her voice sounded.

"Hey, Caitlyn." Alexa sat on the bed beside her and placed an arm around her. "Please don't stay here if you're not happy." She sighed. "I've always worried that we dump too much on you. Don't for one second give up your dreams because you're feeling stuck here." She pulled back and met Caitlyn's gaze. "Go out and do what you want. Open your horse camp. Go to New York and be with Dev. It's not all on you. Jonathan and Jayden are here."

After Alexa left, Caitlyn thought about her words as she showered. In the last week, she'd missed all her board meetings, and the world still went on. She'd managed to take care of things over email. Maybe the new ranch owner wanting to meet her was a blessing in disguise. Perhaps she could offer to buy the ranch from him, or rent the stables to open her horse camp. Then another idea struck her. She dressed for the day and got to work. She'd been working on the wrong goal this whole time.

She didn't need a boyfriend, and she was done mourning Dev. It was time for her to focus on what was really important.

She arrived at the ranch a few minutes early. A rental car was parked in the driveway. Her heart contracted painfully as she drove up to the house. She'd loved it since the moment she'd seen it. It would make someone a nice home. She couldn't bring herself to go inside. Since she was an invited guest, she decided to take a chance on it being okay for her to walk to the back. She strolled toward the horses. They were turned out in the ring. She spoke softly as she approached, and the appaloosa seemed to remember her. He came trotting over. She snatched some clover from the ground and held it out. He ate from her hand. The mustang came over, eager for his share.

"You two are looking a little better. I'm glad the new owner talked to your ranch hand." The troughs inside the ring were full of clean water. It was crazy that this was only her second meeting with these horses. She didn't even know their names, and yet she knew this wouldn't be her last visit with them.

"Their names are Smoke and Shadow."

She whirled. There was no way he was here.

Twenty-Two

Dev loved the look on her face when she turned around. The sun was still high in the sky, and it shone down on her like spun gold. Her hair was pulled back in a ponytail. She wore a V-neck T-shirt and jeans, and even though it had only been a week, it felt like he'd been away from her for a lifetime.

He hadn't responded to her last text, knowing that he owed her more than a text or a phone call. No matter how things turned out between them, he wasn't going to be a jerk like her ex. He was not going to let this all end without letting her know just how amazing she was and helping her make her horse camp come true.

She stared at him as he approached. Her face was inscrutable, and his stomach clenched. She couldn't even spare a smile for him?

"What are you doing here? Why have you returned now?" She looked away from him but he kept walking towards her. When he was standing before her, she looked him in the eyes.

"Did you think I wouldn't be back? Do you think so little of me?" He moved closer but she took a step back.

"Let's not make this harder than it already is. You and I both know that it was never going to work between us. Your father's visit just hastened what would've happened anyway."

"Please let me explain why I had to go. I was never leaving for good."

"Not then, but eventually you will." She looked away from him and he wanted to reach out and touch her but wasn't sure how she'd react.

He rubbed the back of his neck. This conversation wasn't going the way he had planned at all. He hated the way she was looking at him, her eyes full of pain and mistrust.

"I bought this place for you," he blurted out.

Her head snapped up "What do you mean?"

"The night before I left. I bought this place. It's in your name. I bought it for you. No business partnership, no strings attached—it's for your horse camp. Or for you to do with as you want."

She stepped back another pace, her back now against the horse ring. Smoke, the appaloosa, trotted over and nuzzled against her neck. Her eyes were locked on Dev's. She didn't even notice the horse.

"So what is this? A goodbye present?"

Her tone was a punch to his gut. Was that what she thought he was doing? "No. I thought… It's…" He took a breath. "I bought this place for you so you'd know that you are under no obligation…"

"Why would I be obliged to you?"

Everything was coming out all wrong. He should just do what he came to do.

Stepping back, he dropped his knees.

Her eyes widened.

"Caitlyn, you are the love of my life. From the moment I saw you, I knew there was a connection between us. I've loved you from that first night at Alice's house, and since then my love has only grown and solidified. You are kind, you are caring, you are intelligent and being with you has given me the kind of strength I've never had on my own. I don't want to live without you."

He realized he didn't have the ring in his hand, and he pulled it out of his pocket. "This ring belonged to my *nani*, my maternal grandmother. She gave it to my mother to give to my future wife. I came here to ask if you'd marry me."

Caitlyn was staring at him, her eyes shining. Had she decided that she didn't want to be with him?

"How do we make it work between us? How do we split our lives? The first time your father showed up, you dropped everything and left." His heart stopped. Her voice seemed to be coming from far away even though she was only a foot away from him. Had he messed this all up? Had he taken too long to sort things out with his family?

"I'm sorry, Caitlyn. I didn't know how best to handle things. I needed to go, to put things to rest with my family so I could come back here to you. You have to forgive me."

"Where are we going to live? How are we going to make this work, Dev? Love doesn't conquer all. We can't keep ignoring these things."

He was still on his knees. Picturing this moment was what had kept him going through the last week. It was what had given him the strength to stand up to his family. But what he'd dreamed of was her screaming yes and flying into his arms. Had he miscalculated so badly? His knees were wet from the soft ground, and his joints were stiff as he stood. He didn't put the ring away.

He took a step toward her. She placed her hands behind her on the fence, and he retreated.

"I was hoping you might let me live here with you. I'm thinking this would make a really great house for us, and these barns would be great for your camp. I'll open my restaurant at that old Stevens brewery. I'll make it work. If you let me, Caitlyn, we will live right here in Royal, where you can be close to your family."

She shook her head. "I can't do that to you. I won't. I won't take you away from your family. It'll be fine at first, but then you'll resent me. You'll hate the fact that I stuck you in this town, that I took you away from your dreams."

It was time to give up hope that he was going to get his picture-perfect proposal. What he hadn't really thought about was what he would do if she said no. He put the ring back in his pocket.

"I've thought this through. This town will be my flagship restaurant. Then I'll open the chain I was planning. I'll have to travel a lot, and that's something you'll have to put up with. I promise when I come back, I'll make it up to you." He gave her a smile, and his heart skipped a little when she smiled back and took one small step toward him.

"It's not fair for you to give up everything. Your dreams, your family. Why do you want to do that?"

"My dreams have changed Caitlyn, there is nothing I want more than you. If this last week has taught me anything, it's that I can't live without you."

She took another step toward him and held out her arms, palms down. He took her hands, desperate with the need to touch her. Her eyes shone.

"I can't let you do that."

"I want to."

She shook her head. "That's not how it works in a relationship. My family can figure things out without me. My sister, Alexa, lives in Miami. She's here when the family needs her, but she has her own life. I can do the same."

"What about your horse camp?"

"That I'm not willing to give up. But I also don't have to do everything by myself for it. I can steal a ranch hand or two from my father and delegate. The important thing is to have a place for the kids to go, I don't personally have to teach them to ride every day."

What is she saying? "You want to give up your family and your camp for me?"

She smiled. "It's not a matter of sacrificing or giving things up—it's making things work. If you reduce some of your family responsibilities, and I reprioritize my time, we can make this work. In fact, I just resigned from several of my board seats today. There are any number of people who can fill those seats, but there is only one person who can make me happy."

His heart was pounding so wildly in his chest, he was sure it was about to burst. He pulled her close and she came willingly, lifting her chin so he could bend down and kiss her. He kissed her softly, savoring the feel of her lips. "I love you, Caitlyn. I'll do whatever it takes to make it work."

"I still haven't forgiven you for leaving me."

His heart lurched. "Tell me how I can make it up to you. Tell me what I need to do for you to forgive me."

She smiled and stepped back from him. "There is no forgiving you for what you put me through this last week. You're going to have to spend your whole life making it up to me."

Wait, what?

"Does this mean you'll—" He didn't get to finish his thought, because she stood on her tiptoes and pulled his head down, pressing her lips to his.

Twenty-Three

"I'm the only guy here not wearing a cowboy hat," Dev said. "You could've lent me one."

Caitlyn laughed. "Don't worry, I'm sure we'll find some here."

"So what is this place, exactly?"

"It's the Texas Cattleman's Club. Each year they throw this summer barbecue. Everyone who is anyone in Royal will be here, and you're going to have to meet them if you want that restaurant of yours to be a success."

The barbecue was set up on the sprawling lawns of the Texas Cattleman's Club. The day was hot, but a cool front had come in the night before, so there was a slight breeze. A giant white tent held cooling fans, but most everyone seemed to prefer it outside. The air smelled of smoked meat and whiskey.

"Caitlyn, tell me what I'm seeing on your finger is not an engagement ring!" Caitlyn turned to see Chelsea Grandin.

She smiled. "Meet my fiancé, Dev Mallik."

Chelsea smiled at him. "It's nice to see you again. Now let me see that ring." She tugged on Caitlyn's hand and inspected the ring. Chelsea was wearing a summer dress with cowboy boots, her long hair loose around her shoulders. "It's a really unusual stone. Is that a pink diamond?"

"Dev, you have to tell the story. When I first heard it, I started crying." It *was* an unusual ring, with a round-cut stone that had pink and orange hues depending on how the light hit it. The huge stone was set in a simple yellow gold band which just made it look even bigger. Her mother had fanned herself when she saw it, claiming it had to be around ten carats. She'd grilled Dev, who had no idea how many carats the ring was, and then proceeded to tell the story of how he'd gotten the ring.

"The stone is a padparadscha sapphire. They are rare sapphires that are mined in Sri Lanka. My *nani*—that's my mother's mother—was born in Sri Lanka. Her family emigrated to India to flee the famine in Sri Lanka. They had very few possessions, but the one thing they did have was this stone, which was originally set in a necklace that had been gifted to my great-grandfather by the mine owner in return for saving his life from a rockslide. My *nani* was the eldest child, and she wore it around her neck for safekeeping. She had two brothers and a sister, but they all died either during the travel or immediately afterward from disease. My *nani* is the only one who survived. She always held the belief that the stone protected her. Anyhow, she died last year, but before she did, she gave the necklace to my mother and asked her to reset it into a ring and save it for my future wife. Since she knew she wouldn't see me married, she wanted to give this stone as a way of giving our marriage her blessing."

Chelsea put a hand to her heart. "I will not lie, I am so jealous of you right now." They chatted for a few more minutes, then she gave Caitlyn a hug and left to socialize.

Dev steered her toward the tent. It was mostly empty, and the bar inside had no line. They each got a glass of wine. The last few days had been a blissful blur. After she'd accepted his marriage proposal, they'd gone back to her house to announce it to her family. Alexa had offered to fly home, but Caitlyn told her to stay put. She'd have to come home soon enough for whatever happened next with the Thurston claim. Caitlyn hadn't wanted her sister to run herself ragged flying back and forth.

She and Dev had picked out furniture for the Fredrick ranch, which they'd promptly decided to rename Smoke and Shadow, after the horses. Ol'Fred had helped Dev get a contractor, who was going to remodel the old Stevens brewery for his restaurant.

They found a quiet corner. "We've been so busy, you haven't told me how you convinced your dad to make Maya the CEO of his business."

Dev smiled. "A combination of pleading, begging, threatening and cajoling." He took a sip of his wine. "Remember I told you that when I came to Royal, my sister had taken over dealing with the business. Well, the reason my dad came to get me is that Maya's husband had called him saying that his and Maya's marriage was on the verge of divorce because she was spending so much time in the office."

"But you were only gone for three weeks. That can't have been the sole reason."

He nodded. "It wasn't. Maya came to me the morning I arrived. Her marriage has been on the rocks for a while. She gave up everything she wanted to do with her career to help her husband deal with his family responsibilities. She hasn't been happy with her life for a while now, and getting back to work just reminded her of what she really wants out of life. She wants a divorce, and she needed my help to get it."

"Why did she need you?"

"Because shc will be the first person in my family to ever get a divorce. It's not done in Indian families—at least not traditional ones like ours. Maya doesn't want to be estranged from my parents. I had to support her and convince them that Maya's happiness is what's most important to us."

"I'm so sorry. I wish you'd told me before you left. I would've understood."

"I know you would. But at that time, there was so much to deal with in my family, I wasn't thinking straight. It took Maya and me some time to make my parents see that their stubbornness would've caused Maya lifelong grief. But in a way, getting them to see why Maya was unhappy helped my case."

Caitlyn smirked. "Did your mother mistake Maya's husband for a male escort?"

He laughed. "No, that honor will forever remain yours." She punched him playfully. "In all seriousness, they realized that their insistence on Maya marrying someone Indian had led her to choose the wrong the person. I told Maya about you, and she convinced my mother that she could be happy for us and have the opportunity to interfere in our lives, or hold on to her stubbornness and lose me. On the day I was scheduled to leave, she showed up with the ring and asked me to give it to you."

"Dad was really impressed that you asked him first."

Dev smiled. "That's how it's done in Indian culture. My mother would have never forgiven me. It was a bit of a challenge to come see your dad without you finding out."

"Wait, you came to my house?"

He nodded. "Around the time Alexa was leaving. She was dispatched to your room to keep you busy while I snuck in the house to go meet your dad."

"I can't believe Alexa didn't tell me. And she knew how miserable I was without you."

"Yeah, your dad did make me promise that I would make sure he never had to see that mopey look on your face. He also made me promise that I would propose that day, which was a bummer because I had this whole plan that I couldn't put into action."

"And what was that?"

He grinned. "Well, in Indian weddings, the groom rides in on a horse. So, I was going to get the ranch hand to saddle up Smoke for me, and I was going to ride him."

"Do you know how to ride a horse?"

He shook his head. "No, but I wasn't going for a race around the town. I figured I could just sit on him and have him walk a few steps."

Caitlyn sighed. "There is so much I'm going to have to teach you. Starting with the fact that you can't just get on a horse and ride him."

Dev leaned over and pressed his lips to hers. "I look forward to you teaching me all kinds of things." She couldn't resist kissing him back. Since he'd returned, she couldn't get enough of him.

"I see you two have kissed and made up."

Caitlyn turned to see Heath Thurston, and she tensed. Alexa had specifically told them not to speak to him.

Dev held out his hand. "Hey, man, I'm sorry about that night. I was out of line."

Heath took Dev's hand and shook it. "It's okay. I could tell just by looking at the two of you that there was something hot and heavy going on, and I wasn't going to get in the middle of that."

Caitlyn politely excused them and dragged Dev outside. "What is going on with you and that guy?" Dev said.

"That's Heath Thurston, the guy who's making the claim against the ranch."

Dev raised his brows. "Well, then, it's a good thing I rescued you from him the other night."

Caitlyn rolled her eyes.

"Wait, if that guy was Heath, who's that guy talking to your friend?" Dev gestured toward a grassy knoll. The tent door where Heath had gone in was behind them.

Caitlyn turned to look where Dev had pointed, and the sip of wine she'd just taken came spurting out of her mouth. "Oh my God!"

She'd dribbled some on her dress. Dev dabbed at her dress with a napkin. "I guess we're going to have to take you home and get that dress off," he said with a sparkle in his eyes.

Normally she'd be embarrassed, but she was too distracted with what she was seeing. Chelsea Grandin seemed to be in a heavy conversation with a guy who looked exactly like Heath. But Heath was in the tent.

"That's Nolan Thurston, Heath's twin brother."

Caitlyn tried not to stare, but it was impossible. Chelsea was standing close to Nolan, and he was whispering in her ear.

"Those two look awfully chummy. Especially after Alexa told you guys not to talk to the Thurstons."

Caitlyn nodded. What was Chelsea up to? She remembered her own encounter with Heath at the bar. She'd thought she could flirt with him and get information. Was Chelsea doing the same? Didn't she understand how dangerous the game was? After all, Dev was only supposed to have been giving her boyfriend lessons, and here she was engaged to him.

Then another thought struck her. "The Grandins have a lot more to lose than we do. If Ashley is Daniel's daughter, the Thurstons have a blood tie to the Grandins."

"Listen, I've seen this happen in a lot of families. I know your family is friends with the Grandins, but you need to watch out. When it comes to the family home, people will do anything to protect what's theirs."

She nodded. She would call Alexa. They needed to know what Chelsea and Nolan were up to.

"Now, it's nice to see that smile on your face." Ol'Fred interrupted her thoughts, and she grinned at him. "I assume this fella is the reason?" She nodded and held out her hand for Ol'Fred to inspect. "Well, that's a nice sapphire. A rare one, too."

Caitlyn laughed. "Trust you to know jewelry, too."

"So when's the big day? I hav'ta plan for all the fancy stuff you're gonna need."

Caitlyn looked at Dev, who looked back at her. The sooner the better, as far as she was concerned. They had both decided that they weren't going to wait for the wedding to begin their lives. She was flying to New York next week to meet with his parents—the right way. The permits for her horse camp had been filed. Smoke and Shadow were going to make great riding horses, and she'd put out the word in the community for old horses that would make for good trail riders.

"It'll be soon," Dev said. "I can't wait to make Caitlyn my wife."

After Ol'Fred had left, Caitlyn kissed him. "How about we leave this shindig and go practice being husband and wife?"

* * * * *

THE SECRET HEIR RETURNS

JOSS WOOD

Prologue

Sutton Marchant shook the hand of the older of the two nattily dressed lawyers and caught the sneer of the younger one. Probably due to Sutton's ratty sweatshirt, battered Levi's and coffee-cup-and-paper-covered desk. He'd pulled an all-nighter working on edits. Feeling sleep-deprived and rough, he wanted to go to bed and sleep for three days, but, apparently, this meeting was urgent and *could not wait*.

Irritated, Sutton led the lawyers over to the sitting area of his study and gestured them to the love seat. He lifted a box filled with copies of his latest release from a chair, put it down on his hardwood floor and sat down, rubbing a hand over his face.

What the hell could be so important? It couldn't be anything to do with work, since his agent and publishers, thank God, dealt with the legalities. And Sam, his business partner, best friend and brother-in-law, was the CEO of MarchBent, their stocks, shares and crypto trading company. If this meeting had anything to do with MarchBent, Sam would be their first port of call. So…what?

Best way to find out was to ask them. "How can I help you?"

The younger lawyer removed a folder from his brief-case and laid it on the coffee table in front of Sutton. He glanced down at it and lifted his eyebrows. The older man leaned back, undid the button of his black suit jacket, hitched his pants leg and crossed one leg over the other.

"As I said, I am Tom Gerard, senior partner at Ge-rard and Pinkler. This is Albert Cummings, one of our associates. We represent the Tate-Handler Adoption Agency."

Sutton sat up straighter, his heart beating faster. The last time he'd interacted with people from the Tate-Handler Adoption Agency had been seventeen or so years ago, when he and his adoptive parents met with an agency representative. He remembered being handed a brown envelope, and told it contained a letter from his birth mother. He'd coldly, calmly told the representative that he had no interest in who she was or what she had to say.

At eighteen he'd been of the mindset that since she hadn't wanted him then, he didn't want, or need, her now. And nothing had changed his mind.

"I'm not interested in connecting with my birth mother," Sutton told them, his tone cool.

"So you know who she is?" Gerard asked.

He thought of the unopened brown envelope locked

in the small safe behind the painting above his head. "I've never wanted to know. I still don't want to know anything about the circumstances of my birth."

They exchanged a worried glance. "Well, that's a bit of a problem because we're here to tell you that you are the beneficiary of a trust set up by your biological father. As the beneficiary, you own a share in a large company and the control of the trust will pass to you on your thirty-fifth birthday. I believe that is in a day or two?"

Sutton nodded. He rubbed his face with his hands again, trying to force blood into his brain.

"I'm his heir? There are assets?" Sutton looked at the shelf above his desk, where copies of his books were displayed. He was a bestselling author, and the co-owner of a ridiculously successful trading company. He and his sister had inherited millions from their wealthy parents—his father was an internationally renowned economist, his mother a horticulturist—and both were minor branches, twigs really, of England's royal family tree. He and Thea co-owned Marchant House in Sussex, a sprawling estate that had been in the family for over three hundred years that they'd turned into a country hotel.

Basically, he and Thea weren't hurting for money. He did not need anything from his biological father.

"I'm not interested," Sutton told them, leaning back and folding his arms. He'd had parents, and they could never be replaced, by anybody, *ever*. "You can tell him that he can make someone else his heir and beneficiary."

Cummings winced. "It's not that easy, Mr. Marchant. He died shortly after your birth. We have been managing the trust for the past thirty-five years."

Was he supposed to feel sad that a man he never

knew had died over three decades ago? Sutton shrugged.
He'd mourned his parents for years and years. He didn't
have any grief left over for a man he never knew.

"It's not my problem," Sutton said. "I never asked
for the inheritance and I don't want it. Give it to his
other relatives."

"He left instructions that the trust could not pass to
his immediate family."

"Then give it to his wife, lover, friend!"

Gerard shook his head. "That can't happen, either.
The person he was in a relationship with when he died
passed away a few years ago."

"I. Don't. Want. It." Sutton gripped the bridge of
his nose.

"I'm sorry to hear that," Gerard said on a sigh. "But
the only way for you to disperse of the trust is to take
control of it. Once it's under your control, you can liq-
uidate the assets and do with it whatever you wish. You
could, for instance, donate all the proceeds to a charity."

Okay, that was a plan. Sutton placed his ankle on his
knee and linked his hands across his stomach. "Great.
Draw up the papers and I will sign whatever you need
for that to happen."

Sutton glanced at his watch. Mrs. K, his housekeeper—and the woman who'd been his parents' housekeeper for years before they died—would've already
made fresh coffee and would, if he asked her nicely,
rustle up an English breakfast. Then he'd hit the sack for
a solid eight. This afternoon, he'd go for a run and then
have dinner with Adriana, an old flame who dropped
in and out of his life.

Since he was allergic to commitment—thanks to his
parents' early deaths, he was terrified of someone he

loved leaving him—an occasional night of fun suited him just fine.

"Your father—"

"My father and mother died in a car accident, five years ago," Sutton interrupted Gerard, his voice cold.

"Your birth father wanted you to know that he didn't know of your adoption until after the fact. Because of the arrangements your birth mother made with the Tate-Handler Agency, he could not ascertain your identity. He chased down every legal option to get access to you. Obviously, he never succeeded."

Obviously. Sutton squirmed in his chair, feeling guilty that he was even having this conversation. Even discussing the circumstances of his birth made him feel disloyal to his parents.

Gerard continued, "Once you take control of the trust, you can do whatever you want with its assets but—"

Ah, here came the catch. Sutton braced himself.

"—but you can only do that after you spend two consecutive months in Portland, Maine, at a specific inn and attend the annual Ryder International Valentine's Ball."

What? Was he serious?

"If you meet those requirements, you can sell the shares to anyone but your benefactor's brother and disperse his wealth however you see fit. If you choose not to temporarily relocate to Portland for two months, then you cannot do anything with the trust for another fifteen years."

"Wait, let me make sure I understand this correctly— I live in Portland for two months and attend a ball? After that, I can do what I want with the trust? That's…nuts."

"Well, you have to stay at The Rossi Inn for those two months, but yes, that's it."

They both nodded, their faces solemn. Sutton sat up and leaned his forearms on his thighs, dangling his hands between his knees. "He doesn't say anything about me acknowledging him as my birth dad?"

"No," Gerard confirmed, "the will says nothing about you disclosing that he is your father. But you should be aware that there are people looking to discover who owns the shares in the company."

"Why?" Sutton asked.

"The trust owns a twenty-five-percent stake in a multinational, family-run company. Your biological father's brother owns twenty-seven percent, and the rest is owned by shareholders. The brother has wanted to buy your father's shares for the last thirty-five years, but we could not sell to him, or to anybody else. Your biological uncle has been pressuring us for years to disclose the owner but since it's a confidential trust, we cannot, and will not, disclose your identity."

"And I can't sell to him, even if I wanted to?"

Gerard shook his head. "They had a falling-out, and your father's will states you cannot sell to your uncle or any of his descendants."

Family drama—he'd had enough of it in his teens and early twenties. He didn't need it from people he didn't know.

"Look, whether it's now or in fifteen years, you are going to discover who he is. However, if you choose to remain silent about your parentage, you can. You will always be in control of that narrative," Gerard added.

That was something, at least. His mind spinning, Sutton wondered how much money they were talking about. It might be, if he was lucky, a couple of million.

Frankly, his parents' charitable foundation would be happy for *any* additional funds. Looking after vulnerable kids was damned expensive.

"What is his estate worth?"

"Close to a hundred and fifty million."

Holy crap.

He saw the gleam in their eyes, their belief the money was getting to him. It was, but not in the way they thought. His parents were crazy-ass philanthropists and their foundation was running a little dry. He, Thea, and Sam, his best friend, tossed money into it as often as they could, but thanks to the COVID-19 pandemic, the well was running low. If he liquidated the trust, the foundation would be flush for the rest of his life. He couldn't think of a better way to spend his birth father's money than to support the causes his parents had been passionate about.

He could work remotely and didn't have a lover keeping him in London—spending two months across the pond and attending a ball wouldn't be a problem. He just hoped the inn was comfortable. But for a hundred and fifty mil, he'd sleep in a tent.

Sutton scratched his head and looked at the folder on the table. "I presume all the documentation is in there?" After they nodded, he spoke again. "I will discover the identity of my birth father by opening that folder. Will I be forced to find out who my birth mother is, too?"

Gerard shook his head. "No, there is nothing in that folder about your birth mother."

Ah, good. He still had no interest in her. As an adult, he hadn't wanted to exchange his adoptive parents for anyone, anywhere, so what was the point of finding out who she was or why she'd done what she had?

Realizing that the trust was now his problem—or

would be in the near future—Sutton reached for the folder and flipped it open.

I, Benjamin James Ryder-White, a resident of the State of Maine, Cumberland County, declare that this is my will and testament of my wishes.

One

He was here…

Lowrie Lewis parked her ten-year-old sedan next to a very expensive SUV and switched off the engine. She wasn't sure what she'd done to deserve having only one guest to look after for the next two months, but she wouldn't question her good luck. One breakfast, one set of linens changed, laundry for one person…bliss. And the fact that the Englishman had paid a stupendous amount of money to ensure that he had the inn to himself made her want to do a happy dance. The inn was always quiet in the dead of winter but he'd paid her the equivalent rate of having full-to-bursting occupancy, something that never happened this time of the year.

Because he'd paid his enormous bill up front, she

could renovate the bathrooms, replace some linens, give some of the guest rooms a fresh lick of paint.

Lowrie looked over her shoulder and saw that Rhan, her one-year-old, had fallen asleep during their short trip back from the store. Mr. Marchant was earlier than expected, she thought, grimacing. She'd wanted to be here to meet him, to give him a tour of The Rossi. Paddy, bless him, would've just handed him the key and waved him up the stairs.

Her great-uncle Carlo, the original owner of this inn, had been a much better host than the irascible Paddy. He'd been hospitality personified. Carlo would've arranged for coffee and cake, placed a rose in a small vase on the tray and gotten Sutton Marchant's life story within a half hour of meeting the author.

She wasn't overly chatty, but from working here in her teens, and then again when she returned from New York after her life fell apart and before she went traveling, she knew how to make a guest feel welcome. Paddy, who'd inherited life rights to the house from Carlo, did not.

Lowrie looked up at the three-story inn, smiling at the soft lavender color. She loved this whimsical house, perched on the edge of a small cliff. Below the house, the stormy winter waters of Casco Bay pounded the rocks and icy waves slapped the tiny beach they used in summer. The house had wraparound verandas on the bottom level and three of the rooms, including the biggest—now the domain of their guest—had substantial balconies. Black shutters provided the perfect contrast to the lavender, and in summer, the garden was vibrant with color.

The interior was as wonderful as the outside, containing comfortable furniture, amazing art and collectibles. It was a place that begged you to relax, to enjoy the views of the sea and the forest.

She loved it here. It was home.

But it was also her workplace and she had lots to do. Exiting the car, she slammed her door shut and glanced up as she did so. A man, dressed in dark blue jeans and a thick, hooded sweatshirt under a sleeveless parka, walked onto the veranda and over to the snow-covered railing. He jammed his hands into the pockets of his parka, and she examined his profile, trying to ignore her rapidly beating heart and suddenly dry mouth.

Masculine was the first word that popped into her head. Followed by *sexy*. He looked to be in his midthirties and was tall, perhaps six-two or six-three, with wide shoulders, longs legs and big arms. In profile, she could see his long nose and brownish, messy hair. His stubborn chin and strong jaw were covered with a couple of days' worth of stubble.

Ripped, built, hot…

He also looked…intelligent, Lowrie decided. But also a little lost, a smidgen sad. And she wanted to know why.

Lowrie shook her head, dropped her gaze and opened the back door to her car. She undid the buckles holding Rhan in his car seat and lifted her baby up and onto her chest. Sutton Marchant was a guest, and she wasn't looking for a man, any man.

She had her son, a job she loved, her grandmother and aunt down the road. The irascible Paddy. It had been a year since Rex had left her, six since she'd left New York, and her mother and her then fiancé, behind. Her heart was still healing from the pain all those situations had inflicted.

She didn't know if she ever would be open to risk-

ing her heart again. It had been trampled on by many
people, in different ways and too often for her to take
that chance.

Marchant was just another guest and she'd treat him
like one.

*He should kill Maribeth. Look, he liked her, she was
fun and lovely, but she'd outlived her usefulness and it
was time for her to go...*

Sutton Marchant blinked when fingers snapped in
front of his face. He blinked again and slowly the lovely
face of his sister, who was also his personal assistant,
came into focus. The character Maribeth looked a lot
like Thea, he thought. Long blond hair, green eyes, pe-
tite and slim. Unlike Thea, Maribeth was a free spirit.
Maybe he'd keep her around for another chapter or two.
Maybe she could be the one to—

Thea pinched him. Sutton yelped and sent her a fero-
cious scowl. "I hate it when you do that," he muttered,
rubbing the back of his hand.

"I hate it when you zone out on me when I'm talking to you," Thea shot back. Sutton leaned back in his
chair and placed his feet on the corner of his new desk,
crossing his size thirteens. Thea, efficient as always,
was perched on the edge of her seat opposite him, skimming through her iPad.

Sutton looked around his new workspace, which
was attached to his expansive bedroom, squinting at
the mess through one eye. There were at least four un-
packed boxes—containing his can't-live-without-them
books, notepads, reference materials, three dictionaries
and two thesauruses—and he wished he could click his
fingers and have them spring onto the empty shelves of
the small bookcase behind the desk.

Or that Thea would stay another few days and do it for him. But she needed to get back to her family in London. He'd told her he could fly to the States and book himself into the inn, but she'd insisted on accompanying him and they'd spent last night in New York City, eating at her favorite restaurant before flying into Portland, Maine, this morning. He'd rented a Jaguar F-Pace and easily found The Rossi Inn, happy to discover that his temporary housing was a very pretty, luxurious inn right on the edge of Maine's rugged coastline, not that far from Portland's city center.

He'd booked the inn for two months, as per the will, but Thea had negotiated with the owner of the property not to take any reservations while he was in residence and compensated them for the lost revenue.

He had complete privacy and run of the historic place. He wasn't George Clooney famous but he was recognized often enough to make him feel uncomfortable.

"As I was saying, they will serve you breakfast, it's included in the rate, but if you want lunch and dinner you have to arrange it with them. Ahead of time, Sutt, not when you are hungry."

"That's why God invented takeout."

Thea shuddered. "You cannot live on takeout alone. You need vegetables. And fruit."

"Wine is made from grapes and that's fruit," he said, purely to wind up his sister, who insisted upon fresh and organic food.

"Shut up," she told him, standing. She looked around the suite and nodded. "Your laptop is set up, so is your printer and you're connected to the Wi-Fi."

Excellent. As soon as she left, he'd plop himself down at the desk in front of the massive window and get to work. Though he might have to face the wall because the 180-degree view of the rocks, beach and sea, just down the dune, was hella distracting.

But, man, he was looking forward to running along this desolate coastline.

"You have a video chat scheduled with your editor tomorrow at three," Thea told him, looking down at her tablet. Thea was a great personal assistant. She was a perfect pain in his ass but she kept him on track. She maintained his website, his mailing lists and kept his social-media posts up-to-date. She scheduled his appearances at bookstores, conventions and fairs, arranged his speaking engagements and, generally, kept his life on track.

She was the barrier between him and the rest of the world.

"I'll send you a text message to remind you." She tapped the edge of her tablet, her expression worried. "It isn't too late to change your mind and just come back to London, Sutt," Thea told him. "This isn't New York or LA, cities you know well."

Oh, and she also thought he couldn't find his way out of a paper bag. He loved her but, God, she could fuss.

He'd considered staying in London, ignoring the trust. He could simply hand it back to the lawyers to manage for the next fifteen years. But...

"The foundation needs the money, Thea."

"I need you in London, Sutton."

He saw the gleam in her eye, the misery that flashed across her face. And suddenly he realized why she wasn't as enthusiastic about his temporary relocation as he was. He stood up and wrapped his arms around her slim body, then rocked her from side to side. "Are you worried about me interacting with the Ryder-Whites, Thea?"

"No, of course not!"

Yeah, her response didn't sound convincing. He tipped up her chin. "Baby sister, *you* are my family. You and the kids and, at a push, that big lummox you call your husband."

"Also known as your best friend," Thea pointed out.

He waved away her words. "I've never been interested in connecting with my birth family, you know that. Mum and Dad were my parents, and you are my sister. I don't care about the Ryder-Whites."

God, he'd been such a fool as a young man, and if he could go back and yank his head out of his ass, he would. By pulling away and distancing himself from his family, long before his parents' deaths, he'd made his sister feel insecure about his love and his loyalty. Thea sniffed and rested her forehead on his chest.

"Look, Thea, I'm going to get his money whether I want it or not. I don't want it, I don't need it, but the foundation does. And if I need to live in Portland and attend a stupid ball to lay my hands on a hundred and fifty million, then, damn straight that's what I'll do. You know how much the foundation can do with that amount of money."

"We could finally build another children's home, maybe two," Thea told him, sounding excited. "We could also establish more scholarships."

"I need to do this, for the foundation, for Mum and Dad. They'd expect it of me," Sutton told her, resting his chin in her hair.

"Rubbish! They'd be proud of you, but they wouldn't expect it. And you know they would've supported you no matter what you chose to do with the money." She pulled a face and sighed. "They always said it was your right to know your birth parents."

His parents had been shocked when he'd told them he

wasn't interested in finding his birth family, surprised at his vehemence on the subject. They'd protested and had spent so much time reassuring him of their support that he'd started to think they wanted to get rid of him. God, he'd been so damn insecure about his parents' love.

And, yeah, his feelings of loss, grief and rejection by his birth parents still lingered. He still occasionally wondered if his parents regretted adopting him, especially since they'd managed to conceive Thea a couple of years after taking him on. Sutton speared his fingers into his hair, wishing he was one of those people who could compart-mentalize, who could shove his feelings into mental boxes and lock them away. He tried but didn't always succeed.

He'd made peace with his parents, luckily a few years before they died, and he would've been very happy liv-ing out his life not knowing who'd been his birth parents and why they'd given him up for adoption.

He'd had his birth father's identity forced on him, but he had no intention of telling anyone he was Benjamin Ryder-White's son and Callum Ryder-White's nephew. He wasn't interested in becoming the newest member of their wealthy, famous family. The thought made him shudder. He simply wanted Ben's bucks. For the orphans...for all the kids who'd never found their forever home.

But that meant being away from Thea for two months, missing her twin boys' birthday and leaving MarchBent in Sam's capable hands.

"I need to call for a taxi," Thea told him, patting his chest before stepping away.

"No, I'll drive you to the airport," Sutton responded, looking around for the keys to his rental. He saw them on the desk and pushed them into the back pocket of his jeans.

"I need to make a few calls before we leave, I'll slip

into the empty bedroom next door," Thea told him. "Ten minutes?"

"Sure."

Sutton watched her walk away and when she opened the door to leave, she released a little yelp and jumped back. Always protective of his little sister, Sutton bounded across the room and stopped when he saw a slim woman standing in front of Thea, her fist raised as if she was about to knock on the door.

He took in her heart-shaped face, her creamy skin, her made-for-kisses mouth. Her hair—a dark, rich brown—was tucked behind pretty ears and her cheekbones could cut glass. But her eyes... God, her eyes had the ability to drop him to his knees.

They were the color of the Caribbean Sea in bright sunlight. Long, thick black lashes and perfectly sculpted dark eyebrows highlighted the unusual greenish-blue color to perfection.

And talking about perfection... Long legs, a small waist, a very nice set of...

"Hi," Thea chirped. "Sorry to yell, I got a fright!"

The woman smiled, revealing white, even teeth. "No, it's all my fault." Those eyes darted between him and Thea. "I'm sorry, I thought it would be just Mr. Marchant staying with us, but you are, of course, very welcome, Mrs. Marchant. Are you and your husband settling in okay?"

"I'm not staying, but my brother is," Thea said, stepping back and gesturing to him. "I'm Thea Marchant-Bentley. This is my brother, Sutton Marchant."

The woman's eyes drifted over him with no hint of recognition. "Nice to meet you both. I'm Lowrie Lewis and I run this place."

Low... Ree...it was an unusual name. Sutton folded

his arms across his chest and frowned. "I thought Paddy was the manager."

"Paddy owns the business, I run it," Lowrie stated. She glanced around and her eyes widened at the mess in the living area of the suite. "Do you need help getting your study sorted?"

Sutton was about to accept her offer when Thea rolled her eyes and jumped back into the conversation. "Don't touch it or else you'll get growled at! He has a system, or so he says."

"I have a system," Sutton muttered. Sort of. And generally he hated people messing with his stuff, but he wasn't opposed to this sexy woman sticking around a little longer.

"He'll get to it, Lowrie," Thea said, sounding bossy. "He'll ask you to do it, complain and then he'll rearrange everything after you are done, anyway."

God, Thea made him sound like a control freak. And, when it came to his work, he supposed he was.

Lowrie met his eyes and smiled, and Sutton heard his own heartbeat, extra loud in his ears. A long shiver ran up and down his spine and his vision narrowed until she was all that was in it.

Damn. He wanted to haul her into his room, kick out his sister and find out whether she tasted as good as she looked.

Ah, *crap*. He didn't need this distraction now.

"What time would you like breakfast in the morning, Mr. Marchant? And when would be a good time for me to make your bed, tidy up?"

Uh, he couldn't think.

Thea, bless her, jumped into the conversation. "Call him Sutton, Lowrie. My brother is a writer, and works and sleeps at weird hours. So maybe you can play it by car?

Just promise me that if you haven't seen him in days, then bang on his door and check that he's still alive, okay?"

Sutton glared at her. "Funny. I only did that once."

"And that was enough for me," Thea retorted. She pointed a finger at him. "Do not hole up in here for hours at a time. Take a break, get some fresh air."

He ran ten to fifteen miles a day and tried to stretch every few hours. He used a dictation program and when he remembered, did some yoga stretches an ex-lover once showed him. He wasn't a complete slug. But Thea liked to fuss and he let her.

"You were going to make calls, Thea," Sutton reminded her.

Thea nodded. "I was. Nice to meet you, Lowrie."

"You, too," Lowrie stated as Thea walked past her. She glanced at Sutton again and looked at the mess on his floor, and he saw the infinitesimal shake of her head.

"It looks bad now but I will get it sorted in a day or two," Sutton reassured her. And then wondered why. He was hiring this place at a stupid daily rate and if he wanted to cover every inch in paper, he could. But, for some asinine reason, he didn't want this woman thinking he was a slob.

"Dinner?"

Was she asking him out? As much as he'd love to accept her offer, he had to get Thea to the airport and he'd only be back after eight. "I have to get Thea to the airport, but I'll take a rain check."

She stared at him, her mouth forming a perfect *O*. Then she blushed and rocked on her heels. "Uh, sorry, I meant... I was asking if you were in for dinner tonight? We did say that we would provide dinner and lunch if you gave notice."

Shit. Force of will kept him from reddening, experience kept his expression impassive. "Ah, crossed wires.

Sorry. No, I'll grab something. How much notice do you usually need?"

She wrinkled her very pretty nose. "If you are wanting a three-course meal, I'd need to know in the morning. If you require a grilled-cheese sandwich, half an hour."

"Are you a good cook?" he asked, curious.

She shrugged. "I can follow a recipe." Lowrie glanced at her watch. "I need to move along. It was nice meeting you, Mr. Marchant. Let me know if you need anything else."

"Sure," Sutton replied. "And, really, call me Sutton."

She nodded. "Sutton…" She turned to go, then whirled back around to face him. "One more thing…"

He lifted his eyebrows, intrigued by her expression—part pride, part chagrin. "I have a child, he's a year old. He's teething at the moment so if you hear him crying, that's why." She pointed to the ceiling. "I live in the attic space above you, so if you hear me walking or him crying, and we're disturbing you, give me a call and I'll go downstairs or something. My phone number is in the brochure in the desk drawer."

He was a solid sleeper and he rarely heard anything when he was in the zone, so he didn't think it was that big a deal. "Will do."

Lowrie lifted her hand and disappeared in the direction of the stairs. He fought the urge to follow her, reminding himself that he'd made enough of an idiot of himself today. And, yeah, her having a kid made her solidly off-limits. She didn't say whether the kid's father was in the picture, but even if she was a single mom, he didn't date, sleep with or have affairs with women with kids.

Far too much baggage, thank you very much.

Two

Lowrie stepped off the bottom stair onto the harlequin floors of the inn's hallway, grimacing at the drooping heads of the gerbera daisies on the hall table. After removing the almost-dead blooms, she rearranged the greenery and reminded herself to pick up some fresh flowers when she went into town tomorrow.

A massive painting, abstract and colorful, hung on the wall to her right and Lowrie tipped her head to the right, eying the piece. It was fluid, with great composition—she could see the vague outline of a naked woman lying on the settee, but she had to squint to do so.

The colors were just a little off. Cadmium orange deep instead of cadmium orange, ultramarine violet instead of dioxazine purple would've been a better color choice. The slightly different shades would take this picture from good to exceptional.

Turning, Lowrie caught a glimpse of herself in a

sleek oval mirror and grimaced at her windblown hair. The combination of being a single mom and busy inn-keeper left her looking thin and tired. Lack of sunlight had lightened her pale skin to something resembling a ghost.

She was incredibly surprised that the gorgeous man upstairs had accepted what he thought was a dinner invitation from her earlier. Especially since she looked pale, fragile, wispy…

God, what had happened to that ferociously energetic artist, the one who'd paint all day and night and party all weekend? The girl who'd hop on a plane for Cancún or Cartagena, who'd strip naked and roll around on canvas sheets covered in oil paints? The one who'd lived, breathed and sweated paint and color and art and music and sound?

The one who'd lived at a hundred miles per hour?

Lowrie gripped the edge of the hallway table and stared into the reflection of her eyes, chromium-oxide green edged in viridian. They were her best feature but would be more compelling if they weren't accessorized by blue-black stripes proclaiming she hadn't slept properly in a year.

Lowrie was intensely grateful the rich English guy was the only guest in the place until spring. She needed a slower pace, time to breathe, to play with her baby. She could spend the bulk of the day with Rhan, instead of handing him over to her grandmother at the crack of dawn and running down the street to spend time with him when she could.

A couple of months after Rhan's birth, when she'd returned to Portland, she'd needed work and Paddy, bless him, had pulled her into the inn, given her a place to stay and a job. Her Nonna Jojo and her spinster aunt,

Isabel, had scooped up Rhan and lavished him with time, affection and attention, giving Lowrie's battered heart the time and space to heal.

She thanked God every day she was back in Portland, physically better and mentally stronger, and surrounded by the people who loved her...

Lowrie pulled her hair back into a messy knot at the back of her head, securing it with a band she'd slipped onto her wrist hours earlier. She pinched her cheeks to put some color into them and reminded herself to put a tube of lipstick into the drawer of this hall table. Running upstairs to her attic kept her fit and slim but keeping a tube of lipstick down here made sense.

"Is there a reason you are staring at yourself in that mirror?"

Lowrie saw Paddy's hangdog face in the reflection and turned to see her boss, and friend, standing in the doorway to the hall. In his eighties, he had a shock of white hair but his shoulders were rounded and he no longer moved as quickly as he used to. His bright blue eyes were as penetrating as ever.

"Just thinking that I look like a ghost and could do with some lipstick. And maybe blush."

Paddy gave her a long up-and-down look. "You need a haircut and to pick up ten pounds. And, yes, some blush wouldn't hurt."

Wow. "Thanks, I didn't realize I was looking so awful."

"Baby girl, you could dress in a flour sack and you'd still be beautiful, but with a little care you could look stunning." He shrugged, lifting his bony shoulders. "Just calling it like I see it." Paddy tapped his index finger against his cheek. "Would your sudden interest in your appearance have anything to do with the very sexy Englishman upstairs?"

Despite his advanced years, Paddy could still appreciate a sexy man. And, God, Sutton Marchant was Sexy with a capital *S*. Tall, with powerful shoulders and a wide chest, a narrow waist and hips and long, powerful legs. And that face. Up close, it was fantastic and topped with overlong messy hair, burnt umber shot with earthy yellow. His stubble was thicker than she'd thought, his jaw stronger. And his chin more stubborn. But his eyes caught and held her attention. They were manganese blue, a cool, transparent shade with a green undertone. In anger, or high emotion, she thought they'd darken to phthalo blue, one of her favorite colors in the world, elegant and intense.

Lowrie wrinkled her nose. "He is a good-looking guy." She raised her eyebrows. "Gay?"

Paddy, who had come out in the 1970s and never looked back, shook his head. "My gaydar tells me he's a hundred-percent hetero, darling. Why? Are you interested?"

Lowrie snorted. "As if. When Rhan's no-better-than-a-sperm-donor daddy ran out on me in Eureka, I swore I'd avoid the species for the rest of my life."

"That's a bit dramatic, isn't it?"

She shrugged. Maybe. But in her head, every person she ever loved had let her down—her parents, her fiancé, Rex, the aforementioned sperm donor. She'd had her heart broken enough times in a variety of ways, thank you very much.

She didn't think her heart could handle another beating.

"You need to get back on the horse, Lowrie darling."

Lowrie frowned at Paddy. "What does that even mean?"

His intense gaze didn't waver. "You need to date again, sleep with a guy, have some earthshaking sex."

Lowrie fought the urge to slap her hands over her ears. Paddy was the most liberal, open, in-your-face person she knew, but she didn't feel comfortable discussing her sex life—or lack of it—with the octogenarian.

"You need an affair, someone to put some color back into your face."

Despite her parents' open marriage, her wild friends when she was still New York's darling and running with a Bohemian crowd before her pregnancy, she'd never felt comfortable having sex for sex's sake. Hell, she'd only had three lovers in ten years. "Can we not talk about this now, please?"

Paddy shook his head. "When are we going to talk about it?"

"Never?" Lowrie asked, sounding hopeful.

"You are a young, lovely woman who needs to get out of this house, to be in the company of younger people for a change. You need to dress up and feel appreciated. You need to feel like a woman, not a frazzled single mom."

But that was what she was—a frazzled single mom. And she liked spending time with Jojo and Isabel; they were strong, opinionated, wise woman. And Paddy, for all his grumpiness, was fiercely intelligent and widely read. The guests flowing in and out of The Rossi kept her busy.

And Rhan, well, he was her heart.

"Over the next two months, you'll have a great deal more time on your hands as we'll only have one guest to look after."

Lowrie nearly danced on the spot with happiness. "I know! Hiring the inn has cost him a fortune but, God, I'm so grateful for the break."

Paddy narrowed his eyes at her. "And what do you intend on doing with your extra time?"

She shrugged. "Sleep a little later, play with Rhan, paint the empty bedrooms. You said that we could redecorate as well, so I'll be buying new curtains, linens, cushions."

Paddy rolled his eyes. "I was hoping you'd tell me that you'd get a makeover, buy some new clothes, go on a date, fly down to Cancún with some hot man for some fun in the sun."

"That sounds like a plan."

At the sound of the deep voice coming from behind her, Lowrie spun around, her face heating when she saw their only guest standing on the bottom step, unabashedly listening to their conversation. He'd pulled a leather bomber jacket over his hooded sweater and held a pair of gloves in his left hand.

Before either of them could respond, Sutton nodded to Paddy. "Hi, again."

"Are you settled in?" Paddy asked, remembering his innkeeping manners.

"Getting there," Sutton replied, shoving his hands into the pockets of his bomber jacket. "I love this inn with its steep roof, clapboard exterior, the gray shingle roof and black window shutters. Is it old?"

"It was built at the end of the nineteenth century by my ex's ancestors," Paddy replied.

Sutton looked around the double volume hall, his eyes going to the abstract painting Lowrie had been critiquing a few minutes before. "That's a hell of a piece. Is it by a local artist?"

Paddy smiled. "That was one of—"

Lowrie felt hot and cold all over and she spoke

over Paddy. "It's by a local artist, but she doesn't paint anymore."

Sutton frowned. "Pity. She's damn good."

There were so many flaws in that painting that sometimes Lowrie couldn't bear to look at it. There were better examples of her art throughout the house, but Paddy and Carlo had declared that piece, called *Woman Floating*, as their favorite.

God, she'd been so young when she painted it. So young. She'd painted the next in the series years later, shortly after she moved into her own studio in Brooklyn. Had she been eighteen? Nineteen? She'd had a futon on the floor, a two-plate stove and a fridge, and the rest of the space was filled with paints and brushes and canvases of every size and description.

That year, before her career had skyrocketed had been, bar none, the happiest of her life. A time when she felt confident and comfortable.

"I hope you don't think I'm abandoning you, Sutton, but I'll be leaving tomorrow for an extended visit to my sister in San Diego."

Sutton nodded. "I'm sure Lowrie and I will be fine without you."

They heard footsteps on the stairs and Sutton turned around to take Thea's heavy leather briefcase. Stepping into the hall, Sutton's sister smiled at Paddy, and surprised Lowrie by putting both hands on her shoulders and kissing her right cheek, then her left.

"Sutton hates guavas and detests gherkins. He's always grumpy in the morning—give him a vat of coffee before you try to talk to him. Take no crap."

"Hey!" Sutton protested, poking her in the side.

"Just calling it like I see it."

"I see you walking to the airport," Sutton grumbled

as he strolled to the front door. He opened it and waited for Thea to step into the frigid cold of Maine in late January before following her outside.

When the door closed behind him, Lowrie spun around to look at one of the two men she most admired in the world. Great-Uncle Carlo had been one, Paddy was the other. She loved him, but she didn't much like him at the moment.

"Paddy, what the hell? You didn't tell me you were going away! When did you decide this?"

"Three minutes ago," Paddy calmly replied. "You can handle one guest, can't you?"

Were his eyes twinkling? What was the old man plotting? Lowrie sent him a what-are-you-up-to? glare. "But what about my trip to Cancún?"

"We both know that you no longer have the pep, verve or guts to go to Cancún, darling."

"I still have verve. And pep."

"No, you don't. But I can still be impulsive so that's why I'm going to California. Besides, it's much warmer there."

She tried another tack. "You're leaving me alone in this house with a strange man?"

"He's six-four and muscular—I'm over eighty and frail, so I don't think I'm much protection. And I'm a dedicated pacifist so I have no weapons in the house."

"That's not exactly reassuring!" Lowrie stated, her voice rising.

Paddy placed his hand on her shoulder. "He's a famous author, Lowrie. He writes about serial killers—he isn't one. And I think he's a decent enough guy. He has a straight way of looking you in the eye, saying his piece."

"You met him ten minutes ago."

He shrugged again. "Learned how to size up men in

Korea, and it's never failed me yet. You'll be fine. He's also single and he likes you," he added, his expression mischievous.

Lowrie tossed her hands in the air, completely frustrated. "Are you leaving because you think he will strip me naked and ravage me on the stairs?"

"I live in hope," Paddy told her, patting her shoulder before turning to walk away.

"You are irrational, annoying and interfering!" Lowrie told his departing back. "He's not my type."

Paddy stopped and turned to smile at her. "Of course he is. And that's why you stopped by the mirror and decided you needed lipstick. He's the first man who's made you think of how you look, reminded you that you are a woman. And that's why I'm making myself scarce."

Lowrie stamped the heel of her boot on the hardwood floor. "You don't even like your sister!" she shouted.

"Ah, but I do like her next-door neighbor. I might find myself spending more time at his place than at hers."

Lowrie shoved her hands into her hair, dislodged the knot on the back of her neck and released a string of low curses, most of which she'd learned from Paddy.

"If it has tires and testicles, starter motors and stubble, no matter its age, it's gonna give you trouble," Lowrie muttered, repeating one of Jojo's favorite sayings.

Later that day, Lowrie lit a fire in the fireplace, which was original to the house, and placed the fireguard in front of the flames. Picking up Rhan, she walked over to the bank of long, narrow windows looking out onto the rugged Maine coast. Portland was only ten minutes away, but this house, situated at the end of a long road and at the place where the land ran out, felt isolated.

She wasn't, not really. Jojo's house was a couple of doors down, a scant half mile down the road, but on an evening like this, when snow covered the beach and clouds almost touched the sea, the house felt gloomy and atmospheric.

It almost made her want to pick up a paintbrush, prepare a canvas. Almost but not quite.

Lowrie rocked from side to side, holding Rhan's little fist and dropping kisses on his downy head. He'd been bathed and fed and it was almost time to put him in his bed.

She pulled back to look at him, and saw that his eyelids were heavy, and his face was sleepy-soft. He laid his head on her chest and her heart swelled, growing until she thought it might burst.

She'd heard of a mother's love—had never experienced it from her own mom—but only understood the concept once Rhan had arrived in her life. The love she felt for this little soul was all-encompassing, endless, expansive. He was her life and the reason the sun rose for her every morning, the reason it dropped every night.

He was her everything…

He had Rex's blond hair, her generous mouth, his nose and ears. Rhan's eyes, round and bright blue in his moon-pie face, were all his own. His personality was part bully, part charmer, and she wouldn't have him any other way. He wasn't her clone, or his father's—he was just Rhan, sweet and perfect and wonderful.

And now asleep.

Content to stand in front of the window and watch the snow drift onto the wraparound veranda, Lowrie continued to rock him, the motion as soothing to her as it was to him. Tomorrow Paddy would catch his plane out west and she would be alone with Sutton Marchant. And, really, she wasn't worried about sharing a house with the man. She, like Paddy, knew she was in no danger from him.

And, yes, she had cyberstalked him.

He was thirty-five and after years of working on both Wall Street and the London Stock Exchange, he'd written a beginner's guide to investing that rocketed up the nonfiction bestseller charts. Then he started writing fiction and his star kept climbing.

She was more a historical-romance type of girl— sometimes she even ventured into literary fiction and memoirs—but, thanks to running a busy inn and looking after her child, the minute she opened a book at night, her eyes closed. The last book she'd read cover to cover was *What to Expect When You're Expecting*.

Sutton was, according to the internet, a bestselling author and his gorgeous sister was married to his best friend and partner in his investment firm. He lived in the house he inherited from his parents, situated in the fancy suburb of Knightsbridge, and was a fitness fanatic.

Yeah, that was easy to believe. You didn't get a body like that by being a couch potato.

Why was she so curious about a man she'd only met today, spoken to twice? Maybe it was the hints of sadness she saw in those compelling blue eyes, the suggestion of vulnerability beneath that I'm-a-guy's-guy attitude. He was tough, direct, masculine—but she couldn't help thinking that he was fighting a few hard-to-banish demons.

She knew all about fighting demons.

Lowrie heard the front door opening and closing and cocked her head. Paddy was upstairs in his room, Jojo and Isabel wouldn't wander down here in a snowstorm, so that left Sutton. She expected to hear the sound of boots on the stairs, but her heart rate increased as she heard him crossing the hall.

"Do you mind if I join you?" Sutton asked from the doorway.

She turned, noting the snowflakes in his hair and on his leather-clad shoulders. "Sure, come on in and get warm."

He headed toward the fire, then held out his hands over the fireguard. "Hell of a snowstorm."

Lowrie looked at the gentle falling flakes and smiled. "This? This is nothing. Wait until you experience a blizzard."

"I'll pass, thanks."

Oh, dear. "Sorry, but there's a cold front moving in next week and they are predicting whiteout conditions."

"Marvelous." Pulling his hands back, he looked at Rhan. "Cute kid."

"I think so." Lowrie nodded her thanks. "He fell asleep about five minutes ago. I need to take him upstairs and put him down. Did your sister get off all right?"

"Yes, thank you."

He shrugged out of his jacket, draped it over the back of a chair and sat down in one corner of the large leather couch. He leaned back his head and closed his eyes. "God, I'd kill for a whiskey," he murmured.

Lowrie headed to the drinks cupboard in the corner and, using one hand, selected a crystal tumbler. Eyeballing a serving, she dashed in a decent amount of Paddy's best whiskey and carried it over to Sutton, then nudged his wrist with the glass.

He opened his eyes—the man had ridiculously long, thick eyelashes—and groaned in appreciation as his fingers wound around the glass. "Thank you." He sipped and sighed. "That's a good whiskey. But if you'd told me where to find it, I could've gotten it myself."

"Not a problem," Lowrie replied. Nice to know that he didn't expect her to wait on him.

Tipping Rhan so that he was on his side, she sat down on the arm of the chair and darted a glance at the fire. It needed another log, but she needed another hand, and if she put Rhan down anywhere other than his crib, he was bound to wake. "Can I ask you to put a couple of logs on the fire?"

"Sure." Sutton stood up and did as she'd asked.

"Thank you. You're welcome to build a fire anytime you choose—there's plenty of wood." Lowrie looked down at her sleeping son. Should she take him upstairs, put him down and return to talk to Sutton about his expectations for the next few months?

Or should she just plow ahead now?

"What's on your mind, Lowrie?"

Right, that answers that question. "I thought maybe we should have a chat about what you expect? You have paid us an extraordinary amount of money to have the exclusive use of this place, so I just want to make sure you are comfortable."

He looked around, taking in the big, squishy furniture, the fresh flowers and the incredible art—some of it hers—on the wall. "It's a pretty comfortable place. It feels like a home."

It was. It had been Carlo and Paddy's home long

before it had been turned into an inn, and her great-grandparents' house before that.

"Obviously, I'll make your bed every day and do your laundry, make you breakfast. That's standard. But what about lunch and dinner, snacks?" She glanced at the whiskey bottle. "What do you like to drink, eat? Are you allergic to anything? You saw the small study attached to your room but would you prefer to work somewhere else? There are another six bedrooms you can work from, or, if you prefer, you can take over the small library. I use a desk in there but if you want privacy, I can relocate."

Sutton picked up his glass and took a sip of whiskey. "Where's the library?" He frowned. "Can I get you a glass of wine? Something else to drink?"

She appreciated the offer but shook her head. "I'm good, thank you." She nodded to a door behind him. "The library is through there."

Sutton, carrying his glass, walked across the room and stepped into her favorite space in the house. It was an L-shaped room covered in bookcases and had, in her opinion, the best views of the peninsula, beach and forest. She'd be sad to lose her working spot—the window seat was also her favorite place to take a break—but Sutton had paid for the privilege of working wherever he wanted to.

"This is a stunning room."

She heard the sincerity in his voice and his appreciation made her smile. He popped his head around the doorframe. "This is an unbelievable collection of books as well."

"My great-uncle Carlo was an avid reader," Lowrie explained. She stood up, walked around the chair and sat down properly, allowing Rhan to settle in her lap, against her chest. Her arms moaned in gratitude. Her boy was getting heavy.

"Could we move another desk in here?" Sutton called out.

Lowrie dampened her disappointment at losing her favorite room. "I'm sure we can," she replied. When he walked back into the room, she pulled up a smile. "After all, you need another desk for all your books and stuff."

"Ah, no. I was just wanting a desk for my laptop, for when I want to write in there. And I think I'll want to write in there quite often."

She didn't understand. "But then why do you need another desk?"

He sat down again and placed his ankle on his opposite knee. "You use that desk and I can't kick you out. If you don't mind sharing, I'll help you move another desk in there for me to use. There's more than enough room and your presence won't bother me." He sent her a slow, lazy smile that had her stomach doing slow rolls. "I can write on trains, planes, and in busy, noisy coffee shops. Once I'm in the zone, it takes a bomb to disrupt me."

She couldn't help her grin. "So you're not a precocious writer then?"

"Have you met my sister? Do you think she'd allow me to be?"

True. Thea didn't look like she took any nonsense from anyone. "If you'll help me move the desk, I'm happy to share the space. But I will go outside the room for calls."

Sutton nodded his thanks. He stared at his whiskey glass and then at the fire, his thoughts a long way off. She didn't want to disturb him, but…

"I do still need answers about lunch and dinner, what

you like to drink and snack on, what coffee you like and I need to give you a key to the house."

"Paddy already did that, when I arrived," Sutton told her. "Thea wasn't joking when she said that I work crazy hours so I can't give you a definite answer about lunch and dinner. Sometimes I work through, forgetting about food. Sometimes I want something to eat at three in the morning. What time do you and Paddy eat?"

"When guests ask for dinner, we eat at seven," Lowrie told him. "But Paddy is going to visit his sister so it'll just be you and me." She looked away from him, inexplicably embarrassed. "I hope you're okay with that?"

He took a while to answer her and eventually Lowrie looked at him. As soon as their eyes met, he spoke again. "I think the question should be whether you are comfortable in the house with *me*?"

"But you're the guest."

"But you're a woman, half my size," Sutton said, sitting up straight. He leaned forward and held her eyes. "I would never hurt you, Lowrie, but I don't expect you to take my word on that."

Yet, strangely, she did. She pulled in a deep breath and nodded. "I'm fine with you staying, Sutton."

"Good," he replied, his tone matter-of-fact. "I'm not allergic to anything and I eat everything, bar the aforementioned guavas and gherkins. If you make yourself something for supper, make extra and if I don't respond when you call, leave it out for me to find. If you can buy some frozen meals for the times you don't feel like cooking, that would be great. I'll have an order of whiskey and wine delivered, I like both. I run most days, sometimes at night, sometimes during the day." He glanced toward the windows and pulled a face at the falling snow. "Is there a gym anywhere close by?"

"Portland is ten minutes away, but if you only need the basics, there's a minigym next to the pool house."

"You have a pool? Where?" Sutton demanded.

"Jeez, didn't Paddy show you around when you arrived?"

Sutton stood up to pour himself another drink. "I told him I'd see everything later and time ran away from me."

"I'll take you on a tour in the morning. Yes, there's a lap pool, to the side of the house. It's heated so you can swim anytime you want." She swam most mornings, but the pool was big enough for the two of them. "The gym is next to the pool and we have a treadmill, a weight bench, a couple of other machines. It'll do if you aren't superfussy."

"Not fussy," Sutton assured her. So far, he was turning out to be the dream guest. She was sure, as they got to know each other, that would change. Nobody was as easy and amiable as Sutton Marchant appeared to be. And living with someone stripped away the masks people wore.

"I didn't choose this inn, but damn, this spot isn't too shabby," Sutton said, sliding down in his seat and stretching out those long, long legs.

What did he mean by that? Lowrie pulled her eyes off his muscular thighs and flat stomach to ask, but Rhan let out a little cry and wiggled in her arms. She glanced down and saw his eyes fluttering. Rhan only liked to be cuddled for a set amount of time and then he wanted to be in his crib, where he could stretch out.

"I need to put him down," Lowrie said, scooting to the edge of her seat. She started to push herself up and was surprised when Sutton stood up and held out his hand for her to grip. Placing her hand in his, he pulled her and her son up with ease.

"Thank you," she murmured. She looked up, into his eyes, which were intensely blue and glittering with an emotion she couldn't identify. Whatever it was, it made her feel warm and tingly and a little strange.

Lovely strange. Attracted strange.

Which wasn't good.

Lowrie tightened her grip on Rhan and forced a polite smile onto her face. "If you haven't eaten, I have beef soup on the stove. There's also sourdough bread."

"Thanks, but I'm fine. I grabbed a pizza at the airport," Sutton replied.

Lowrie nodded, murmured an "excuse me" and walked past him, cursing herself for feeling disappointed. He might be her only guest but he was still a guest and distance should be maintained.

No, physical and emotional distance *had* to be maintained.

Whenever she got close to people her heart ended up being bruised and battered and she'd never let that happen again.

Three

Penelope

Penelope dug her nails into her biceps and looked at her husband of thirty-plus years, the icy fingers of fear skittering up and down her spine. How did one reveal a three-decades-old secret? How could she be as open with him as he'd been with her?

He'd just informed her that he wanted to acknowledge his son, a son he'd had with his father's personal assistant before Penelope and James were married.

Because she was human, she wanted to rail at James for keeping his son a secret, for never telling her that he'd had an affair with Emma. But she couldn't, not when her own secrets eclipsed his…

It's not a competition, Penelope.

James thought she was scared of the consequences of him acknowledging Garrett Kaye as his son. James's father, Callum, would push James out of the business and them out of the family. But she agreed with her husband's plan. Like him, she was tired of being dictated to by Callum Ryder-White.

"Walking away from Callum doesn't scare me, James," she said, a shrill laugh following her words.

"Then what does, Pen?"

"Your reaction to what I'm about to tell you. Sit down, darling, you're not the only one who has a bombshell to drop."

James perched on the edge of his chair, his eyes wary. Her eyes were a more unusual shade of light blue, surrounded by a darker ring. She'd been complimented on them all her life, but neither of her girls had inherited her intense eye color. No, the only person who had the same eyes was that little boy so long ago…

"Talk to me, Pen. There's nothing we can't do together." James looked and sounded earnest.

Oh, God, he was so sweet and, despite closing in on sixty, was still too kindhearted. There were some things that couldn't be solved with a smile and a hug, things that could come back to haunt them.

The son she gave up for adoption was a case in point.

Despite so many decades passing, she still expected him to drop back into her life, and if he did, she knew the lives of all the people she loved would never be the same again.

Penelope looked out the window and her eyes immediately went to the patch of trees by the tennis court, overlooking the cove. The memory of that long-ago day was still crystal clear.

After a week-long affair, she hadn't been able to make contact with the man who'd impregnated her and then, not unexpectedly, she'd seen him again at the Ryder-White Fourth of July celebration eighteen months later. He'd made a stupid comment about her engagement, something about keeping it in the family, and she responded by railing at him for ignoring her many calls and letters.

He'd curled his lip, told her she'd been a way to pass the time, to alleviate his boredom. And that, by sleeping with her, he'd finally came to terms with the fact that he preferred men.

Hurt and anger had crashed over her like a tidal wave. Being young and vain, she thought he was just trying to hurt her, and needing to wound him in return, she'd told him—a little gleefully—that she'd given up his son for adoption.

His immediate and visceral anger had scared her. How dare she make that decision without him? he'd snarled. He'd wanted to know where the boy was, what was his name. Caught off guard by his intense reaction, she'd told him about the agency in London and the name of her case worker. Then, two months later—after coming out to his family and creating a storm of epic proportions—he was dead.

Although he'd never disclosed that he had a child, Penelope had no doubt that in those two months he'd made plans. He wasn't the type to leave events to play themselves out.

She'd made sure to leave her contact details with the agency, was fairly certain that her son's father would've done the same. So why hadn't her boy contacted her or contacted his father's family? It made no sense.

"Pen?"

She didn't know if she could bear to see the disappointment on James's face. He might not have been her first choice for a husband, but she'd come to love him.

She liked his kindness, his patience and his affectionate personality. She found his new quest for indepen-
dence from his controlling father sexy. She didn't want
to lose her husband, and she feared that revealing her
secret might lead to exactly that.

She wasn't ready, wasn't strong enough, couldn't be
on her own...

Penelope lifted her fingers to her forehead, conscious
of her pounding head and her dry mouth. She lifted her
eyes to meet James's, feeling awful about the confusion on his face. He was waiting, but she wasn't ready,
not yet.

She waved her hand in the air. "I do have something
to tell you, but... I can't, not yet."

James placed his hands on his knees, disappointment running across his face. "Can you tell me why
not? Don't you trust me?"

"I *do* trust you, I just need some time. Everything is
moving so fast and things are changing."

"You've never been good at change, Pen."

Oh, God, wasn't that the truth? "I know. I thought I
was ready to tell you, but I'm not."

James nodded, staring at his hands. He pulled in a
deep breath, the way he always did when he had un-
pleasant news to break, something tough to say. "Pen,
in case you are thinking of confessing to past...indiscre-
tions, I'm begging you not to. I don't need to know, any
more than you need to know about mine." He dragged
his hand down his face. "I think we might be getting to
a point of finally having an honest relationship. Let's
not spoil this new beginning, okay?"

She swallowed her hysterical laugh. Affairs? That's
where he thought she was going? If only. But because
he'd given her an out, she'd take it. So she nodded, tried

to smile. "I have a headache. I think I might go and lie down for a while, wrap my head around the idea that I have a ridiculously wealthy, successful stepson."

James stood up and placed his lips on her forehead. He kept them there for a long time before stepping back. "There's nothing we can't handle, Pen. Just remember that, okay?"

Oh, God, he really believed that. But some things, as Pen knew, weren't so easily dealt with. Or forgiven.

A week later, Lowrie was surprised to hear boots heading toward the kitchen, where she was making herself and the very elusive Sutton Marchant a chicken salad, in between feeding Rhan pureed vegetables.

She looked up as Sutton stepped into the massive country kitchen, dressed in a pair of designer jeans and a black sweater, sleeves pushed up past his elbows. A pair of wire-framed glasses on his nose made him look like a very sexy professor.

"Hey," she said.

Sutton surprised her by laying a gentle hand on Rhan's head as he passed to sit down at the big table in the center of the kitchen. "Hi back."

Lowrie pointed her knife to the salad she was making. She was becoming used to making food, covering it with Saran Wrap and leaving it in the fridge, only to find the empty plate in the dishwasher a couple of hours later. "Would you like some lunch?" she asked him, expecting him to say no.

"Yeah, that would be great," Sutton replied. "Thanks."

Wow, they were going to share their first meal after a week of living together. No, not living together, sharing the same house. She was his temporary housekeeper, nothing more, nothing less.

Lowrie fed Rhan a spoon of baby goop then carried on assembling the salad. "How's the writing going?"

Sutton pulled a face. "Better. I've just finished edits on a book due next week."

Sutton got up, reached for a glass and shoved it under the tap. After drinking, he filled it again and asked Lowrie if he could pour her something.

She refused, fed her little openmouthed bird and started to shred cold chicken.

Sutton leaned against the counter opposite her and crossed his ankles. "What do you know about the Ryder-Whites?"

Lowrie looked at him, frowning. "Portland's princesses?"

"Who?"

"That's what they call Kinga and Tinsley, the Ryder-White daughters… Portland's princesses."

"They are that well-known?" Sutton asked, resting his glass against his huge biceps. She'd love to see him shirtless… Hell, naked. She wanted to see if his stomach was as ridged as she imagined, whether his erection was as impressive—

Dear God, it's one thirty on a Tuesday afternoon, Lewis!

Maybe Paddy was right—maybe she did need to have an affair, to get back into the groove. But the only man she could imagine getting naked with was her guest. Which wasn't going to happen.

She met his eyes and saw that he was waiting for an answer. Right, they'd been talking about the Ryder-Whites.

"The Ryder-Whites are East Coast nobility," Lowrie

explained. "They have the bluest of blue blood and can trace their family tree right back to the first European settlers in Yarmouth. Why are you asking about them?"

"Ah, because I am attending their Valentine's Day Ball this Saturday?"

Her knife stopped abruptly and she looked up at him, her mouth agape. "Seriously?"

He shrugged. "Yeah."

Right, she didn't know much about the ball, but she did know it was one of the world's most exclusive social events. Princes and celebs, billionaires and sheikhs, fought for tickets. The price of the tickets were a closely guarded secret and it was said that if you had to ask how much they cost, you couldn't afford to attend.

"I've been meaning to look them up, but I've been swamped. What do the daughters do?" Sutton asked.

Lowrie had only been back in Portland for a year and she'd been far too busy to keep up with local gossip. But, invariably, there were some things you couldn't help hearing, especially since her grandmother and aunt were huge followers of the local news. "They run the PR division of Ryder International. They are responsible for organizing and hosting the Valentine's Day Ball in Manhattan."

Sutton's attention sharpened. "It's in Manhattan?" he demanded.

"For someone who's forked out a lot of cash to attend the social event of the year, you don't know much about it," Lowrie commented, more than a little confused.

"You are not wrong," Sutton conceded. "In my defense, I've been snowed under and left the arrangements to Thea."

Rhan banged his little hand on the table and Lowrie

hastily shoved another spoon of food into his mouth. He grinned at her and gummed his food.

"Do not get in the way of my son and his food," Lowrie said, then returned to the subject at hand. "The first Ryder-White ball was hosted decades ago by Callum Ryder-White's brother, I can't remember his name, and it's morphed into an annual, not to be missed, event. To be fair, the ball might be horribly exclusive but it does raise lots of money for their foundation."

"They have a foundation?"

"They are the richest family on the East Coast, Sutton—of course, they have a foundation. I think the brother set that up, too," Lowrie said, reaching for ingredients to make a simple salad dressing. That done, she pulled two bold blue plates out from the cabinet and set the table. Sutton sent her a smile of thanks as he pulled his phone from the back pocket of his jeans. "Give me a minute," he asked.

Lowrie shrugged, scooped up the rest of Rhan's food and popped the spoon in his mouth. He grabbed the spoon out of her hand and proceeded to bite down on it. Damn, he always did that when his teeth were bothering him. She hoped they weren't in for another night short on sleep.

"Thea, hi," Sutton said. He listened for a moment, smiled and leaned back.

They spoke for a few minutes and then Sutton raised the subject of the ball. "I remember seeing an email but confirm that all the arrangements are in place for me to attend Ryder International's Valentine's Day Ball?"

Despite being across the table, Lowrie heard Thea's reply. "They are. It wasn't easy getting a ticket at the last minute but I pulled some strings, dropped a couple of names, used your title."

"You have a title?" Lowrie demanded.

Sutton's reply was to create a tiny space between his thumb and index finger. Was he an earl? A marquess, a viscount? Her familiarity with aristocratic English titles was due to all those historical romances she'd once had the time to read.

Lowrie dished up some salad, tossed some dressing over it and dug in. Sutton shrugged, told Thea that she was on speakerphone with Lowrie in the room and placed his phone on the table next to his glass.

"How much was the ticket?" Sutton asked, winking at Lowrie. She leaned forward, curious to know the answer, and lifted both her hands to indicate ten thousand dollars. He shook his head and mouthed, *Fifty*.

"Before I tell you, I want to remind you that you said I had to pay what I had to, that it was imperative that you go…" Thea said, sounding a little choked up.

"Yeah, yeah…how much, Thea?"

"Because you bought it so late, the week of the event, you had to pay a penalty," Thea explained. "The ticket cost two hundred and fifty thousand dollars."

Sutton coughed, choked and reached for his water. "What?" he croaked, his eyes wide. Lowrie's mouth dropped open as well.

"That's the cost of a ticket, Sutton," Thea replied. "As I keep saying, it's a premier social event."

"It's bloody highway robbery," Sutton sputtered.

"If it helps, all the money from the ticket sales go to their foundation. They get sponsorships and Ryder International pays a hefty price for hosting the ball," Lowrie told him, trying to wrap her head around the fact that Sutton could afford to spend a quarter million on one evening's entertainment. "I heard that from my grandmother. She follows local news, and the Ryder-Whites in particular."

"Why?" Sutton asked her, after disconnecting his call to Thea.

Lowrie handed Rhan his teething ring. "Why what?"

"Why does she follow the Ryder-Whites in particular?"

Lowrie laid down her fork, sat back and looked at him. "I have no idea, actually. My great-uncle Carlo, Jojo's brother, was the same. They were, to put it mildly, obsessed with everything that family did."

"Did they know Benjamin Ryder-White?" Sutton asked, in a tone that was so casual it immediately raised Lowrie's curiosity.

"Is that the name of Callum Ryder-White's brother?" Lowrie asked. Seeing Sutton's nod, she shrugged. "I don't think they knew him."

They ate in a silence, although it was occasionally broken by Rhan banging the spoon on the plastic tray of his baby chair.

"Two hundred and fifty *K*," Sutton said mournfully after he'd demolished most of his salad. "I could've bought a holiday home for that, or a nineteen-sixties Shelby Cobra."

The most expensive painting Lowrie sold, at the height of her so-called fame, was for a hundred thousand, but after Kyle, her agent-slash-fiancé, and her gallery-owner mother took their cut, she only saw just over half of that.

Lowrie's eyes widened. She assumed he was wealthy but not crazy rich. "Sorry, but that's stupid money."

She could buy an art shop with that money. Or a gallery. An amazing painting or sculpture by an incredible artist...

"It is," Sutton agreed.

"Then why are you going?" Lowrie demanded.

"Reasons," Sutton replied, before finishing his salad. He pulled a funny face at Rhan, who laughed, and returned his attention to his food. Right, he didn't want to explain his interest in the Ryder-Whites. Message received. Loud and clear.

Sutton caught the shadowy figure out of the corner of his eye and slowed down, lifting his head out of the water to watch Lowrie slip into the pool beside him. He saw that she was wearing a one-piece swimsuit, and a cap over her long hair, hoping to keep it relatively dry. But it was her body that caught his attention—tall and slim, with muscled legs and arms, and a flat stomach. And, yeah, great breasts.

Sutton ducked his head back into the warm water and powered to the other end of the pool, easily passing Lowrie. She had good form, he noticed—much better than his. It was easy to see that she'd had some training.

Being a night owl, he frequently worked and exercised late at night, but he could afford to play with his working hours. As an innkeeper, Lowrie couldn't, and because it was past midnight, he wondered why she wasn't in bed asleep. Pulling into a breaststroke, he noticed the baby monitor on her towel quite close to the pool. He slowed down, drew level with her and spoke. "Do you often take midnight swims?"

She grimaced. "Rhan is teething and he woke up crying. I gave him some pediatric pain medicine and he's asleep but I'm now awake. You?"

"Things."

He caught her smile. "Writing things or Ryder-White things?" she asked.

God, she was perceptive! He thought about lying, then did a mental shrug. "Both."

"Why are you so interested in the Ryder-Whites?" Lowrie asked him, her breath visible in the cold air. "Are you using them for research?"

It was as good as an excuse as any but he didn't give her a definite answer. "Are they that interesting?"

"Some would think so," Lowrie quietly replied. "I'm just not impressed with fame and fortune."

He believed that. She knew he was a writer and he had no doubt that she'd done a little research on him. Even the most cursory of internet searches would tell her that he was one of the most successful authors around. Hiring out the inn and instructing Thea to pay for his ticket to the ball would tell her that he was seriously wealthy.

Yet, she'd never once suggested she was impressed. That both annoyed him and intrigued him.

He was used to woman falling over themselves to date him, to pull him into some sort of relationship or arrangement. Uninterested in settling down, he'd had a lot of practice dodging them. But Lowrie treated him as just another bloke, someone who could pay a king's ransom to have an empty house and give her a mini-break from cooking and cleaning.

Sutton did a tumble turn at the wall and sped up into a fast freestyle, leaving Lowrie behind. But his thoughts remained on her. She hadn't always been in the hospitality game, of that he was sure. He wondered where she'd gone to college and what she'd studied, where she'd worked before she landed at The Rossi. He could see her as a kindergarten teacher. She was incredibly patient with her son. Or he could see her working as an event planner, as nothing seemed to ruffle her composure.

She was definitely more of a people person than he was, but he'd noticed that sometimes, especially when she was looking out at the incredible view of the storm-tossed ocean, she had a look in her eye that suggested she was miles away, in the zone. Creatives, he smiled, easily recognized members of their own tribe.

Sutton increased his pace, irritated that she was taking up so much of his mental headspace. He was here to fulfill the conditions of the will so he could donate his birth father's money to his parents' charities. He just needed to hang out at the inn for another seven weeks and attend the Valentine's Day ball, and then he would be done with the situation.

And make his parents proud.

That hadn't been his goal in his late teens and twenties, he'd be the first to admit that. In hindsight, he knew that his parents had treated him and Thea equally, and even back then, he'd intellectually understood that to be true. But deep inside, way down, a small voice insisted that they had to love her more because Thea was *theirs*. They made her and she carried their blood.

When Thea did something amazing—aced a test or nailed a dance routine—he stepped back, watching to see if they praised her more, rewarded her in some way that they didn't him. He couldn't remember a single instance of inequality, but the thought that he was a cuckoo in the nest refused to go away.

Instead, that feeling had grown bigger and bigger and he started to put more distance between himself and his parents. By the time he left school, he was barely on speaking terms with his mum and dad. In his twenties, he pushed away his guilt at his lack of contact and concentrated on establishing a kick-ass career in finance.

He'd dodged their calls, missed birthday celebrations and holidays, always finding something better to do, somewhere else to be. He worked sixty-to-eighty-hour weeks, often worked weekends too, and used his schedule as an excuse to avoid his parents and sister. Yeah, he felt guilty but, wrapped up in himself, he figured they were better off without him.

He found solace in writing and when Sam, his oldest friend, became frustrated by dealing with clients who didn't know the difference between a unit trust and a share, he suggested Sutton write a book for beginner investors. He did, had it published and it was a runaway success. He acquired an agent, banged out three chapters of a thriller, had that picked up and a year later he was working as a full-time writer.

It took nearly ten years and his father rocking up on his doorstep and giving him a come-to-Jesus talk that yanked him back into the family fold and opened the door to a new relationship with his parents. Not being a talker, he never explained his insecurities about being adopted, but their relationship did improve dramatically. He had lunch with his mum, played golf with his dad, made every family occasion for two years. He thought he'd have another thirty, forty years with them but, on a sunny afternoon in June, they died when a truck slammed into their side of the car he'd been driving.

They'd been killed instantly and he walked away with minor scratches.

He'd wasted so much time second-guessing their love, second-guessing them. But, despite his confusion, he'd never once in the ten years they'd been estranged, or before or after, wanted to find his birth parents. He had a family; he just hadn't known how to relate to them. And a scant two years after he realized that all they'd wanted from him was his time and at-tention, they were taken from him.

And his world fell apart.

Completely and indescribably.

It had taken him a long time to crawl out from under the grief, to get back to work, to start living again. He and Thea grew closer, and he was grateful that she never once blamed him for the accident. But it left him with a series of invisible scars and a couple of hard truths.

He'd had a family and had lost it. Thea, Sam and the twins were his family now and they were all he needed. He never wanted to lose someone he loved again. And, this was harder to admit—although he knew his parents loved him, he still didn't know *how* much they loved him. Less than Thea? The same? Did they regret adopt-ing him, especially once they knew they could conceive naturally? Would they have liked a biological son?

He never wanted to question someone's love for him again, so it was easier not to love, to keep his circle small, to stay away from the what-ifs and the doubts and the am-I-good-enoughs.

Sutton felt Lowrie tug on his ankle and he abruptly stopped, dropped his feet so that they hit the floor of the pool and looked across to her. "What?"

"You've been swimming for almost an hour, Sutton, and at a hell of a pace. Enough now."

He looked at his waterproof watch, saw that she was right and noticed that his chest was heaving, that his arms felt heavy and his legs tired. He'd been push-ing himself harder than he thought, and he'd been so wrapped up in his thoughts that he'd lost track of time and what he was doing to his body. While he hated being told what to do, he admitted she was right. It was time to stop.

He swam over to her and watched her as she climbed out of the pool, reaching for the warm toweling robe that was lying on a nearby chair. The air temperature hovered around freezing, so he was happy to stay in the warm water and watch her pull her robe over her lovely body, then shove her feet into slippers. She pulled off her cap, allowing her damp hair to fall to her shoulders.

"Damn, it's cold," she muttered, scooping up her baby monitor. She rocked from foot to foot, peering down at him in the low light. "I'm going to make myself a boozy hot chocolate. Do you want one?"

Hell, yes.

"I'll see you in the kitchen in ten minutes."

Sutton glanced at his watch again and saw that it was close to one in the morning. It was, he decided, the perfect time for booze and chocolate.

Four

Sutton offered to build a fire while she made the hot chocolate and Lowrie agreed. She ran upstairs, thought about changing into jeans and a nice sweater. Nope, Sutton would think she was trying too hard, that she was trying to impress him, so she pulled on her favorite pair of men's pajamas and fluffy socks. She towel-dried her hair and left it to fall as it would, into a tumble of curls.

She peered into the mirror of her bathroom and decided that she definitely needed a facial, to shape her eyebrows and trim her hair. There was nothing like having a sexy man in the house to realize that you looked like a wreck.

Not that she was sure he even saw her as a woman. Oh, there were times when she felt his eyes on hers but he kept his expression so impassive she had no idea what he was thinking. She had stretch marks on her tummy and her boobs definitely weren't as perky as they had been five years ago.

Why are you even thinking like this, Lewis?

She wasn't looking for a man or a relationship and even if she was, Sutton had No Entry signs flashing in his eyes. If, somehow, she did get naked with him, it would be on a just-for-fun basis.

Could she do that? Could she be that live-for-the-moment girl? She didn't know. She wasn't sure she wanted to find out.

What she didn't want to do was fall for another unsuitable man. Her fiancé had been unaffectionate, controlling and too ambitious, happy to use her hard work and talent to enrich his own pockets. When she told him that she was taking a break from art, that she wasn't going to exhibit for the next few years, he'd dropped her like a hot coal, taking her cash with him when he walked.

Her parents, on hearing the same news, also lost their shit.

Lowrie tossed ingredients into the pot, threw in a decent amount of liquor and stirred. She was tired but also wired, and she hoped the hot chocolate would help her sleep. And that Rhan wouldn't wake up at the ass crack of dawn. She needed a solid six, maybe eight, hours of sleep to feel human again.

Lowrie poured the hot chocolate into mugs and took them into the sitting room. Sutton, dressed in a pair of navy track pants and a long sleeved T-shirt, was crouched in front of the fire, poking the logs with a poker.

Despite the thick windows, she could hear the sound of the waves pounding the rocks, and heard the house settle and sigh. God, she loved it here.

And drinking hot chocolate late at night with a hot guy wasn't a bad way to pass the time, either.

Lowrie handed Sutton his cup and curled into the corner of the couch, tucking her feet under her butt. She wrapped her hand around her cup as he settled his big frame next to her, his bare feet pointed toward the fire. He lifted his cup to his mouth and Lowrie waited, interested to see his reaction.

His eyebrows lifted momentarily, but, to his credit, he took another sip.

When he looked at her, she saw glinting amusement in his eyes. "When you said boozy hot chocolate I expected whiskey or rum, not chili and...tequila?"

She laughed. "I got the recipe from a bartender I follow on social media. Do you like it?"

He looked at his cup, considering her question. "I do, actually," he told her. "It's different. So, do you always take midnight swims?"

"Not that often and rarely in winter. I thought a long swim would make me tired. I'm surprised you aren't swaying on your feet, since you swam for close to an hour and at top speed."

"I always do when I've got a lot on my mind."

"Your new book?"

"That's part of it," Sutton replied, an answer that told her nothing.

He wasn't a guy who easily let people in, and Lowrie knew he wasn't going to spill his soul, but a part of her wished he would. He needed a friend, a nonjudgmental someone who'd give him another perspective, a differing opinion. But he didn't seem the type who told his secrets to strangers...or anyone.

"Did you ever consider giving your son up for adoption?"

His question was so out of the blue that she jerked in surprise, spilling a couple of drops of hot chocolate onto her hand. She grimaced and placed her cup on the side table to her left. She started to stand up to go wash her hand, when Sutton lifted his T-shirt, giving her a glimpse of his rock-hard abs, and gently smoothed the fabric across her hand. "Okay?"

"Sure, but you've now dirtied your shirt."

"It's a few drops, not a deluge," Sutton told her, wiping her hand again. He was so warm, and his scent—a mixture of a citrus cologne and chlorine from the pool—drifted up her nose. Sitting back, he stretched out his legs, crossing his feet at the ankles.

"I'm sorry if my question startled you. I'm being nosy—you don't have to answer me."

"No, I don't mind. It was just unexpected. Ah, did I ever want to give him up for adoption? Well, in those first few weeks after hearing I was pregnant, I considered all the options. My boyfriend at the time, well, he wanted me to get an abortion and he pushed pretty hard for that to happen. I refused. I'm pro-choice, but my choice was to keep my baby."

Sutton stared at the fire, but Lowrie knew he was listening. "I did think about adoption, for a few weeks. But once I felt him kick, I fell in love with him and I didn't want anyone else raising him but me. He was mine, you know?"

Sutton turned to look at her, his expression enigmatic. "How long did your guy stick around for?"

"Until I went into labor," Lowrie answered, her voice cracking just a little. "He called an ambulance for me, told me that he'd follow as soon as he locked up the house." It still hurt. It shouldn't but it did. "I waited, and waited some more. I called him and his phone went straight to voice mail. An hour passed, then two, then three. Eight hours after leaving the apartment, Rhan was born, but my boyfriend didn't show. When I went back home, he'd cleared out his stuff and disappeared."

Sutton released a low series of curse words, and because he was a writer, his insults were intensely creative.

"I think that when I went into labor, it got very real. Rex was a Peter Pan character and he couldn't cope with the idea of being a father, being responsible."

"Does he, at the very least, pay child support?" Sutton demanded.

"Ah, well, I'd ask him, but I'd need to find him first." And didn't she sound like a fool admitting that? "I tried to track him down, but he ditched his phone, scrubbed his social-media accounts and simply dropped out of my life. Judging by the fact that I cannot find a Rex Hensley anywhere in California—he said he was born in Orange County—I can only assume he gave me a false name."

Sutton stared at her, his expression bemused. "This sounds like something that would happen in a book."

"All too real, I'm afraid. So, Rhan is mine, and I'm good with that."

"How did you get from California to here?"

Lowrie took a sip of her drink, enjoying the kick of chili against the taste of tequila and warm, rich chocolate. "I called Jojo, my grandmother. She and her oldest daughter, Isabel, who is my mom's sister, flew out the day Rhan was born. They packed up my meager possessions while I held Rhan and sobbed."

"Did you love him?"

Now that was a hell of question.

"God, what is love? What does the concept even mean? He was fun, sociable, charismatic and compelling."

"And if he walked back into your life tomorrow?" Sutton asked.

"I'd kick him in the balls and show him the door."

Sutton's lips twitched, as if he was trying to hold back a smile. When he turned to face her again, his expression was remote and altogether too serious. "I'm glad Rhan stayed with you, that you didn't give him up for adoption."

She wrinkled her nose. "Me, too. It's been tough but Jojo and Isabel are my safety net. They've given me so much support. Paddy gave me a job, a place to stay and something to do."

He played with her fingers and Lowrie looked down at her hand, expecting to see tiny fireworks exploding on her skin. "I was adopted, and while I loved my parents, I didn't like being adopted."

Uh…what? Wow, he was opening up.

"I—"

"Why didn't you call your mother when you went into labor? Why your grandmother?" Sutton asked, dropping her hand and reaching for his hot chocolate.

And he'd slammed that door closed again. Well, what did she expect? For him to reveal his deepest secrets? She knew that wasn't going to happen.

"Uh…well, my mother and I are at odds. And because I'm at odds with her, I'm also at odds with my father."

"Been there, done that," Sutton murmured. "What did you do?"

She leaned forward and punched his biceps. It had as much effect as a bee banging against a glass window. "Why do you think I was the one who did something?"

"Because I messed up in my twenties—it's what your twenties are for."

She mock glared at him. "For your information, I wasn't at fault."

"Tell me what happened," Sutton gently commanded.

"You're awfully curious about my life," Lowrie grumbled.

He smiled, unrepentant. "I'm a writer, I'm curious about everything."

"If I tell you, will you put it in a book?"

"It depends how interesting your story is," he replied. "Most people think their lives are interesting but they rarely are. Does your story involve skeletons in cupboards or dead bodies?"

"Literally or figuratively?"

He laughed, a sound as rich, deep and dark as her chili-tequila hot chocolate. Amused, he looked a lot younger, his eyes crinkling at the corner and his lips revealing straight, white teeth. He had a great smile, Lowrie thought.

She wanted to know how it felt under her lips. Lowrie felt her nerves tingling, and that secret place between her legs throbbed. The urge to erase all distance between them pummeled her. She needed to touch and explore.

There were a million reasons why kissing him would be a bad move but she didn't care. For the next few minutes she wanted to feel alive, to feel like a woman, sexy and confident.

"I'm sorry, I have to," she told him, pushing up so that she was kneeling on the couch.

"Have to what?" Sutton asked as she swung her thigh over his and settled into his lap. She lifted both her hands to hold his cheeks, loving the feel of his stubble on her palms.

"Kiss you." Lowrie pulled back to look at him. "Is that okay?"

His big hands gripped her hips, his fingertips burning into her skin through the fabric of her pajamas.

This was a mistake. She knew it was. She wasn't mentally ready to dive into an anything with anybody, but his mouth was a temptation she couldn't resist. Just one kiss, so she could stop wondering, stop fantasizing...

Lying to yourself, Lewis. You know you want more than a kiss.

But a kiss was all she could have.

"This works better if you actually kiss me instead of just staring at my mouth," Sutton murmured, his words low, slow and sexy as hell.

Lowrie smiled, lowered her head and placed her lips against his. He allowed her to explore, play, and when she sucked his lower lip between hers, he released the smallest of growls. He lifted his hand to cup the back of her head. Gently tugged on her hair to pull her head back so he could look into her eyes.

"Is that all the game you've got, Lowrie?"

Seeing the challenge in his eyes, she held the side of his face and placed her lips on his, sliding her tongue along the seam. He opened his mouth and she slipped her tongue inside, enjoying the sensation of being in control. It didn't last long because Sutton's grip on her head tightened and, on a low groan, he took over, sweeping her into a passionate kiss that had her head swirling and her heart thumping.

His tongue twirled around hers, and her blood superheated. His thumb brushed over her nipple and her blood started to boil.

She wanted him, of that she had no doubt. No one

had ever made her feel so alive, so quickly. He shut down her brain and circumvented her common sense, and she was okay with that, as long he kept kissing her, touching her.

She slid down so that the space between her thighs was flush against his erection and she couldn't help wriggling a little, trying to hit the spot. The world could end, a bomb could detonate, but as long as those apocalyptic events didn't stop her from making love to Sutton on this couch in front of a fire, she didn't care.

Lowrie sighed as his mouth traced the contours of her cheekbone, whispered over her jaw, sighed when his tongue sucked on the delicate flesh between her neck and ear. Impatient, she pulled up his T-shirt, her fingers dancing across his muscled stomach, her thumb brushing through the line of hair that disappeared beneath his pajama pants.

This was sweet madness...

Sutton took her mouth again and she tasted chili and chocolate, tequila and temptation, as she sucked on his tongue, arching her breasts into his hands. Her womb pulsed, her soul whimpered with need and she knew that when he lifted his mouth to allow her to speak, she'd ask him to take her to bed.

In his arms, for the first time in over eighteen months, she felt like a woman. Desirable. Having a delicious man tell her she was hot reminded her that before she was a mother, she was Lowrie.

Before she was a mother...

Something deep inside her, intuition or a mother's sense that something was wrong, had her pulling away from Sutton to cock her head. She looked over to the baby monitor but it was silent.

"Come back here," Sutton told her, reaching up to cup her neck.

She held up a finger… Three, two, one…

Waaah!

Lowrie slammed her eyes shut and tipped back her head to glare up at the ceiling. Her son had awful timing…

Waah, waah, waah.

Right, that was a where-are-you-need-you-right-now wail. He wouldn't settle down and go back to sleep. In fact, she was pretty certain he was climbing to his feet and holding the sides of his crib, tears running down his face.

He was either scared or in pain, possibly both.

Lowrie grimaced and met Sutton's eyes. "Sorry."

He lifted his hands in a what-can-you-do? gesture. Lowrie climbed off him, straightened her pajama top and, out of the corner of her eye, saw him adjusting the fabric of his pants. He sent her a pained smile.

"Babies have the worst timing in the world."

"No problem," Sutton replied. "He's your top priority, I get that." He winced when Rhan turned up the volume. "I can't believe something so small can make so much noise."

She sent him a grateful look before walking over to the baby monitor and picking it up. "I'll see you in the morning."

"Good night, Lowrie."

Feeling frustrated, Lowrie walked toward the hallway. When she reached the stairs, she ran up one flight, then another and walked into her extensive upstairs apartment, and through its open-plan living room. She walked into the smaller of the two rooms and there he was, tears running down his little face. She swung him up, sighed when he buried his face in her neck and patted his little bottom.

"Mommy's here, baby. She'd much rather you were sleeping and she was on the couch with Sutton exploring his delicious body, but she's here. Shhh, baby boy."

Lowrie, for various reasons, got very little sleep that night.

Why was he sent to The Rossi? Why did Benjamin Ryder-White want him here, at this small, lovely place on the outskirts of Portland? What was the connection between Benjamin and this place?

The next morning Sutton stood on the covered porch off his bedroom, his hands jammed into the pockets of his sleeveless parka. It was the first clear day in ages and the air was bitingly cold but bearable. He'd recently returned from an eight-mile run and he needed to get to work, but the urge to take ten minutes to suck in the view couldn't be ignored.

The sea was gunmetal-gray, hinting at violence beneath its surface, and weak sunlight danced on the sand of the small beach between the boulders.

Sutton brushed snow from the balcony railing and leaned his forearms on the wood, his thoughts bouncing from the intensely passionate kiss he'd shared with Lowrie last night to the mystery of his birth father.

It was easier to think of his birth father than it was to think of Lowrie, as he'd already spent half the night reliving what was probably the hottest kiss of his life. He'd been surprised when she'd climbed onto his lap, unable to believe she'd made the first move. But very damn grateful. Her skin felt like silk beneath his hands, her mouth like the ripest, sweetest fruit, and he'd felt the heat of her core beneath their clothes. It had taken everything he had not to strip her down and take her on the carpet in front of the fire...

He was doing it again, giving those few minutes holding her far too much mental energy. Sutton scrubbed his hands over his face and glared at the rocks below.

Move the hell on...

Right, Benjamin Ryder-White.

When he came to Portland, he'd resolved that he was here for one reason and one reason only: the bucks. One hundred and fifty million, to be precise.

The money he was on the brink of inheriting would fund the running costs of the children's home his parents established for yet-to-be-adopted orphans and at-risk kids for a long time, with change to spare. The home had been so important to his parents, and he and Thea had taken their seats on the charity's board when they passed on. Thea with enthusiasm, him with trepidation.

He'd never felt comfortable with the idea of a charity to support orphans; it struck too close to home. Would he have been one of the kids who ended up there, or in the system, had his birth mother not been rich, if she hadn't found the Tate-Handler Agency? Where would he be if his mum had fallen pregnant before they adopted him? He couldn't help imagining that other baby, the one they'd been thinking of adopting when they heard that Thea was on the way... What had happened to him? Or her? Had someone else taken him? Was he raised in a crappy home, or a place like The Marching Ant House?

His parents, God bless them, had high standards for their orphanage, its name a play on their surname. All caregivers were carefully chosen for their kindness and empathy. Young babies and toddlers were given all the attention and love they needed. Small groups of younger children were placed in the care of a foster mother—or father—and that person was their "parent" until they left the facility at eighteen. Teenagers were also matched with older brothers and sisters, people to guide them.

The Marching Ant House was a happy place, but it was only one and there were hundreds, thousands, of kids who weren't raised in such a loving environment. And, yeah, if Benjamin's money could build, establish and fund another two or three houses, that's what Sutton would use it for.

But why The Rossi? Why did he have to stay here for another month and a half?

Why did he care? It. Didn't. Matter.

They'd chosen to give him up; he'd chosen not to find out anything about them.

Simple enough.

Sutton heard a baby laughing and looked down to see Lowrie stepping onto the veranda from the sitting room, little Rhan gripping her finger and toddling beside her. He held a stuffed giraffe beneath his arm and plopped down on the cold floor. Sutton watched, fascinated, as a massive mop of a dog ambled onto the veranda and sat down next to Rhan, laying a gentle paw on the little boy's thigh. Rhan wrapped a handful of the dog's corded fur in his hands, hauled himself up and snuggled into its huge chest. Sutton smiled when the dog's paw snuck behind the boy to hold him in place.

Rhan laughed again, pulled away and toddled off toward the railing. The dog immediately put himself between the boy and the railing, as if to protect him. Rhan couldn't fall through the slats but Sutton was impressed with the dog's strong instinct to guard Lowrie's son.

Lowrie, holding a mug in her hand, praised the dog, gave it a biscuit that she pulled from her jacket pocket and turned to speak to someone inside.

"It's actually lovely outside," she said, her words drifting up to him.

She was lovely, he thought, happy to watch her. She wasn't his usual type—a little too thin, a bit nervy—but God, he'd never been so aware of a woman in all his life. She was…*magnetic* and he couldn't pull his attention off her.

Lowrie had pulled her hair into a ponytail and wore a little makeup this morning, maybe mascara and a peach-colored lipstick. Her long legs were covered in tight, black denims that disappeared into low-heeled, knee-high boots. Her sweater was a cheery red. A cream, sheepskin aviator jacket ended at her shapely hips—hips he'd held in his hands last night.

Two ladies, one a lot older than the other, stepped onto the veranda. Sutton watched as Lowrie took a tray from the younger woman and placed it on the wrought-iron table. Sutton looked down at the tray and saw cinnamon buns, steam rising off them.

Cinnamon buns? Where were his?

Lowrie stepped back into the house for a minute and when she returned, she spread out a thick blanket on the floor next to their chair and tipped out a box of toys for Rhan. He looked at them, ignored them and walked his giraffe along the enormous dog's back.

Lowrie suddenly looked up and their eyes connected, then clashed. She blushed and he grinned, amused by her embarrassment. They were two consenting adults and they hadn't done anything illegal. They'd kissed…

Though that was a very weak description of the way

he'd inhaled her, how he'd fought to keep from stripping her naked and plunging inside her.

Sutton took a couple of deep breaths and reminded himself that he wasn't fifteen anymore. When he felt more in control, he spoke. "Can you spare a cinnamon bun?" he asked, resting his arms on the railing.

"Come on down and meet my grandmother and aunt," Lowrie told him, her hands on her hips. "Would you like a cup of coffee?"

"Sure, but I'll make it." He turned to walk away but stopped, thinking of the dog. "If I come down there, will I be attacked by the oversized mop?"

Lowrie's grin was like fireworks exploding in a night sky. "Maybe. How much do you want a cinnamon bun, Marchant?"

Home-baked and still warm? Hell, he'd take his chances.

Five

In between being interrogated about his books—Lowrie was unaware that her grandmother and aunt were into crime novels—Sutton ate three of Jojo's famous cinnamon buns and drank two cups of coffee. He kept a wary eye on Charlie, and Charlie treated him with supreme indifference.

She wished she could say the same.

Sutton was a difficult guy to ignore, and not just because he was tall, broad and big. This morning he wore dark blue Levi's that cupped his butt in the most delicious way, waterproof boots and an ivory-colored hoodie. He hadn't shaved—after living with him for over a week, she realized he wasn't a fan of scraping his face daily—and his hair was its usual mess.

Supersexy man.

Lowrie sighed, annoyed with herself.

She'd promised herself that she'd be the consummate

host this morning, that she'd treat him like any other guest, and she was trying, she really was. But he'd had his tongue in her mouth, his hands had covered her boobs and traced the contours of her ass with immense skill. If Rhan hadn't cried, there was no doubt that she would know what it felt like to be loved by him, to have him slide inside her, rock her to heaven.

Lowrie ran her hand over her eyes, sighing. She wasn't on the pill. Dressed as he was, it was obvious that he hadn't had any condoms on his person and they'd been so into each other that birth control might've been forgotten. It certainly hadn't crossed her mind. With Rex, she'd been dogmatic about taking the pill, but a dose of antibiotics messed with her protection and that's how she got pregnant with Rhan.

But she hadn't been on the pill in ages, so if she and Sutton got it on, they'd need to use condoms. If they got it on… Yeah, her mind, or more likely her needy body, wasn't moving off the possibility.

She wanted him more now, knowing what an excellent kisser he was, how he'd set her body alight with one slide of his hand and a few hot-as-lava kisses.

This wasn't good, this wasn't good at all. He was just another man who'd dropped into her life, and he was only in the country for the next six weeks. He wasn't, she was sure, the type who wanted to stick around.

But she didn't want one of those, did she? She wasn't looking for a man to marry, to help her raise her son, a man to love. She'd loved enough people in her life who'd let her down, so why would she want to add one more to the list?

But sex would be good. Sex with Sutton would be, she was convinced, a mind-bending, soul-touching, body-melting experience.

She just had to let her body have some fun without allowing her heart into the party…

"Don't you think so, Low?"

On hearing her grandmother say her name, her head snapped up. "Sorry, what?"

Jojo's eyes narrowed with speculation. "You haven't listened to a word we've said."

Lowrie tried to recall snippets of their conversation to refute her accusation but came up with nothing. She shrugged, saw Sutton's lips twitch in amusement and glared at him. "Sorry. Miles away."

"I was saying that there's an art exhibition at the Portland Museum of Art. Gavin Price? Wasn't he a friend of yours from New York?"

"No, Mama, Lowrie had an exhibition with him," Isabel corrected.

Sutton's gaze sharpened and Lowrie wrinkled her nose. Her past as an up-and-coming artist wasn't a secret but neither did she blab about it. How did she tell people that art had started making her feel sick, that she'd found herself falling apart under the stress of being one of the country's most exciting painters? That her life collapsed when her agent-fiancé threatened to ditch her at her lowest moment, telling her that he wasn't interested in dealing with children having temper tantrums.

She'd asked for help and got none, and the only way to survive had been to drop out, to disappear. She still associated painting with panic attacks, racing thoughts and feeling out of control. She hadn't picked up a brush or a palette, not even a pencil, in over six years.

She couldn't go back there, to that terrifying place where she was solely judged on the work she produced, the money she made—for her fiancé and her gallery-owning mother—and the reputation she was building.

"You're an artist?" Sutton asked her, his index finger tapping against his coffee mug.

"I *was* an artist," Lowrie replied, mentally grimacing at her short reply.

"Lowrie had a few exhibitions in New York and was regarded as one of the most exciting artists of her generation," Jojo explained, her tone proud. "Of course, art runs in her blood. My brother was an incredible artist, as is my daughter. She owns a gallery in Lenox Hill—Lily Lewis…?"

Since her mom's gallery was one of the most famous in the city, Lowrie wasn't surprised at seeing Sutton's immediate recognition of the name. "Your father is the sculptor Roscoe Lewis."

Lowrie nodded and looked away. She really didn't want to talk about this anymore. She missed her art, missed creating, but she didn't miss feeling panicky or pressured to perform.

"What can you tell me about this house, ladies?" Sutton asked.

Lowrie darted a look his way, grateful to him for changing the subject. He half smiled at her and reached for another cinnamon roll. Was that his fourth? Where did he put all that food? He winked at her as he took a huge bite out of the pastry.

"What do you want to know?" Isabel asked, surprising Lowrie with her question. Her grandmother was feisty, never afraid to speak her mind, but Isabel was a quiet soul and shy around strangers. She hardly ever instigated conversation. It was strange for her to be so at ease with Sutton. Or any man.

Sutton lifted one powerful shoulder in a shrug. "When was it built?"

Jojo jumped in, telling Sutton the history of the hundred-year house, that her grandfather built it and that her brother Carlo inherited it over forty years ago.

Jojo gestured to her. "Carlo didn't have any kids and Lowrie is the only grandchild so it will be hers one day."

Sutton frowned. "I thought Paddy owned it."

"Paddy has the right to live in it until he dies, but it will be Low's, then Rhan's," Jojo insisted. "It's a huge place and it requires upkeep so Carlo and Paddy turned it into an inn twenty years ago."

Sutton swallowed the last of his cinnamon roll and linked his hands across his flat stomach. "I can understand that. My sister and I inherited a house in Sussex from my parents that's been in the family for hundreds of years and we converted it into a small hotel so it could pay its way. These old houses suck up cash."

Jojo nodded. "Great minds think alike."

Sutton placed his ankle on his opposite knee and played with the laces in his boot. "Lowrie told me you are a fount of knowledge about local families and you follow the local news. What can you tell me about the Ryder-Whites?"

Jojo didn't hesitate. "Kinga Ryder-White is dating Griff O'Hare, the singer. You know, the one who threw a chair through a hotel window in Dubai?" Lowrie shook her head, amazed by the things Jojo remembered. "Good-looking boy, but trouble. All good-looking men are trouble."

Lowrie coughed to cover her laugh and although Sutton's expression didn't change, she saw amusement in those extraordinary eyes.

"Tinsley and her ex-brother-in-law, Cody Gallant, are organizing another event to celebrate a hundred years of Ryder International being in business. James and Penelope Ryder-White—"

"Callum Ryder-White's son and daughter-in-law?" Sutton interrupted.

Jojo nodded. "Right. Well, they attended a fundraising dinner for cancer last week. Very into fundraising is Penelope. She runs the Ryder Foundation."

Thinking that her relatives would get a kick out of knowing that Sutton would be attending the Ryder-White ball later tonight, Lowrie told them the news.

They laughed with delight, clapped their hands together and demanded to know who he was taking—no one—and why he was going, but he dodged that question. They insisted that he take photographs and tell them everything. Everything, you hear.

"And if you want to get Griff O'Hare's autograph, that would be okay, too," Isabel murmured.

Jojo hooted. "Isabel has the biggest crush on Griff O'Hare! She could be his mother, but there it is."

"I've got a crush on him, too, Is," Lowrie told her aunt and it wasn't a lie. O'Hare was one sexy man. "It should be illegal for a man to look that good."

The hell of it was, and she would never admit this, but if given the choice between the bad boy of rock and roll and Sutton, well, the broody man opposite her would win that toss.

Dammit.

"Yeah, yeah…got it," Sutton grumbled. He dropped his leg, sat up and leaned forward. His expression turned intense. "Do either of you know if Benjamin Ryder-White has any connection to this house?"

Jojo's mouth fell open and Isabel released a little squeak. They both, perfectly synchronized, stood up, and Jojo snapped her fingers to call Charlie. "It's time to go," Jojo said, picking up her handbag. "Thanks for coffee, darling Low. Nice to meet you, Sutton."

Sutton looked from Lowrie to their departing backs and back to Lowrie again. "Was it something I said?"

Lowrie sent him a ya-think look and shrugged. "Good to know that mentioning Benjamin Ryder-White's name will clear the room."

"But why?" Sutton asked.

"Good question," Lowrie said. She scooped up Rhan, placed him on her hip and followed her relatives into the house, determined to find out.

When Lowrie returned, a good forty-five minutes later, she was minus her child. Sutton had moved into the library, built up a fire and was looking at an email of two potential book covers, neither of which he liked.

He glanced up, watching as she went to the fire to warm her hands. It was close to noon and she was normally in the kitchen at this time of day, making food for Rhan and for him.

"No Rhan?" he asked, leaning back in the ergonomic leather office chair he'd had delivered. Yeah, it was pricey, but he was a big guy and he spent a lot of time with his ass plastered to the seat so it was a good investment.

"Jojo and Is kidnapped him for the afternoon, possibly the night," Lowrie told him. "They adore having him and, much as I love him, it's nice to have a break now and again."

"Did they give you an explanation for their bolting out of the room at me mentioning Benjamin Ryder-White?"

Lowrie shrugged. "I asked, they ignored me. It's weird because they are pretty chatty people."

"Yeah, I gathered, especially your grandmother." He laid a hand on his heart and tapped it. "If she were forty years younger…"

Lowrie grinned. "I know, right? She's a firecracker."

Sutton looked at her, enjoying her wide smile as she talked about her relatives. "But what is a four-foot-nothing Italian nonna doing with a dog the size of a baby cow that looks like an old-fashioned mop?"

Lowrie turned her back to the fire and Sutton wanted to suggest a better way of warming her up but managed to keep that asinine suggestion to himself.

"Isabel found Charlie on the side of the road, a couple of months before Rhan was born. He was just a puppy and they brought him home, not knowing what he was or how big he'd get."

"Apart from being ninety percent mop, what breed is he?"

"He's a Komondor, also known as the Hungarian sheepdog. Quite rare and we have no idea how he came to be lost or abandoned because he's definitely purebred."

"You're very comfortable with him being around your kid."

Lowrie pulled out her phone, flicked through it and walked over to him to show him the screen. He looked at the photo of Charlie, sprawled out, and a newborn Rhan lying between his chest and front leg. Both dog and human were fast asleep.

"I have dozens more. Charlie has been besotted with Rhan from the moment they met. Now that Rhan is becoming more mobile, he's an amazing pair of second eyes."

Yeah, he'd noticed that. Lowrie took back her phone, placed a hand on his shoulder and looked at his big monitor, filled with the two images of the competing book covers.

"Nice," she said, her tone polite.

He shook his head. "Do you think so? I don't know

if I like either of them." He stared at the screen and attempted to be casual. "You're an artist, what do you really think?"

Lowrie crossed her arms over her chest, stared at his screen and contemplated the first image. "It's too busy, for one. I'd make the background black and white so it comes across as spookier, more atmospheric. I'd change the white writing to red, maybe have a couple of droplets dripping off the last two letters." She glanced at him. "It does have dead bodies, right?"

"Many," Sutton confirmed. He cocked his head to the side. "I agree with you. I'll send your suggestions back and see what they come up with. Thanks."

"Pleasure," Lowrie said as she sat down behind her messy desk. Their desks faced each other but if he looked left and she right, they both had an exceptional view of the bay.

"I'm going to pay some bills, do some admin," Lowrie told him. "I'll be quiet so as not to disturb you."

"Don't worry about that, I'm done with work today. I'm going to be leaving for the airport in a couple of hours."

Lowrie nodded. "Right, the Ryder International Ball."

"Mmm." He really wasn't looking forward to it. Spending his evening in a room full of strangers, making small talk, dressed in a penguin suit, wasn't his idea of fun.

"Poor boy, drinking the world's best champagne, eating amazing food, listening to Griff O'Hare sing," Lowrie said, tongue firmly in her cheek.

"He doesn't have quite the same effect on me as he has on you. And Isabel," he muttered, annoyed that he was just a little jealous.

"As I said, talented and hot. It's a killer combination."

Sutton propped his boots on the corner of the desk, leaning back in his chair. He really didn't want to rush off to Manhattan and spend the night in a cold hotel room, but what choice did he have? If he wanted Benjamin's money, it was what he had to do...

But maybe he wouldn't have to spend the entire evening alone. "Come with me."

Lowrie looked up, her expression puzzled. "What?"

"Come with me to New York City," he said. "I've got to make an appearance at this bloody ball but no one said I had to stay for the whole thing. I'll hang around for an hour, maybe two, and then we can go to dinner, walk the streets, ride around Central Park in one of those carriage things."

"They are called hansom cabs," Lowrie replied, slitting open an envelope to pull out a bill. "And no. But thank you."

"Why not?" Sutton demanded.

Lowrie rolled her eyes. "Well, I have a young son I can't leave—"

"You said that he might stay the night with your grandmother and aunt."

"But I like being close by. They live just down the road and I can be there in under five minutes if there's a problem."

"True enough. But what's going to happen with a guard-dog-slash-babysitter in the house and two very eagle-eyed, doting women?"

She looked tempted. And excited. Then she shook her head. "It's a silly idea, Marchant."

"It's a *great* idea, Lewis. I already have a hotel room booked at the Forrester-Grantham, and my plane is waiting for me at Portland Jetport. My suite has a hot tub and awesome views of Central Park. I'll order you wine and sushi, or anything else you want to eat, and you can kick back in the hot bubbles while I go and meet boring people downstairs. I'll do my thing and then we can spend the rest of the evening exploring Manhattan."

"Sutton, I can't just go to New York on a whim with a man I don't know."

"You know me," Sutton calmly stated, holding her eyes. "You might not know what my favorite color is— mint green, by the way—or what music I like, jazz, but you know that I would never harm you." He smiled to lighten the mood. "Besides, we've been living together for nearly two weeks now."

She didn't look convinced.

"Lowrie, take a break. You're a great mom, and I get that you are worried about leaving Rhan, but he's in amazing hands. Take an evening for yourself—" He looked at his watch. "In fact, if we leave now, we can be there in a couple of hours and we'll have time to do whatever you want to do."

"Would we have time to—" She stopped and waved her hands around. "Don't worry, stupid question."

"Time to do what?"

She lifted her stubborn chin. "It doesn't matter because I'm not going."

Oh, she was thinking about it. "Time to do what, Low?"

She looked out the window and released a little sigh. "Visit the Frick Museum."

He moved his mouse, pulled his keyboard to him and asked the internet when the museum closed. He did some calculations and worked out that if they hustled, they could have two hours at the museum before it closed. That would still give him more than enough time to shower and change and get downstairs to the Forrester-Grantham ballroom.

"We've got time. C'mon, Lowrie, come play with me."

She bit her bottom lip, scratched the back of her neck. "When you say *play*, what, exactly, do you mean by that?"

He saw the flash of vulnerability in her eyes and sighed. He knew what she was asking... How was he expecting to be paid for this unexpected trip? Man, she had to start hanging out with better men.

"There's no quid pro quo here, Lowrie. I'm going to Manhattan, anyway. My sister booked a suite, but if there's no second bed, I'll sleep on the couch. I'm not expecting payment, in any shape or form."

She rubbed her forehead with her fingertips. "I don't know, Sutton."

He stood up and walked over to her desk, placing his hands on its surface and lowering his head so his eyes were level with hers. "Call your grandmother, ask her what she thinks. Find out if she's happy for you to go, happy to look after Rhan, and if she is, come and find me, okay?"

Knowing that if he pushed her further, he might lose her, Sutton left the room, thinking that he had, maybe, a thirty percent chance of her company.

Well, it was still a chance.

In the bathroom of his suite at the Forrester-Grantham Hotel, Sutton threaded cuff links through the buttonholes of his white dress shirt and rubbed his smooth face. The last thing he wanted to do was go downstairs and be sociable, but needs—specifically The Marching Ant's needs—insisted he must.

He'd much rather stay here and slide into that hot tub,

preferably naked, with Lowrie. Sutton reached for his toothbrush and paste, thinking about the fun afternoon they'd spent looking at art in the Frick Museum. Being with her was like having his own personal tour guide, as her knowledge about art history, techniques and design was encyclopedic. She might not have a college degree, but she knew her subject inside out.

She was intelligent, interesting and had a dry sense of humor he found incredibly attractive.

Getting her to spend the evening with him in Manhattan had been difficult—she'd second-guessed her decision to leave Rhan right until the plane took off. When they landed, she checked her phone for messages, called Jojo and immediately offered to catch the first plane home. Jojo insisted Rhan was absolutely fine and that she stay in New York City. He'd be buying Lowrie's grandmother an enormous bouquet of flowers when he returned to Portland.

Lowrie didn't call her grandmother again, but he did see her exchange a number of text messages to check up on Rhan. Her son was everything to her.

Lucky kid.

He'd been lucky, too, but he'd been so wrapped up in his own insecurities, so intent on protecting himself from his parents' unlikely but possible rejection, that he hadn't noticed how involved his parents were in his life. They attended parent-teacher meetings, sports matches. Every evening they gathered around the dinner table and talked about their day, what was happening in their lives. Thea rattled on, telling them everything, but they'd had to pry every nugget of information out of him…

Even back then he'd found opening up difficult.

He was surprised he'd told Lowrie he was adopted; it wasn't a subject he ever raised. Even more shocking was his desire to tell her the whole story, to blurt out why he was really going to this ball, why he was staying at her inn for the foreseeable future.

He never opened up; it wasn't what he did. He dealt with his issues alone, or on the pages of a book, and never let people into his headspace. He wanted to confide in her and didn't know why.

What was it about the single mom, onetime artist and current innkeeper that drew him like a moth to a flame?

She was...authentic, Sutton decided. She was just trying to win life, not wrapped up in the bullshit of ego or success. She wanted to be a good mom, do a decent job running the inn. She seemed content with her life.

But why had she given up on art? Trailing behind her in the Frick Museum, he'd seen her passion, watched as her eyes sparked with interest, admiration. Noticed how her brow furrowed when she tried to work out how an artist created a particular effect.

He suspected a lot of the art in the inn was hers, and that the massive painting in the hallway was one she'd done years ago. He'd love to see more of her work, and when he had some time, he'd see if he could track down her art.

In the bedroom, Sutton slid his tuxedo jacket off the hanger and walked into the lounge area of the suite. Beyond the massive windows was an impressive view of the city and Lowrie was standing there, a glass of red wine in her hand.

She lifted the glass. "I hope it's okay that I ordered a bottle."

He smiled. "Very." After tossing the jacket over the back of the couch, he walked over to her, plucked her glass out of her hand and took a sip before handing it back to her. "I'm sorry to be leaving you alone tonight," he told her, reaching up to tuck a curl behind her ear.

"It's fine," Lowrie assured him. "Thanks for being

patient this afternoon at the museum and sorry if I bombarded you with too much information."

"I enjoyed it," he assured her. He grinned. "And during those few times you stopped talking, I was thinking that a famous, fictional museum would be a perfect place to stage an art theft and a murder."

Her eyebrows raised. "Uh...seriously?"

"Mmm. There would be a table in the dining room where I'd pose a dead body, dripping blood onto a priceless Persian carpet. Obviously, the walls would be stripped of their art. My police detective would be stumped by how the thieves and murderers rearmed the place when they left. Or maybe the murderer used the theft to cover up his crime."

She scratched her forehead. "I was thinking light and technique, and you were thinking dead bodies?"

"It's what I do." Thinking this was the perfect segue into a topic he wanted to raise, he leaned his shoulder against the glass window, his eyes on her lovely face. "Talking of, why don't you paint anymore?"

"How do you know I don't?" Lowrie demanded.

"I've been living with you for nearly two weeks and I haven't smelled paint on you or turpentine. I haven't seen paint on your hands. And I've explored most of the inn and seen no canvases, no easels, no hint of creativity."

Shutters dropped over her eyes, blunting the color. "It's a long story and you're going to be late."

Sutton looked at his watch and grimaced. She was right—if he didn't hustle, he'd be walking in when everyone was seated. He wanted to observe the Ryder-Whites, not bring attention himself.

He played with his yet-to-be-tied bow tie, a little discombobulated by the thought of seeing his blood relatives for the first time ever. Up to this point, the thought of meeting them had been an intellectual exercise, but now it was about to become reality. Would he look like them, talk like them? Would they see the connection? Would he be just another face in the crowd? Probably.

Sutton squared his shoulders, straightened his spine. He was making too big a deal of this. The Ryder-Whites were not his family...

He'd lost half of his family five years ago and they could never be replaced.

"You've turned pale," Lowrie said, putting her hand on his arm. "Are you feeling okay?"

No, unfortunately he felt just the smallest bit sick. But, because he was not someone to show weakness, he pulled up a nothing-to-see-here smile. "Sure, why?"

"Liar," Lowrie told him. She raised her glass, sipped and handed it to him. "I'll make you a deal, Marchant."

"And what might that be?"

"You tell me why you're here in the States, the real reason, and I'll tell you why I don't paint anymore."

It was tempting. He wanted to dig and delve beneath her fake-cool surface but he didn't know if he was ready to tell her, or anyone else, about his birth family and Benjamin's ridiculously enormous bequest. He considered her suggestion. "I'll tell you what I can," he said as a compromise.

Lowrie tipped her head to the side and smiled but didn't say anything.

"No deal?" he asked, disappointed.

"Actually, you gave me more than I expected. You aren't what anyone would call a chatty guy."

He gripped her biceps and stepped closer to her, dropping his head so that his temple rested against the side of her head. "I'm not. But I can ask for what I want."

She angled her head so that her lips were a fraction from his mouth. "And what might that be, Sutton?"

"While I'm gone, will you think about sharing my bed? I can't promise you anything, I don't do relationships, but I promise to make it good for you."

Her lips drifted across his before she pulled away. "I'll think about it," she murmured.

"Fair enough," Sutton replied, kissing her head before stepping back. "I must go. Aré you good?"

She raised her glass. "I have wine and I'll order room service when you leave. Then I'm going to hop in that hot tub outside."

"So you brought your bathing suit? I meant to remind you."

The corners of Lowrie's mouth kicked up. "I didn't, actually, but that's not a problem since, despite being on the balcony, the hot tub is quite private."

He closed his eyes at the image of her long, slim and very naked body sliding into the hot bubbles. He started to grow hard and he groaned. "Thanks for that image," he grumbled. "You just shot my concentration to hell, Lowrie."

Lowrie laughed. "It's a ball, Sutton, why on earth do you need to concentrate? Drink some fancy whiskey, eat the amazing food, dance with a pretty girl."

She tugged at one end of his tie, which was lying flat against his chest. "Don't forget about this," she told him.

He couldn't resist brushing his lips against hers. "I wish you were coming with me." He really did—this would be so much easier with her hand in his, her steady gaze grounding him, having someone in his corner.

For a man who was ruthlessly independent, those thoughts scared the crap out of him. So he walked away and did what he always did—thought about something else.

Unfortunately that something else was a naked Lowrie in the hot tub and that made for an extremely uncomfortable trip down to the ballroom.

Six

Sutton watched as Kinga Ryder-White approached their table, the fabric of her red ball gown swishing around her ankles. The brown-eyed blonde—would she be his first or second cousin?—radiated happiness and Sutton knew it had something to do with Griff O'Hare. He had excellent observational skills, but one would have to be clueless not to notice that Kinga and Griff only had eyes for each other.

Isabel would be heartbroken.

Sutton and Garrett Kaye stood up as Kinga approached them and she smiled, before plopping down in the chair his other cousin, Tinsley, had vacated at least an hour before. Neither Tinsley nor Cody Gallant had returned to the ball and Sutton doubted they'd be seeing them again that night. Electricity had arced between them all night, as it had with Garrett Kaye and Kinga's friend, Jules Carson.

Sutton had spent the evening dodging lightning bolts between the potential couples and it was a bloody miracle he'd yet to be electrocuted.

Garrett introduced Kinga to Sutton and when they were all seated again, Kinga rested her chin in the palm of her hand. "Are you guys having fun?" she asked.

"Surprisingly, yes," Garrett said.

Instead of being offended by his blunt reply, Kinga just laughed. "And you, Sutton?"

He said he was and it wasn't a complete lie. He had enjoyed his evening, more than he'd expected to.

"We seated you at this table partly because this is the singles table but mostly because Tinsley and I are huge fans of your work," Kinga told him, smiling.

Sutton thanked her, thinking that he'd enjoyed the company at the table. He'd met Garrett Kaye years ago through Sam—Kaye Capital and MarchBent had done business together— so seeing him sitting at the table was a pleasant surprise.

He instinctively liked Cody Gallant, the owner of an international events company. Jules Carson, a semifamous mixologist, was both lovely and funny, and he'd found Tinsley quietly charming.

Kinga radiated soul-deep happiness. Good for her.

Kinga ordered a glass of champagne from a passing waiter and looked toward the empty stage. She glanced at the diamond bracelet watch on her left wrist and released a quiet sigh.

"Long night?" Sutton asked her.

She smiled and he saw the exhaustion in her eyes. "Honestly, it's been a long year. I can't wait until this evening is over and I can sleep for a week."

Sutton looked around the exquisitely decorated ballroom, recognizing a German princess and a European industrialist. A Danish politician was talking to an Arab sheikh and two A-list celebrities—not married to each other—were making out on the dance floor. The ball had most definitely lived up to its hype and Sutton was impressed. "You and your sister did an impressive job, Kinga."

Kinga's smile was tired but appreciative. "Thank you. Oh, God…"

Garrett raised his eyebrows. "Problem?"

She shook her head. "My grandfather is bearing down on us, with an I-need-to-talk-to-you look on his face." Trepidation shimmered in her eyes and Sutton felt his protective instincts rise.

Callum Ryder-White—tall, stooped and flint-eyed— approached them, his son James two steps behind him. Sutton noticed the long look James exchanged with his daughter, and had he not been looking so closely, would've missed the small shake of James's head.

Right, things were about to get interesting, Sutton thought, climbing to his feet again.

Kinga introduced him to Callum and James, while Garrett stood back, his expression sardonic. It seemed Sutton wasn't the only one who had issues with the Ryder-White men.

"Welcome to my ball, gentlemen," Callum said in his raspy voice.

His ball? From what he'd gathered, Callum's grand-daughters had worked their tails off to create the event and his daughter-in-law was the powerhouse behind the Ryder Foundation. The old man had no problem claiming credit he wasn't due.

"And what's your line of work?" Callum asked Sutton, his tone just the wrong side of bored.

If he wanted to impress him, Sutton could disclose

he held a minor royal title, was the co-owner of a property that had been in his family for over four hundred years, had a degree from Oxford and was the founder of an exceptionally lucrative and very respected investment firm.

But because he was contrary, and instinctively didn't like this man—his uncle—he slowly smiled. "Oh, I write blood books."

Callum's already frosty eyes narrowed. "Blood books?"

"Sutton is an international bestselling author of crime novels, Callum," James informed him, smoothing over the awkward moment. Sutton suspected he did a lot of that.

"So you just play with words?"

Play? He wished. Sutton shrugged, not bothering to explain the long hours, frustration and sheer bloody hard work entertaining readers entailed.

Callum harrumphed—huh, Sutton had never actually heard someone do that before—and turned away to look at Garrett Kaye. Sutton saw the amusement in Kinga's eyes and winked. She coughed to cover her giggle.

"Mr. Kaye, I hear that you have an exceptional hacker on your staff."

Beside him, every inch of Garrett's massive frame tensed. "You heard wrong, Mr. Ryder-White."

Callum frowned at him. "But Emma said—"

"My mother misunderstood, sir."

Garrett's voice suggested that Callum not argue, and Callum, obviously not used to being shut down, lifted his nose in the air and stalked off. They watched him go and when he was out of earshot, Garrett looked at James. "I would suggest that you inform your father that openly seeking a hacker might make certain regulatory bodies, like the goddamn police, start looking his way."

James briefly closed his eyes and shook his head. "I swear he's losing it. And what the hell is Emma thinking, passing along that sort of information?"

Kinga nudged Sutton's arm with her elbow. "Garrett's mother is Callum's longtime personal assistant."

Right, that explained why Callum felt comfortable asking Garrett about a hacker. Obviously, he just thought Sutton was an idiot and beneath his notice.

Garrett asked the burning question Sutton himself had been dying to know. "What does Callum need a hacker for?"

James and Kinga exchanged a long look before James shrugged. "It's public knowledge that a quarter of Ryder International's shares, shares that were originally owned by his younger brother Benjamin, are held by an outside party—"

Do not react, dammit, and do not *draw attention to yourself.*

"Callum has been obsessed by those shares for decades and he wants to own them, to keep the bulk of RI stock under family control."

"And by family, my dad means under Callum's control," Kinga muttered.

Wow. Callum Ryder-White wasn't a popular guy. Sutton couldn't understand why, since the man had *such* a sparkly personality.

"So find the owner and make him an offer," Sutton suggested, deliberately sounding obtuse.

James, to his credit, just smiled at his exceptionally naive statement. "His identity has been hidden from us in a trust and we can't access it. I presume that's why

Callum is talking about hacking." James ran his hand around the back of his neck, obviously agitated.

"Well, I suggest you talk him out of it, James." Garrett said, his voice hard. "Prison orange is not his color."

James nodded and turned away, taking Kinga with him. Garrett rubbed his hand over his lower jaw and watched them go. "I need a whiskey," he told Sutton. "You coming?"

"Yeah." Not because he needed a drink but because he needed to know whatever Garrett Kaye knew about the Ryder-Whites. Sutton knew that if Old Man Ryder-White was so desperate to hire a hacker to find out who owned his shares—Benjamin's shares—Sutton was running out of time. If Callum got hold of his name and launched some sort of court application to have Ben's will declared invalid, Sutton could be tied up in legal problems for years, possibly a decade or more. It didn't matter whether the case was legitimate or not—sometimes just having pots of money was enough. If the lawyers found a cash cow, they'd keep finding reasons to milk it.

Sutton had seen enough to know how long it took legal challenges, especially ones of an international nature, to make their way through the courts. If he didn't get Ben's money soon and sell the shares, his parents' charities would not see any money for a long, long time.

Not happening. Not on his watch.

Lowrie looked at her watch—it was past eleven. Sutton had been at the ball for three hours, which meant he would be back soon. That meant she had to decide whether to sleep with the man or not.

She wanted to—he was a great-looking guy, fit and sexy. He kissed like a dream and if he brought the same skills to the bedroom, he'd more than exceed his promise to make it good for her.

She had no fears about whether she'd have a fun time, but she did worry about the potential emotional fallout.

She was going to be all but living with the guy for the next six or so weeks, and if he got bored of her, or bored of sleeping with her, how would they be able to face each other across the breakfast table? How would she be able to treat him like another guest?

But how could she pass up this opportunity to be the spontaneous person she missed being? While she hadn't slept around, she'd dated extensively, got a little hot and heavy with a few guys. Did she want to sleep with Sutton because he made her feel more open, less anxious and way more adventurous than she normally was?

When she was with him, she was reminded of the woman she used to be. She missed that version of herself.

You're overthinking this, Lewis.

Sex with Sutton would be a step out of time, an escape from her day-to-day routine. And sure, knowing that Sutton wanted her was a balm to her shaky self-confidence, reminding her that she was a woman and not just Rhan's mom and Paddy's innkeeper. Just hearing his request had lit a small fire in her stomach, telling her she was desirable and attractive.

Hooking up with Sutton would be a lovely, light, superficial connection. All good things…so why was she still hemming and hawing?

Since Rhan's birth and returning to Portland, she hadn't met many men—or any she wanted to date—and she'd been too busy with Rhan and the inn to go out. She could've embraced technology and registered on one of the popular dating apps, but she didn't have the time or energy to wade through the stalkers and the weirdos to find a connection with someone decent.

And, yes, maybe she had been hiding out, because it was too painful and risky to emotionally connect. She couldn't handle it—after being rejected by her mom, her fiancé and Rex—to love and be left again.

With Sutton, she knew he wasn't looking for more than a hookup—he'd told her exactly that—so she'd be a fool if she wanted more from him than he could give. But could she remain emotionally distant while handing him her body?

Was she going to regret this in the morning? Would her heart start misbehaving and start thinking of happy-ever-after, tossing out how-can-we-make-this-work? questions?

Lowrie heard the door to the room opening, heard him place the key card and his phone on the hallway table. By the time he appeared in the doorway of the living room, his tie was pulled loose and he'd shed his jacket. His hair was messy from running his hand through it and his mouth was tight with tension.

So the ball hadn't been fun. "Hi," she murmured from her position curled up in the corner of the couch.

Sutton's head spun around in the direction of her voice. "Hey."

In the light of the hallway, he navigated his way over to her and sat on the edge of the couch, his thigh pressing into her hip. "Why are you sitting in the dark?"

"Thinking," Lowrie replied.

"About?" When she didn't answer, he laid a hand on her thigh and squeezed. "Everything okay at home? Is Rhan okay?"

She so appreciated him thinking of her baby boy.

"He's absolutely fine. No, I was thinking about what answer I'd give you when you walked in here."

His hand tightened on her thigh. "No pressure, Low. I hope you know that?"

"I do," Lowrie replied. She lifted her hand and her fingers drifted down his jaw. "Tough evening?"

He half shrugged. "Not as bad as I expected, actually. Food was good, Griff O'Hare, your idol, was fantastic, I met the Ryder-Whites."

"And what do you think about Portland's first family?" Lowrie asked.

He tipped his head back, thinking. "Callum is a prick. James is, I think, a nice guy and the family peacemaker. I didn't meet his wife, Penelope. The princesses weren't half as snotty as I expected them to be," Sutton replied, his hand stroking her thigh from hip to knee. "I sat with Tinsley Ryder-White and Cody Gallant, Garrett Kaye and Jules Carson—she's a mixologist."

Lowrie nodded. "I follow her on Instagram. She's very beautiful."

"Yet my mind was full of the woman I left upstairs, and I kept looking at my watch, wishing I could leave and come back up here to be with her," Sutton said, his deep voice lower than usual. He dragged the tip of his index finger between the lapels of her oversize robe. "I'd hoped to catch you in the hot tub."

"Would you have joined me?" Lowrie asked him, her tone flirty.

"If you asked me to," Sutton replied.

This was it…do or die. Ask or don't. *Step forward or step back, Lewis?* She might regret sleeping with him in the morning, but there was a damn good chance that she'd regret *not* sleeping with him more.

One night, just one night of being loved by him. Then

they'd go back to normal. She suspected—*knew*—she wouldn't, but she was more than happy to ignore that insistent voice.

"A fun night? No strings?" She'd forced the words up her tight throat, over her lips.

Sutton's light eyes darkened with lust. "Yeah."

Lowrie scooted past him and stood up. Looking down at him, she undid the sash and allowed the sides of her robe to fall open, giving him a hint of her shadowed curves and dips. His eyes wandered down her body, a slight smile hitting his lips when he noticed the small tattoo on her ankle.

He surprised her by bending down to lift her foot onto his knee. Embarrassed at what he could see—pretty much everything—she gathered the lapels together and ignored his quirking lips. But instead of speaking, he ran a finger over her brightly colored tattoo.

"Why a sunflower?" he asked.

"It's a happy flower, always looking for the sun," Lowrie replied.

"Got any others?" Sutton asked, his hand running up the back of her calf.

"Underneath my right breast, on my hip."

"Can I see them?" Sutton asked, lowering her foot to the floor.

He was looking at her like she was Édouard Manet's *Olympia*, Gustav Klimt's Adele Bloch, Andy Warhol's blue Marilyn Monroe. She was the *Mona Lisa*, Venus, every stunning woman painted in oils or watercolors on canvas or vellum. Desired, made to feel beautiful.

The admiration in his eyes gave her the courage to push the robe off her shoulders so that it hung behind her back and off her arms, exposing her to his gaze. She turned slightly, allowing him to see a delicate rose on her ribs, mimicking the curve of her right breast. She then pulled the robe aside to show him the teeny-tiny bee on her left hip.

"For me, the more inconspicuous the tattoo is, the sexier it is. It's like I've been allowed in on a very private secret," Sutton told her, his hands coming to rest on her bare hips. He pulled her toward him and laid his lips on her skin, just above her belly button.

"Got any of your own you want to share?" Lowrie asked, pushing her hand into his soft hair.

Sutton looked up at her and grimaced. "I'd love to get a couple but I'm dead scared of needles."

Lowrie laughed. "It's not that painful."

"That's what everyone says, but the one time I made it to the tattoo artist's chair, I nearly punched him when he lifted the gun," Sutton confessed, moving his lips to kiss her little bee. "So sexy."

Lowrie looked down at his bent head, not quite able to believe that she was standing in front of him, all but naked. In fact, there was no point to the robe anymore, so she allowed it to drop to the floor. She fought the urge to cover her breasts, her groin, feeling vulnerable while he was still dressed.

Sutton stood up, clasped her face in his hands and brushed his lips across her mouth in a kiss that was as tender as it was sweet. "I'm a wordsmith but I can't tell you how much I want you, Low, how much I need you."

She held his wrists, sighing as his tongue slid inside her mouth. Ribbons of pure pleasure, hot and sweet, ran down her spine, into her nerves, across her body. Needing to touch him, to feel that glorious skin under the palm of her hands, she tugged his shirt from the waistband of his pants and slid her hands under the hem to touch his hard stomach, to dance her fingers against his ribs.

Growling with frustration, Sutton stepped back and grabbed the back of his shirt by its collar and pulled it over his head, then tossed it away. He toed off his shoes, bent down to pull off his socks and, not giving her a word of warning, swept her up and held her against his chest.

"Bedroom?" she asked breathlessly.

"Eventually," Sutton replied. "We're taking a detour first."

Sutton, still holding her, stepped into the hot tub in his suit pants and gently lowered her into the water, the bubbles popping around her. Sitting on the step, he turned her to face him, pulling her knees so that they rested on either side of his hips.

He wanted to remove his pants—of course, he did—but for the first time since his teens, he didn't know if he could stop himself from plunging inside her, losing control.

Lifting wet hands, he smoothed her hair back from her face, taking in her fine features, her flushed-with-anticipation skin, her take-me-now eyes.

"You are so very lovely, Lowrie," Sutton told her, tracing her feminine shoulder with his big hand.

She dropped her head to place an openmouthed kiss on his shoulder. "You're not too bad yourself, Sutton," Lowrie told him, her hand trailing down his stomach to find the snap of his pants. After fumbling briefly, she unhooked the tab, eased down the zipper and burrowed her hand under his briefs to find him, hot and heavy and needing her touch. She wrapped her fingers around his erection and smiled. "And so, I have to say, is this."

Unable to speak with her hand on him, Sutton ducked

his head to close his lips over her nipple, sucking the perfect bud into his mouth. Through the chlorinated water, he could smell the perfume on her skin. Her hand gripped his head, holding him in place as he pleasured her. Needing no barriers between them, he released her and shoved his hands under his briefs, then pushed them and his trousers down his hips, tossing the wet fabric over the side of the hot tub. Water sloshed onto the floor but he didn't care.

Sutton pulled her into him, and her core hit his, hot and wet and indescribably wonderful. She wrapped her arms around his neck, took his mouth in a hot, open-mouthed kiss and rubbed herself on him, using his shaft to pleasure herself. While he had no problem with being used like this, he had a better way to bring her to orgasm.

Using his bulk and strength, he gripped her hips and easily lifted her so that she sat on the edge of the tub, her damp hair streaming down her chest, over her breasts. She shivered.

"Too cold?" he asked, watching goose bumps pebble her skin.

"I'm sure you have an idea of how to warm me up," Lowrie said, looking down at him.

"I do, indeed." He picked up her hands, told her to grip the edge of the tub and then slowly spread her knees. He looked down at her thin strip of hair, her plump feminine lips, and sighed. So pretty.

He dragged his finger down that narrow strip, watching her eyes deepen with intense pleasure as he slipped his finger between her folds and found her button. She released a tiny scream and she tipped back her head, panting softly.

Her skin was flushed, her breaths were irregular, and despite not spending a lot of time pleasuring her, he knew she was close to coming.

He'd use his mouth later, he thought. This first time he wanted to watch as her orgasm hit her, wanted to see the pleasure he gave her.

He reached up with one hand to play with her nipples then slid two fingers into her channel and placed his thumb on her clit. Lowric screamed again and ground down on his fingers, looking fierce and wild and wonderful.

He was throbbing, his cock aching, but he'd wait, he needed to wait. This was too lovely to miss.

Lowrie put her arms behind her head, her spine arching, lifting her breasts. She held herself there, lovely and luscious while his fingers worked her. His thumb brushed her clitoris again and he felt her shudder, her channel throbbing against his fingers as the waves of her intense orgasm crashed over her.

She sobbed, covered her eyes, bore down again and he felt her come again, not as strong this time but good enough to make her gasp.

She was the most beautiful thing he'd ever laid eyes on. And the memory of her losing control, the lights of the city blazing behind her, would always be etched into his memory.

Sutton pulled his hand away and reached up to pull her back into the water. She sighed when her body hit the heat, her eyes closed as she buried her face in his neck. "Wow."

"Good?" Sutton asked, incredibly pleased by her one-word statement.

"No…amazing," Lowrie said, leaning back and wrapping her long legs around his hips. "But I think you should take me to bed, Sutt. And if you don't have condoms, I might scream."

He brushed strands of damp hair off her face. "I have condoms. And you very definitely are going to scream."

Seven

In Lenox Hill, Lowrie placed her hand on Sutton's arm, tugging him to a stop on the sidewalk. Standing at the bottom of a set of concrete steps leading up to an ornate black door, she took in the discreet sign. What was she doing here? Why was she returning to the one place she said she never would?

Because, lying in Sutton's arms last night, after two bouts of truly exceptional lovemaking—Sutton had exceeded his promise to make it good for her—she'd thought about being back in New York City and how that made her feel. Honestly, not as bad as she'd expected.

She'd always believed that returning to the city would make her anxious, but she'd yet to feel that way. Maybe it was the fact that she was older, a little wiser and had different priorities now, but the thought of being back in the city she'd once called home didn't send her spiraling.

And while she was feeling strong, maybe it was time to exorcise a couple of ghosts.

The sign was new: Lily Lewis Gallery. Opening hours 10:00 a.m to 6:00 p.m. She checked her watch and saw that it was five minutes after ten. She and Sutton could be in and out in thirty minutes, and her mother, who never graced the gallery before noon, would never know she was here.

She didn't know if she'd ever paint again, but in this building were ghosts she needed to put to rest.

Biting her bottom lip, Lowrie walked up the steps, yanked open the door and stepped into the vestibule of the gallery. Taking a deep breath, she pushed through the next door and stepped into the double volume room, the low heels of her boots tapping against the laminated wood floors.

She felt Sutton's bulk behind her and appreciated his hand on her lower back, grounding her. A terribly thin, terribly haughty woman walked over to them, dressed in black, her long hair pulled into a bun. Her mother wore brightly colored couture, but her assistants, she decreed, were to wear black.

"Can I help you?" the woman asked, looking down her rather long nose at Lowrie.

Lowrie smiled, wondering how she'd react if she told the woman that she was Lily's daughter and the artist who'd catapulted this gallery into being one of the city's best.

"We'd just like to look around," Lowrie told her.

The assistant turned to Sutton, that red mouth curling into a come-to-me-baby smile. "Let me know if I can help you with anything."

Lowrie was very sure that she would've gotten the cold shoulder if she'd wandered in here on her own.

After shrugging out of their coats, they draped them over their arms and Lowrie led them into the main viewing space, the center of which was dominated by a series of abstract sculptures. She recognized the work immediately. The figures were her father's and they were stunning.

Sutton looked at the plaque with the artist's details and sent Lowrie a look. "Your dad is incredibly talented."

She couldn't argue with that statement, he really was. "My mom is also an artist—no doubt we'll come across a few of her paintings—and she also owns this gallery."

"I gathered that." Sutton captured her hand in his and raised her knuckles to his mouth. "You're looking a little pale. Are you okay?"

Lowrie shrugged. "Trying not to let memories and ghosts swamp me."

Sutton wrapped his arm around her waist and pulled her into his side. She leaned into his strength, his solidity. "Must've been hard trying to live up to two successful artists in the family."

She released a low, bitter laugh. "Trust me, it was harder to outstrip them in talent and selling power."

She felt Sutton tense, heard his sharp intake of breath. She lifted her head to look at him, her chin lifting at the shock in his eyes. "My grandmother mentioned my talents but I'm pretty sure you thought she was exaggerating, as any doting grandmother would."

"For about seven years, between the ages of sixteen and twenty-three, I was an art sensation," she explained. "Hard to believe, right?"

Sutton rubbed his hand over his lower jaw, scratchy

with stubble. She knew it was scratchy because he'd rubbed it against various parts of her body earlier, and in the most delightful way.

"Not really. I know I've only seen one painting of yours, but it's amazing."

"I did that when I was fourteen and gave it to my uncle Carlo for Christmas."

Sutton's eyes widened. "Fourteen? You painted that at fourteen?"

"I was precocious," Lowrie told him. "I thought I was so sophisticated, painting him a naked lady for his bedroom. I wanted to shock the establishment and I thought it was sexy, which it isn't. Anyway, I was mortified when Jojo pulled me aside and ever so gently told me he was gay."

Sutton's lips twitched with amusement. "It's still an incredible painting, but I don't understand why you don't paint anymore."

"That's a long story and not one I want to get into right now," Lowrie told him, sliding her hand into his and leading him deeper into the gallery. "Let's look at art."

She was grateful that he didn't push her for information, or demand to know why they were here and why she'd turned her back on the art world. Lowrie stopped in front of a mammoth oil, ten feet high and at least fourteen wide, surprised at the relatively realistic view of the New York skyline from the Brooklyn Bridge. The painting leaned into being an abstract but the view was instantly recognizable and the colors equally realistic. It was safe and, dare she say, boring.

Sutton cocked his head to the side. "Do you like it?" he asked.

She wrinkled her nose and pulled a face when she saw the price tag. "At fifty thousand I should, but I don't."

"The artist is going to be an incredibly big name in the art world in a couple of years and it's a solid investment."

The raspy words had Lowrie spinning around. In the doorway to the space marked Staff Only, she saw her mother, dressed in a tangerine-colored suit and skyscraper heels, blond hair immaculately coiffed. She didn't look a day older than she'd looked the last time she'd seen her, six years ago in this very space.

"Lowrie?"

Lowrie stepped closer to Sutton, and reached for him, feeling calmer when his big hand encircled hers. "Hello, Mom."

"What the hell are you doing here?"

Such a gracious welcome!

Lowrie shrugged. "This is Sutton Marchant. Sutton, my mom, Lily Lewis."

Thankfully Sutton didn't release her hand to shake Lily's. Lily barely acknowledged Sutton's existence. "Unless you have at least twenty works ready for exhibition, you're not welcome here, Lowrie."

"I told you that I'd never exhibit again, Mother." Lowrie's voice, to her horror, was thin and insubstantial.

"Then we have nothing to say to each other," Lily told her, her eyes granite-hard.

"Oh, I can think of a few topics of discussion. You could ask about your grandson, your mom, your sister," Lowrie stated, gripping Sutton's hand, hanging on.

"They chose their side."

"Rhan is a year old, Mom, he doesn't take *sides*," Lowrie said, furious at the burning sensation in her eyes. She blinked it away and sucked in a hard breath. "How's Dad?"

Lily gestured to the sculptures behind them. "Working, busy, creative, productive."

Unlike you...

Lowrie heard the unspoken words. *Yeah, got it, Mom, I'm not forgiven. Never will be.*

Lowrie turned her back on her mom and looked at Sutton, whose eyes were flashing with annoyance. The man was pissed, but Lowrie knew his anger wasn't directed at her. He opened his mouth to speak but Lowrie squeezed his hand, begging him not to rush to her defense. Apart from the fact that she didn't need him to fight her battles, her mom was never going to change. There was no point in wasting his words or his energy.

The fact that he wanted to protect her was enough.

God, it felt amazing to have someone standing in her corner. "Let's go, Sutt."

Sutton stroked his thumb across her knuckles. "In a moment," he said. He turned to look at another, quite small painting on the wall at right angles to where they stood. "Is that a Cordyn?" he casually asked Lily.

Her mom straightened. "It is. Do you know his work?"

"I have a couple of his pieces hanging in my home in Knightsbridge."

Knightsbridge, one of the most expensive suburbs in the world. It wasn't like Sutton to name-drop so what was he doing?

"You own a Cordyn?" Lily asked, sounding doubtful.

"I do. I own *Darkness Approaches* and *Darkness Within My Soul.*" Sutton pulled his hand from hers and walked to the painting to look at its inscription. "This is *Darkness Before the Dawn*, the third in the series."

Lily's eyes sparked with greed and her lips curled into her salesperson smile. "It was the last painting he did before he died. I acquired it from his wife a few weeks after his funeral." Lily stepped up to join Sutton in front of the painting, Lowrie forgotten. She folded her arms and glared at their backs and reminded herself to be an adult. Sutton was allowed to buy a painting from her mother...

"It's for sale for two hundred thousand dollars," Lily told him. "But since you're a friend of Lowrie's, I'll give you a two-and-a-half-percent discount on that price."

"Don't involve me in your horse-trading," Lowrie muttered.

Sutton looked over Lily's head to wink at her. "That's a kind offer, but...no. I'd rather not purchase from you."

Lowrie couldn't help her wide grin.

"But, but..." Lily spluttered. She waved at the painting. "It's the final in the set! You might never get a chance to buy it again!"

Sutton shrugged. "Then I don't get the chance to buy it again. It's a painting, not a lifesaving kidney." He held out his hand to Lowrie. "Shall we go? I think there's a little boy back in Portland who's missing his mama."

Lowrie placed one hand on her heart, the other in his hand, and sighed. He'd stood up to her mother, walked away from a painting he liked...for *her*. She had to be careful or else she could fall for this man, fall hard.

She just hoped she could stop her heart from doing something that would hurt like hell later.

Sutton led her across the gallery floor toward the front door, pulled it open and gestured for her to precede him. On the steps, in the frigid New York air, they pulled on their coats and wrapped scarves around their throats.

"'Do you really have the other two paintings by Cordyn?" she asked as they hit the pavement.

Sutton nodded to the coffee shop across the street. "Do we have time for coffee or are you desperate to get back to Portland and Rhan?"

She wanted to be with Rhan, that was natural. But she also, selfishly, wanted a little more one-on-one time with Sutton. Surely she could take another couple of hours before rushing back? "Coffee sounds great."

"Well?" she asked after Sutton ordered and they were seated at a small table. "The paintings?"

"I do own them."

Lowrie lifted her hand to her mouth in shock. "I thought you were bluffing!"

He shook his head. "Nope. They hang on my bedroom wall and you can see the progression of light in the paintings. The third would complete the story."

Lowrie reached across the table to grip his hand. "Go and buy it if you want to, Sutt. Please. Don't miss out on the opportunity to own the third painting because of me."

Sutton shook his head, looking obstinate. "As I said, it's just a painting, Lowrie. And I refuse to pad the pockets of a woman who treats her daughter like crap."

So sweet but horribly misguided. "They were just words, Sutton. I've heard worse from her over the years."

His expression darkened. Right, he definitely wasn't going to buy the Cordyn now. Dammit. She hated the idea that he'd lost out on something he'd been looking for because of her.

"Why?"

Lowrie raised her eyebrows. "Why what?"

"Why does she treat you like shit?" Sutton demanded, impatient.

"Ah…that." Lowrie wrinkled her nose and tapped her index finger on the glass table. She looked down, saw that her legs were intertwined with Sutton's beneath the table and liked seeing them like that. It felt…right.

Don't go there, Lowrie.

"Talk to me, Low."

"I don't know how to explain without sounding like I'm blowing my own trumpet," Lowrie said, her voice hesitant.

"Blow away," Sutton said, leaning back so the waitress could place his coffee in front of him. Lowrie smiled her thanks and picked up her teaspoon, dunking it in the frothy milk.

"My parents are good artists, very good, but I am… better." She saw his skeptical expression and rubbed the back of her neck. "Honestly? I was very talented."

"One of the best artists of your generation…" Sutton murmured, repeating Jojo's words.

"So it was said. My dad encouraged me, but the older I got, the less my mom could handle it. I was offered my first exhibition when I was fourteen by a small gallery in SoHo and I sold out. I raked in a ton of money that night. And that's why my mom opened her gallery… That way, she could not only control the sale of my work but she could earn off it as well."

Sutton locked his eyes on hers, his attention completely focused on her.

"In public, she talked me up, but in private she mocked my work, told me I was riding on her and my father's coattails, that it was derivative and that it helped, immeasurably, that I was pretty."

"And your dad?"

"He's a quiet guy, soft, you know? He hated us arguing so he retreated to his studio and left us to fight. Then he moved out to an artist's colony in Arizona and I haven't seen much of him since my late teens."

Anger flickered in his eyes, but he didn't speak and for that Lowrie was grateful.

"I had another show at seventeen, but I started garnering real attention when I exhibited at my mom's gallery in Chelsea shortly after my eighteenth birthday. I had a show every six months for the next six years, and my mom moved her gallery three times on the back of my shows, ending up there." She nodded to the building across the street.

"So she did well off you," Sutton murmured.

"She did *very* well off me and as my star rose, so did hers. She started attracting bigger names. She's now regarded as one of the most powerful gallery owners in the city."

"I still don't understand how you came to give up something you were incredibly good at," Sutton said, wrapping his big hand around his mug of coffee.

"My mother hired a business manager to look after my money and, God, I was earning a ton of it. Together, they controlled pretty much everything I did, what I earned, where I invested the money… I got an allowance."

"You got an allowance?"

She nodded. "Kyle, my business manager, paid all my living expenses, but if I wanted spending money, I had to ask for it." She shrugged, thinking that sometimes it felt like years ago, other days it felt like yesterday. "I was young and I wanted to please them, but I also wanted to paint and not be bothered, so him paying the bills felt right. But they pushed me to paint more and more, to keep the money rolling in, so that's what I did. I worked, all the time."

"That sounds a little like forced labor," Sutton said, anger in his eyes.

"I did, eventually, start to rebel, telling them that I needed to get out, to party, to have a life. So Kyle and my mom concocted a plan to give me what I wanted. Kyle started taking me out, to parties and shows, flirting with me and treating me like a princess.

"I was pretty sheltered and overprotected and I hadn't had a boyfriend so I loved the attention I received from him. He was older and charming and sophisticated, and he made me feel amazing."

Sutton winced. "And after a great night out, he'd push you back into your studio and tell you to paint?"

Basically. She nodded. "I thought I was in love, but every year I became unhappier. Kyle proposed, I accepted and I thought that would make me happy, but it didn't. I'd paint and party with him, with his friends, attending all these celebrity events with artists and creatives and movers and shakers. And I hated every minute. I hated the art I was doing, I thought I was rubbish and I lost control of my stress levels."

"What did you do?" Sutton asked.

"I asked for help, I didn't get it. I told them I wanted to change direction, they talked me out of it. I couldn't sleep, barely ate, and I would randomly start crying while I was working. I was constantly terrified of letting them down or having them not love me if I didn't give them what they wanted. Their opinions meant everything. Because they kept telling me that they didn't understand the hype around me, that I was a fad that would fade away, that I needed to milk my fame while

I remained in the public eye, I kept working at a fre-
netic pace."

She released a long breath before continuing. "But
the quality of my work dropped and my heart wasn't
in what I was painting. At times I felt I was going in-
sane, my mind raced constantly and I kept imagining
running away." She'd never told anyone, not even Rex,
this much about her past... God, did her son's father
even know that she was once a semifamous painter?
She didn't think their conversations had ever gone that
deep. And how sad was that?

"So what was the final straw, Lowrie?" Sutton asked,
leaning forward.

"It was the opening night of my newest show, in that
very room we were just in. I arrived late and Kyle crit-
icized my outfit in front of a bunch of art critics, and
my mom agreed with him. I felt something crack inside me and I went to the bar and tossed back a tequila
shot. Then another."

Sutton winced and she nodded. "Yeah, not clever. I
wasn't drunk, but I did become uninhibited."

"What did you do?"

"I went up to a couple of art critics, listened to them
dissing my work and I agreed with them. I told them
that it was derivative and silly and that I was just churning out my greatest hits. Basically, I shot myself in my
own foot."

Sutton winced.

"I walked away from them, went into the ladies'
room and had a panic attack. Kyle and my mother found
me and I begged them for help, begged them to take
me to a doctor, but they just shouted at me and left me
there, feeling like I was going to die. One of my mother's assistants called an ambulance and I was taken to

the hospital. They diagnosed a panic attack, gave me a sedative and I spent the night in the hospital. The next morning they insisted I call a family member so I called Jojo and she came down, picked me up and took me back to Portland."

Sutton stroked the inside of her wrist. "Get it all out, Lowrie."

"Jojo moved me into her house, and I started therapy. Lily and Kyle wanted me to return to Manhattan, but I refused and Jojo told them to leave me alone. Kyle told me I was being childish and irrational and called off our engagement. My mother told me I was spoiled and selfish and was behaving like a brat. I was numb for a couple of months, and because nobody told me to paint, I didn't. And when I finally felt the urge to, I picked up a paintbrush and the anxiety hit me again. I couldn't breathe, my heart felt like it was about to burst out of my chest, so I walked away. Jojo suggested that I go traveling, that I be a kid for a while and I did. I was in Thailand and I emailed Kyle, asking him to transfer funds from my investment account and he refused."

Sutton tensed. "What? Why?"

"He said that I had no funds available, that he'd paid himself and my mother what they were due and used the rest to break the lease on my studio and pay off my debts. I wasn't aware I had any debts."

Sutton lowered his mug, his expression reflecting his shock. "You've got to be kidding me!"

She wished she was. "They took their cuts before I saw any money and I thought I had a million invested, but there was nothing. I sued them and it's still working its way through the court system, with delays and arguments and with the lawyers just getting richer."

Sutton lowered his cup to place it on the table. "I

have no idea what to say," he said, shaking his head. "Except that I'm sorry you went through that. That you're still going through that."

"I don't care about the money, to be honest. I've been thinking about calling a halt to the legal proceedings for a while now."

"Why haven't you? Your legal fees must be killing you."

"I can't afford lawyers and I'm not paying the legal bills, Jojo is. She's very wealthy in her own right and refuses to let it drop. She is still furious at my mother for not getting me help, for not seeing that I was burned out, for pushing me so hard. She says it's unconscionable that they took every cent I earned."

"It is," Sutton insisted. "It's your creativity, your talent, and they already took their percentage. It's theft, Lowrie."

Lowrie shrugged. "I gave him power of attorney. I gave him the right to access my funds."

"That doesn't make his actions acceptable and the fact that your mother was party to it astounds me."

"Yeah, well, Jojo is quite sure Lily was swapped at birth," Lowrie quipped. She waved her hand in the air. "Well, that's my why-I-don't-paint-anymore story."

Sutton leaned back in his chair and folded his arms, frowning. "Did you love it?"

She shook her head. "No, I didn't. I adored it. I lived for it. It was my way of making sense of the world."

He didn't speak for a minute, maybe more. "No, you couldn't have loved it that much," he told her, his tone nonconfrontational.

"Before Rhan came along, art was all I cared about!"

"Then why did you give it up? Why, when the panic attacks eased, did you never pick up a palette, a brush, prep a canvas? Was it because you still had their voices in your head, because you still believed that you are second-rate, that you didn't deserve the fame and success you did? You're still marching to the beat of their drum."

"I am not!" Lowrie protested. How dare he say such a thing?

"Yes, you are, or else you would never have let them take away something so important to you."

"I didn't have the money to buy paints or supplies," Lowrie protested, feeling hot and cold.

Sutton's amiable expression didn't change. "Are you seriously telling me that at no point in the past six years you could spare some cash to buy paints, a canvas, a brush? Watercolors? Colored pencils? Charcoal?"

Lowrie glared at him and slouched in her chair, her temper bubbling. "I—I—" Dammit, he was right. And even if she didn't have cash, Jojo would've bought her everything she needed had she said the word. In fact, she did. She recalled Jojo buying canvases, paint and brushes years back and Lowrie had refused to use them. Were they still in the storeroom, where she'd stashed them five years ago? Probably.

"I'm not saying you should produce art to sell, to become the superstar you obviously once were, but don't let them take away your passion, Lowrie."

"I don't know how to paint for fun, Sutton, I never really have." She shrugged. "Maybe when I was a kid. But from my early teens, it was a serious business."

He leaned across the table and literally got in her face. "Then make it unserious, do it for fun, because it makes you feel good. You might not get your money back from them but you can reclaim something you love, something that's yours!"

His words pierced through her defenses, made her take another look at her anti-art stance. She did miss it, but she was scared she'd lost her talent, lost her ability to create. What if she tried to paint something and it was utterly terrible? What then? "I won't be as good as I was before," Lowrie admitted, her voice soft.

She expected Sutton to tell her that she'd be fine, that her talent was just lying dormant, but he didn't. "Of course, you won't be good—you haven't done anything for six years! Whatever you paint or draw will probably be dreadful."

"Well, thank you for that," Lowrie muttered.

"But that's not the point, Low. The point is losing yourself, the point is loving it, the point is finding yourself in the strokes, not how good you are. It's about reclaiming a part of yourself you've denied because your ex-fiancé and mother are awful people." He flashed his megawatt smile. "And have you heard about a concept called practice? I guarantee you'll get better the more you paint."

"And if I get a panic attack, what then?"

"Then you'll get a panic attack and you work through it and deal with it. But I'm willing to bet that the less pressure you put on yourself, the less chance you have of having a panic attack."

He was right, dammit. Her panic attacks were a result of stress and anxiety, and if she went back to art looking to have some fun, with an attitude of kindness toward herself, she probably would be fine.

"Excuse me," Sutton told her, shoving his chair back and heading to where the bathrooms were. She stared as he walked away, annoyed and frustrated with him, but grateful, too. Jojo had tried to talk to her about taking up painting again but she'd shut her down, as she had Paddy. All her attention was dedicated to Rhan, she'd told them. She didn't have time to paint. But she'd left Rhan for nearly a day—something she hadn't done often—and this Manhattan jaunt had shown her that she could leave him for a morning, an afternoon, a couple of hours. She could step away to do things that made her heart sing.

And, God, art did make her heart sing. And dance and twirl.

Maybe, just maybe, she could try again. She wouldn't tell anyone. If she failed, she wouldn't have to give embarrassing explanations. But Sutton was right, she owed it to herself to try.

Because only *she* could reclaim what she'd lost.

Eight

They got back to Portland around two that afternoon and, after parking his luxury SUV in the four-car garage, Lowrie climbed out and immediately dashed down the road to pick up Rhan from Jojo and Isabel.

Smiling at her half walk, half run, Sutton gathered up their bags and took them inside.

He walked into the library and sat on the edge of his desk, taking in the view of the point and the forest, the sea and the sky. He glared at his blank screen, thinking that he needed to do some work, check his emails, call Thea.

Sutton rubbed his hand over his lower jaw, thinking of the last day and a bit, and trying to make sense of it all. He'd thoroughly enjoyed being with Lowrie, much more than he'd expected to. She was one of the few women he knew who didn't rush to fill silences with inane chatter, who was happy to stare out of a window and be with her thoughts. And when they did talk, their conversation was never forced.

He would never have guessed that such a passionate creature existed under that calm facade. She was smoking hot in bed, confident and lusty, and she made his head swim. Sex had been off-the-charts fantastic, the best he'd ever had.

Would he have the honor of sharing her bed again? He didn't know and he couldn't presume. He hoped so, about as much as he wanted to keep breathing. All he could do was ask...

He had known they'd be good in bed—hadn't imagined they'd be fantastic together—but their mental connection *did* surprise him. He'd asked her to tell him about why she didn't paint anymore, but he'd never expected the story he got, was still shocked at how successful she'd been and how her ex and her mother had treated her. He'd been angry—still was—and was astounded by her mother's lack of love, empathy and support.

Jesus, some people were not supposed to procreate. They just weren't good at it, were not able to put their children's needs above their own. Thankfully for Rhan, Lowrie was an excellent parent and he had no doubt Rhan would always come first in her life.

Sutton's adopted mother had been brilliant. In hindsight he could see how involved she'd been in their lives, but what about his birth mother? Had she just been young and dumb? The Tate-Handler Agency only dealt with girls from good families, rich families, so why hadn't she kept him? Was having a baby an embarrassment? What sort of support structure did she have? Was she someone without resources?

There was an envelope in the side pocket of his suitcase—all he needed to do was slit it open, read the letter and find out. But he wasn't ready to do that…not yet.

Maybe not ever.

Sutton stood up and started to pace the L-shaped room, idly looking at the walls covered in old photographs, some of them going back to the early part of the twentieth century.

He remained uninterested in his biological parents, despite meeting members of his birth family last night. Autocratic Callum, easygoing James and Sutton's cousins, Kinga and Tinsley. They seemed nice enough, polite, charming, very glitzy.

But dark waters frequently lurked under placid surfaces.

He'd had a family, a fantastic mother and father, and he'd lost them in an accident. In his teens and twenties, he'd pushed them away, intent to make his own way, laboring under some sort of misguided idea that he wasn't as loved as Thea, that he wasn't really a part of the Marchant family. When they confronted him about his emotional and physical distance, he'd seen the pain on their faces, the sorrow in their eyes.

They weren't at fault—he was, for being so caught up in himself, so damn insecure in his position as their son. But he had been *theirs*, in every way that was important. After his mental and emotional turnabout, he'd tried to be the son they wanted, a son to be proud of, to show them how much he loved them. But he'd only had two years and he hadn't come close to making it up to them.

He didn't have the right to another family, and he wasn't sure he was cut out for one of his own. He worked too hard, wasn't great at communicating or showing love and, frankly, could never be half the dad to his kids his dad had been to him. And if he couldn't give his children what his dad had given him and Thea, what was the point? And, yeah, he really didn't want to have more people in his life he was scared to lose.

Losing his folks nearly killed him; losing a wife and child *would*. He wasn't brave enough, he really wasn't.

So, no. He'd stick to the plan and just do enough to fulfill the terms of the will, to get his hands on Benjamin Ryder-White's cash. He'd attended the ball, but he still needed to stay at the inn for another six weeks.

He didn't need to know who his birth mother was, why she gave him up for adoption or how Benjamin was connected to this house. It wasn't important…was it?

But he was curious.

Hell, that couldn't be helped. He was a writer, after all. But not all questions had to be answered, not all situations had to be controlled.

"Hey," Lowrie said, walking into the study with Rhan on her hip. He gripped a hank of her hair and was chortling, happy to be back in his mom's arms.

Sutton couldn't help smiling at the pretty picture they made. "Hi." He nodded at Rhan. "Everything okay?"

"Absolutely fine," Lowrie replied on a wry smile. "I doubt he even noticed I was gone."

Sutton walked over to them and ran a hand over Rhan's head, returning the baby's one-toothed smile. Then Rhan leaned away from Lowrie and toward Sutton, waving his hands in the air. Sutton raised his eyebrows at Lowrie. She shrugged. "He wants you to take him but don't worry, I'll grab a box of toys and put him on the mat."

"I don't mind," Sutton said, placing his hands under Rhan's arms. Rhan laughed as Sutton swung him up and tucked him under his arm like a football.

"It's obvious that you've had some contact with kids," Lowrie said.

"Thea has twin boys, they are seven now. I babysit when she and Sam want to have a date night or a dirty weekend away. We eat junk food and play *Mortal Kombat* or *Assassin's Creed*."

Lowrie didn't hesitate. "I play *Call of Duty* with Rhan—he's pretty good."

Busted. He grinned at her. "Thea would skin me alive. We play *Minecraft* and Xbox soccer."

"Who wins?"

He pulled a face. "They kick my butt, every time. And no, I don't let them win…where's the fun in that?"

Lowrie looked out at the low-hanging clouds and grimaced. "We're in for snow later. Jojo sent me home with a chicken casserole—is that okay for dinner?"

He lifted his free hand and cupped the side of her face. "Are we back to being guest and innkeeper?"

She raised one shoulder and bit her lip. "I don't know… I've never done this before."

She was looking tense again and he knew, by Rhan's suddenly alert body, that he felt it, too. "I loved being with you, Low, and I'd love to be with you again. But that's totally up to you and always will be. Your choice, sweetheart."

"So no offense if I say no?"

His heart clenched at the thought. Damn, being an adult sucked. "No offense. I might pout, but I'll get over it."

She smiled and placed her hand on his waist, resting her forehead on his chest. "Thanks for taking me with you to New York City."

"Thanks for coming with me," Sutton replied, stroking her slim back. He placed a kiss on her temple. Not knowing whether he would be sleeping alone later, he decided to ask. "So, are you saying no, sweetheart?"

She stood up on her tiptoes and brushed her lips across his. "Because Rhan sleeps in his room next to mine, you'd have to temporarily relocate to my bed. Is that okay with you?"

Relief cascaded through him, hot and sweet. And it was strange, because he'd always shrugged off rejection easily before. "Sure," he told her, keeping his voice even while doing cartwheels inside.

Before he could deepen the kiss, as he wanted to, Lowrie stepped back and nodded at Rhan. "Can you entertain him for ten minutes or so while I make coffee?"

"Sure," Sutton replied. He looked at Rhan and made his eyes go squinty, and the baby laughed. "Want to go and watch *Texas Chainsaw Massacre*, kid?"

"He'd prefer something from this decade, Marchant," Lowrie told him, not batting an eye.

Yep, he thought, eying her very nice butt as she walked away, his girl was quick.

Lowrie, glaring at the canvas she'd prepared earlier, was becoming more and more unhinged. It had taken four weeks and a lot of courage for her to dig her paints out of storage and prepare the canvas. She'd arranged for Rhan to spend the day with Jo and Is. Sutton was in the study, pounding his keyboard. She had lots and lots of uninterrupted time to tiptoe back into painting.

Lowrie squinted at her canvas, scowling. Was that a stick insect or a tree? God, the color was horrendous! She'd mixed ultramarine blue and cadmium orange to make brown but it looked too insipid. And, yes, she was out of practice, but her tree looked like a five-year-old had found a tube of beige lipstick and drawn on a wall.

The blue under it for the sea was too dark and too thick. It looked flat and, worse, uninteresting and amateurish.

Lowrie placed a hand on her stomach and dropped to her haunches, staring at the floor. She'd set up her easel in a corner in front of the window. She'd thought she'd start on something familiar, something she'd painted a hundred times before, thinking that muscle memory would take over and she'd fall back into the zone.

But her zone was a car crash.

Had she lost all her talent? Had she forgotten how to paint, to use color? Years ago, she'd mixed paints by instinct, knowing exactly how many squirts of this added to a squirt of that made a particular shade, but judging by the canvas above her, all that knowledge had fled.

She couldn't paint anymore…and the thought was a one-two mental-and-body blow.

Lowrie plopped onto her butt and placed her elbows on her bended knees, her face in her hands. This was a bad, bad, awful idea and she wished she'd never listened to Sutton. Art was part of her past—being Rhan's mom and The Rossi's innkeeper were where she should be focusing her attention. Painting was part of her "before" life. She now lived in the real world and she didn't have time to fool around mixing paints and producing…crap.

Lowrie heard the bedroom door open, but didn't turn around, not wanting Sutton to see her tearstained face. She was angry at herself, angry at him, angry to have gotten her hopes up only to have them so brutally crushed.

"Well, that's pretty bad," Sutton said.

She turned slowly and looked up at him, furious at the amusement she saw on his face. She leaped to her feet and threw her paintbrush onto the small table she'd set up by the easel. It rolled off the table and splattered brown paint on her floor.

"If you've come up here to mock me then you can just piss off!"

Sutton lifted his hands. "Not mocking you, just stating a fact. It's awful."

"I know!" Lowrie yelled at him. "I've got eyes, don't I?"

Sutton ignored her outburst. "And when I say it's awful, I mean it's awful for you. If anyone else painted it, it would be a perfectly good painting."

"That's not making me feel any better!" Lowrie snapped.

He tucked his hands into the back pockets of his jeans and rocked on his heels. "So what has you so riled up? The fact that you didn't produce an award-winning painting six years after last picking up a paintbrush?"

Yeah, well…exactly! "I didn't expect to be able to paint something good, I just didn't expect it would be so bad. I can't remember how to mix colors the way I used to, my grip on my brush is tight, my perspective is off."

"Yeah, yeah…you're crap," Sutton told her, grinning.

Lowrie punched his biceps. "You are not helping! Go away!"

Sutton wrapped his arms around her waist and rested his chin on her hair. "You're being too hard on yourself, sweetheart. And instead of jumping back into oils, and your type of painting, which requires subtle combinations of color, why don't you ease into it?"

Lowrie scowled. "What, should I get one of those paint-by-number kits?"

Sutton dug the tips of his fingers into her lower back, pushing into tense muscles. "How can you create when you are so damn tense, Low?"

Lowrie released a moan and arched her back, enjoying the way his thumbs pushed into the muscles above her butt.

"And I bet you keep stopping to see if your breathing is shallow, if you feel a little panic."

Yeah, she had being doing that. She had been constantly checking in with her body, testing her lungs, waiting for desperation and stress to flood her system.

"You're being too tough on yourself, Low," Sutton told her, tugging her over to the bed. "You need to trust yourself, and, man, you need to relax. Nobody is judging your work except you."

"You said it was awful," Lowrie pointed out, sighing when his hands slid up under her sweater to dance his fingers over her stomach.

"What do I know?"

"I've always been my own harshest critic," she admitted as he sat down on the edge of the bed and pulled her into the space between his knees.

"And you're judging your work to the standard it was when you were painting constantly and were in high demand, when you were the art world's darling." Sutton lifted her shirt and dropped an openmouthed kiss on her stomach, just above her belly button. "You can't expect to paint to the same standard, six years after not painting at all."

"I'm not. I just don't want it to look like a dog's breakfast," Lowrie muttered.

"It's a perfectly good attempt for your first time. The second time will be better, the third a lot better… It's like sex. The more we practice, the better we'll get."

Lowrie ran a hand over his burnished head, sighing as his hand slid between the fabric of her panties and the skin of her butt. "You're supposed to be writing, Marchant."

"And you're supposed to be painting. Let's do something else instead."

Oh, yes, please. "*Scrabble*? *Monopoly*? Poker?" she asked, teasing him.

"I'm excellent at *Scrabble*, hate *Monopoly* and I can hold my own in poker. I'll happily show you, later." Sutton looked up and sent her a tender smile. "Take a break, Lowrie, and let me love you."

Lowrie nodded, pushing her fingers in his hair and lowering her head to kiss his mouth. Sutton's hand gripped the back of her head, holding it in place. She slung her leg over his knees and slid down his lap, her doubts, her temper and her frustration melting away. There was only Sutton and what he was doing to her, how he made her feel.

Sutton's hand came up to undo the buttons of her shirt and it fell open, revealing the cups of her lacy, almost transparent baby blue bra. She looked down to see his tanned, broad hand against her pale skin and blue fabric, and sighed. God, she loved the way he touched her, making her feel powerful and feminine and lovely. His hand disappeared beneath the cup of her bra to cover her breast. Her nipple poked his hand and he rubbed her, slowly and gently, building her anticipation.

Lifting her up and off him, he stood and quickly stripped her of her clothes, shoes, socks and yoga pants, dropping her shirt to the floor so that she stood in her matching underwear. He sat back down on the edge of her bed and removed his hiking boots and his socks. She loved his feet—like his hands they were broad, with long toes and neatly clipped nails. Impatient, Lowrie tugged his Henley up his broad chest and over his head, pulling it down his arms. She stroked her hand through the light smattering of hair on his chest, tracing the path that disappeared into his pants. She flat-out adored his body, the strength he exuded.

Looking past his shoulder, she saw that it had started to snow. Big, fluffy flakes drifted past her window to fall on the Juliet balcony outside her room. God, she wanted to capture that blue-white haze, the gray of the sea, the gunmetal-blue of the clouds.

She wanted to paint again—no, she *needed* to paint. Right damn now.

Lowrie spun back to the table that held her paints and reached for the Payne's gray and pushed a blob onto her palette tray. She grabbed viridian and indanthrone blue, and rapidly mixed them, adding a touch of Portland gray. Yeah, getting there...

Picking up a palette knife, she spread a thick strip across the lower half of the canvas, angling it up to suggest the curve of a wave. Yeah, that was the color—she'd tip it with more gray.

The wave wasn't at the right angle so she smeared her finger through the paint, liking the flow. Sutton came up behind her and placed his hands on her breasts and she stilled, turning to look at him over her shoulder.

"No, don't mind me, carry on," he said. "I'll do the same."

She was excited, her mind hopping between the sensation of his fingers tweaking her nipples and being bombarded by color. Her hand trembled as she mixed paint again, great big blobs of blue and gray and green. She glanced out the window and grabbed a brush, dashing strokes on the canvas, moaning as Sutton's hands dipped down beneath her panties, his fingers working to devastate her control and concentration.

She squinted at the canvas and dragged her brush through some paint, panting as she felt his hard erection pushing into her back, his fingers in her panties, another finger rubbing her nipple—where was her bra and why did she not notice him taking it off?—and soon she couldn't help her harsh breathing as she climbed up and up. Paint splattered on her chest as her hand shook, but she needed to capture the exact roll of that wave about to hit the rock. How should she create that turbulence, capture the power?

In a way, she was trying to paint her orgasm, the buildup to the crash, the intense power locked inside her.

"Open your legs, Lowrie," Sutton said and she did as she was told. Sutton stepped between her and the painting, and dropped to his knees in front of her, his eyes that intense shade of blue she so adored. "Keep painting," he told her, his breath hot on her mound.

"I can't," Lowrie moaned.

"Do it or else I'll stop."

His mouth, hot, wild and experienced, dropped back onto her sex and she bucked against him, her cries the only sound in the room. Lowrie cursed him but she reached for Portland gray and squeezed the paint directly onto the canvas, before adding the dark blue, then green, to the mix. She picked up her palette knife, mixed it and screamed when Sutton's mouth landed on her clitoris. She stopped, dropped her hand to his head and he immediately pulled back. "Paint!"

She looked down at his head, shook hers and dragged her eyes back up to the canvas. She dragged her thumb through the paint, used her palette knife again, and waves started to appear on the canvas, rumbling and grumbling, looking to crash.

God, could she stand it? But Lowrie obeyed his instruction. Immediately her other senses were heightened: she could hear the faint tick-tock of the grandfather clock in the hallway, feel the thud of every heartbeat, smell the acrid turpentine in the bottle on the table. Sutton built her up and up, using his clever mouth and fingers buried deep inside her, as she added white to the tips of the wave…moaning as he stoked her pleasure.

She was going to come…

She slapped her hand against the painting, slid her palm through the paint, then gripped Sutton's bare shoulders, streaking his skin with viridian green and Portland gray. She tipped up her head and lifted her hands to her breasts, playing with her nipples to increase the sensation. She was building, building, about to crash…

Her wave smacked into those rocks, splintering into shards of intense pleasure. Lowrie screamed and shook, and before she was done, Sutton surged to his feet. He scooped her up and tossed her on the bed. Spreading her knees, he slid into her with one smooth stroke, burying himself inside her, and she felt her storm whip up again, another set of waves rushing for shore.

He pulled out and she took him in her fist, guiding him back so that his tip was at her entrance. His biceps bulged with the effort of keeping from ramming himself inside her.

"No condom," he muttered, his arms shaking. He reached across the bed, yanked open a drawer and pulled out a box of condoms. She heard the thud of the box hitting the floor and moaned when Sutton pulled back to sit on his haunches and roll the condom down his length.

"It's so much nicer without a condom," she told him. "Hotter, sexier..."

"Riskier," Sutton muttered, lowering himself down and sliding into her hot, warm channel. "God, you feel so good."

She dug her nails into his butt, laid her mouth on his shoulder and licked his hot, warm skin. She tasted something strange on her tongue and realized it was paint. She laughed and pushed her hands into his hair. They'd be wiping each other down later and wearing turpentine as a perfume, but it was a small price to pay to experience fantastic, mind-blowing, midmorning sex.

"Love me, Sutt," she murmured in his ear.

"I do," Sutton replied as he surged into her, setting off a tsunami deep inside her.

Nine

"I'm going to frame that painting," Sutton said, leaning back against her headboard. "I think it's the best work you've ever done, or ever will do again."

Lowrie looked across to the easel and laughed. Standing up, she walked, naked, over to the painting, picked up a brush and pulled it through the paint mixture on the palette. Writing quickly, she stood back and gestured to her signature in the corner.

"I even signed it for you."

Sutton laughed and patted the bed. He watched Lowrie as she walked back to him, sliding under the covers to nestle into his side. He saw there was paint on her bedspread, across her neck, on her chest. He had no doubt he was dotted with color, too. He couldn't care less.

What he was worried about was whether Lowrie took his words, uttered in the heat of the moment, seriously.

Love me, Sutt.

I do.

And he had, at that moment, never loved anyone or anybody more. But it had been said in the heat of passion and now that reality had returned, those words didn't translate in real life. He liked Lowrie, a lot, but he didn't love her, wouldn't *let* himself love her. He wasn't looking for a lover, or a relationship and, even if he was, she came with a kid, which would mean stepping into an instant family.

He wasn't ready for that, for any of it.

This was a fling, a couple of months of fun, nothing serious.

He had no interest in being Rhan's daddy. He didn't want kids, and he especially didn't want to raise a kid who wasn't his own. His adoption, on the surface picture-perfect, had created many emotional issues, ones he was still working his way through.

Lowrie was the first woman he'd ever met who'd even raised these thoughts in him. Hypothetically, if he and Lowrie fell in love and—very hypothetically now— if they went on to have a kid, maybe more, would he love Rhan as much as he did his own flesh and blood? He didn't know, he wasn't sure, so he'd never put the kid in that position. He wanted to believe that he could but he wasn't certain, so he'd never take the risk.

It wouldn't be fair to Rhan, or to Lowrie, and it would eat him up inside.

But what if he fell for her, realized he couldn't live without her, and what if she, in a year or two or ten, decided he wasn't what she wanted? Would his heart recover from another rejection? Doubtful. No, it was better to avoid pain, put on the brakes and create some emotional distance.

But hell, he'd never had a more exciting, more responsive lover. Passionate, impulsive, creative...

He was definitely getting that painting framed. When he was old, he'd look back and remember their fiery lovemaking on this icy winter morning.

Lowrie kissed his shoulder. "I know you didn't mean it, by the way."

"Pardon?"

She raised those exceptional eyes to his. "You know what I'm talking about, Sutton. I know that you didn't mean it when you said you love me."

Ah.

"You're right, I didn't mean it." He felt her tense and cursed himself for being so blunt. But he didn't know any other way to be. He turned his head away to look out the window. "Love is hard for me, Lowrie," he added, surprising himself. "I'm not good at relationships."

Lowrie reached for the thin blanket at the end of the bed and wrapped it around her torso like a sarong. She sat cross-legged on the bed facing him, her one bent knee resting on his thigh. "Why? Can you tell me that?"

Could he? He didn't know—he wasn't great at talking, but he could try. "I told you that I'm adopted, right?"

Lowrie nodded, her chin in her hand.

"So, Thea, my sister, is the biological child of my adoptive parents. She came along four years after I was born, during a time my parents were trying to adopt another child. She was a complete surprise, as they were told they'd never have kids."

"I've heard that happens," Lowrie said, nodding. "More often than people realize."

"Anyway, Thea is just awesome and she always

has been. She quickly became the center of our world. There's a family joke that Thea has an overdeveloped baby finger from winding us around it. As a kid, she was sweet and happy and outgoing and extroverted."

"I was not. I was shy, introverted, supersensitive, but proud with it. People found it difficult to get to know me."

"Found?"

He winced at repeating his use of the past tense. "Was, am. I don't let people in."

"But your parents were good to you? They loved you?"

"Yes." He nodded and rubbed his hand along his jaw. "They loved me as much I would *let* them love me."

"I'm not sure what that means," Lowrie stated, her brow wrinkling.

How to explain? He placed his hand on her thigh and traced patterns on her skin with his thumb, the connection calming him. "I must've been six, maybe a bit older, and I remember my folks sitting down with me and telling me I was adopted. I can't remember the words they used, but I do, distinctly, remember my mom saying that one day, if I wanted to, they'd help me find my *real* parents." He looked away from her, irritated at the ball of emotion in his throat. "Isn't it weird how one little word can have such a massive impact?"

"I don't understand, Sutt."

He loved it when she shortened his name, spoke in that low, sexy, caring tone. "She said she'd help me find my real parents. I've always been sensitive to words and by using the word *real*, to me at age six, that meant they were pretending. That they weren't mine or were only mine until I found my *other* parents. That I didn't have the same relationship with them as Thea did, that I was different."

"I'm sure they didn't mean it like that, Sutton," Lowrie told him. "I'm sure it was just a slip of the tongue."

"It was, I know it was, but it formed the basis of how I saw them for the next twenty-odd years." He lifted his knees but kept his hand on her thigh. "It wasn't something I thought about all the time but it was there. The next time my adoption slapped me in the face was when Thea ran into the house, crying because she'd been told I wasn't her brother. Mom explained about me being adopted, but Thea was so angry and I thought she was mad at me."

"Why?"

"Because in my head, she had a right to have her parents to herself."

"And you're thinking this at what, ten or eleven?" Lowrie asked, puzzled.

"Yeah, I was always an overthinker."

"And far too smart for your own good," Lowrie told him. "What other overly imaginative conclusions did you come to?"

He couldn't object to her phrasing because her words were spot on.

"Because I had this idea they didn't consider me to be a *real* son, I looked for reasons to back up that theory. Did my mom taking Thea shopping mean that she loved her more? If my dad canceled an outing with me, did that mean he didn't want to be with me? I couldn't be honest with them, or vulnerable, because I thought they were looking for an excuse to kick me out. I never disobeyed them, threw a temper tantrum, lost my shit, because I didn't want to lose them."

"Hell, Sutt, it doesn't work like that."

Of course it didn't, but the mind was a powerful weapon when it worked against you. "When I was eighteen, the adoption agency contacted me and my folks and I went to meet with them. They had a letter for me, from my birth mom, but I refused to look at it, to find out who she was or where I came from. My folks pushed me to find out, and, thanks to those childhood fears, I thought they were trying to get rid of me, trying to move me on. I was scared and confused and I took it out on them."

"What did you do?"

"Pulled back, pulled away, tried to put as much distance between myself and them as I could."

"That must've hurt."

"It did, them and me. But in my mind, I'd imposed on them long enough."

God, it hurt to say this out loud, to show her what an idiot he'd been. But she needed to know why he wasn't long-term material, why he could never be in a functional relationship. He bottled everything up, found communicating difficult and created problems for himself and the people who loved him.

"Did your relationship with your parents improve?" Lowrie quietly asked.

He nodded and smiled a little. "But only when I was a lot older. It was shortly before Christmas and I was trying to get out of some family function, I can't remember what. Anyway, my dad drove down from Marchant House, stormed into my office and tore sixty strips off me. He rarely lost his temper, so I just stood there, dumbfounded. He let rip. He told me he was done, that I was hurting my mom with my lack of interest and told me that I had to pull my head out of my ass and act like their son, to be the man they raised me to be. While he stood there, shouting at me, I felt relieved, you know. He wouldn't be this upset if he didn't love me."

Lowrie smiled, understanding.

"Things changed after that and I had two years with them, enjoying every minute of being their son. One Sunday, I was driving them to a local restaurant for lunch and we were in a car accident, a delivery truck T-boned my car. They were killed instantly, and I walked away without a scratch."

She winced, her eyes flooding with tears. "Oh, Sutton, I'm so sorry."

He was, too. "I miss them every day—it's like a hole that won't heal."

"You don't blame yourself for their deaths, do you?"

"No, but I do for distancing myself, for wasting time, for being a self-involved jerk for most of my life. If I'd just told them how I felt, that I felt like a cuckoo in the nest, that I was scared, I wouldn't have so many regrets about how I treated them."

Lowrie stared at him, wrinkling her nose, obviously deep in thought. "I know you probably don't want to hear this, Sutt, but maybe they were at fault, too. Why didn't they push harder to find out why you were distancing yourself? Why didn't they sit you down and demand to know what the problem was? Why did they let nearly ten years pass before your dad lost it? If there's blame to be cast, which I'm not trying to do, then it should be equally shared."

Her words made him feel a little better, a little lighter. "Being English, and upper class, they believed in sporting stiff upper lips, not airing their dirty emotional laundry. As a result, heart-to-heart conversations weren't their thing."

Lowrie smiled. "I can see where you got that from."

She turned, lying down on her stomach, and played with the tassels of the blanket. "So have you categorically decided against finding out more about your birth parents?"

"They were just egg and sperm—my family is who raised me. I'm their real child. It took me far too long to realize that."

"Finding out about your birth parents doesn't change that. You can still be your parents' son and explore the circumstances of your birth."

He looked away from her lovely face and debated how to answer her question, considering whether to tell her about Benjamin Ryder-White and his inheritance. When she put it like that, she sounded so damn reasonable and, yeah, he'd be lying if he said he wasn't curious. But he couldn't tell her the whole story yet. He wanted to know why his birth father had sent him to this inn before he discussed Benjamin with her or anyone else.

But he wasn't ready, not yet.

"Why are you really in Portland, Sutton? Why this inn?"

The blaring ringtone coming from his jeans pocket had him leaping out of bed, and he was deeply grateful for the interruption. Saved by the proverbial bell…

"Please ignore it, Sutton, and answer my question," Lowrie insisted, sitting up again. He couldn't, not yet. He'd told her so much already—he couldn't tell her the whole story. Not because he didn't trust her, but because he *did*. He was starting to value her opinion a little too much, seeking her counsel too often. He wasn't a sharing-caring guy. He worked out his own issues by himself. It was the only way he knew how to be.

He shook his head, saw it was a number he didn't recognize and punched the green button. "Marchant."

He watched Lowrie leave the bed, her expression a combination of irritation and resignation. She picked up her clothes and walked into her en suite bathroom, closing the door behind her.

He grimaced and turned his attention back to his call. "Sutton, this is Kinga Ryder-White."

Kinga? Ryder-White? What did she want with him? "Hi there," Sutton said, keeping his voice neutral.

"I'm so glad I caught you! I hear you are still in Portland. Would you like to join me, my siblings and their partners for dinner on Saturday night? And please, feel free to bring a date."

Uh…what?

Looking down at her paint-splattered hands, Lowrie twisted her lips as the hot water of the shower pounded her shoulders. Despite knowing she needed turpentine to remove the paint, she rubbed the bar of soap between her hands, hoping for a miracle.

Sutton had ducked answering her question about why he was in Portland, specifically at this inn. What was he hiding? And why could he tell her deeply personal stuff from his childhood, yet not tell her about why he was in the States?

He'd been far too quick to pounce on that phone, and oh-so happy for an excuse not to answer her question.

You are getting in too deep, Lowrie, allowing yourself to fall.

Sutton was not whom she was looking for, wasn't an answer to her prayers. In fact, he was the last guy in the world she should fall for because he could never give her what she needed.

He buried all his emotions, didn't communicate and wasn't interested in being a dad to her son or to any other children. He was gorgeous and a wonderful lover but he'd rip her heart in two if she was fool enough to give it to him.

So she wouldn't.

Besides, she knew how fickle love could be. Kyle, her manager-fiancé, had misappropriated her money, her mother had abetted him—both were supposed to have loved her. Rex left her when times got tough. No, the only person she could rely on was herself, so she'd stay on her emotional island, her and Rhan, enjoying visits from her grandmother, Isabel and Paddy. Allowing anyone else to take up residence on the safe little patch of earth she'd carved out for herself would be stupid in the extreme.

Sutton was a fling, someone whose body she could enjoy for a few more weeks, and then she'd kiss his cheek and let him go. They were both scarred and scared, and she was old enough to know that two battered, half-alive hearts couldn't make a whole.

Sutton rapped on the door and, not waiting for her reply, stepped inside. She eyed him through the steam, looking at him standing there, his jeans pulled up but not buttoned, his hair messy.

"That was Kinga Ryder-White."

Lowrie looked at him, intrigued. "I wasn't aware that you two knew each other."

"We don't," Sutton said. "We met briefly at the Valentine's Day Ball but that's all the contact we've had. She invited me to join her and her siblings for dinner on Saturday night."

"She only has one sibling—Tinsley," Lowrie said, correcting him.

"That's what I thought but she definitely used the plural."

He'd obviously misheard. If Portland had a prince,

they all would've heard about it by now. "So are you going to go?"

He stared down at his bare feet, a million miles away. "Yeah, I think so." Right, so it would be her and Rhan in this huge house on Saturday night. Good to know.

What is wrong with you, Lewis? You've spent plenty of time in this house alone—in fact, you love it! Be honest. It wasn't that she minded being alone—she minded that Sutton was going out to dinner without her.

Grrr...she was acting like she had a claim on his time and attention, and she didn't. They were having a fling, so he owed her no explanations.

"Will you come with me?"

She blinked, unsure of what he'd asked. "Sorry?"

"She said I should bring a date. Will you come?" Sutton asked her, scratching at the streak of paint on his shoulder. "Will Jojo and Isabel take Rhan for the night?"

"I'm sure they will but...are you sure you want to take me?"

He frowned. "Why wouldn't I?"

She shrugged. "Because I'm a single mom innkeeper and they are Portland royalty."

He frowned at her. "Yes, and you are also an incredibly talented artist and an interesting woman, Lowrie. Stop putting yourself down."

Right. Okay, then. She wanted to argue with him but he was right. There was nothing attractive about self-bashing. "Is the dinner at a fancy restaurant?"

"I'm not sure. She said she'd text me the directions. So is that a yes?"

She nodded. "Yes, please. And thank you."

Sutton grinned and gestured to her torso. "You have gray paint on the side of your left breast. And on your stomach."

She lifted up her hands for him to see. "And you have it on your shoulder and down your back," she told him. "Can you grab the turpentine and the rag? I'll get yours off if you remove mine."

His smile turned wolfish. "I like the way you think, Lewis."

"I'm talking about paint, Marchant," Lowrie told him, keeping her voice prim.

"I'm not," Sutton replied, turning away to get the turpentine and the rag. She sighed and hoped he remembered to grab a condom. After such a physical morning, she might just need a nap.

Kinga Ryder-White opened the door to her apartment and welcomed them. Sutton took Lowrie's coat, introduced her to Kinga and followed Kinga into her apartment, his eyes bouncing from person to person in the room. Tinsley stood by the fireplace, a glass of red wine in her hand. She was laughing at something Jules Carson was telling her. Garrett Kaye, the venture capitalist, sat on the arm of Jules's chair, his hand lightly cupping the back of her neck. Sutton had thought they'd been sparking off each other at the Valentine's Day Ball and they were now, obviously, together. Good to know he wasn't wholly unobservant.

Sutton shook hands with Garrett, Kinga's fiancé, Griff O'Hare—the announcement was headline news for a couple of days—and Cody Gallant, who stood with his arms around Tinsley's waist. Right, everyone was loved up...

Good for them.

He looked across at Lowrie, who'd been tugged down to sit between Jules and Kinga and had accepted an offer of wine from Griff.

"Sorry about the lack of space," Griff told him, when he had a drink in his hand. "Kinga and I are looking for a bigger place but we haven't found anything yet."

"Are you going to build?" Cody asked him.

"Maybe," Griff replied. "But I'm doing a minitour in a few months and we'd have to meet with an architect and come up with plans before that happens. And then Kinga would have to supervise the build and she's got more than enough on her plate right now."

Garrett wandered over to join them, his face relaxed and happy. "Nice to see you again, Sutton. How goes the writing?"

Sutton winced. His word count lately was dismal. But because he hated to whine, he just shrugged. "It goes." He looked over to Jules, who was laughing at something Lowrie said. Wanting to get the spotlight off him, Sutton recalled a long conversation at the ball about a gin-making company out west.

"What happened with Crazy Kate's? I remember us discussing its downward spiral at the ball. Was it liquidated?"

Garrett smiled. "We managed to pull a rabbit out of the bag and Crazy Kate's was saved. They are back in production with Kate, Jules's second mother, at the helm. Kate also has a new financial adviser who keeps her on the straight and narrow."

He said the words with such fondness that Sutton had no problem working out the subtext. "You?"

Garrett nodded. "Me. In between being the co-CEO of Ryder International and Crazy Kate's adviser and trying to keep up with Jules, I'm exhausted."

He might be tired, but the guy looked happy. Good for him. Hold on...

"Wait…what did you say? You are involved in Ryder International now? How did that happen?"

Garrett sipped his whiskey. "Well, you know Callum had a heart attack, right?"

He'd heard that along the way. "Yeah, but he's okay, right?"

"He's still in the hospital, slowly recovering after picking up an infection. Anyway—"

"Food is ready!" Kinga called from the kitchen area of the open-plan space.

"Hold that thought," Garrett told Sutton as Lowrie asked Kinga whether she'd cooked.

Kinga tossed her bright blond head and laughed. "No, I don't like to poison my dinner guests. Griff and I love a little Italian place down in Old Town called Benito's—"

"I know it, my uncle used to take me there as a little girl," Lowrie told her.

Kinga flashed her a smile. "My dad used to take us, too. He told me *his* uncle introduced him to Benito. I know it's been around for more than seventy years. Anyway, it's their lasagna. And garlic bread. But I made the salad."

"Avoid the salad, people," Griff teased her, walking past and stopping to drop a kiss on her temple.

Kinga tried, unsuccessfully, to swat him with a kitchen towel.

Ten minutes later they all sat around the too-small dining table, bumping elbows and jostling for food, finding space on the crowded table for wine bottles and glasses. Lowrie sat opposite him, in between Griff and Garrett, a huge smile on her face.

He caught her eye and mouthed, *You okay?*

She nodded and slid her eyes to the left, to where

Griff was sitting next to her, and placed her hand on her heart, closing her eyes. He rolled his eyes. "Funny girl," he said, remembering their conversation about Griff's hotness.

"Isabel is going to hate me forever," Lowrie told him, grinning. Seeing that the rest of the table were now listening to their exchange, he sat back and grinned at Lowrie, lifting his eyebrow in a challenge to explain.

She didn't hesitate, just turned to Griff and shrugged. "You ring my aunt's bell. She's never going to forgive me for being thigh-to-thigh with you."

Both Kinga and Griff laughed, as did the rest of the table. Griff turned to Kinga and winked at her. "Competition, babe."

"Yeah, yeah…" Kinga rolled her eyes. "Trust me, I will not miss your inability to pick up your clothes or replace the toilet roll."

"We've been engaged like ten minutes and she's already nagging me," Griff complained good-naturedly. He turned to Lowrie. "What do you do, Lowrie?"

"I run an inn, situated on the water in East End." She looked at Sutton and he frowned, silently telling her to own her art. "A long time ago I was an artist, a painter. I was pretty successful."

Sutton winked at her, there was admiration in his eyes, and she shrugged, embarrassed.

"Do you not paint anymore?" Jules asked, interested.

He wondered how she was going to answer. "Ah, I was young and I didn't know how to handle the pressure, the success and the attention. I had a bit of a meltdown and I went traveling for a long time. And then I got pregnant so my uncle's ex offered me a job at the inn they converted on the bay."

"You have a baby?" Jules asked, clapping her hands.

"Yes, a boy. He's a little over a year. His name is Rhan."

"I'd love to see a picture," Tinsley said, and Lowrie picked up her phone, scrolled through the gallery and then passed it around. He caught a picture of Rhan, toothy smile and dark eyes, and his heart turned over. He was such a gorgeous kid, happy and chill.

"Have you seen Callum lately, Cody?" Garrett asked, tearing off a piece of garlic bread from the loaf in front of him.

Sutton's attention moved away from the conversation about Rhan and he waited for Cody's answer.

"He's still frail but getting terser with every interaction. I presume that means he's getting better," Cody replied. "When I saw him yesterday, he went on a ten-minute rant about James and his inability to track down the owner of Benjamin's shares. Then he spent another ten minutes bitching about the fact that he can't get his DNA results back from that genealogy company."

"What is the holdup?" Kinga asked, tuning back into the conversation. "We swabbed our mouths on Christmas Eve, it's now the third week of March and we've heard nothing. Other people have gotten their results within a week or two of submitting their samples."

Tinsley saw his and Lowrie's confusion and laid a hand on his arm. "Sorry, quick explanation. Our grand-father is obsessed with his DNA and the fact that he is the last of an unbroken line of Ryder-Whites—"

"Well, technically, Dad is," Kinga corrected her.

"Yeah, but Callum doesn't like Dad, so he considers himself the reigning king... Anyway, he gave us the present of having our genealogy traced by a local company and we can't get the results back."

Sutton frowned. "That's strange. My sister had it done in the UK and it was quick."

Kinga shrugged. "I know, that is what we're having difficulty with."

Sutton picked up his wineglass, sipped and decided to return to his earlier conversation with Garrett. "Garrett, you were going to tell me how you came to be involved with Ryder International?"

Garrett pushed a hand through his hair. "It's not public knowledge yet..." He trailed off. He looked at Kinga, then Tinsley.

Kinga nodded and spoke. "You can tell Sutton, Garrett. I don't think he or Lowrie are going to run to the tabloids. And if they do, so what?"

Garrett shared his smile between the sisters, his expression a little tender. Not an emotion Sutton expected to see on the hard-as-nails venture capitalist's face.

"My mother is Callum's personal assistant and from the time I was a teen, I thought Callum was my father. It turns out that James is my dad," Garrett explained.

Sutton raised his eyebrows in astonishment. "Really?"

"Yeah. When Callum had his heart attack, he told James to find someone to run Ryder International. He and James have a fraught relationship and there isn't a great deal of affection between them—"

"Or any at all," Kinga interjected.

"Despite knowing that it might jeopardize his inheritance, James decided to reveal that I was his son. James also offered me the Ryder CEO job and left it up to me whether or not to acknowledge him as my father. I have, privately, and he, Kinga, Tinsley and I are running Ryder International together."

Well, that was bombshell news.

"Will Callum go back to work at Ryder International?" Lowrie asked.

Garrett shrugged. "I'm sure he will, at some point. Hopefully by then we will have locked in some permanent changes, changed some of his old-fashioned policies."

"Like?" Sutton asked, obviously interested. He owned a significant share of the company in question. Or shortly would.

"We want to restructure the company and streamline it. Worldwide, upper and middle management is top-heavy and there's a massive overlap between jobs. We want equal pay for equal work. It's nonsense that men earn fifteen percent more than their women colleagues," Kinga said, sounding crisp. "Paternal leave, better employee benefits. We've encountered some resistance to the changes from the old guard of managers and are expecting more from Callum's cronies on the board of directors."

"James sent a letter to the lawyers representing our silent-but-powerful shareholder, asking him for our support for these changes. If he sides with us, we'll have enough votes at the upcoming board meeting to push them through."

Kinga smiled and looked at Lowrie, seeing her confusion. "Someone out there controls what used to be my uncle Benjamin's shares in Ryder International. We don't know who it is—he hides behind a blind trust."

Sutton started to object to the word *hides* and then remembered that they didn't know he was on the cusp of taking ownership of the shares. And he wasn't about to disclose that at a family dinner, the second time he'd been in the company of the Ryder-Whites. He caught

Lowrie's frown and watched her tip her head to the side. He wondered what she was thinking.

Sutton took a large sip of his wine and forced himself to lift a forkful of lasagna to his lips. He chewed, tasting nothing, and when there was a gap in the conversation, he spoke again. "So your uncle Benjamin was Callum's brother?"

Tinsley picked an olive off her plate and popped it into her mouth. "Mmm, he was a great deal younger than Callum, fifteen or twenty years I think."

"And did they get along well?"

"God, no, they hated each other! Well, Callum hated Ben, and really loathed that he wouldn't marry and settle down," Tinsley replied. "Callum never accepted Ben being gay and thought he could switch his sexual preferences at will."

"He was *gay*?" Sutton spluttered. That couldn't be right. He was here after all.

Seven pairs of eyes hit his face, all cool. He immediately lifted his hands, not blaming them for assuming he was intolerant. But he couldn't tell them that he'd just found out that his birth father was gay. Or, he thought, as his brain restarted, at the very least, bisexual at some point in his life.

"Sorry. That came out all wrong…" He cleared his throat, annoyed to feel heat in his cheeks. "I'm not that guy, I promise. I don't give a toss what people do in the privacy of their bedrooms."

"He's really not," Lowrie assured them and he smiled his thanks when six spines relaxed.

"By the way, my uncle Carlo was gay and he and my uncle Paddy established the inn together. They were together for more than thirty years. The LGBTQ commu-

nity in Portland back then was smaller than it is now. I
wonder if they knew each other?"

"What was his surname?" Tinsley asked.

"Rossi," Lowrie said and frowned when Tinsley and
Kinga both gasped.

Tinsley's knife falling onto her bone china plate shat-
tered the silence.

"Oh, my God," Kinga said, placing her hand on her
heart.

Lowrie hunched her shoulders and looked from them
to Sutton, as if asking him what she should do. He had
no idea so he shrugged. "I'm sorry, we don't understand."

"Our uncle, the one we were talking about? Well,
he had a lover named Carlo Rossi. They were living
together when he died, living in Carlo's house somewhere on the bay," Kinga explained.

"My uncle and your uncle?" Lowrie demanded, her
eyes wide.

Kinga clapped her hands together, her eyes sparking with the thrill of the unexpected. "Oh, my God, can
you believe it?"

Sutton stared at his plate while the table erupted.
Well, now he knew why he'd been sent to spend time
at Carlo's inn.

Ten

Because he wasn't the chattiest kid in the sandbox, nobody noticed that Sutton, as the evening progressed, got quieter and quieter and retreated into an all but unreachable space. Oh, he answered when he was spoken to, spoke just enough so nobody realized anything was off, but because she'd been living with him for nearly two months, Lowrie saw the distance in his eyes, the pull of his lips, the tension in his shoulders.

He was upset, but she couldn't fathom why.

Leaning back in her seat as Sutton drove them home, she thought back on the evening. She'd had a lot more fun than expected and would love to hang out with the group a little more. Instead of being the prissy princesses she expected, Kinga and Tinsley were down-to-earth and lovely, strong women, but not without empathy. They were quick to laugh, quick to tease.

Lowrie had been so sure that being alone on her emotional island with Rhan was what she wanted, but now, after seeing the way the extended Ryder-White clan interacted, she wasn't so certain. She could do with a couple of girlfriends, lunches and coffee dates, feminine conversation that rambled and rolled along. She'd been so busy with Rhan, with the inn, but now she felt like she was missing out. She wanted more people in her life who loved her, or at least liked her. She wanted to socialize, to laugh and tease. Have more people her own age in her life.

And, God, the relationship those women had with their men! There was no doubt those couples were all deeply in love, that they'd found their forever partners. Lowrie and Sutton were sleeping together, that much was obvious, but there was a mental distance between them that was easy to discern. They knew each other in bed, but emotionally? They'd barely connected at all.

And Sutton was doing what he always did—he was blocking her out and trying to unravel the mystery on his own. Oh, she knew he was a loner, that his career as a novelist was both lonely and, sometimes, unexplainable, but he didn't have to figure out everything solo. Why wouldn't he let her in? Let her help?

She was crazy about him, Lowrie admitted. Might even be on the way to being neck-deep in love with him. She loved his body, his small smiles, his occasional sense of the ridiculous. She loved his confidence, his I-don't-give-a-crap attitude. He was a strong man but, at his core, he was a loner…

She'd fought for love her whole life, banged on people's doors asking them to love her—not her talent or her success—and she was damned if she'd ever do that again. A life spent with Sutton would be spent prodding and prying, trying to get him to open up, to let her in. And, as she'd been taught, love not freely given wasn't love at all.

They didn't have a future. It was time to accept that—and God, it felt like a thousand hornet stings. But even accepting they weren't a couple, she knew he was her friend. She was utterly unable to sit here and let him stew on his own.

"Want to tell me why you are rattled?" she asked, turning to look at his strong profile.

"I'm fine," he politely answered. "Did you have fun?"

"I did and you know it. And you are trying to change the subject," Lowrie said, too tired to play games. Sutton signaled to turn onto her road and she winced. She'd left this conversation far too late and they were home. In the car he was a captive audience, but now that they were back at the inn, if Sutton didn't want to talk, he could remove himself to more than a dozen rooms in the building and there was nothing she could do about it.

"I need a drink," Sutton told her, pulling into the garage. He exited the vehicle, walked around to her side and opened the car door for her. His action was instinctive, but his expression suggested she should leave him alone.

Well, that wasn't going to happen.

Sutton opened the side door, entered through the utility room and shrugged off his jacket. Without putting on any lights, he walked through to the sea-facing lounge, his back ramrod straight.

Lowrie hung her coat on the coat stand and flipped on the hallway light. She hung up her scarf and handbag on another hook and debated whether to let Sutton stew.

No, when he stomped around too much in his own head, he overanalyzed and overthought, and that wasn't healthy. Besides, she thought she might be in love with him—Damn! Damn! Damn!—and she'd do anything to ease his pain.

Because he was in pain, any fool—or any woman foolish enough to fall in love with the man—could see it.

He stood at the tall windows, his forearm resting on the glass above his head, and stared down at the ink-black rocks. He cracked a window and an icy breeze sent shivers down her spine. Sutton held a whiskey tumbler in his other hand.

Lowrie sat down on the arm of the closest chair and crossed her legs, linking her hands around her knees. "Talk to me, Sutt."

He didn't reply but she did catch the quick shake of his head.

"You told me that had you communicated better when you were a kid and young adult, then you wouldn't have jumped to so many conclusions about your parents, that you wouldn't have wasted so much time."

He spun around, his expression bordering on mean. But she wasn't scared—he would never, ever hurt her.

"That's a low blow."

She shrugged. "It's the truth." And the truth could hurt in a thousand different ways. "Tell me about why you are here in Portland, staying in my house."

He turned his back on her again, his spine rigid with tension. She waited and then waited some more. Five minutes passed, then a few more, and Lowrie finally realized that he didn't trust her enough, respect her enough or care for her enough to let her in. Right, she didn't need him to draw her a picture.

She didn't need to love someone who couldn't love her back, who kept her on the outside looking in. She'd done that all her life—with her mom, with Kyle, with Rex. They'd loved her on their terms, not hers. She'd never again settle for less than everything—a mental and emotional connection and complete trust. Maybe she was shooting for the impossible, but she'd rather be alone than have less than what she wanted.

Lowrie stood up and started walking to the door, her shoulders hunched and her hands in the back pockets of her smart woolen pants. She blinked away the moisture in her eyes, annoyed to find her eyes wet. He wasn't worth her tears.

"Benjamin Ryder-White is my birth father."

His words reached her, his tone low and confused. It took her a good thirty seconds to process what he'd said, and when she did, she softly whistled. Right, well, she hadn't expected that.

Lowrie walked over to where he was standing and leaned her shoulder into the wall, her eyes on his profile. "How long have you known?"

"Mid-January. I turned thirty-five and the adoption agency lawyers met with me."

She had a million questions running through her head. "How did the adoption agency know he was your birth father?"

"I can only presume that my birth mother told him and he contacted the agency."

Eh, okay, that made sense. But she still didn't understand why Sutton was here, in Portland. So she asked him. A muscle jumped in Sutton's jaw as he lifted the glass of whiskey to his lips. It was nearly half-gone, she noticed. Sutton wasn't a big drinker so seeing him put back so much liquor at one time was a good indicator as to how upset he was.

"I'm about to inherit a crapload of money from him,

as well as his twenty-five-percent share in Ryder International."

"The same shares that were discussed earlier, the ones that Callum Ryder-White is so desperate to get his hands on?"

He nodded.

"God, you're seriously rich."

Her asinine comment almost made him smile. "I was rich before, but yeah, this puts me up a level."

"Are the shares why you are in Portland?"

He rocked his hand up and down. "There were two codicils to me inheriting his wealth. The first is that I had to spend two months here, at this inn. I can only think that Benjamin wanted me to be here, to find out about him and his life through Carlo. Judging by the hatred between Benjamin and his brother, I think he wanted his story to be told by someone who loved him. The other proviso was that I attend the Valentine's Day Ball, I presume because it, and the foundation, was something he started and was proud of."

Lowrie shrugged, thinking it was so sad that Carlo had passed and couldn't tell Sutton about the man he'd loved such a long time ago. She thought for a minute. "Paddy and Carlo were together for thirty years, Sutton—maybe Paddy knew Benjamin? Or knew about him from Carlo?"

"I doubt Carlo would've spent any time talking about his old lover to his new lover," Sutton muttered, dragging his hand through his hair.

"Paddy and Carlo knew each other all their lives, they were friends long before they became lovers. Maybe Paddy even met Ben, knew him."

"But I don't need to know anything about Benjamin, Lowrie!" Sutton turned anguished eyes onto her. "You keep mistaking me for someone who cares. I don't care about anything except fulfilling the terms of the will, getting my hands on that fortune."

"So you're just in it for the millions?"

He shrugged, not bothering to dispute her statement. No, that couldn't be true. Sutton, who wore casual jeans and sweatshirts, wasn't that into money…but God, what did she know? It wasn't something they'd spoken about. And if she was wrong about the money, what else had she misconstrued? What was his real reason for being with her?

"Then what am I? A side benefit?"

He didn't look at her. Lowrie pushed her hands into her hair and tugged at the strands, not sure whether or not to smack him. He was hurting, of that she was sure, but he was also acting like a prime-grade jerk.

But she did sense that this was a watershed conversation, something that would make or break them. He'd either knock down some of his walls and talk to her, or he'd layer another brick on top, making entry into his inner world impossible.

"Come and sit down, Sutton, and talk to me. Let me in, let me talk this through with you. I can see that this has upset you—"

He whirled around, his eyes blazing. "This? You've got to be joking! In the scheme of things, this is barely a scratch. This means *nothing*. Compared to losing my parents, my real parents, this doesn't even blip on my radar! She gave me up, he gave me up… I don't give a shit about them!"

Oh, he cared more than he thought. "Then why are you shouting?"

"I'm shouting because you won't stop bugging me! I'm shouting because you won't leave me the hell alone! And yes, you were a side benefit to being in this cold-as-hell place, a way to pass the time, to relieve the boredom."

She knew he didn't mean that, not really, but his words came too close to others she'd heard before—*you're a meal ticket, you're a fun time*—and they stung like the slash of a steel-edged whip across her soul. Lowrie lifted her head and her eyes, roiling with anger and frustration, clashed with his. And an emotion she couldn't place, something hard and feral.

Maybe he did mean it. Maybe she was simply someone he'd been using.

Because, if she was honest, she was the ultimate fling. She not only washed his clothes and tidied up after him as his housekeeper, but she also warmed his bed at night. He didn't have to make any effort to see her, to make plans with her, since she was always available. Living in the same house, he didn't need to lift a finger...

God, she'd been such an idiot to think he was different! She was simply convenient.

Hurting everywhere, from the tips of her hair to the nails on her toes, she cursed her burning eyes. She walked in the direction of the door and bumped her knee into the side table.

She felt movement behind her, heard him calling her name.

She spun around. "Don't! Don't you dare apologize. It'll mean nothing and my respect for you, already skimming rock bottom, will drop exponentially. Stay in your messed-up mind, Sutton. Be on your own. Keep using people, stay apart, be the loner you so desperately want to be. But know that when you are eighty or a hundred, and sitting in your study surrounded by musty books, you'll regret me. You'll regret not allowing love into your life."

"You haven't let love into your life," Sutton pointed out, his voice raw with emotion.

"Because I fell for another man who couldn't give me what I need! A repressed Englishman who thinks too much and feels too little," Lowrie snapped. "Your parents loved you, but you were too scared to accept that love. I'm crazy about you, but yet again, you are running away. There's another family out there who'd be happy to let you into their lives—Kinga and Tinsley are lovely people—but because you are so damn scared, you'll take Ben's money and run back to your ivory tower. I only realized this earlier tonight, but do you know what I would do for sisters, friends, for more people in my life to love me, to love Rhan? You can never have too much love in your life, but somehow you're above all that!"

He opened his mouth to speak but shut it again and shook his head. Yeah, talking to him, shouting, was like shouting at a brick wall. "Stubborn, stupid man!" she muttered before spinning on her heel and storming out of the room and into the hallway.

She grabbed her coat, wrapped her scarf around her neck and stepped into the cold night, needing to get to Rhan and Jojo. To Isabel.

To be with the three people who loved her, no questions asked.

Sutton followed her down the road to Jojo's, just to make sure she got there safely. That she didn't, in her anger, slip on some ice, crack her head and lie on the sidewalk for the rest of the night.

From the shadows of the hedge, he saw the front door

to her grandmother's house open and watched Jojo pull her inside and into her arms. He was too far away to see, but he knew that Lowrie was crying.

He'd done that. And so much more.

Walking back to the inn, Sutton scrubbed his hands over his face, as cold on the inside as he was on the outside. What an intense, soul-disturbing evening.

He jammed his hands into the pockets of his coat and stared up at the star-filled sky. He wasn't a praying man, but he could do with some divine guidance because, God, his life was so fucked up.

He was Benjamin's son. He liked his second cousins—a lot—and a part of him wanted to get to know them better. He liked their men and thought he and Garrett could become good friends. Thea would adore them all. They were her type of people—smart, funny, direct…down-to-earth. He had, if he wanted it—if they wanted him—a family…

But it wouldn't fill up the hole that had been carved out when Lowrie stormed away. If he had to choose between her and the Ryder-Whites, between her and anyone else, ever, he'd choose her. But she came with a kid and that little guy—that gorgeous kid—scared him like no other. Sutton wouldn't just be living his life with Lowrie, he'd also become Rhan's stepdad, his role model, his dad but *not* his dad. In his life but not his blood.

Sutton and Lowrie were adults. They could choose whom to love, but their choices would affect Rhan. What if Sutton raised him and then things fell apart with him and Lowrie? How would Rhan feel, what would he do? How would *Sutton* feel?

Or, if Sutton and Lowrie had other kids, would Rhan feel less loved, not as good? And what if Lowrie, in a couple of years, left Sutton? He wouldn't just lose her, but Rhan, too. Sutton jammed his fist into his sternum, trying to push away the sharp pain.

He couldn't think about Lowrie, couldn't deal with her and the complications loving her pulled to the surface. Before he tackled Lowrie and her place in his life—or his in hers—he had to sort out the Ryder-White mess.

He needed to get all the facts, face the truth of his birth and how he came into this life, once and for all. He'd been picking and choosing his puzzle pieces, trying to fit them into a picture where they didn't belong. He needed to put the right pieces in the right places and go from there.

He needed to face the truth, find out who his birth mother was, what caused her to give him up and deal with any emotional fallout.

Until he worked out how to deal with his past—all of his past—he wouldn't be able to construct his future.

The future that had just stormed out of this house and down the road, the future that included the baby boy he was damn sure she was cuddling.

Sutton arrived back at the inn, shed his coat in the hallway and walked up the stairs to his room. He walked over to the freestanding wardrobe, pulled down his suitcase and flung it on the bed. Lifting the lid, he saw the outline of the envelope in the inside pocket, his throat Sahara-dry.

God, he wished Lowrie was here, sitting next to him, her hand on his back as he perused its contents. But because he was a selfish, silent prick with the communication skills of a cactus, she'd bolted. And he only had himself to blame.

Get on with it, Marchant.

He dipped his hand inside the pocket, pulled out the envelope and walked over to the comfortable chair in the corner. He sat down and stared at his trembling fingers. This was it.

He looked across the room to where a photograph stood of his parents, wrapped in each other's arms, laughing at the camera.

It's okay, Sutton, you can do this. And you will always and forever be ours.

Sutton blinked away his tears, grateful to hear his mother's voice in his head, suddenly sure that if she knew of this, she'd be here, supporting him. The woman in the envelope might've birthed him, but those were his parents, the people who'd made him the center of their world.

He loved books because his mom read to him every night, knew how to crack an egg one-handed because he'd watch his dad make breakfast every Sunday morning—eighties rock music blaring—for eighteen or so years. He loved Monty Python, astronomy, watching Wimbledon tennis because his parents did. So much of what was important in his life, his opinions and his values, he'd inherited from that couple who didn't pass on a single strand of DNA to him. And as he later learned, the day she heard about him being adopted, Thea cried because she'd been terrified someone was going to take her big brother away.

He was a Marchant, and always would be. Nothing in the envelope could change that. Nothing ever would. Feeling calmer—heart still aching but calmer—he ripped open the package and pulled out a thin envelope. He looked at the corner, saw the stamps on the expensive stationary and saw that the letter was postmarked the first day of the New Year, the year he was born.

Removing the rubber band, he picked up the letter, his heart pounding. Forcing his finger under the seal, he pulled out the thick, expensive paper.

Dear Sutton...

I hope they've kept the name I chose for you. From the time I was little, I wanted a boy and two girls. I just never expected to have a boy under these circumstances... I know that you are a boy, don't ask me how.

It's winter in London and I turned nineteen a few months ago, a year older than you are now, assuming you're reading this on your eighteenth birthday. I am sitting in the apartment my parents hired for me in Mayfair, and it's a cold, bleak day. I can feel you moving around inside me, and they say you are going to be a big baby. Honestly, I'm a little terrified of how I'm going to push a six-pound baby into the world. But I will, I have no choice. Just like I have little choice but to be in this apartment, on a rainy Monday in January.

I suppose I am the embodiment of a "poor little rich girl." I'm an only child of a timber industri-alist and his society wife, both active in con-servative politics and the leading lights of East Coast society. Blue bloods, if you will. We're the American equivalent of royalty, or so my parents and their friends like to think. We live by a code, anything—drugs, promiscuity, alcohol, bad busi-ness deals—is acceptable provided we don't get caught, that our peccadilloes don't become public knowledge. We must be seen as above reproach, perfect in every way. Hypocritical, I know.

Falling pregnant by a man fifteen years older than me is not acceptable. Neither is an abortion. I have tried to talk to your father, but he's managed to avoid me for the past nine months. You can do that when you are rich and powerful. As a result, I am reliant, in every way possible, on my parents. They have the money, the power and, should I buck their wishes, I will be the poor girl without a place to live or a cent to my name. I wish you and I could just run away, but how would I feed you, us? How could I work and look after you? I want to think that I am brave enough to try, strong enough to struggle, but I'm not. I'm quite spoiled, you know.

So I agreed to come here to London, to engage with an agency who specializes in dealing with little rich girls who get themselves in trouble. My friends back home think I'm at finishing school in Switzerland. It's 1987, for God's sake, who goes to finishing school anymore?

Anyway…adoption it is. I know a little about the people who are going to take you, though not their names, and they seem like good people. They are, I'm told, so excited to take you home, to make you theirs. You'll have a good life with them, of that I am sure.

I wish I was stronger, better, less spoiled, more resilient. But I'm not, and I can't pretend to be. I only hope that your new mother and father raise you to be a better person than I am.

My name is Penelope Freya Jackson and the man who made me pregnant is Benjamin

Ryder-White. Should you wish to, when you are
an adult, you can track me down. I imagine I'll
be easy enough to find.

Penelope Ryder-White, Kinga and Tinsley's mother,
was his mother, too.

They weren't his cousins, but his half sisters.

Sutton stood up, intent on telling Lowrie the news,
desperate to share this information with her. He looked
around, remembered that they weren't talking—might
never again—and sank back down onto the bed.

Holy, holy shit.

What the hell was he going to do?

Eleven

Penelope

The last time Penelope had met with her private investigator, it had been in this same coffee shop. And young KJ Holden had ordered an espresso that time, too.

Today, Penelope hoped there was more information to share.

"So thank you for meeting with me today." KJ leaned forward and dropped her voice so that she couldn't be overheard by people at the adjacent tables. "As you know, I tracked down the adoption agency and I asked them for information on your son. I wasn't surprised when they refused to entertain my inquiries. They told me that if he wanted to contact you, he knew how to do that."

Penelope swallowed down her impatience. Of course, she knew this, found it incredibly frustrating. How could she control events if she had no cards to play, and wasn't even sitting at the poker table?

KJ tapped her finger against her coffee cup. "Imagine my surprise when the lawyer representing the agency contacted me and told me that your son is looking for a meeting."

What?

Penelope jerked back her head, feeling like she'd been slapped. Immediately, she glanced toward the door, wondering how long it would take her to stumble into the cold air, to find her car and start driving. And driving. And driving.

"They asked me to facilitate a meeting between you and the son you gave up for adoption."

Penelope was going to meet her son; her secrets would come to light. She didn't know if she could bear it. Her friends, her family, her girls... *James.*

God, she still hadn't told him. How would he react? Would he hate her, yell at her, refuse to talk to her?

No...wait! James told her that they were stronger together. There wasn't anything they couldn't handle. She just had to believe that. She hadn't held his past against him; he would deal with hers. She had to trust him.

As for the girls, well, they were more resilient than she'd ever imagined. But how would Callum react? Did she even care? She'd never liked her father-in-law and no longer gave a hooey about his feelings!

Penelope met KJ's sympathetic eyes, then straightened her spine and lifted her chin. She was a Jackson by birth and a Ryder-White by marriage and blue bloods didn't buckle.

"Say what you need to and get it done," Penelope told her through gritted teeth.

"Up until this point in his life, he had no intention

of meeting you. But circumstances are dictating that he makes his presence known, and this specifically relates to the shares he owns in Ryder International."

She *knew* it, knew that Ben would've made provisions for him, made sure that *his* blood inherited *his* share of Ryder International. The Ryder-White men shared a craving for continuity.

"Who is he?" Penelope asked again, her voice high and tight. "And when am I going to meet him?"

KJ looked toward the door of the diner. "Right now, if that suits you. If it doesn't, then you can meet at some point in the future." She pulled a face. "I have been asked to tell you that, due to circumstances, you will probably run into each other quite frequently so maybe it's best to get this over with."

Get this over with? *This* was only meeting her child, the son she never knew! Penelope fanned her fingers over her heart and took a deep breath, looking for her courage, telling herself she couldn't cry, wouldn't cry.

She would not embarrass herself like that. *Stiff upper lip, dammit!*

"Who is he?" she whispered.

"His name is Sutton Marchant and, when you are ready—*if* you are ready—he's waiting outside," KJ softly told her. "I just need to call him and he'll either come in or go away."

Penelope closed her eyes and bit the inside of her lip, so hard that she drew blood. She opened her eyes, leaned back in her chair and finally nodded. "Call him. Do it now before I change my mind."

Sutton stood outside Callum Ryder-White's study at his home in Yarmouth and leaned his shoulder into the wall, waiting—as were James, Kinga, Tinsley and Garrett—for Callum to admit them into his inner sanctum.

The old codger was taking his time.

Sutton ran a weary hand over his face and wanted this day done, this part of his life over. He was sick of living with a woman who barely glanced at him, who only spoke to him to inquire whether he wanted fresh coffee, or what he wanted for dinner.

He was sick of being treated like a guest in a house he'd briefly considered his home.

The day after his and Lowrie's fight, he'd tried to ask her to give him some time, but she'd shut him down, telling him quietly and proudly that their association was over, to please forget they'd slept together. She intended to keep her distance and treat him like the guest he was. He protested, but she just left the room. That became the pattern for every interaction they'd had since. He'd raise the subject, she'd look at him with blank eyes and leave the room.

He hadn't managed to finish one nonguest question in more than ten days. And he was done. He was tired of looking at Lowrie and wishing, desperate to wrap his arms around her and never let her go. He was tired of hearing her laugh with Rhan and wishing he could be part of the joke, sick of watching her, Rhan and Charlie walking on the beach and wishing he was part of her circle. Exhausted from lying in bed and physically restraining himself from going to her.

No, he had to stay away from her until he could give her what she and Rhan needed. Security, love and understanding…his loyalty and his life. Besides, he wanted to walk into a new phase of his life, hopefully with her and Rhan, carrying as little baggage as he could.

"You okay, Sutton?" asked Garrett, who was standing next to Kinga, his hands in the pockets of his suit.

Sutton shrugged and brushed a piece of lint off the sleeveless parka he wore over a black cashmere sweater. Jeans covered his legs and fell over his battered hiking boots. His half sisters, uncle and Garrett were all wearing corporate boring, but Sutton wanted Callum to underestimate him because, well, that would be fun.

"I'm not a fan of waiting," he replied and got an answering grimace in response. Neither, it seemed, was Garrett.

Emma, Garrett's mother, opened the door to Callum's study and frowned at them. "He's ready for you now. I'd like to remind you all that he's still recovering from a profoundly serious operation so make it quick and *don't* upset him."

Sutton raised his eyebrows at her directive. She sounded more like a wife than a personal assistant. Had he missed something along the way?

But, unfortunately, there was no chance of not upsetting Callum, Sutton thought as they trooped into the office, lining up in front of his desk like errant school children at the principal's desk.

Callum, tapping on his keyboard, didn't bother to acknowledge them. After a few minutes, Sutton, who wanted to get this over with so he could move on to winning Lowrie back—he was sick of their cold war—rapped his knuckles on Callum's vast, antique wooden desk.

Callum sighed and finally leaned back in his chair, pushing his fingertips together. "Who are you?" he asked Sutton, forgetting that they'd met before.

"I am Benjamin's son, Sutton Marchant," Sutton replied. Certain Callum's heart could handle it, he dropped another conversational grenade. "And I own a quarter share of Ryder International."

Color rushed into, and out of, Callum's face, but his eyes remained steady and as cold as ice. He took a moment to speak, and when he did, his voice was deep and steady. "Name your price."

Sutton lifted his eyebrows. "For the shares?"

"Of course, for the shares," Callum retorted. "What else?"

Sutton spread his hands. "No 'welcome to the family'? No 'where did you come from?' Nothing?"

"The shares," Callum said through gritted teeth. "Name your price and I'll arrange for payment."

Sutton jammed his hands into the pockets of his parka and rocked on his heels. "Even if I wanted to sell you the shares, and I don't—I can't."

"Why not?" Callum demanded, his face mottled with fury. Sutton doubted he'd have a heart attack, but was starting to think that Callum exploding was a distinct possibility.

"The terms of Benjamin's will forbid it. He specifically stated that I could not sell to you."

"I… What… You…"

James sat down in one of the two chairs opposite Callum and looked across to Emma, who was standing next to Callum, her hand on his shoulder. "I'd like notes of this meeting, Emma."

Emma narrowed her eyes at him and shook her head. "Callum is my boss, not you."

"Mom, this isn't the time to be difficult, but this will do," Garrett said, removing his phone from the inner pocket of his jacket. He laid it on the edge of Callum's desk and Sutton saw it was recording their conversation. Like a lawyer's deposition, Garrett explained who was present and recited the date and time. He placed his hand on James's shoulders and squeezed, silently encouraging his father.

"Callum," James said, looking the Ryder-White patriarch in the eye. "As you know, a Ryder International board meeting is scheduled for tomorrow night."

"I know, I'm working on the agenda," Callum retorted.

"We've already set the agenda, Callum, and I will be chairing that meeting," James told him, his voice steady and uncompromising.

Talking over Callum's splutters, James continued. "The five of us have decided how Ryder International will be run going forward and you are no longer part of that equation. In fact, we would like you to tell the world that, following your heart attack, you have retired and will be resigning from Ryder International, as CEO and as chairman of the board."

Callum's bright blue eyes narrowed. "That will never happen. This is my company, my legacy. And who will run the company? *You?*"

James nodded. "Absolutely me. But, unlike you, I am not an egotistical ass and I am happy to take advice and support and direction from my son, my daughters and my nephew. I will be the face of the company, but they will very much be part of Ryder International going forward."

"I will fight you on this! I will wipe the floor with all of you and you will be ruined by the time I am done with you!"

It was a threat they'd expected and it didn't scare any of them. Sutton and Garrett shrugged, Kinga and Tinsley looked stoic and James smiled. It was his son's smile that pushed Callum to his feet. "Get out of my office! All of you! Emma, call my lawyer."

"That's your prerogative." James didn't move except to take out a piece of paper from his jacket pocket. "Before you do that, there is one more thing you should know, Callum."

Callum looked down at the paper, frowning. "What is that?"

James tapped his finger on the envelope. "None of us could work out why it took so long to get our DNA results back from the genealogy site WhoAreYou. We should've had them back ages ago and last week, when I phoned to inquire, I was given the runaround, a million and one excuses. I eventually threw my weight around—I learned to do that from you—and reached the CEO.

"He told me that he would rerun them immediately and that we'd have our results the very next day. I asked him to run Garrett's and Sutton's DNA as well, anticipating the legal challenges you might throw our way. I didn't want any queries about bloodlines to cause a holdup in the legal fight I knew you'd embark on."

Callum's eyes darted between the paper and James's face, excitement brimming in those depths. Excitement or madness? Sutton couldn't tell. "I presume there were many matches between us and the Delaware cousins, and the Boston Ryder-Whites? Where do we come from, originally?"

Sutton exchanged a puzzled glance with Garrett. It seemed to him that Callum had forgotten that they were trying to oust him from the company. All his attention was on his ancestry.

"What other connections did they find? Let me see!"

James sent Kinga, then Tinsley a should-I-be-doing-this? look and Kinga placed her hand on his, squeezing.

"If we don't tell him, Dad, he will just rerun the tests himself and find out, anyway. Just tell him. Quick and clean," Kinga told James, and Tinsley nodded her agreement.

James nodded, swallowed and spoke again. "The thing is, Callum, me, Kinga, Tinsley and Garrett do *not* carry the Ryder-White genes. Sutton, through Benjamin, does."

Callum dropped into his seat, seemingly smaller than he was when he'd stood up a few minutes ago. "What are you saying?"

"Your mom was either pregnant when she married your father or had an affair when she was married to him because the man you thought was your father, James Callum Ryder-White, isn't."

"Maybe Benjamin wasn't his son, did you think about that?" Callum shouted.

"We did consider that, but Sutton is related to the other Ryder-Whites, Callum, and you aren't." James stood up, buttoned his jacket and made eye contact with each of them before looking at his father. "The thing is, Callum, we don't care about DNA, about what some test says or who populates our family tree. We're a family, by choice, not by blood. We choose each other.

"Don't fight us, Callum, you'll lose. Your choice is either to retire, resign and remain part of our ragtag, non–blue blood family or die a lonely, resentful old man, fighting a legal battle he will not win and dealing with the world knowing that you aren't, by blood, a Ryder-White," James continued.

"You're blackmailing me?" Callum demanded.

James shrugged. "*Blackmail* is an ugly word. Think

of it as us giving you a reason to retire gracefully. You have until tomorrow morning to decide."

James inclined his head and moved toward the door. They followed him out.

Sutton looked at James's back and realized there was a new head of the Ryder-White family. They were being led by a good man, a decent man.

Yeah, he could maybe hang around this family a little longer.

Lowrie wasn't sure how much longer she could live with Sutton without losing it. She wasn't sleeping, couldn't concentrate and was less patient with Rhan than usual.

But what she was doing, surprisingly, was painting. She was using oils and color to paint out her frustration and sadness, creating vibrant, messy works that were technically useless but full of passion and anger and desperation.

Standing on the veranda in the weak sunshine, she nibbled the end of her paintbrush and looked at a half-dead vase of peonies. The flowers were a metaphor for how she felt—droopy, low on energy, washed out.

She missed Sutton, missed sleeping in his arms, his quirky smile, his deep voice and God, she missed his blunt way of talking and his strength, mental and physical. She missed their conversations, the rumble of his laughter, the way she sometimes caught him looking at Rhan, wonder and fear on his face.

Her heart felt heavy, her soul full of stones. She'd told herself not to fall in love but she hadn't listened. And yeah, she did love Sutton, in ways she'd never loved Kyle or Rex, in ways that were unexpected and delightful and heartbreaking.

Lowrie jabbed her brush at the canvas, scowling. Well, she'd fallen in love with him so she could damn well fall out of love with him. And yeah, that was a good idea because his reservation was almost at an end and it was time to start taking in normal guests.

Returning to life as she knew it.

Lowrie turned at footsteps and smiled at her Paddy, walking toward her carrying a neatly wrapped brown paper parcel under his arm. He'd returned from San Diego a few days ago and apart from shaking his head at overhearing a biting conversation between her and Sutton, hadn't commented on their frosty relationship.

She wasn't expecting his silence to last.

"What do you have there?" Lowrie asked, nodding at the packet.

"Feels like a frame," Paddy told her. "It came with a thick envelope embellished with the fancy logo of your Manhattan lawyers."

Right, she'd been expecting the delivery but was surprised it had all happened so quickly. Amazing what you could accomplish with the right incentive, Lowrie thought.

"Are you going to tell me what's going on?" Paddy demanded.

Lowrie shook her head. "No, not now." Maybe one day but today she was feeling a little too raw.

"Fair enough," Paddy replied. He angled his head. "Had a walk-in, looking for a room. He's in the front lounge."

She frowned at him. "We're still closed, Paddy, you know that. Couldn't you have sent him on his way?"

Paddy shrugged. "You're the manager, so manage. Where's Rhan?"

"With Jo," Lowrie said, wiping her paint-streaked

hands on a rag. She took her parcel into the house, shaking her head. Men! They could occasionally be as useless as a glass hammer.

Lowrie stomped to the living room, saw the outline of a shadowed figure by the window and spoke before waiting for her eyes to adjust, trying to be cheerful. "Hi there. Sorry, the inn is temporarily closed and we're not taking additional— Sutton? What the hell?"

He stepped away from the window and her heart went into free fall. He was so good-looking, so masculine, the only man she could imagine in her life.

But she was just a side benefit.

Lowrie lifted her free hand. "Sorry, mistake. Paddy said a guest walked in looking for a room." She turned to leave but his low voice stopped her.

"He wasn't wrong. I *am* looking for a room."

She glared at him. "Well, then you're shit out of luck because I wouldn't rent you a bucket if your boat was sinking." She placed the painting on the seat of the nearest chair and shook her head. "Go back to England, Sutton, and let's all go back to normal, okay?"

"Not okay," Sutton replied. "Nothing is okay anymore. Or normal."

"Can't help you with that," Lowrie said, aiming for flippant and not hitting the mark. God, she was tired. Tired of feeling miserable and heartsore. "I've got to go, Rhan is—"

"Rhan is with Jojo and I bribed Paddy to get you in here and then to give us some privacy."

Lowrie scowled and leaned her shoulder into the doorframe. "Why? To say goodbye? It's easy, one word… 'Bye.'"

Sutton had the balls to smile at her. "I'm not leaving,

Low, not until you and I have had a proper chat, an old-fashioned heart-to-heart."

Lowrie snorted. "You? Having a heart-to-heart? *Sure.*"

"I'll admit I'm a useless talker for a writer, but we *are* going to talk, Lowrie, so sit your pretty ass down."

Her spine snapped at his command and she was about to stomp away when he spoke again. "Please, Lowrie. Let me talk and then if you still want me to go, I will, no questions asked."

She pushed her fingertips into the skin of her forehead and cheekbones, knowing that Sutton was stubborn enough to follow her around until she let him say his piece. It was easier to just let him speak and get it done.

God, it hurt.

Sighing loudly, she turned and met his eyes. "Speak. Make it fast."

Relief jumped into his eyes and he asked her to sit down but she refused. Nodding, Sutton took a moment to gather his thoughts before telling her about his father, that he was, by birth, a Ryder-White and the only reason he wanted Benjamin's money was to fund his parents' charity—a home for orphans—back in the UK. He told her that Callum Ryder-White had resigned from Ryder International, that James was the new CEO and chairman of the board and that Sutton, Kinga, Tinsley and Garrett Kaye would be James's advisors. That his parents charity would be, from this point onward, funded by the Ryder Foundation and the profits he earned from Ryder International would be split between the two foundations.

"My birth mother runs the foundation and we came to an agreement."

Reeling under a deluge of information, Lowrie held up her hand. "You met her?"

Sutton jammed his hands into the back pockets of his jeans and rocked on his heels. "Yes."

"And?" Lowrie demanded, unable to stop the questions tumbling from her lips. "How did that feel? Was it weird? Are you going to spend time with her?"

Sutton's eyes, when they met hers, reflected his confusion. "She was young, very spoiled. Benjamin hadn't yet accepted the truth about his sexuality and shortly after their affair ended, he met Carlo, your uncle, and fell completely in love, according to Paddy. Penelope tried to tell Benjamin about me but he refused to listen. He didn't want her, or any other woman, tainting what he had with Carlo."

Lowrie gasped. Penelope? "As in Penelope Ryder-White?"

He nodded. "Fantastical, right?"

"I had a long talk with Paddy and you were right— he did know Ben and knew a lot about his and Carlo's relationship, but nothing about the trust and the shares," Sutton continued. "Ben and Carlo lived here, together, for a year, maybe a little more. They were, by all accounts, blissful."

Yeah, she was happy for them but she was more concerned about the man she loved and how he felt meeting his birth mother. "We were talking about how *you* feel about Penelope, Sutt."

He met her eyes again. "I'm not sure. Neither of us knows what to feel or how to deal with each other so we're kind of in a holding pattern. But I don't think I'm ever going to be able to call her Mom, or feel like she is my mother, if that's what you're asking."

"Of course you won't because you had a mom and

Penelope can't take her place. Just like Ben can't take your dad's. You're a Marchant, not a Ryder-White."

Sutton started to smile, and it just grew bigger and bigger. "God, I love you."

The words came out of nowhere and were a bucket of icy water. Her eyes filled with tears and she stared down at the Persian carpet. "That's cruel, Sutton."

She heard him walking to her, felt his palm cradling her cheek, his knuckle lifting her chin. She forced herself to meet his surprisingly tender eyes. "I do love you, Lowrie. I will keep saying it until you believe me."

"But…" She waved her hands in the air. "But I'm a diversion, remember? A way to pass your time?"

He nodded and her heart sank. "You are and you will be because I intend to spend the rest of my life passing my time with you. And Rhan."

Uh…

"Look, I'm not sure where we're going to live, here or in the UK, or, I imagine, splitting our time between both, but wherever you and Rhan are is where I want to be."

He was going too fast—she couldn't keep up. "You want to be with *me*?"

"And Rhan."

She shook her head, not understanding. "You don't want kids, Sutton, neither do you want a relationship. You said that."

Sutton ran his hand down her arm, regret flickering in his eyes. "I said a lot of stupid stuff, Lowrie, all of which I regret. Let me make this clear… I want a relationship with you. I want to be Rhan's father. I want more kids. But only with you."

Lowrie, needing something to hold on to—her knees were definitely liquifying—gripped his sweatshirt in her fists and twisted the fabric around her hands. "I don't know what to say, Sutton."

Her heart felt like it was about to leave her mouth and her stomach felt like it had dropped to her toes. Her world was inside out and upside down, but in a good way, in the *best* way.

"Say you love me. Or if you don't, tell me you think you can love me…"

She met his eyes, saw the vulnerability in those depths and bit down on her bottom lip at seeing him exposed, brave and open to rejection.

"Tell me you want to spend your life with me, making books and babies and paintings. Making me happy." His thumb skated along her cheekbone, sending sparkles of excitement dancing along her skin. "Because I sure as hell intend to make you happy, Lowrie."

Lowrie loosened her grip on his sweatshirt and it took all her courage to step away from him. Glancing around, she tried to reorientate herself, surprised to see that the furniture was still where it had always been, that the sun hadn't turned into a ball of sparkly colored diamonds and that the sea still pounded the rocks and the beach. Shouldn't the world have changed? At least a little?

Reaching for Sutton's hand, she tugged him over to the chair and gestured to the professionally wrapped parcel she'd received from her lawyer. "That's for you."

Sutton handed her a little frown. "I'm giving you my heart and you're giving me a… What is that? A painting? This doesn't bode well."

She placed a hand on his arm and squeezed. "Open it, Sutton."

Sutton frowned again but bent down to rip the paper off the frame. "Did you frame the painting you did while we had sex? I'm warning you, if that painting goes with me, so do you."

"Open it, darling."

It was the *darling* that did it and Sutton ripped away the paper to look down at the painting, his mouth falling open with astonishment. "It's Cordyn's *Darkness Before the Dawn*." He stood up, his eyes darting between her and the painting. "This is an expensive painting, Low. Why do you have it?"

She smiled, her eyes a little blurry. "I knew that I needed to move on from my past, from what my mom and Kyle did, from what Rex did, or didn't do. I told my mom and Kyle, through my lawyers, that I would settle, go away, if my mother gifted me that painting in lieu of what they owed me."

She released a small smile. "Jojo, as you can imagine, pitched a fit. She said I deserved millions, not a painting by some artist she'd never heard of."

"I happen to agree but we'll discuss that later." Sutton looked at her, his eyes intense. "Why this painting, sweetheart?"

She sniffed and dashed away a tear with the back of her hand. "Because it belongs with you, with the others you own. But mostly because I wanted something of mine to go with you when you left."

Sutton took her hand and rubbed his thumb across the ring finger of her left hand. "I'd far prefer it if we *all* stayed, or all left. You, me, Rhan, the painting, the other painting…"

Lowrie lifted her hand to trail her fingers down his cheek. "Are you sure?"

"Never been more certain of anything in my life. I'll love you, Lowrie. I'll love Rhan. I'll love him as much, maybe more, than any other kids we have. I know that now."

"I know that, too, Sutt. You wouldn't have it any other way. You just needed time to realize it," Lowrie told him, curling her hand around the back of his neck, and pushing her breasts into his chest.

"Okay," she murmured, standing on her toes to whisper the words against his lips. "Let's do this."

"Do what, darling?"

"Love each other, Sutton. Here, there, everywhere."

Epilogue

Lowrie sat, with Sutton, at the head of the long, exquisitely decorated twenty-five-seat table and looked up through the branches of the ancient woodland trees at the velvety, cloudless sky. Organizing an outdoor reception in the United Kingdom was a risk, but this small wood bordering Marchant House was a magical spot, full of history and mystery. Lanterns, candles, fairy lights and flowers—peonies, roses and camellias—added to the *Midsummer Night's Dream* theme and she wanted their special guests—friends who were family and family who were friends—to experience the magic of this spot where Sutton proposed just a few months ago.

Lowrie glanced down at her stunning engagement ring—sixteen diamonds surrounding a whopping rare blue, oval diamond—still unable to believe that she was now Sutton's wife, that her son would soon become a

Marchant and that she had more family, and friends, than she knew what to do with.

Sutton, dressed in a tuxedo and open neck shirt, turned to face her and managed, somehow, to pull Rhan from her lap while dropping a hot kiss on her lips. He pulled back and smiled at her, his eyes tender. "You're looking a bit shell-shocked, my darling. Are you okay?"

Lowrie placed her hand on Rhan's chubby knee and looked up into her husband's gorgeous face. "I feel like I am having a bit of an out-of-body experience, to be honest. I can't believe this is my life."

He tipped his head to the side. "So you're happy then?"

Sutton adored her and her son, was a fantastic lover and her best friend. Happy didn't come close to describing her level of euphoria. She held her thumb and index finger an inch apart and grinned at him. "Maybe just a little," she teased.

Rhan pushed his hands against Sutton's chest in a bid to escape his grip and Sutton lowered him to the floor. He immediately toddled off on chubby legs, gleefully evading adults who wanted to scoop him up for a cuddle.

Sutton draped his arm across her lap and held her opposite thigh in his big hand. She rested her head on his shoulder and looked down the table at the laughing, happy crowd.

Jojo, who'd walked her up the aisle earlier, sat next to James and Penelope Ryder-White. Paddy was regaling Garrett and Cody with one of his tales, and Isabel was deep in conversation with Griff. Despite receiving an invitation, Callum was absent from the festivities, as were her parents.

Their choice…

Sutton dropped a kiss on her head before leaning back and looking at their ragtag family. He released a huge sigh when he saw Kinga, Tinsley, Thea and Jules huddled together, deep in conversation. "Look at them, I am sure they are planning world domination. Three sisters, Low, three!"

Lowrie laughed, not fooled by his mournful tone. He adored his sisters, and Jules, but Thea, naturally, would always be his favorite. She leaned back, crossed her legs and placed her elbow on the table, her chin in the palm of her hand.

"They are probably bouncing around ideas for the Ryder-White Christmas Ball," Lowrie told him. The ball would be smaller than the Valentine's Day one, though no less luxurious and it would take place in the ballroom of Marchant House a few days before Christmas. "I can't wait to dance with you under the mistletoe, Sutt."

Sutton stood up and held out his hand. Lowrie stood up and turned at the gentle sound of a strumming guitar. She looked around to see Griff leaning against a majestic oak, a guitar in his hands and a smile on his handsome face.

Sutton wrapped his arm around her waist. "Dance with me now, Low?"

Griff's rich voice filled the forest and Lowrie nodded. Of course she would…

Because in his arms, in his life, was the only place she wanted to be.

* * * * *

COMING SOON!

We really hope you enjoyed reading this book.
If you're looking for more romance, be sure to
head to the shops when new books are
available on

Thursday 9th June

To see which titles are coming soon, please visit
millsandboon.co.uk/nextmonth